In a secret stronghold of sorcery and black magic, a meeting was being held of the inner circle of the world's most dangerous devil cult. Dangerous because they not only sought, they *knew*.

What did they know? They knew that ghosts and demons, vampires and werewolves, and other creatures from Beyond are real, and if properly called, will come. That which is summoned may be forced to obey, if the caller's binding spells are strong enough. If not, the Beyond will have its own . . .

THE DEVIL'S BROOD

The New Adventures of Dracula,
Frankenstein & the Universal Monsters

DAVID JACOBS

Based on the Classic Universal Monsters

BERKLEY BOULEVARD BOOKS, NEW YORK

THE DEVIL'S BROOD: THE NEW ADVENTURES OF DRACULA,
FRANKENSTEIN & THE UNIVERSAL MONSTERS

A Berkley Boulevard Book / published by arrangement with
Universal Studios Publishing Rights, a division of Universal Studios
Licensing, Inc.

PRINTING HISTORY
Berkley Boulevard edition / June 2000

The Penguin Putnam Inc. World Wide Web site address is
http://www.penguinputnam.com

ISBN: 0-425-17365-8

BERKLEY BOULEVARD
Berkley Boulevard Books are published by The Berkley Publishing Group,
a division of Penguin Putnam Inc.,
375 Hudson Street, New York, New York 10014.
BERKLEY BOULEVARD and its logo
are trademarks belonging to Penguin Putnam Inc.

PRINTED IN THE UNITED STATES OF AMERICA

10 9 8 7 6 5 4 3 2 1

PART 1

ONE

In a secret stronghold of sorcery and black magic, a meeting was being held of the inner circle of the world's most dangerous devil cult. Dangerous because they not only sought, they *knew.*

What did they know? They knew that ghosts and demons, vampires and werewolves, and other creatures from Beyond are real, and if properly called, will come. That which is summoned may be forced to obey, if the caller's binding spells are strong enough. If not, the Beyond will have its own . . .

The site of the meeting was called the White Room, an underground wide circular space with a low domed ceiling and curved walls. It combined elements of a surgical operating theater, an electronics lab, and a place of worship. Dark worship—a satanic chapel, starkly modernistic, minimalist in design.

The cultists were grouped in an open space on the floor under the center of the ceiling. They were thirteen: the High Priestess and her coven of twelve disciples.

The followers were evenly divided between males and females, with ages ranging from young adult to elderly. This was the cult's Western European headquarters, and in its background and makeup the membership of the inner circle was not unlike that of the board of directors of any other successful Euro-firm.

Among them was an industrialist, a banker, a chess grandmaster, a cleric, a government minister, a nuclear physicist, a shipping magnate, and other persons of power and influence who had enjoyed great success in their chosen fields.

Also among them was murder, betrayal, blasphemy, incest, rape, torture, necrophilia, necromancy, and evil in all its multiform guises.

They were steeped in sin but paled in comparison to their mistress, the High Priestess, Countess Marya Zaleska.

She stood at the head of the group, a tall, slender brunette with an exquisite fine-featured face and a ballerina's body. Over a chic, simple dress she wore a black velvet robe, the hood of which was down, the long, straight garment draping to her ankles.

The others, too, wore long black robes over their civilian clothes, which made them look like judges or members of a church choir.

The Countess said, "The powers and principalities of Darkness can be as stupid, greedy, and self-serving as those of the mundane world. This is the natural outgrowth of our prideful natures. The intrigues they give rise to hold all in check, preventing any one from growing so great as to devour the rest of us.

"When that balance is threatened, all must act. All of us of the Dark. That is Law!"

Her voice rang sweet and clear, like chimes. Crystalline, bright, and piping, but without warmth.

Overhead, recessed indirect ceiling lights shone down on the open center space, bathing it in a soft white glow. Outside the glow cone, the chamber was dimly lit, thick with shadows.

Shimmers of reflected light played across the followers' shiny black robes, but the velvet robe of the Countess was blacker than black, absorbing all light. Her white oval face, swan neck, and languid, long-fingered hands seemed to be floating in midair.

4

She said, "There is one who would devour us all, if he could. You know who he is."

She looked each of the others briefly in the face, her gaze sweeping all in the circle. All looked away, unable to meet her eyes, some nodding, all squirming.

"You know," Marya said, enjoying their discomfort. "You know, but you're too afraid even to speak his name, for fear that you might call him up!"

Her laughter was girlish, merry. But she, too, avoided saying the Name.

The laughter stopped, abruptly bit off. "This much is known: his actions have created a crisis," she said. "I trust no one here is fool enough to think we can ignore it."

Not being a question, her statement required no reply.

She went on: "Before we can act, there must be a Seeing. In order to lift the veil, we must perform the Red Orb rite."

The followers stirred, anxious and aroused. A Red Orb rite was no small thing, even to these jaded devil worshipers. This was real magic, the Power.

All was in readiness for the ceremony. At the head of the circle of light, at a place corresponding to a point due north on the compass, stood a slab of machinery about the size and shape of an office filing cabinet, divided into two sections. The upper half's curved metal housing bulged with various clear flasks, containers, and tubes, while its front panel was faced with banks of gauges, dials, and switches. Coils and loops of plastic and rubber tubing bristled from its bulk like whipping tendrils. The machine's boxy bottom half held electric motors and pumps behind louvered side panels. From its rear emerged a wrapped bundle of black power cables, snaking across the floor to an outlet in the shadow zone.

A few feet in front of the machine stood an elongated brass tripod, shoulder-high, topped by a delicate gold birdcagelike structure which held a pumpkin-sized clear crystal bowl, sealed at the top by a flat disk-shaped golden lid.

They made quite a contrast, the brute twenty-first-century

machine and the delicately wrought tripod-mounted globe, product of a lost age of fine Old World craftsmanship.

Marya said, "Bring forth the donors."

Some of the followers went into the shadows, returning with a pair of wheeled hospital-type carts, each bearing a body. The carts were placed lengthwise on either side of the globe-and-tripod.

The bodies lay with their heads close to the machine. They were teenagers, a male and a female, clad in white hospital gowns. They lay on their backs, arms at their sides, eyes open, unblinking. Only the slow, measured rise and fall of their chests as they breathed gave any indication that they were not dead.

The cultists formed up around the teenagers, drawing in.

"The rite calls for two virgins of both sexes, to assure the proper polarities," Marya said. "Considering the scarcity of the commodity, you can see the seriousness of the situation."

The cultists pressed closer still, eager, avid, some breathing heavily.

The teens both looked sickly and starved, with thin, pinched features and an unhealthy grayish tinge to their skin. The boy's mouth, cheeks, and chin were dotted with acne; the girl's thin brown hair was lank, lifeless. Their eyes were glassy marbles, staring fixedly into nowhere.

Marya said, "For best results, their blood must be pure, untainted by drugs. They are under hypnotic control. The restraint straps securing them to the tables are necessary only as a precaution against involuntary muscular contractions or spasms during the process."

Standing at the machine, hunched over the controls, was a man with thick round glasses and a turnip nose, his hands encased in rubber gloves. The cuffs of stiff white trousers and white shoes with gum-rubber soles peeked out from under his ceremonial robes.

Marya turned to him. "Begin the procedure, Dr. Gregor."

"At once, Countess," he said. He fixed a long thin needle in the stoppered end of a tube attached to the machine.

6

He went to the girl, his rubber-soled shoes squeaking. The noise seemed to make him self-conscious and he took small, mincing steps to minimize it, making him look like he was skulking.

He swabbed alcohol on the side of her neck, a pointless antiseptic precaution, considering . . . Still, in medicine as in magic, procedure is paramount.

He inserted the needle into a blue-snake vein in her neck. She did not even blink. He used strips of surgical tape to hold the needle-tipped length of tubing in place. The tube fed into a metal nozzle at the base of one of the machine's forward-mounted flasks.

Unwrapping a fresh needle, he fitted it to the end of another tube and went around to the boy. This time he moved quickly, squeezing loud squeaks from his rubber-soled shoes, but now he ignored them, intent on what he was doing.

He stuck the needle into the boy's neck, taping it down. The tube was connected to another flask on the machine.

When he was done, Gregor straightened up, taking a step back, holding himself ready for the next step.

Marya's nod cued another acolyte to open the vents of a brazierlike object that contained burning incense, releasing thin pale clouds of sweet-smelling smoke that quickly spread through the space by hidden ventilator ducts. The heady mix was laced with psycho-concentrative chemicals that narrowed the focus and heightened the receptivity to suggestion of all but the Countess, who was immune to it.

She said, "The exsanguination, Gregor."

He ducked his head, making a bobbing head bow, and threw a switch on the machine. Motors whirred, pumps started pumping.

He turned a valve on top of a nozzle sticking out of the bottom of a flask. Connected to the nozzle was the tube which was attached to the girl's neck.

The pumps pumped. Blood spurted from the girl's neck into the tube, so dark that it was plum-colored, with red highlights. The purple-red column climbed up the IV tube, sucked into the flask like a blood transfusion in reverse.

7

Gregor did the same to the boy, whose blood began filling the second flask. A second set of tubes stretched from the tops of the flasks to the golden disk-topped crystal globe, the tips threaded through a pair of intake ports controlled by a bow-tie-shaped handle.

The other cultists leaned in, fascinated by the spectacle of the lifeblood being drained from the two hypno'd youths. The victims grew visibly pale, networks of blue veins standing out against their translucent white skin. They became restless, as if suffering bad dreams.

Blood reached the tops of the flasks, filling them.

Marya turned the bow-tie handle, opening the valves. Immediately blood began flowing from the flasks through the tubes to the crystal globe.

Mixed streams of blood flowed down the inner walls of the globe, coating it, puddling at the bottom. It was the color of cherry cough syrup and thick as paint.

The pumps cycled steadily, the globe filling up quickly with blood. The dark fluid seemed to be alive—lurid, crimson, and iridescent, as though firelight shone through it.

Gregor blinked behind his glasses, his eyes burning, tearing. The incense, of course. He felt light-headed, dizzy. After a few heartbeats, the feeling passed . . . yet did not quite pass. Some remnant of the psychoactive smoke clung to his brain, his vision. Colors seemed brighter, shadows darker.

The cultists could see that the teenagers' bodies were deflating, shriveling, the fleshy envelopes shrinking to bare the skeletal outlines beneath the skin. The duo squirmed, thrashing and moaning. It was the will to live flaring up one final time, as if their subconscious minds realized that the life was running out of them and urgently tried to shake the sleepers awake.

But they were not asleep, they were entranced. As their restlessness reached its peak, Marya made some mystic passes over them with her hands, muttering binding spells and words of power under her breath.

The victims ceased their unconscious strugglings, slip-

8

ping into a comalike state of consciousness from which there would be no awakening.

The cultists hung over the scene like vultures, visibly brightening as the two youths sank into near death.

Now the globe was almost full of blood, the blood of two virgins, mixed and swirling, turning the crystal container ruby red. It gave a scarlet tint to the soft light fanning down from overhead, and to the incense clouds that tumbled and unfolded in the beams. It cast an illusory glow of ruddy good health to Marya's cold, white, flawless face.

She pulled her hood up over her head, swathing it so that only the face showed. The hood came to a point on the end, with a tassel on the tip.

The others donned their hoods, which were similar to hers, but had no tasseled tip.

Marya stood within arm's reach of the globe, the others moving in around her—but not too close. Facing the orb, her back to the others, she spoke certain words of power, Names and invocations. She spoke them low, so only she could hear them . . . she, and those who were summoned.

Outside the circle of light, shadows stirred, thick, coiling like a mass of serpents. The darkness deepened, pressing on the fan of light in the middle of the room.

The Red Orb glowed, not with reflected light, but from an inner fire that was quickening to life at its heart. It brightened, outshining the overhead lights, painting the scene with a bloody glow.

The liquid in the blood bowl began to seethe at its center, where a dark purple-red mass was slowly taking shape, a semisolid core the size of two fists held together.

For a brief moment the congealing mass of liquid redness hung there, floating, quivering. Then, abruptly, it spasmed, as if squeezed by an invisible hand, lurching into a steady series of rhythmic pulsations, expanding and contracting. Pulsing with a life of its own.

The blood heart began to extrude thin threadlike tentacles from all parts of its surface at once. The filaments expanded outward in a sunburst pattern, stretching toward the inner walls of the crystal globe.

The thin rivulets touched the glass shell of the container, bending, splitting, dividing and intertwining, weaving an intricate pattern of veinlike threads on the inside of the globe.

Then the design seemed to coalesce, taking shape, etching a map of the world on the orb's inner walls. Oceans and continents, seas and islands appeared, outlined in blood fire, accurately imaged and to scale.

Marya stood facing it, with her hands crossed at the top of her chest. On the fourth finger of her right hand was a massive, ornate gold ring, like a signet ring of the type favored during the Italian Renaissance by nobles at the court of the di Medici princes.

The ring fit her finger perfectly, but otherwise seemed too heavy and oversized, as if it had been made for a much larger hand. The stone was jet-black onyx, bearing a royal crest etched in gold: a Gothic letter *D* bordered by the images of a bat and a spike.

Marya was a cold one, but the ring felt icy even through the layers of her garments where it touched the top of her chest. She rubbed the stone with her left hand, as if to stroke some warmth into it.

—*Astral communication being facilitated by touching some object that has been in intimate contact with the one being sought.*

"Find him," Marya said, clasping her hands, her fingers entwined in an ancient yogic channeling grip.

Spidery dark blotches, each of them hand-sized, appeared at the north and south poles of the globe. They sent bands of black-red tendrils thrusting vertically on the globe, reaching for each other, meeting at the equator.

A longitudinal line, finger-thick, now stretched from pole to pole. Inside the globe, on its inner surface, the world map began to turn, rotating eastward. Land and sea rolled under the rootlike vertical locator line.

Western Europe, the British Isles, the Atlantic Ocean were all swept past the line, the global view slowing as the east-

10

ern seaboard of the United States came into view. The movement became slower still as the Caribbean and the Gulf of Mexico appeared, halting in the West Indies, at an island group that lay west of Jamaica and east of the Yucatán.

"Isla Morgana, his magic island kingdom. For many years he's been there in a kind of voluntary self-exile, which suited our plans, if not his," Marya said. "But now, like Alexander the Great, he longs for new worlds to conquer.

"The results could be catastrophic."

She stood up very straight, her back rigid, body immobile but dynamically charged, outlined in a bubbling black aura.

In the orb, a bright crimson diamond appeared on the map, marking the Isla Morgana chain.

Abruptly she unclasped her hands, letting them fall open in front of her, palms up.

The red diamond flared up, expanding swiftly, wiping the map clean off the globe. The light faded with equal quickness, swallowed up by the dark bowl of blood.

Marya's eyes blazed red, glowing. Neither the pupils nor the whites of the eyes could be seen, only a pair of red-hot balls of blood.

In the orb, clotted burgundy blackness swirled, thick with ruby-red points of brightness that blazed like red dwarf stars streaming through a black nebula.

In its heart, a pair of eyes winked into being, bright hot bloodfire eyes, like Marya's. They might have been reflections, but after a pause, they began to take on a life of their own, as though peering beyond the confines of the crystal globe to see—what?

"Find him," Marya urged, her lips barely moving. "Find him, seek him out—but softly!"

Eddying currents in the orb made the fire eyes waver, rippling and fading away . . .

—And pictures took form, in a head space where the Red Orb and the mind's eye met!

A cascade of images, seen as if in flashes of red lightning:

The sea, islands, boats, beaches, villages, mountains—a city in the sea, with a sunken bell tower—the walking dead, a lycanthrope—no, two lycanthropes, a man-made monster, a sleeping Eve, a giant vampire bat—

Marya stiffened, bracing herself against the onslaught of images. She clamped down a protective mind shield, throttling the flow of mental pictures to a trickle.

This was strong magic. The cultists had absorbed only a fraction of the raw energy force which the High Priestess had handled, but they were mere mortals and it had hit hard. Some had bloody noses and a few were picking themselves up off the floor.

Dr. Gregor took off his glasses, pinching the bridge of his nose, his eyes squeezed shut. He felt as if he had been stabbed in the forehead with a knife.

Not for the first time he wondered about the powers which the Countess was able to summon. Was this truly a manifestation of mystical power, of metaphysical control, or were he and the others under the thrall of an extremely potent brand of mass hypnosis, designed to make them believe in the existence of the supernatural?

When he put his glasses back on, he discovered that the right lens was cracked, splintered with spiderweb cracks.

A most potent illusion! he thought.

A new scene took shape in the Red Orb, catching his attention, compelling him to move closer and watch, along with all the other cultists, who were similarly compelled . . .

The image was distorted by the curvature of the crystal bowl, creating a funhouse-mirror-like effect, with weird foreshortening and distorted perspectives.

It showed a nighttime vista of a seaside estate, where a white-columned mansion stood in the middle of sprawling, overgrown fields.

An eerie bloodlit glow made the scene visible in the darkness. The mansion was long-abandoned, decayed. The grounds were thick with weeds.

Behind the back of the structure was a graveyard, both house and gravestones revealing the style of some two centuries earlier. The perimeter of the cemetery was partly enclosed by an iron spear fence. Above, bats lurched and flitted beneath a crescent moon.

Gravestones and marble statuary were tilted at steep angles, thick gnarled roots grew out of cracked graves, a mausoleum sagged at the corners, its marble walls pitted and stained.

A fit setting for the thing that shambled into view, its Titan form outlined against the sky, blotting out a mass of stars.

A manlike thing, gigantic, seven feet tall, with a square-topped head and the face of an animated corpse. It lumbered toward the mausoleum, as rude a caricature of the human form as any that had ever been scratched on a lavatory wall.

A section of fence that got in the way was trampled down, kicked aside like cardboard by gunboat-sized hobnailed boots. A huge strangler's hand gripped a tree branch for support, showing stitches on the wrist where it had been sewn onto the rest of the arm. Its weight was too heavy and tore the branch off the tree.

The creature reeled, flailing long arms for balance, harried and frustrated to the point of madness.

Marya announced, "The Frankenstein monster!"

"I thought it was destroyed!" a cultist said.

"It was lost for half a century. Obviously someone found it. And it's just as obvious who that 'someone' is," she said.

Dr. Gregor crowded closer, eager, excited. "This is something I never dared hope to see—the living creation of the genius of Henry Frankenstein!"

"Better had you not seen it, Gregor."

"But why, Countess? This is an invaluable scientific find, a walking marvel to be studied, analyzed—"

"'Monster' is no idle term. It has brought destruction down on all those who would be its master."

Somebody else said, "Looks like he's hurt."

The Monster staggered, clutching his side, where his garments were in rags and so was the flesh beneath, wet and shiny with greenish-black blood.

13

"He *is* hurt!" Gregor said, peering through one cracked lens and one good one as the Monster slumped against the side of the mausoleum, leaning on it for support.

"He's weak, wounded. Undercharged, too—barely enough to be ambulatory!" Gregor said, sounding offended.

Marya gestured subtly, adjusting the orb's angle of vision, widening the view to take in more of the surroundings. Beyond the graveyard were more weedy fields and some dark, shedlike outbuildings.

Over a rise in the middle ground, a pack of demon dogs came loping into view. Not dogs, wolves—though no less demonic.

They had pointed ears, glowing eyes, and slavering fanged mouths. They burst out of nowhere, a half dozen or so, silently charging the Monster, going in for the kill.

He threw himself forward, meeting them head-on, wielding the broken tree branch which he still clutched, using it as a club. He swatted down one wolf, then the others were upon him.

The pack savaged him, their thrusting fanged snouts slashing everywhere, ripping and tearing. The Monster wrung the neck of one and broke the back of another, but the survivors were getting stronger while he grew weaker.

His back to the wall, his knees buckled as the wolves dragged him down. Now they could really get at him. Green blood flew, splattering the wall, drenching the graveyard dirt.

The wolves tore open his belly, spewing massive quantities of green blood. They eviscerated him, rooting out his guts.

After a time the Monster's feeble stirrings ceased, and he went inert, motionless, like an engine that had run out of fuel.

The wolves eased off the attack, their ferocity spent now that the alien inhuman thing was dead. Occasionally they would return to worry the Monster's parts, more out of reflex than anything else. The outbursts became steadily more infrequent. The animals sniffed around the pools of green blood, finding it repellent.

". . . dead!" a cultist said, astonished.

"It wasn't a fair fight," Gregor said, angry. "If Franken-stein's creation had been charged to even a fraction of his full strength, he'd have brushed aside the pack like so many gnats!"

Reacting to some unseen cue, the wolves suddenly all jerked their heads up at the same time, turning them in the direction from which the stimulus had come.

There, at the edge of the graveyard, a figure emerged from behind a tall tilted obelisk-shaped monument. Stepping into view was a devil in the shape of a man, tall, power-fully built, deep-chested, and long-limbed, a vigorous adult male in the full prime of—not life, but Undeath.

His glossy black hair was slicked back in a widow's peak, his skin was dead white, and his facial expression was one of supreme arrogance and hatefulness. His eyes were blood-red and glowing like Marya's, only hotter and brighter.

He was a thirsty corpse in old-fashioned formal wear, with a black dinner jacket and pants and stiff white shirt-front wrapped with a scarlet cummerbund, and a scarlet-lined black cape that trailed him like batwings.

He gestured curtly and the wolves scattered, trotting off. He gloated over the fallen Monster, sneering, baring a leer-ing fanged mouth hungrier and infinitely more feral than those of the wolves.

"Dracula!" Gregor's voice was thick with outrage. "The mad fool! Only he could destroy such a priceless creation!"

"But why?" someone asked. "I thought the Monster was his slave—"*

"Who knows? Perhaps he did it merely to show that he could," Marya said, shrugging. "Dracula was never one to deny his whims, no matter how murderous.

"If he revives the Monster again, it will fear him and serve him better. It was ever his way to terrorize his slaves into obedience."

Her words seemed to inspire Gregor. "Yes," he cried, "it

*See *Return of the Wolfman* (Berkley Boulevard Books).

15

can live again! Henry Frankenstein was a genius and no one since has plumbed the full depths of his creation."

Without warning, Dracula turned away from the Monster, looking off to one side, glaring.

A cultist cried, "He sees us!"

Marya motioned for silence. "No, but he sees something . . ."

Dracula started to stalk away, shuddering with fury, his face twisting with naked hatred that made his previous expressions seem benign. He rushed out of the graveyard and over the rise, crossing to the largest of the nearby outbuildings.

The orb tracked him, eyeing him from above, as though the scene were being viewed by some airborne observer, some flying spirit.

The building loomed up before Dracula, a gloomy pile of stone a couple of stories tall. It was an old mill house, where long ago the cane had been brought to extract its sugar. At ground level a door was open, exposing a dark entryway. Dracula went inside, his cape streaming after him like a tattered black banner, and was lost from sight.

The unseen observer whose viewpoint was imaged in the Red Orb now rose straight up in the air, zooming to a height where it hovered, looking down on the mill-house roof.

There was a hole in the roof, a big one, one that had clearly been there for a long time. Moonlight shone through it, into the structure. A horde of bats flew out of it, spooked.

The phantom eye dropped through the hole, into the cavernous space of the main building. Below, Dracula was locked up in hand-to-hand combat with an agile and deadly foe. Hand-to-claw combat, really, since he fought with a man-beast. They grappled, biting and tearing, rolling around on the floor.

"The Wolfman," Marya said, nodding. "Now I begin to understand. He and Dracula are old enemies—I almost said, *mortal* enemies. It was an evil time for Dracula when he first crossed paths with the lycanthrope. The Wolfman disappeared at the same time as the Monster, and it was thought that they perished together.

"I can guess the rest. Dracula found the Monster, somehow freeing the Wolfman at the same time. With the sureness of the beast, the Wolfman has tracked the vampire to his lair to try to put an end to him!"

Dracula stopped rolling around on the floor with his foe long enough to get his feet under him. He picked up the Wolfman and slammed him into a fallen millstone, bending him back over the edge of it, trying to break his spine.

The Wolfman got his claws into Dracula's face, ripping it, striping it like a tiger mask. The deep gashes failed to bleed.

Still, Dracula was hit hard where it hurts, in his vanity. He was proud of his dark good looks, now temporarily spoiled, disfigured. The sight of his dead shredded flesh clinging to the undersides of the Wolfman's talons did little to improve his temper.

But Dracula was off balance and the Wolfman had the momentum. The lycanthrope grabbed two clawed fistfuls of Dracula's front and lifted him up, so that his feet were off the floor. He swung him around, Dracula kicking empty air, groping for the Wolfman's throat but unable to reach it.

Beside the millstone stood a half-collapsed framework of old timbers and beams, part of the clockwork machinery of wheels and rollers that once helped grind the cane. A wooden wheel the size of a wagon wheel was part of the scaffolding, parts of its iron-sheathed rim having broken away to expose a row of sharply pointed wooden spokes that protruded like stakes.

The Wolfman whirled Dracula toward the broken wheel, Dracula glancing over his shoulder just in time to see himself being borne toward the longest, stoutest, and most sharply pointed spoke.

Hate, rage, even chagrin showed on his face. Then he was impaled on the spoke, hung up on it by the Wolfman like a carcass stuck up on a meat hook.

The spoke's splintered tip speared through his back, penetrating him and bursting out of the front of his chest. Staking him through the heart, such as it was.

The look on Dracula's face was like that seen on animals as they chew a leg off to escape from a steel trap. He grabbed the sharp point where it protruded six inches past his chest, gory with the blood he'd drunk earlier this night. The blood was slippery, making it hard to get a grip. His feet were off the floor, so he couldn't get any leverage. He tried to pull himself off the spoke by the strength of his arms alone.

He might have done it, if not for the Wolfman, who shoved him farther down on the spoke, until eighteen inches of it jutted from the vampire's chest.

Dracula was stuck, pierced through the heart. The staking ruptured his center, nullifying his shape-shifting abilities, preventing him from changing into a bat, a wolf, or a pillar of mist. All that remained was immediate dissolution.

"The Impaler impaled!" Marya intoned, awed despite herself.

Dracula's face contorted in a shriek, his body imploding. He melted like a wax dummy under a blowtorch. The flame was Time. For five hundred years of unnaturally prolonged Undeath, the vampire had existed in a diabolic bubble outside the timestream, immune to the natural rhythms and universal cycles of birth, aging, and death.

Now Time reclaimed its own. Dracula writhed, twisting into grotesque contortions, withering, shrinking on the spike. His hair turned gray, then white, cobwebby. His skin was yellow and brittle. His nose caved in, leaving a triangular hole above fretted, crumbling lips.

His eyes receded into the depths of ever-widening sockets. Dry bones broke, thrusting brown jagged ends out through the dwindling papery flesh.

Dracula came apart, breaking up into a man-sized whirlwind of powdery gray ash which flew off the blackening bones. The bones disintegrated into a cloud of black flakes that was sucked into the spinning dust devil. Graveyard dust.

Last of all to go were the eyes, Dracula's fire eyes that sputtered and shrank to tiny orange embers, motes.

The Wolfman slunk away, smacking his chops, grinning.

The dust devil rose, whirling, funneling up into the air, rising to the roof, where it bumped up against rafters and planking before finding the hole.

It popped outside, corkscrewing up into the moonlight, a horde of whirling specks like a cloud of flies.

Then it was gone . . .

A cultist said, "Dracula—is dead!"

"Ceased to exist, perhaps. He *died*, literally speaking, five hundred years ago," Marya said, tentative, unsure.

In the room, the blackness of occult darkness lightened, the shadows ceasing to be creeping things of evil and becoming only shadows. The inner fires of the Red Orb were extinguished, turning it back to a mere bowl of blood.

On the tables lay the two virgins, drained, white, and dead.

Someone pressed the question: "Is Dracula destroyed, then?"

Marya thought about it, concentrating, touching the side of her forehead where blue veins stood out. An intimate psychic link existed between her and Dracula. Always before, even when he was on the other side of the world, she could sense his presence in some corner of her mind. It was a kind of pressure, like a storm boiling just below the horizon of her awareness.

Now that presence was gone, the pressure lifted. Scanning the bandwidth of her supernatural mind force, she found only emptiness in the space formerly occupied by Dracula.

Emptiness, and yet not quite emptiness. There were traces there, ghostly echoes, some psychic residue perhaps of the entity who had crowned himself Lord of Vampires.

She narrowed her focus, trying to zero in on those traces, but the harder she concentrated, the more elusive they became, so that she was unable to tell if they were signals or just background noise.

Yet despite her frustrations, there was a curious lightness to her mood, as if some heavy weight had been lifted from her mind.

19

She said, "Dracula is silent."

A cultist asked, "But is he done, annihilated?"

From the way in which the others hung on that answer, it could be seen that the end of Dracula would be a good thing, hoped for even by these devotees of evil.

Marya felt that way herself. And yet . . .

"He is silent. I can say no more than that. But remember, Dracula has cheated what looked like sure doom many times in the past—the devil takes care of his own," she said.

She drew back her hood, baring her head, the others following her cue. The red glow had left her eyes and they seemed normal enough now, as long as they were not looked into too deeply.

The orb was dark, and all that remained was a bowl of still-warm blood and two fresh young corpses.

Indicating them, a cultist whose tastes ran in a necrophagous direction said, "Shame to let them go to waste. Might as well make a party of it."

Marya shrugged. Her tastes generally ran to living prey, but she was broad-minded and did not begrudge others their little pleasures.

"Why not?" she said.

The cultists had clustered around the cadavers, ready and eager to begin their feast, when, suddenly—

A bell struck, a phantom bell with a dull, heavy leaden stroke that froze them all on the spot, filling them with dread. The gonging note hung in the air, reverberating, groaning, with eddying overtones that were like shrill, mocking laughter.

The deafening wash of sound died away, and the hearts of the mortal cultists once more resumed beating.

In reality, there was no bell in the chamber, though from the loudness of the stroke, a massive iron bell might well have been booming there. Yet there was no such bell in the building housing the White Room, nor in any of its neighbors.

Someone tried to speak, managing only a croak. Someone else stage-whispered, "What—what is it?"

20

"The bells of hell, tolling for the vampire lord," Marya said, her voice clear but hushed.

The invisible bell struck again, its mournful mocking clangor beating down on the cultists. Some covered their ears with their hands, fruitlessly attempting to muffle the leaden gong.

In all, the bell tolled thirteen times.

Breaking the long, strained silence which followed, Marya said, "Dracula is done."

TWO

Luck comes in streaks and Steve Soto's was trending downward. Earlier tonight he'd dropped a bundle at the tables of the island's only casino. With hard, dogged "play," he'd managed to recoup most of his losses, all but a couple hundred bucks. Instead of trying to break even, he decided to write it off and call it a night. The way he'd been going lately, that practically counted as a win.

He felt beat, hollow. Maybe some fresh air would help. He looked around for his sidemen, Tony Paul and Dennis. He didn't have to look far, not in this high-rolling money crowd thronging the main floor of the gambling room. Among all these well-heeled heels they were just plain heels, hard guys down from the States for a little island adventure. Tony Paul was kibitzing a card game and Dennis was badgering a cocktail waitress.

Soto could use a break from them, too. Like everything else on this crummy island, they were starting to get on his nerves. Abruptly he shoved off from the dice table he'd been hovering over, heading out without telling the others. What were they, his keepers, that he had to clear his every move with them?

The big room had green carpeting and white walls with gold trim. There were roulette wheels, craps tables, and high-stakes poker and blackjack games. All were ringed with milling clusters of players, and no place at the action remained vacant for any longer than it took the next in line to fill it.

Soto crossed the floor, making for a row of glass doors in the opposite wall. The carpet was the color of money. He weaved past knots of deep-pocketed men and sleek, expensive women.

The glass doors opened onto an outdoor patio overlooking the harbor. Set out on the flagstoned terrace were some tables and chairs. The tables were topped with beach-type umbrellas, folded down now for the night. Some strategically placed planters and shrubs broke up the space, creating a few semiprivate nooks and niches on the sidelines.

There was a handful of people on the patio, mostly amorous couples who had retired to those sidelines for more intimate conversations, and a couple of loners who stood off by themselves. It was a big patio and Soto didn't have any trouble finding a place where he could be alone.

A waist-high wall bordered the patio and Soto sat on the edge of it, looking out at the water. Sited on the shores of the natural harbor was the town of Magdalena, capital and only real settlement of any size on Isla Morgana. South of the curving shoreline was a jewellike little cove with a good, deep anchorage—Coral Cove.

Jutting into the water was a rocky spit, on whose flat top sat a long, low Spanish mission–style building with a tile roof, wheat-colored walls, and lots of ornamental wrought-iron grillwork.

The island had changed owners many times, and when it had been a British possession, the structure had been the home of the Coral Cove Yacht Club. Now it housed the casino.

Sea breezes, warm and moist, played over Soto. He didn't like it. It felt like somebody was breathing on him.

He lit up a cigarette, the lighter flare underlighting his hard hawk face. He looked worried, preoccupied. He was lean, wiry. He wore a jacket, open-necked sport shirt, casual slacks, and expensive tasseled handwoven Italian loafers.

He took a couple of long drags on the cigarette, sucking the raw unfiltered tobacco smoke deep into his lungs so that it hurt good. He blew the smoke out over the wall, where it hung like a cloud in the moonlight for an instant before the breezes tore it apart.

When he was done, he flicked the butt out over the water, watching the orange ember arc out and down before hitting the sea. The cove looked like a scene from a tourist post-card: tropical night, moonlit palm trees, colored lights mir-rored on dark waters. A privately owned pier extended from the landing into the water, with motorboats and water taxis dropping off and picking up casino guests.

Farther out, five or six sleek white yachts were moored offshore, millionaires' toys, pleasure craft of the ultrarich who cruised the islands on the café society circuit, a kind of seagoing jet set. The brightly lit multitiered white yachts sat in the water like floating wedding cakes.

What wasn't on the luxury boats could be found in Mag-dalena: gambling, vice, drugs, and other, less pleasant di-versions. The town was wide open. So was the island.

That's why Steve Soto and associates were here.

Wasn't it?

"I wish to hell I knew," he said to himself.

The sea lapped at the shore, sloshing on the rocks. From inside the casino came the sounds of games of chance: a ball clicking in a roulette wheel, the slap of cards being dealt on a table, dice tumbling, ice cubes rattling in a glass, the ceaseless rising and falling of voices in conversation, sighs and gasps marking the big wins and losses of play ...

Soto flipped the butt of his second smoke into the sea and started back inside, crossing toward the glass doors. Lights from inside threw pastel rainbow-colored bands on the flagstones.

A door opened outward and he stepped aside to let a cou-ple exit, holding the door for them. An older man with a much younger woman. Nothing novel about that arrangement, in the casino or anywhere else.

But there was something distinctive about them and he remembered having seen them before, if only in passing. The man had a smooth-shaven oblong face and lead-colored hair worn flat against the scalp, like a skullcap. He wore a gold-buttoned navy blazer, shirt with ascot tie, canvas slacks, and deck shoes.

The woman was in her mid or early twenties, a brunette beauty in a red dress and red shoes. An elaborate hairstyle heaped masses of chestnut-brown tresses on top of her head, piling it up like a crown. A remote, modellike face was sparked by a pair of long green eyes. The strapless, low-cut red gown sheathed a high-breasted, long-legged body.

The man was hanging on to her arm, a little unsteadily. He was sweating, pasty-faced.

Soto asked, "You okay, buddy?"

"Yes, yes," the man said, without conviction. The young woman said, "He's fine," steering him out onto the patio.

The man wobbled, knees buckling. Soto grabbed him by the arm, above the elbow, holding him up and keeping him from falling.

The woman gasped. "Uncle Basil!" Her face tightened and her eyes widened, showing white circles around the irises. She clutched his other arm, the one Soto wasn't holding.

Soto said, "You need a doctor?"

"No, no, nothing like that," Uncle Basil said. "If I could just sit down for a minute . . ."

"You sure?"

"Yes. No doctors, please." Uncle Basil smiled loosely, but his eyes were frightened.

Soto and the woman walked him to the nearest table. Soto held him at a distance, not wanting to bump up against him because he, Soto, was wearing a gun on his hip, a snub-nosed .38 in a clip-on holster fastened to his waistband and hidden under his jacket. He had an in with the local power brokers and an okay to go around armed, but why call attention to it?

Uncle Basil slumped into a chair, holding on to the curved arm rails. The woman hovered over him, putting her hands on his shoulders. She said, "Are you all right, Uncle?"

He put a hand on hers, patting then squeezing it. "Yes, Dorian. Don't worry about me, dear. It's nothing—nothing at all . . ."

"Is it? Is it really, Uncle? . . . Or did you *see* something?"

At these words, a sudden expression, hard and sharp, flashed across Uncle Basil's face, and he straightened up in his chair. He and Dorian exchanged glances, then looked at Soto.

Indicating the casino, Soto said, "There's a doctor on duty inside. Want me to get him?"

"No, thank you," Uncle Basil said, holding up a hand. "No need to call the good doctor away from his rounds ministering to cardiac victims who keel over at the tables. Of which, I assure you, I am *not* one."

He turned to the young woman he had called Dorian. "Now that you mention it, dear, I believe I did see something—"

"What!"

"Stars. I saw stars," he said slyly.

"You're impossible," she said. She leaned forward, fussing over him. Soto took the opportunity to look down the front of her dress. He was still looking when Uncle Basil turned his face up to him.

"A slight dizzy spell, brought on by a touch of sun and too many gin and tonics, I'm afraid. But it's better now."

And it was true: he looked better. The wildness was gone from his eyes and most of the color had returned to his face. He relaxed into a more comfortable position in the chair.

The people on the patio who'd been watching now realized that the incident, such as it was, was over. They went back to what they were doing.

Uncle Basil murmured, "So grateful for your kindness, Mister . . . ?"

"Soto. Steve Soto." He could see that the name meant nothing to them. *Good.*

"I'm Basil Lodge, and this is my niece, Dorian Winter."

Basil Lodge held out a hand. Soto took it. The palm was moist. Closing his fingers, Soto shook it, not squeezing it. Lodge seemed to prefer it that way. He wasn't a hearty-handshake kind of a guy.

Dorian shook hands, too. Her hand was cool, her grip firm. Soto said, "Pleased to meet you."

"Most men are," she said.

Soto smiled with his lips. He said, "Didn't I see you two coming out of the Ministry this morning?"

Lodge answered. "Why, yes. Did you have business there, too?"

"You can't do business on this island without the Ministry getting involved."

"Quite true." A faraway look appeared in the older man's eyes, as if he was searching his memory. He came up blank. "Odd . . . I don't recall seeing you there, and I pride myself on remembering faces, especially those of fellow Americans."

"I saw you through the window when I was in Stafford's office," Soto said.

"Ah, you know Sir Hugo," Lodge said, brightening.

"Sure. And I'm not above dropping his name, either."

Lodge cackled, leaning forward. "Better and better! I assure you that it's a name worth dropping, if you want to cut through useless red tape."

"That's me. I'm a direct actionist."

Dorian frowned, looking at Soto with hard clear eyes, appraising him. At least that was a change from her frozen-faced indifference. She was still frozen-faced, but now she seemed to be thinking . . . calculating. Lodge looked like he was doing it, too, only he hid it better.

That was okay with Soto. He was busy figuring the angles on them.

Lodge indicated a chair. "Have a seat and join us, Steve. Let me buy you a drink."

Dorian gave him a look. "Don't you think you're over-doing it, Uncle?"

"Not at all."

"Your health, I mean."

"Nothing wrong with me. I'm sound as a dollar—and that means something these days, eh?" Once more, Lodge indicated the chair. "Steve—please."

"All right." Soto pulled out a chair at the table and sat down.

Dorian said, "You didn't look so hot a minute ago, Uncle Basil, when you almost passed out."

"A shock to the system, my dear. A sudden shock, that's all. A drink will set things right."

There were no waiters nearby, so Soto got up to look for one. He opened a glass door and stepped into the casino. Looking across the crowded floor, he spotted Tony Paul on the other side of the room. Tony Paul was looking around for somebody, too—Soto, who else? But he was looking in the wrong place.

Trailing a pace or two behind Tony Paul was Dennis, stupid-faced and weaving. He held two drinks, one in each hand, alternately drinking from each of them.

Waiters in tight short gold jackets and wide shiny black trousers circulated around the room. Soto flagged down the nearest and gave him the order, telling him to bring it out onto the patio.

Tony Paul was still looking for him in the wrong places when Soto slipped back outside, unobserved. *Some body-guard,* he thought. But then he didn't keep the big goon around for brainwork. Soto was the brains. Tony Paul was muscle. He would do what he was told to do, *no matter what.*

As for Dennis, he was just some young punk who was along strictly to handle the donkey work, as stooge and er-rand boy.

Soto wouldn't have been surprised to return to an empty table, but Dorian and Lodge were still there. Their heads were together, talking. When he joined them, their heads were apart and the talk was done.

"You folks boat people?" Soto asked, waving a hand toward the yachts.

Lodge shook his head. "Afraid I'm not much of a seagoing man. We've taken a house by the beach, out on Claw Cape."

Dorian said offhandedly, "Are you a yachtsman, Steve?"

"Are you kidding?"

"Well, yes."

He grinned at her. Lodge said quickly, "Where are you staying, Steve?"

"The Casa Grande."

"Good choice. It's the only decent hotel on the island."

"Drop by sometime when you're in town."

"I might just do that."

"You're both welcome. I'll buy you a drink."

"I hope we don't have to wait that long." Lodge turned toward the glass doors, craning to see inside. "Seems they've forgotten about us out here."

"They're a little backed up at the bar, but they should be here directly."

Lodge turned away, facing Soto. "You gave me the impression that you were down here to do a little business, Steve. What is that business, if you don't mind my asking?"

"My company handles a lot of currency transfers, so I'm checking out the local banking setup."

Dorian's face showed her disbelief. "If I may say so, you don't look much like a banker, Steve."

"I'm not. I'm an expediter."

"An expediter? What's that?"

"I make things happen fast."

"Direct actionist."

"That's me," Soto said.

Lodge asked, "What company are you with?"

"An outfit on the East Coast. You wouldn't have heard of us. We're low profile, but we're into a little bit of every-

29

thing—banking, construction, trucking, vending machines, service industries, import export.

"How about you? You a businessman, Mr. Lodge?"

"In a way. And please, Steve, don't stand on formality. Call me Basil."

Dorian said, "You can call me Ms. Winters."

"These youngsters today." Lodge sighed, shaking his head.

"I'm over twenty-one."

"As I said, a mere child."

Soto said, "Okay, Basil, what's your line of work?"

"Futures."

"What, like commodity futures?"

"Just futures," Lodge said, airily waving his hand. Dorian was smirking.

The waiter arrived with a trayful of glasses, setting the drinks out on the table. They were free, compliments of the house.

"Why not? With all the dough they've gotten out of me, they can afford it," Soto said. He tipped the waiter, saying, "Might as well spread it around."

Before the waiter left, Lodge told him, "Don't be a stranger. Come back before we get too thirsty."

The waiter went away, and they went for their drinks. Dorian's was something pink and frothy that looked more like an ice-cream soda than an alcoholic beverage. Lodge's sixteen-ounce glass held mostly pure gin peppered with some ice shavings, a splash of tonic, and a twist. He drank it like it was water.

Dorian said, "Whoa."

"Don't nag," Lodge said.

Soto had a rum and Coke. The trick was to keep adding rum until it killed the sweetness of the cola.

"Rum should go good with this place," he said. "Used to be some kind of pirate base way back when, right?"

Lodge held his glass, peering over the top of it, looking owlish. "That's putting it mildly. At one time this was one of the centers of piracy in this part of the world."

"The more things change . . ." Dorian said. She took a sip

30

of her drink through a skinny red plastic straw held clutched between her glossy red-painted lips.

Lodge went on, "Claw Cape used to be twice the size it is now. It reached out into the harbor like a hook, or a claw—thus its name." He curved his drinking arm into a crescent shape to illustrate the point, gin sloshing over the top of his glass and spattering on the flagstones.

"Whoops! I'm leaking fuel," he said, taking a few big gulps. When he stopped, there wasn't much chance of what was left in the glass sloshing out. "Ahhhh . . . Where was I? Oh yes—Freetown," he said.

"Freetown? Don't think I've seen that one on the map," Soto said.

"It hasn't been, for over three hundred years," Lodge said. "You see, Freetown was a pirate port, a safe haven for the buccaneers. They built it out on the tip of Claw Cape, fortifying it with cannons and strong walls so they couldn't be dislodged. They sold their stolen booty in the market—including slaves—and merchants from all over the Caribbean and the Gulf came here to buy.

"Oh, it was one of the wickedest cities in the New World, in its day! But then that day came to an end, as all good things must."

"What happened to it? Pirate catchers?"

"No, Steve, something more basic than that, more elemental. The earth moved. I should say, the seabed moved. You see, the sea basin in this area is shot through with fault lines, and apparently the island sits right on top of one. One day there was an earthquake, er, sea-quake, that sent half of Claw Cape to the bottom, taking Freetown with it. It vanished literally overnight, with no more than a handful of survivors managing to escape."

Soto swallowed some of his drink. "Remind me not to invest in any of the local real estate."

"Don't worry, there haven't been any more quakes recorded in the area in the last three hundred years," Lodge said.

He stretched out the arm holding the glass, pointing out

to sea. "About a half mile out from where the cape now ends there's a cay, a pile of coral and rocks that's visible at low tide. It's a navigational hazard, marked off by buoy lights.

"That was the top of the highest hill in Freetown before it sank. The rest of it is underwater, forty fathoms down—the city in the sea."

Soto leaned back in his chair. "You should be a tour guide, Basil. You really know the local history."

"Thank you. I have a passion for ancient things." Lodge chuckled to himself, ignoring Dorian's sidelong glance. "There's more," he said. "The islanders believe that sometimes at night, when the moon is full and the sea is calm, you can see the lights of the sunken city, the ghost lights of drowned pirates cavorting underwater. But beware that they don't drag you down, to claim you for their own.

"That's the superstition, anyway."

Dorian said, "All these islands have local legends. The tourists love them."

"Maybe so, but I for one wouldn't care to be out there on a boat on a moonlit night, just in case the legend is true. Besides, I don't even like water as a chaser for my drinks!"

Lodge raised his glass. "Speaking of which, I seem to have run dry. This talking is thirsty work." He looked around for the waiter. "Where's that boy? I'm ready for another."

The waiter was hovering nearby, and came when he saw Lodge looking around. He approached quietly, standing at Lodge's elbow. Lodge didn't see him at first, and when he did, he did a double take.

"Don't sneak up on a fellow like that, you gave me a start!" He turned to his tablemates. "Who's for another? Dorian?"

She shook her head. "I'm okay."

"Steve, how about you?"

"Sure, why not?"

"That's the spirit!"

The waiter took the order and went away. Resting his

forearms on the table, Soto leaned in toward Dorian. He said, "How long does it take you to get your hair that way?"

"Why do you ask?" she said.

"Looks like a lot of trouble to maintain."

"It is. This humidity is terrible for my hairstyle."

Lodge said, "Our Dorian is a creature of artifice and sophistication. She's hardly what you would call a natural girl."

"That depends," she said.

Soto said, "You're high-maintenance, huh?"

Lodge murmured, "How true."

"High-performance, too," she said, looking directly at Soto.

"That remains to be seen," he said.

The waiter returned with another round. It didn't look like Dorian or Lodge was going to, so Soto tipped him again.

While the waiter was still within earshot, Lodge chided, "You shouldn't throw your money away like that, Steve; it only spoils them."

"I didn't want to stiff the guy. I've been a workingman myself," Soto said. "Anyway, that's the only thing I've been feeding money to in the casino that's giving me any kind of return."

Lodge said slyly, "You should try throwing some Dorian's way. She's money-mad."

"That's one thing we've got in common—I like to spend money on women."

Dorian said, "That's one way of getting them."

Lodge raised his glass. "That sounds like a reasonable basis for negotiation. Here's to beauty."

Soto raised his glass, toasting, "To luck."

"When it comes to beauty, Steve, money beats luck every time!"

Dorian toasted, "To money, then."

They all drank, but before they could set their glasses down—

A bell rang.

A phantom bell, unseen, heard as much as felt, its major tone one of stern desolation, finality, doom. Its sobbing, shud-

33

dering vibrations hung shivering in the air, counterpointed by high, shrill, mocking chords.

Dorian and Lodge started when they heard it. Soto was surprised, and irked, by the sound, but showed little reaction. His nerves were good and he kept them under control, and most of all, he had no idea of the bell's origin and what its tolling meant.

To him, it was an annoyance and nothing more—a damned loud one. When the sound died away, his ears were still ringing.

He said, "What the hell's that, the dinner bell?"

The bell tolled again, rattling the table and chairs. The glass slipped from Lodge's hand and fell, shattering on the patio stones. The sound of it breaking was drowned out by the gong.

Others on the patio were standing up and looking around, frankly puzzled as to the source of the sound, which seemed to come from everywhere and nowhere.

Another stroke tolled. That made three. Soto found himself counting.

Lodge sat upright in his chair, leaning at an angle with his head tilted, like a dog cocking an ear to his master's voice.

People came out of the casino to see what it was all about.

Another stroke sounded.

Dorian was stiff-faced, utterly motionless, her unseeing eyes bulging.

Stroke.

More people were coming out of the casino, crowding the patio and stepping down into the garden pathways. Decks and terraces adjacent to other parts of the building were also starting to fill up with the curious.

Stroke.

Some people stared out to sea, others rubbernecked the night sky, while still others looked toward town. Each time the bell tolled, they looked in a different direction. The people who'd been looking out to sea looked up into the air, the people looking in midair turned toward the town, and so on.

Stroke.

They were crazy, Soto thought. The tolling was as loud as if they were right up in a church bell tower. Now, if the casino had a bell tower, or there was a church nearby, that would have added up. But this—

Stroke.

One person alone looked for the source not out to sea, not at the sky, and not toward the town. One person: Lodge. His face was turned toward the interior of the island, to the dark fields and hilltops overlooking the coast highway south of town.

Stroke.

Dorian sat stock-still, staring straight ahead at nothing. What looked to be a nervous tic fired off at the corner of her tight-lipped mouth.

Stroke.

Glancing inshore, following the sweeping curve of the waterfront district, Soto saw tiny antlike blurs that were people gathering on the streets, come outside to see what was what.

Stroke, stroke, stroke, stroke!

Tolling with metronomic regularity, the phantom bell counted the cadence, ringing out the count:

Thirteen.

The last and final stroke, the thirteenth, was heavier and more ominous than the rest.

Seconds passed and Soto realized that he was holding his breath, waiting for another stroke. There were no more. Finally he exhaled.

The crowd outside was in a strange mood, excited yet constrained, like spectators at a three-alarm fire watching somebody else's house burn down. When the final gong faded away into nothingness, there was some mock applause and shrill whistling.

Lodge's eyebrows were raised. He looked expectant, thoughtful. Dorian sat rigid, tightly wound.

Soto's drink was barely touched, a big tumbler of solid rum as yet undiluted by cola. He pushed it across the table to Dorian.

He said, "Here, you look like you could use a real drink."

The glass apparently showed up on Lodge's internal radar, snapping him back to reality. Before Dorian could react, he reached over to her place, scooped up the tumbler, and tossed back the rum in one gulp.

"Thanks, I needed that," he said.

Dorian snapped out of it, coming back into focus. The rigidity poured out of her body, leaving her slumped in her chair, looking sick.

Soto said, "What was that, the starting bell?" His voice sounded funny to him because his ears still rang. "Church bells in the middle of the night? It's a little late for services . . . except maybe a midnight mass."

Lodge shook his head. "Not church bells. Not the kind you mean."

"What other kind is there?"

"There's churches and then there's churches."

"I guess so. I've got to admit, that wasn't the most festive thing I've ever heard. Sounded weird, like somebody died."

"That may well be the case," Lodge said, nodding significantly.

Dorian turned to him. "Is that what you felt before?"

"I sensed something was in the air. Call it intuition—a premonition, if you will."

Soto asked, "This kind of thing happened before?"

"Never, in my experience," Lodge said.

"Must be some kind of gimmick for the tourists. Although from the way the casino cleared out, the owners can't be too happy."

Somewhere in town, emergency sirens sounded. Fire? Police?

"What I can't figure out is how they rigged it. The sound seemed to come from everywhere and nowhere," Soto said.

36

"Must be some concealed speakers planted around the grounds."

Just then a couple of vehicles topped with red flashing lights showed on the coast highway, turning onto the casino's access road and arrowing toward the structure at the end of the rocky spit.

People started trickling back inside the building, but there were still plenty of them milling on the decks and wandering through the grounds.

Two police cars drove up, big black hulking sport utility vehicles with portable red flasher emergency lights mounted on the rooftops. They jerked to a stop in front of the casino, tires barking. Doors flung open and a half-dozen-or-so uniformed policemen piled out of each one. Some of them took up guardposts around the vehicles while the others formed a wedge that went through the front entrance into the building.

Soto saw signs of their coming before he saw them. Through the glass doors he could see a disturbance inside as people jostled and pushed each other in their haste to get out of the way. They peeled off to the sides, opening a center lane in the middle of the gambling floor in advance of the oncoming squad.

Soto could see them now, a six-man wedge making their way past the midpoint of the floor, heading straight for the glass doors and the patio.

"Uh-oh," he said.

The people outside were all watching to see what would happen next. The island *policía* didn't have the most savory reputation. Standard practice was for them to handle the money crowd strictly with kid gloves, but mistakes happen.

The rank-and-file police wore military garb, plastic helmet liners, olive-drab fatigues, web belt and sidearm, and combat boots. They looked like soldiers, not lawmen. On the island, the two job categories tended to blur into each other.

In the center of the wedge was an officer, his command status signified by a black-visored cap, khaki uniform, and Sam Browne belt. Of all the squad, he and he alone wore sunglasses, an odd touch.

The squad crossed the floor, climbing three shallow steps to the glass doors. The man at the tip of the wedge palm-heeled a door, straight-arming it open and holding it that way as the others quick-marched out to the patio.

The squad members fanned out, making way for their leader, the khaki-clad officer in dark glasses.

He was *the* senior officer in the police establishment, the chief, Major Quantez, a burly bullish man with dark curly hair sticking out from the cap over his ears and a droopy black walrus mustache. Only custom-tailored khakis could have fit him as well as they did. They were starched and pressed with sharp creases. His brass shone and his black patent-leather gun belt and harness and spit-shined shoes glimmered.

Standing at the center of his squad, he struck a dramatic pose, fists on hips, slowly scanning the scene, his gaze sweeping across the patio.

The sunglasses must have hampered his vision, because he couldn't seem to find what he was looking for as long seconds dragged by. All the people on the patio were frozen in place, nobody wanting to make a move in the presence of the notoriously quick-triggered police.

Quantez was ripely middle-aged, while his men were much younger, some of them looking like teenagers. Their expressionless hard-eyed faces showed they were nothing to fool with, though.

One of them leaned into Quantez, speaking low behind a hand, pointing toward the table where Soto, Lodge, and Dorian sat.

Whatever the beef was, Soto figured it wasn't a matter of life and death, not yet, otherwise the squad would have come with drawn guns. All the same, he kept both hands on the table, open and in plain view.

Quantez stepped toward the table, leaving his sidemen behind. He loomed up beside Lodge, who seemed not only totally unconcerned but bemused.

The major smiled, the lower half of his face showing a shark's grin with strong white teeth, capped and polished. They gleamed, too.

He nodded to Dorian, leaning over her, then to Lodge. "Good evening, señorita . . . señor."

Dorian acknowledged the greeting with a tight little head bob. Lodge drawled, "Ah, Major . . ."

Soto was out of the loop and glad to be there. The law could ignore him as much as it pleased and that was all right with him.

Quantez rested a meaty hand on the back of Lodge's chair. "You heard the bells?"

"Who didn't?" Lodge countered.

"You know what it means?"

"Trouble. It means trouble."

"That much I know."

Lodge reflexively reached for the tumbler of rum, raising it to his mouth before realizing it was empty. "Damn."

He set it back down, then looked up at Quantez. "You know, Major, the Baron's troubles are not necessarily our own."

Quantez thought that one over. "No?"

"No," Lodge said.

"There's no answer at the plantation. The men don't reply."

Lodge shrugged. "There's nothing to be done about that until daylight."

"We can plan. I've called an emergency meeting at the Ministry," Quantez said. "Calexa and Alba are already there."

Lodge pulled a face. "Those charlatans! Who needs them?"

"That's what they said about you when I went out to find you."

"Hmmph! Well, in that case, we mustn't keep them waiting."

"My sentiments exactly, señor."

Lodge pushed back his chair and stood up, rock-solid, all signs of tipsiness or unsteadiness vanished. "To the Ministry, then."

Quantez stood over Dorian, lifting the bottom of his dark glasses so he could see better down the front of her dress.

"Come along, dear," Lodge said.

Dorian rose, moving stiffly. She was more unsteady on her feet than her uncle, not so much from the alcohol as from tension.

Soto got up, too. What the hell, it was polite. Mindful of the squadmen, he moved slowly and easily, making no sudden movements.

Lodge smiled. "Afraid we'll have to call it a night, Steve. Delighted to make your acquaintance. We must make a date for Dorian and me to show you the sights of our little island."

"Sure."

"Let's do it soon, shall we? I promise we'll give you the grand tour."

"I'm looking forward to it."

Dorian said, "You think so."

Soto said, "You know where to find me. And if you don't, I'm sure Major Quantez will."

Quantez nodded, smiling, acknowledging the pleasantry. "I like to know the whereabouts of all our distinguished guests."

Soto nodded back. Quantez said, "You have arrived at a most interesting time, señor. Big changes are in the wind. A clever man will choose his friends with care."

"I'm a friendly guy," Soto said.

"We are all friends here on Isla Morgana."

Quantez took Dorian's arm, steering her away from the table toward the glass doors. "With your permission——"

He, Dorian, and Lodge crossed the patio, the woman flanked by the two men. Soto called after them: "'Night."

A couple of the squadmen hopped to it, opening doors and holding them for their chief and his two companions. Soto noticed that Lodge's movements were straight and steady. He didn't seem drunk at all.

The trio went inside, with squadmen before and behind them, the ones in front clearing the way as the group crossed the gambling room toward the far wall.

Soto lost sight of them, but after a moment he saw the

two police SUVs drive away, going the way they came. This time their red flasher lights were dark. Only when they were on the coast highway heading back to town did the casino crowd begin to loosen up and move freely, and then mostly to make their exit.

Elegantly dressed couples and groups streamed out of the building, descending the zigzagging flights of wooden stairs to the brightly lit pier, where their boats and water taxis awaited.

A hulking figure stepped out of the shadows, trailed by a tall, skinny companion. They sidled over to Soto, who nodded at them. The big bearish guy with the crew cut was Tony Paul and the other guy was Dennis.

"The bad pennies always turn up," Soto said.

Tony Paul said, "We was right here, watching the whole thing."

"That's a comfort."

Dennis said, "I thought the general was going to put the arm on you and haul you off to the slams."

"That's no general, he's a major. And when he collars you, the next and last stop is the torture dungeon of Seaguard Castle."

Tony Paul said, "We had him covered, Steve. Dennis and me was set so we would've had him in a cross fire. One wrong move, and we'd have put the blast on him—and his boys, too."

"That would've been funny, considering he's the guy that gave the okay for us to pack heat in the first place."

Dennis asked, "Hey, Steve, who's the babe?"

"Some wacko. And if you think she's weird, you should meet her uncle Basil. If he is her uncle."

"I'd rather meet her. She's hot."

"Too skinny," Tony Paul said. "You can't trust those skinny broads—they're hungry."

Dennis scratched his head. "What was that bit with the bells? Some kind of publicity stunt?"

"Beats me, but I can tell you this—it's got the bigs rattled," Soto said. He shook a smoke out of the pack and stuck it between his lips, and while Dennis was fumbling for a light, Tony Paul had his lighter out and flaming, torching the end of the cigarette.

Soto vented smoke clouds. "Quantez picked up Lodge and his screwball niece to whisk them to some emergency meeting at the Ministry. It wasn't a bust. Lodge's got plenty of juice in his own right with the powers that be down here."

Tony Paul said, "Who is this guy Lodge and how does he rate so high?"

"Damned if I know. I'm a stranger here myself. But I'll find out."

Dennis said, "No mystery about why the niece rates— she's hot! I'd like to take a meeting with her!"

Tony Paul shook his head. "You better take a cold shower instead, kid."

"It's this tropical climate, it's gotten into my blood."

Soto said, "Try quinine." He stood facing the town, smoking and thinking for a minute.

He said, "Don't forget why the Boss sent us down here. He's got a couple million in hot cash that needs laundering and the island bankers say they can do it. Maybe so.

"But something happened tonight that's made the insiders jumpy. I don't know what it is, but I'm damned sure going to find out. Not a nickel of the Boss's money moves offshore until this place gets a clean bill of health."

Dennis stroked his chin, rubbing his hipster goatee. "Maybe it's political, like a revolution. They're always having revolutions in these hot countries, right? The bells could have been a signal for the workers to rise up and overthrow the government."

Tony Paul said, "They could have been a signal to drop dead, because that's what they sounded like."

"They were kind of depressing."

"Weird."

"Yeah, man, weird."

Soto laughed. "Don't get spooked."

THREE

Like nature, power abhors a vacuum. For decades the un-natural power of Dracula had laid a blight on the land, serving as a magnet for evil shadows and things of darkness. Now, with Dracula gone, the dominant will that had held those sinister forces under sway was no more, and so—

"Zombie girls are no fun," Gaston said. "They can't feel it when you're doing things to them. Not like you, sweetheart."

He did something then to the girl and she screamed. It was early yet and he was just starting in on her, so her screams were loud and clear. He added a special little finesse at the end of what he was doing and her shrieks shrilled up into a high falsetto register of pain.

He let go of her and she fell to the floor and lay there curled in a fetal position, too scared to sob. She panted, gasping, unable to catch her breath.

Gaston stood over her, not really excited yet but interested, enjoying himself. He was wide-built, stocky, with short curly black hair, a spade-shaped face, and pointed-arch eyebrows.

Bessamo stood beside him, eager to get in on the fun. He was a steroided-out bodybuilder with a neck as thick as most men's thighs. He wore a sleeveless skintight black muscle shirt and baggy pants.

Nearby but over to one side sat Haze, a lanky cocaine cowboy in a cowboy hat, vest, and jeans. He sat with his chair tilted back, resting his pointy-toed cowboy boots on top of the old scarred wooden desk in the office part of the shack. He held a well-worn copy of a paperback western, but he was doing more watching than reading.

The girl on the floor was named Kristen and she was young and still pretty even after all she had already endured. She was a free spirit and fun seeker from the States who had come to the island on a pleasure-cruising yacht filled with party people. When the yacht weighed anchor and sailed away, it was minus more than a few of its original passengers. Those who had been left behind were all young, attractive, and wouldn't be missed if they dropped out of sight. Like Kristen.

There was a lot of that sort of thing going on around the island, so much so that there was a surplus of attractive young people to stock the brothels, live sex shows, and private slave auctions that catered to those with specialized tastes and the ability to pay for them.

Because of the surfeit, the powers that be could afford to toss some of the human chattel to their underlings, the ordinary workers and soldiers that made up the bulk of the organization.

That's why Kristen had fallen into the hands of Gaston and his associates, as a kind of bonus for guarding the compound on the edge of the plantation, up here in the hills overlooking the sea.

The four of them were in a big one-room wooden shack with a flat tilted roof. It served as the guardhouse. One side of the space was a kind of office area, with a massive beat-up desk, some chairs, and a couple of dented filing cabinets. No paperwork was kept here at the compound and the cabinet drawers were stocked with weapons, ammunition, whips, prods, prongs, and bottles of rum.

44

The other side had a table and some chairs and a couple of iron cots with bare stained mattresses lining the walls.

Up here in the hills, there were no power lines and they were off the Magdalena grid, but the shack had electric lights, thanks to a gas-powered generator in a shed leaning against one of the walls. Its chugging was a constant background noise, and the place stank of gas fumes that leaked in through the cracks.

At the compound, so close to the plantation, light was a necessity. Nobody wanted to be without it, not with the things that were liable to be walking around in the dark.

Unshaded lightbulbs filled the shack with hot yellow brightness. Lots of screened windows and a screen door did little to ease the heat, while a couple of electric fans moved the air around without cooling it.

The space stank of sweat, tobacco smoke, gas fumes, and rum.

Gaston and Bessamo loomed over Kristen, who lay huddled on her side on the warped plank floorboards. Bessamo said, "I think she fainted."

Gaston snorted, nostrils flaring. "Hell, no! She's just scared."

Hunkering down beside her, he grabbed a fistful of long tangled yellow hair, pulling it by the roots, jerking her head up, and lifting her face off the floor. She stared at him with eyes of horror.

Actually, she wasn't too bad off yet. She'd been through the mill but she was lucky: she still had all her fingers and toes and no disfiguring marks.

Gaston was loving it. "We're going to do whatever we want to you, sweetie, and when we're done, we'll toss you to the zombies."

She screamed, "No!"

Bessamo said, "Those stiffs wouldn't know what to do with a warm one. I say, feed her to the wolves."

Gaston said, "Maybe we'll make you a zombie, doll."

"NO!"

45

"Then you won't feel a thing. Because you'll be dead, but walking around."

Bessamo said, "You feeling anything, Gaston?"

"I'm starting to."

On the desk a portable radio was playing calypso music, a jaunty tune, not too loud.

Gaston crouched over the girl, pulling her hair, leering at her, when the screen door opened from outside and a man stuck his head in.

He was fair-haired, with a soft face the color and consistency of whitefish and dull brown eyes. He stood outside, just sticking his head in, a man in a hurry. He showed no surprise or change of expression at the sight of the brutalized, half-naked girl.

He said, "Come on, let's go."

Gaston said, "What's up, Flume?"

"You better see this. All of you."

"What—"

"The barracks. Now. Move it." Flume pulled his head outside and stepped away, not waiting to see if they followed. The screen door banged shut.

Gaston stared at it and called Flume a dirty name when he was sure the other couldn't hear him. Haze swung his feet to the floor, rose, and stuck the paperback in his back pocket. His jeans were tight and he had to jam it in.

Gaston gave the girl's head a bone-rattling shake and then flung her aside by the hair. "Later for you, sweet cheeks."

He'd been squatting on his hams for a while and he groaned as he rose. Haze stood at the doorway, holding the screen door open. Bugs flew in, big ones, lots of them, flapping and circling the electric lights.

The other two started outside, Bessamo hanging back. He said, "What about her?"

"What about her?" Gaston asked.

"You just going to leave her?"

"Sure."

"What if she runs away?"

"Where could she go—the plantation? If she's crazy enough to run around here after dark, then too bad for her."

Bessamo nodded, as if that made sense. The three went out, with Gaston calling back, "Keep it warm for me, honey. Those zombie girls are soooo cold!"

They went away laughing.

The compound was in a hollow on the other side of the dirt road leading to the plantation. It had been built to shelter the workers who came to cut the sugarcane at harvesttime at the plantation, and the buildings were at least fifty years old. There was a long shedlike barracks, a handful of small outbuildings, and the guardhouse. Some Jeeps and pickup trucks belonging to the guards were parked in a dirt yard near the guardhouse.

On the other side of the rise was the road, and beyond, the plantation. The mansion was set far back from the road and was further screened from the compound by a line of trees.

Gaston, Bessamo, and Haze crossed to the barracks grounds, where floodlights blazed. The floodlights had their own generator.

The barracks building was a converted curing shed, a shoe-box-shaped building with a peaked roof. The windows were shuttered and the solid doors were reinforced. The unpainted wood was silvered with age.

Flume and six other guards were grouped around the building's nearer long side. The guardhouse trio joined the group.

Gaston said, "What is it?"

Then he saw what the others were already gaping at, the barracks walls and locked shutters straining, swelling, and heaving, as though whatever was inside was trying to get out.

A guard named Hector turned to face Gaston. He said, "They're restless."

"They can't be restless. They're dead," Gaston scoffed. "Why, they don't do anything unless you tell them to."

"Well, they're doing it," Hector said. "Listen . . ."

47

Gaston didn't have to strain his ears to hear; he realized that he'd been hearing it all the time, but he just hadn't noticed it until Hector singled it out.

From the barracks came a clatter that sounded like nothing so much as a barnful of cattle, milling, stomping their hooves on a wooden floor.

"Damn!"

"It just started a few minutes ago, after the bells, Gaston. We've heard all kinds of hell at the plantation tonight—worse than usual, even . . ."

"Yes, yes, get on with it, Hector."

"And all through the shrieking and the howling and all the rest of it, the barracks was dead quiet, as always."

"Like a tomb, yes, I know."

"But the bells, Gaston! After the bells rang, they started moving by themselves. By themselves!" Hector's voice rasped, his face was drawn so tight it was twitching. "The bells—they rang *doom*."

"Shhh! Not so loud. It's best to turn a deaf ear to what you hear from the plantation. If you're smart, Hector, you'll dummy up."

"If the zombies are free, they'll destroy those who made them zombies. What mad sorcery of the Baron's is this—"

"Shut up, shut up."

Flume came over to them, fists at his sides. Without warning, he punched Hector in the face. Gaston winced. Hector's head snapped back from the recoil, but he stayed on his feet, staggering. Flume waited, his fists up. Hector had no fight in him and put his open hands up in front of his face.

Flume lowered his hands. "Never mind about Baron Latos. Keep your mind on your work and your trap shut about things that don't concern you, unless you want to end up on the wrong side of those barracks walls."

Hector nodded, head bobbing, holding his hands to his face, nursing a bloody nose. Flume gave Gaston a hard look.

"I didn't say anything," Gaston said.

Flume held the look a few more beats, then walked on. He'd gone only a few paces when a shutter near the front of the building popped open. A plank was banged out from inside, nails squealing as they were pried out of the frame.

A clawlike hand reached through the hole in the shutter, taking hold of the plank and tearing it off. More fists hammered at what was left of the shutter, battering it down.

In the now-empty window frame, the rectangle of blankness was filled with the torsos of the walking dead. The zombies were a dry lot, mostly, leathery, all moisture long since burned out of them. They looked like people carved from driftwood.

One of them threw a leg over the sill, a skinny gray man with a potbelly and a pair of colorless tattered knee-length breeches. He flailed around in the window, his stiff angular limbs thrashing.

Flume said, "Don't let him get out."

"I got it," a man holding an ax handle said. He trotted to the window, whose sill was about four feet off the ground. Somebody called to him, "Careful, Turk!"

Turk swung the ax handle like a baseball bat, slamming it into the zombie's leg that was outside the window. There was a loud crack but it didn't slow the zombie down any. It scrabbled for a grip on the outside of the window frame, to pull itself out.

Holding the club like a spear, Turk made short, savage thrusts to the zombie's middle. Another zombie stretched a sinewy arm around past the one in the window and got a grip on the end of the club.

Turk stopped thrusting and started pulling, trying to free the club. He struggled to break the zombie's grip. He spread his feet on the ground, dug in, and leaned back and heaved, putting his weight into it.

The zombie's arm snapped off at the shoulder and came flying out the window, still clutching its end of the ax handle. There was very little blood, only a few splashes of thick dark syrupy stuff.

Turk kept going backward and sat down hard. When he saw that the zombie arm was still attached to the club, he threw it away, shouting, "Arrgh!"

Gaston and a few of the others snickered. Turk put his hands on the ground, bracing himself to rise, but before he could get up, he got a lapful of zombie as the thing in the window came tumbling down on top of him.

This one had two good arms, though one of its legs wasn't working too well where Turk had clipped it with the ax handle. It shoved bony hands into his soft parts and started digging while Turk kicked and screamed.

Two more zombies came flopping out the window, crashing to the ground. They got up, moving like stick-legged insects. More crowded the window, clawing to get out.

Turk's screams rose to a wailing pitch, then were suddenly choked off and he fell back, dead.

Gaston drew his gun, a big-bore revolver, opening fire on Turk's killer. Each shot sounded like an artillery shell being fired. He shot at point-blank range, bursting the zombie's head. It fell back, still moving.

Other guards pulled their guns and started shooting, pouring it into the two zombies on the ground and the ones in the window. Spear blades of fire flashed from gun muzzles, puffing gun smoke. A hazy cordite-stinking blue-gray cloud hung in the air at chest height.

The zombies twitched and jerked and fell as the bullets tagged them, but not all of them fell, and those who did picked themselves up once the bullets stopped hitting.

More came out the window.

The barracks door went convex, bowing outward on its hinges. Flume rounded up a couple of guards, getting behind them, herding them toward the building.

He shouted, "Block that door!"

They'd almost reached it when it burst apart, exploding outward in a mass of splintered planks and snapped beams, falling down like a drawbridge.

Out came the zombies, a mob of them. Their hair was stringy like dried seaweed. They had skull faces and wasted bony bodies and alligator-hide skin. They exited the barracks, about twenty-four in all, all of them going for the guards.

They were surprisingly quick, and any one zombie could absorb a gun's full load and keep on coming. Most of the guards were already low on ammo before the mass onslaught from the barracks.

Pretty soon after that, they were low on life.

In the shack, Kristen was weak from abuse and near-paralyzed with fear. What got her moving wasn't the sound of gunfire; it was the screaming that began when the shots trailed off. That reached her, even in her shell-shocked condition.

She was shaking too hard to stand up, so she crawled on hands and knees toward the doorway. She was stiff, numb, freezing. The swirling patterns of the wooden floor planks stood out with crystal clarity, like details in a black-and-white photo.

The radio played on, now featuring a peppery salsa tune with lots of drums and brass. When the trumpets hit the high notes, they dueted with the screaming outside.

Gaston came crashing through the screen door, staggering inside. He was in red, a bloody mess of tattered flesh that looked like the work of a jungle cat.

A spring-coil hinge caused the door to swing back, closing on a zombie who was closing in on Gaston. The zombie held out a spread-fingered hand, spearing it through the top screen panel.

The zombie got tangled up with the screen door but kept on coming, tearing it off its hinges and knocking it aside. Kristen was crouching squarely in its path and threw herself out of the way as it bore down on her.

It ignored her and kept after Gaston, a few paces behind him. Gaston stumbled to the office area, bouncing off the desk, falling on a filing cabinet with both arms. He tore at the top drawer, frantically trying to open it, fear and loss of blood making his hands clumsy. Looking over his shoulder, he saw the zombie reaching for him.

The zombie was a female, naked except for a ragged, faded Club Med T-shirt. She was all broomstick limbs and dried-out yellowed skin, eyeless but able to get around as easily as if there were eyeballs in her hollow sockets. She had good teeth, on display where the skin around her mouth had rotted away.

She put a hand on Gaston's shoulder. He screamed, pulling something out of the top drawer as he dodged to the side. He broke her grip and got away, her claws raking long deep slashes through his tattered shirt and into his shoulders and chest.

He fell back behind the desk, back to the wall. He'd grabbed a sawed-off shotgun from the cabinet and held it now cradled in both hands as she came at him.

It was a double-barreled job and he jerked both triggers at once, cutting loose on the zombie's middle when she was almost in reach of him.

There was a tremendous blast of fire, smoke, and noise, cutting the zombie in half—literally. There wasn't much of her there to begin with. She was severed between rib cage and hips. The top half fell to the floor. The bottom half, from the waist down, remained standing for a few seconds before toppling.

Gaston couldn't believe his luck. As it sank in, he started laughing. There was something crazy in it, but not all the way. He still had something left inside, and that might make all the difference.

A cloud of gun smoke hung in his corner. Looking past it, he saw Kristen on the floor. An audience, the only thing that could make his triumph still sweeter.

"See, girl, no zombie bitch can kill me. I'll get out of this yet," he said.

He should have been watching instead of gloating, because while he was bragging to Kristen, the zombie's upper half was stirring into motion on the floor.

Walking on its hands, trailing a length of severed spinal column like a wriggling tadpole tail, it scuttled over to Gaston and started climbing up his legs. Clawing handholds through his pants into his flesh, the she-zombie scampered squirrellike onto his trunk and then started biting and burrowing.

52

Gaston clubbed it with the butt of the weapon, screaming and screaming. As he fell down behind the desk, kicking and screaming, Kristen got up and ran out the door, suddenly stopping short to keep from colliding with a zombie just outside the guardhouse.

She shrieked, ducking to the side. The zombie ignored her, stalking into the shack, from which screams, while weak, were still emanating.

A half-dozen zombies were walking around nearby, in the shadow zone between the guardhouse and the barracks. A glimpse of what was happening to the guards at the barracks grounds sent Kristen abruptly lunging in the opposite direction.

She ran up the rise, leaving the compound behind her. She was barefoot but oblivious of the sharp stones that cut the soles of her feet. As she climbed to the top of the hollow, she saw figures off to her left, about a stone's throw away.

A couple of guards ran across the moonlit ridge, chased by twice as many zombies. Kristen peeled off to the right, running away from them. The ground leveled off and she cut onto a dirt road at a tangent, the road to the plantation.

Clouds blew in, streaming across the moon, hiding the stars. The moonlight became murky. The road was a strip of grayness stretched across a deeper darkness. Kristen followed it, away from plantation and compound.

Farther up the rise, Bessamo and Haze ran across the road toward the plantation, a posse of zombies behind them. Haze was in good condition and jogged steadily along, a couple of lengths ahead of Bessamo. The bodybuilder wasn't a jogger and he was laboring, sucking wind.

The clouds rifted and the moon came out, its light brightening, revealing vast empty open fields of hard-packed dirt stretching from the roadway to the mansion a couple of hundred yards away. The mansion was dark.

A long thin shadow appeared on the ground in front of Bessamo, a giant's shadow, startling. He squawked, breaking stride, almost tripping and falling.

He looked back, sobbing for breath. The nearest zombie was a hundred feet away, with the others straggling behind. They weren't built for speed, but they were tireless, relentless.

Panting, he started forward, jolted again by the sight of the weird giant shadow stretching out in front of him. It was his own shadow, cast in the moonlight. He followed it, trying to catch up to Haze, who was still loping along.

"Haze . . . wait . . . *wait! Haze!*"

Haze kept going, not slowing, not looking back. Bessamo saved his breath for running, pouring on an extra burst of speed to cut the distance. His chest heaved, lungs burning, limbs leaden.

Haze was up ahead, slowing, pausing. Bessamo reached him, nearly tripping over his own feet, reeling. He stood leaning, bent forward, holding on to the tops of his thighs, gasping like a man saved from drowning.

Haze put a hand on Bessamo's shoulder, pointing toward the mansion. "Look!"

Bessamo raised his head and looked up, sweat stinging his eyes. Ahead, a handful of figures wandered around in front of the mansion, shambling and slouching.

"Zombies guarding the house! Can't go there," Haze said.

The zombies ahead turned toward the guards, then started forward. Bessamo said, "Oh, God, they're coming after us, too!"

The zombies were closer to the mansion than they·were to the guards, but that was still too close. Also, the zombies from the compound had regained the ground they lost when their quarry had raced ahead on the flat.

Haze indicated a thicket of woods on the right, about two hundred feet away. "The trees—maybe we can lose them in there."

Bessamo was too winded to do anything more than nod and say, "Yeah—yeah . . ."

Haze took off. Bessamo paused to catch his breath, and when he did he saw how close both groups of zombies were to him. It gave him a burst of adrenaline that sent him zooming after Haze.

Haze was far ahead but paused near the edge of the woods, uncertain. Bessamo caught up with him, holding on to him to keep from falling.

Haze broke loose. "Get your hands off of me, boy!" He looked back. The two groups of zombies had formed into one and they were coming, shambling along, hopping and weaving and flailing.

Haze said, "Where's the trail, where's the trail?"

Moonlight picked out a gap in the woods about thirty feet to the left. Haze went to it, Bessamo following. The gap was the mouth of a trail. The two plunged into it.

The trail was a tunnel through thick tropical growth, winding deeper into dark thickets. A man standing with his arms extended straight out from his sides could have brushed the foliage on both sides of the pathway with his fingertips.

Haze went on ahead, Bessamo struggling to keep up with him. Haze's light-colored shirt stood out in the dimness. Moonbeams shafted through gaps in the interlacing canopy of boughs, the twisted branches hung with moss and strangled with snakelike lianas and furry vines.

There was a thick smell of green decay and moist earth. The trail zigzagged, never traveling in a straight line for more than a few paces before making a sharp turn around a blind corner. As the men continued, it trended downward, hairpinning down the side of a hill. The growth was quite thick here, the overhead branches sometimes shutting out all moonlight, so the trail was in blackness.

The fugitives made a lot of noise going down the hill, breaking branches, knocking rocks loose, panting, cursing. At the bottom of the slope, at right angles to it, lay a broad shallow trough, the bed of a dry gully. The far side of the gully was lined with more woods.

No trees grew in the sandy soil of the gully, only chest-high bushes and ankle-high grass. Moonlight picked out some zombies at the top of the hill Haze and Bessamo had descended, then clouds covered the moon, darkening the hillside. The zombies could be heard crashing downhill through the brush.

The gully was closed off by boulders on the right and open on the left. Haze and Bessamo went left, weaving around bushes, tripping over roots, falling, getting up, and going forward.

The gully curved right, then left, circling around far to the left, under the base of a wooded knoll. On top of it, rising from a mass of foliage, could be seen part of the roof of a tall building.

Haze said, "I think that's the mill."

"No . . . not that way," Bessamo said, wheezing.

"We can't go back the other way."

"They—they coming?"

"I can't see them, and I'm not going to wait until I do," Haze said, starting forward.

Bessamo held his hands against his barrel-vault chest. "My heart . . ."

"Those suckers'll *eat* your heart, buddy," Haze said, over his shoulder. Bessamo lurched after him, groaning.

On the far side of the knoll, the gully reached its head in a couple of low mounds and a long sloping rise. The duo climbed it.

At the top was a line of trees, tall and slender, about fourteen feet tall, screening off what lay beyond. Haze and Bessamo pushed through to the other side.

They stood at the edge of a marshy field about fifty feet wide. On the one side of it was a graveyard, a very old one, desolate and overgrown. On the other, beyond the graveyard, rose the back of the mansion.

There were no zombies in sight.

Haze crouched beside the trees, head turned back the way they came, listening. "Stop breathing so hard, I can't hear."

"I—I can't help it," Bessamo said, panting.

"Try." Haze listened some more. "I don't hear them."

"Maybe . . . maybe we lost them."

They spoke in hushed voices, whispering, poised to run. Haze gripped Bessamo's meaty arm. He said, "We'll sneak around the back of the house, then double back along the opposite side of the fields to the road. They won't be looking for us there."

Bessamo had finally caught some of his breath. "Hell with that. I'm not going near that house, or the graveyard, either."

"I'm going," Haze said, stepping off. He hadn't gone more than a few steps before the other had fallen in beside him.

"This is crazy," Bessamo complained.

"Shut up," Haze said.

They crossed the field, marsh ground squelching beneath their feet. They skirted the perimeter of the graveyard, emerging on a strip of land running between it and the mansion. The ground was harder there. Once it had been part of a landscaped garden, but now it was just weeds and dirt. A path made of paved stones ran through it, paralleling the back of the mansion. Weeds grew through the cracks in the stones.

Haze and Bessamo walked softly on the path, the walls of the mansion rising up on their left, hemming them in on that side. On the right was the graveyard.

Haze said, "No wolves around . . . maybe they ran off."

"Now you think of that," Bessamo said. "At least a wolf is something normal. Alive. You can kill it."

They were at the midpoint of the path. Ahead on the right, bordering the graveyard, stood a small private chapel, of an age with the mansion. It was oddly shaped, with stone octagonal walls. A big tree that had been uprooted by some long-ago storm had fallen on the chapel roof, crushing part of it. It was still there, thick with decades-old growth.

The mansion was a bleak squalid ruin, sinister and black-dark. No glimmer of light showed anywhere in it. The roofline sagged, the uprights slumped, and the blank gaping windows were like open mouths turned down at the corners. The walls were stained, dingy.

Clouds thickened around the moon, dimming it to a pale white smudge, deepening the darkness along the path. Haze cursed. The brightest thing in sight was his light-colored shirt. Bessamo followed it closely as they kept on going, but more slowly.

A patch of moonlight played on the chapel walls, flickering as the clouds streamed across the sky. Haze and Bessamo drew abreast of the structure. The moon was hidden behind clouds, but the patch of pale, silvery light glowed brighter than before.

It was the unearthly glow shed by three females who glided out from behind a corner of the building, crossing the men's path. A thick milky mist cloaked them, luminous mist that globed them in soft greenish-white brightness. A corona of swirling streamers seemed to boil off the edges of the glow.

There was no mist anywhere else in the surroundings.

The women were veiled and wore what looked like lacy negligees, one red, one white, and one black. Their veils and slippers were the same colors as their gowns. The veils were gauzy things made of see-through netting, worn over the head and trailing in long loose gauzy folds, covering them from crown to throat.

Behind the veils the women's eyes were red and their faces blurred. The eyes burned brighter, the faces growing vaguer and more indistinct, until at last there seemed to be three pairs of hot coals hanging in midair in front of the faces of the two men.

Having been caught by those hypnotic eyes, Haze and Bessamo could not look away. They forgot to run and just stood there, rooted with stupefaction.

The three females laughed, sounding like mischievous schoolgirls.

The one in white said, "Sisters, I am famished!"

The one in black said, "Young, strong, the rich red blood!"

The one in red said, "Ahhhhhhh . . ."

They lifted their veils, baring blood-eyes and wickedly fanged mouths. They were starved, hollow-cheeked, hauntingly beautiful in a morbid way, with lithe, electric bodies.

They were female but not human women. They were Undead vampires, Dracula's harem.

They fell on Haze and Bessamo.

FOUR

I am DRACULA. I was a prince and warlord of the Szekely folk, in whose veins runs the blood of Attila and his Huns, greater than any witch or devil. I was of the same generation as the last emperor of Byzantium, born over five centuries ago. I led the Order of the Dragon's iron knights against the sultan. Only Muhammad II, who sacked Constantinople to end its thousand-year reign, could kill me, and then only by treachery and deceit. He killed me but did not defeat me. Even Death could not defeat me. Of all powers of earth, heaven, and hell, I acknowledge only Satan as my liege lord. I am immortal, I can not die.

I am Dracula—

But Dracula was no more.

Wasn't he?

Dracula was a cloud of graveyard dust hanging in midair above the old mill. The dust glowed like radioactive particles. The cloud tended to hold together, resisting the breezes that sought to disperse it.

Any vampire is a kind of satanic miracle, requiring the intervention of dark powers to suspend the natural processes of life and death. Like all such devilish gifts, Undeath has its price. The vampire must sustain itself on the blood of the living.

But Dracula was no mere vampire. He was a Lord of the Undead, claiming his title not by birthright but by untrammeled force, destroying all challengers to his rule, be they living or dead or something in between.

Success breeds its own continuity and his existence over more than five centuries had made him a nexus of diabolic power. He was a true Vampire Lord, one of that rare and potent breed that could transform himself into a bat, a wolf, or a cloud of mist.

But not when he had been staked through the heart, the time-honored antidote for Undeath. Vampires are supernatural creatures, not mortals. They don't breathe, their hearts don't beat, and the only blood flowing through their veins is that which they've sucked from the living.

Dark forces bind the complex energies of vampirism, and the heart corresponds with that place on the astral body where those energies find their source and core. Those who know the yogic concept of *chakras* or primal energy centers will understand.

When that core is penetrated with a wooden stake, the binding energies are disrupted and come undone, causing the vampire to cease to be. Wood is prescribed for the stake rather than metal, because, having once been part of something that lived, it is lethal to the vampire's antilife energies.

When the Wolfman hung Dracula up on a stake through the heart, the core of his astral being was ruptured. The tremendous energies loosed by this act were impossible for the vampire to control. This was not the transformative process that could change his material body into a bat or mist—this was disintegration.

Dracula was powerless to stop it, unable to check the chaos of coming apart. His body crumbled into dust and his spirit was smeared into the sky as a hate-cloud.

Vampires sleep in their coffins during the day and even dream in order to preserve what's left of their sanity. Dracula had never been that sane to begin with—witness his penchant for impaling his enemies. During long centuries of

Undeath, he coffin-slept always with one small corner of his mind aware and awake, ever-vigilant for outside threats.

Now he knew oblivion. Was oblivion. Not death, but nullity, pure negation. That vast, seething, scheming mentality that was Dracula, lusting and hating—wiped out.

That incredible rage, that pure hate, hung in the air with the cloud of dust. Drifting.

Hordes of vampire bats took to the air, fleeing the plantation. They steered clear of the cloud.

Rats poured out of the mill, mansion, and chapel, streaming across the ground in squealing waves, running away.

His mastery vanished along with Dracula himself, and the zombies were freed to take revenge on their tormentors.

His three vampire wives were now held in check solely by their own feverish appetites.

And the bells of hell rang.

All these things marked the passing of Dracula. All that remained was a death-dust hate-cloud. And yet . . .

The cloud basked in the moonlight, soothing balm for its chaotic energies. There was occult power in the moonlight for those of the night world.

Moonbeams shone on the graveyard. The hate-cloud followed them down. The beams fell on the mausoleum and the inert gutted Monster that lay sprawled before it.

The aura of pain and fear and death attracted the cloud, drawing it down. And there was blood, massive amounts of it pooling on the ground. Monster blood, but still blood.

And the blood is the life.

Puddles of liver-colored blood shimmered with iridescent green highlights, welling out from the gutted carcass. The hate-cloud hung in the air above them.

The Monster's body was of no use to it. It could not possess another's body, wearing it as a host, least of all a physical shape as gross and alien as that of Frankenstein's creation.

But the blood beckoned. The hate-cloud hung over it, shaking out flakes of sooty graveyard dust. Where they touched the blood they dissolved, sending up strings of smoke, thin streamers six to eight feet long, which rose vertically, tethered to the puddles.

A torrent of graveyard dust fell into the blood, dissolving into grounded vapors, the blood-dust compound fizzing and hissing.

There was a sense of unease, of restless motion eddying in the air. Tree boughs shook and weeds rustled.

The hate-cloud sank into the blood like mist melting into a pond. The compound glowed, shining with phosphorescent light.

Corpse light.

Weird chemical and alchemical reactions were taking place where the dust of Dracula joined the blood of Frankenstein. Greenish-white fumes boiled off the hybrid, thick and curling, like the smoke off a cake of dry ice.

The compound foamed, bubbled and grew, becoming a kind of bloblike plasma, semisolid, writhing in a cradle of raw crackling energy.

The long vertical tendrils of smoke fell back on the plasmoid, wrapping around it, banding it. The mass heaved and shuddered, taking shape, becoming solid.

The flooding phosphorescence ebbed, faded, went dark. The plasmoid blob still had a slight lunar glow, shimmering through the spiraling bands of smoke that wrapped it.

The smoke blew away, revealing something new under the moonlight.

It looked like a maggot, but it was the size of a man. A sluglike thing with no head, arms, or legs. It lay squirming on the ground, a crawling thing. It was cigar-shaped, the thickness of a man at its middle, tapering to a triangle-shaped tip at both ends.

There was something of the single-celled organism in it. Its outer "skin" was a glistening semitransparent membrane that pulsated wildly, quivering from the shock of its creation. Inside, it was all liquid protoplasm, streaming and flowing. In its center was something that looked like an egg yolk the size of a covered serving dish. This was the nucleus, the controlling center.

In the past, Dracula had been resurrected by quantities of fresh human blood, transforming it into the building blocks of a physical body. But this was Monster blood.

The result was something new and strange, bearing the same relationship to Dracula as a larva does to a fully-formed insect. The creature was mindless, with no conscious awareness, but it did have instincts and appetites and bundles of nerve receptors that sensed things at a distance and responded to stimuli.

It was a creature of the night, it hungered for blood, and it was not alive but Undead. In this much at least, it bore Dracula's stamp.

It was not Dracula, no more than a seed is a plant.

For classification purposes, it could be called the Drakon, the Dracula-who-is-not-Dracula.

It set off in search of prey, moving by rhythmically wriggling its flattened underside, gliding speedily over the ground, an undulant blood-slug.

It moved away from the plantation. That was a place of walking-dead zombies and Undead vampire wives. The Drakon needed live prey, fresh hot blood.

It slithered out of the graveyard and around to the front of the mansion, moving speedily with a wicked whipsawing motion. Moonlight tingled on its gelid outer skin.

It scuttled through the dirt fields. A lizard got in its way and the Drakon rolled over it and scooped it up, passing the reptile through its semipermeable membrane and swallowing it inside, where digestive enzymes went to work dissolving it.

In an instant the lizard had been sucked dry and reduced back to its basic components. It had provided only a squirt of blood, but all of its elements could be absorbed to build more Drakon-stuff.

The Drakon wriggled onward, questing for real prey, something big, with lots of blood, preferably human. It operated purely on blind instinct, without calculation, responding to stimuli.

Live blood attracted it, dead things repelled it. These were

63

forces, operating on it like gravity or magnetism. One stimulus pulled, another pushed.

It sensed zombies nearby and abruptly changed course, angling away to avoid them. Yet the Drakon was too new and unsure of its powers to try them, so it avoided them instead.

It slithered into the brush, gliding over the bumps and hollows on the ground, under arching roots, over fallen trees, thinning itself to flow through narrow places and tight spots.

Along the way it scooped up toads, frogs, iguanas, field mice, and rats, popping them into itself and absorbing them. It did so by reflex. They weren't much of a meal. The Drakon was just grazing.

After a while it came to the end of the thicket, crawling over grassy ground until it reached a road. It paused, its nucleus rippling like a jellyfish jetting water through itself.

It sensed blood, human blood. Flattening itself like a carpet, it glided over the road, its outer edges waving and fluttering. A shark can smell blood in the water a mile away, and the Drakon's receptors were sharper than a shark's.

Its underside throbbed with tiny starbursts of hot pleasure each time it touched a drop of blood. It soaked up the blood like a sponge. There wasn't a lot of it, really only a tiny quantity, a sparse scattering of match-head-sized droplets sprinkled along the road. To the Drakon, each drop was a promise and a lure.

The trail took it down the road, away from the compound. The tantalizing sweetness of the wholesale bloodletting going on there was almost maddening, but the anticipatory pleasure was poisoned by the taint of the hostile zombie presence.

Besides, the trail was fresh and the blood-scent was hot. The creature quickened, sidewinding down the dirt road, leaving a distinctive zigzag track.

Nosing down the crest of a rise, it sensed the immediate nearness of its prey. It launched itself downhill with a fresh burst of speed.

Kristen was walking on the side of the road, limping, the

soles of her feet sore and bleeding where she'd cut them on sharp stones. The adrenaline which had helped power her escape from the compound had worn off and she was weary and staggering.

She heard something moving behind her. She froze, her heart squeezing into a knotted fist, then racing wildly. Crouching, ready to run, she looked back up the road, where the sound had come from. A rustling, sifting sound, like something heavy being dragged through the dirt.

Something long and sluglike came gliding downhill, wriggling on its belly. At first she thought it was the limbless trunk of a still-live human, a not unreasonable expectation in light of what she'd already seen tonight.

But it was too lively for that and besides it had no head, unless that shovel-shaped appendage sticking out of its front was one. It was low like an alligator and about the same size and there was something reptilian in its S-curve slitherings as it advanced, but the rest of it was like nothing on earth, even on Isla Morgana.

It glimmered pale yellow white, this lens-shaped thing with a rounded upper side and a flattened underside. Its slick outer surface shone with rainbow swirls, like a soap bubble.

Kristen picked up a rock and threw it at the thing, hitting it. The rock sank into the gelatinous mass with a wet plopping sound, punching a hole in it a foot deep.

It kept coming. The hole shrank, filling in, sealing itself, spitting out the stone. All the while the Drakon's speed never slackened.

Kristen said, "Oh, God!" She started to run, the Drakon a few paces behind her heels. For a while they raced down the hill, the gap between them staying the same.

Kristen ran all-out, arms and legs pumping. She started to pull ahead of the Drakon, getting away.

But then the flat shovel-shaped fluke at its front pointed its tip upward at her, launching itself up and outward at the end of a long whiplike tentacle that lashed out toward her.

It got her, too, like a frog's tongue zapping a bug in midair.

The tentacle hooked her around the neck, the flat shovel-shaped fin at its tip clamping onto her head. It jerked her to a halt, hauling her backward, off her feet.

She fell not on hard ground but on the thing itself, splashing down back first into a yielding bed of quivering yellow-white jelly. At first cushioning her fall, the jelly then engulfed her.

There was an instant's resistance, then the Drakon's outer membrane adjusted to let her pass through, swallowing her up inside. The membrane sealed itself and then there was Kristen, floating inside it, suspended in clear yellow-white jelly, looking out.

She struggled, but it was like trying to swim in mud. No matter how frantic her thrashings, how wild, the stuff adjusted to her movements, infinitely flexible and yielding, yet relentless.

It was like drowning in mud. That's what she thought in the final instant before the Drakon unleashed a flood of digestive enzymes, caustic acids that would break down flesh and blood into a nutrient soup that the Drakon could use.

She did not struggle long.

The Drakon paused in the middle of the road, absorbing the girl's body, making her substance its own. It took what it could use, which was almost everything, ejecting a mound of bleached pitted bones, hair, and some organic residue that looked like lumps of melted wax mixed with seaweed.

The entire process took less than half a minute. The Drakon was a lusty infant with a raging appetite, and its digestive juices were stronger than fifty gallons of the most highly concentrated industrial acids.

It was bigger now, bulked up by what it had taken from Kristen. The feeding was pure fuel for it, making it faster, stronger, more efficient.

And hungrier.

The Drakon moved on, following the road that led out of the highway to the coast. The route was littered with the wrecks of long-abandoned farmhouses and shacks, deserted a half century earlier when the vampire first came to the valley to make it his own. No life there—no blood.

But beyond the valley lay the coast highway, the roadway to Magdalena and its teeming human masses . . .

Along that highway a truck was heading north toward town, a two-and-a-half-ton job with a rail-sided flatbed holding eight riders in the back and a driver and two passengers in the front cab. They were workers returning from an extended shift on a construction project out on Claw Cape, building a private dock for the beachside home of one of the rich foreigners who'd been buying all the property on the island's choicest piece of real estate. They didn't like to work after dark, but the owner wanted the job done double quick and was willing to pay the bonuses necessary to keep them on-site after the sun went down.

After the phantom bells rang, the workers called it a night and started packing up their picks and shovels. Even the greedy crew boss, Victor, was for once immune to the blandishments of the home owner, who offered to pay more if they would continue to labor on the dock under the lights.

In the truck cab now were Victor, his fourteen-year-old nephew, Carlito, and the driver, Alfonso. Victor sat on the passenger side, leaning an arm out the window. He and Alfonso were passing a pint bottle of rum back and forth, drinking it, letting Carlito take a swig every now and then.

In the back of the truck, the crew members were passing around a couple of quarts of cheap potent rum, fortifying themselves for the night ride. They rode standing, holding on to the side rails as the vehicle jounced along the roadway. It was an old truck, and the springs and suspension were shot, and each time it hit a pothole there was a bone-jarring thud.

Behind, the limb of the cape where it curved out into the sea was ablaze with the bright lights of the palatial homes and estates of the new gentry lining the beachfront. The highway itself was dark, with no lights except the truck's headlights. Heading back to town, the truck had the hills on its left and the shoreline on its right.

Ahead, coming up on the left, could be seen the mouth of the road leading to the valley and the plantation. Beyond that, the curve of a hill temporarily blocked the view of the town of Magdalena, the glow of whose lights could be seen shining around the bend.

As the junction neared, Alfonso tilted the bottle, taking a long pull of rum before handing it off to Victor. He took hold of the wheel in both hands, leaning forward, speeding up as much as the old truck would allow, which wasn't much. It was laboring while the speedometer's red needle bounced around just under forty miles per hour, unable to top it.

The valley road was in sight now and there was a strained silence in the truck cab and the flatbed. Then it was past and the driver let out his breath as the truck swung around the bend, bringing the lights of town into view.

Suddenly something darted out of the brush and slithered across the road, square in the path of the oncoming truck. There was a quick flashing glimpse of its long streamlined torpedo shape glistening in the headlights before the truck ran over it.

There was no time to stop, even if Alfonso had put on the brakes, which he hadn't, not liking the looks of the thing or the place where it had appeared.

The truck ran over it twice, once with the front wheels and again with the rear wheels. It was like driving over a speed bump. One of the riders in the back wasn't holding on tight enough and the double impact catapulted him out of the truck, pancaking him onto the highway.

The others shouted, banging on the cab and yelling for the driver to stop. Victor had seen the thing, too, and he motioned frantically for Alfonso to keep going, yelling, "Don't stop!"

When the truck didn't slow down, the men in back really started pounding on the cab, shouting angrily. When some of them started reaching through the window to get at the driver, Alfonso reluctantly put on the brakes.

The truck stopped a couple of hundred feet from where the man had fallen out. The crew was outraged. Some of them climbed down to the pavement, tearing open the door to confront Alfonso.

A burly spokesman for the group said, "Raul fell out of the truck! Why didn't you stop?"

"I didn't know he fell out," Alfonso said.

"You deaf or something? We were all yelling!"

"I thought it was because of the thing on the road—"

"What . . . !"

"You didn't see it?"

"You drunk, or just loco, man?"

"The—animal—that crossed the road, the truck ran it over . . ."

"We didn't see a thing!"

Victor had sat silent throughout this exchange. Now he said, "Never mind about that, what about Raul?"

Somebody said, "Some of the men went back to get him."

Victor got out of the cab, stepping down to the pavement, Carlito following, sticking to his heels. Alfonso stayed at the wheel, leaning out of the open door.

The crewmen milled around the back of the truck, looking back down the road the way they came. A couple hundred feet back, some workers had reached the place where Raul had been thrown out of the truck.

Victor put a hand beside his mouth, shouting, "How is he?"

The reply: "He's not here!"

"What!"

"We can't find him!"

"Impossible! He must be!"

"He's not!"

Victor reached into the cab, fumbling for a flashlight. He tried it, making sure that it worked. It did. He joined the men behind the truck.

He said, "We ran over a snake or alligator or some damned thing. It might still be alive, so be careful."

The men had brought their tools back from the work site.

69

Some of them climbed into the back of the truck and started handing down crowbars, pickaxes, and sledgehammers.

Victor shouted down the road, "Find him?"

"No!"

Victor went around to the front of the truck, the driver's side. He said, "'Fonso, turn the truck around and turn on the high beams. We'll use them to find him. But where the hell did he go?"

"Remember where we are, *jefe*," Alfonso said. "The valley—"

"Never mind about that. We're safe enough as long as we stay on the road." He turned to his nephew. "Carlito, you stay in the truck."

"I'm not afraid, I want to go with you."

"I know you're not, but do as you're told."

Carlito got back in the cab. Victor and the men who'd stayed behind formed up on the roadway, grouping in an irregular line that stretched across the pavement, with Victor in the center.

Alfonso jockeyed the truck around, doing a K-turn so that the vehicle was pointed in the opposite direction, away from town. Dark smoke puffed from the rusted tailpipes, laying down a pall of exhaust fumes.

He switched on the high beams, their yellow-white brightness pushing back the dark. Alfonso said, "You saw it."

"I saw something," Carlito said. "It looked like a big snake, the biggest I ever saw."

"There are no snakes that big on the island."

"Well, you ran over something."

"That I did—but what?"

· Victor and the others were a dozen yards or so ahead of the truck, fanned out across the highway in a straight line. The high beams shone at their backs, bright and hot, casting giant elongated shadows that stretched for a hundred yards or so before being swallowed up by the dimness farther down the road.

The truck beams cast a zone of light in the middle of the curving asphalt tube of darkness that was the highway, bounded in the far distance by the lights of Cape Claw and at the other end by the skyglow of Magdalena shining around the bend.

The men moved forward, the truck following at a crawl. Victor said, "Look around in the brush on both sides of the road. Raul must have fallen in them somewhere and now he's hurt and maybe unconscious, so he can't call out to let us know where he is."

The searchers fanned out to the sides, poking around in the weeds and bushes bordering both sides of the road.

"Watch where you step. That snake might still be around and not too happy about being run over," he added.

Some of the men who'd gone deepest into the weeds now backed off, getting closer to the road.

The line advanced, the truck creeping after, closing the distance to the place where Raul had fallen out. Three of the men who'd first gone back to look for him now stood in the center of the road, waiting for the others to arrive.

The two groups linked up, the truck standing about thirty feet away, its engine idling heavily.

The original trio of searchers stood waiting at the edge of a broad slimy patch of stuff smeared across the pavement.

Victor asked, "Raul?"

"Can't find him," one of the trio said.

Another, toeing the edge of the broad streak of slime, said, "Look at this."

Mutters sounded from the men in Victor's group and one man asked, "What is it?"

"It's not blood," Victor said. "It looks like jelly . . . it must have come from the thing we hit."

"What did we hit?" somebody asked.

The men huddled closer to each other, avoiding the shiny patch. Sea breezes picked up, gusting, sweeping dirt and chaff across the pavement with a sifting sound, rustling the weeds at both sides of the road.

One of the first men to run back for Raul now looked around, turning his head in all directions, squinting against the high beams' glare, peering into the dark places at the roadside where the light failed to reach.

He was so obviously agitated that Victor asked him, "What's wrong?"

"Now Escobar is missing!"

"What?"

"He was looking for Raul a minute ago, and now he's gone!"

Some of the men shouted Escobar's name. He didn't answer.

"If this is some kind of a joke, I'll skin him alive," Victor said. "Escobar! Escobar, Escobar!"

In the truck, Alfonso said, "I knew we shouldn't have stopped." Carlito, scared and excited, fidgeted on his side of the seat, nervously kicking the door panel.

Outside, the men stood around, unsure what to do next. Somebody said, "We should get out of here before any more of us get disappeared!"

"We can't leave our friends here—they could be hurt, and counting on us to find them!"

"You would say that. Escobar's your cousin."

"That's right, and I'm not leaving without him. Or Raul, either!"

Victor stepped in. "Nobody's getting left behind. Two men can't just simply vanish without a trace."

"They can around here," said the man who had first spoken of leaving. "Or have you forgotten where we are, so close to the valley of the zombies—"

"Shut up. Just because you don't have any *cojones,* Mendoza, don't try to cut them off the rest of us," Victor said.

He went to the man who'd first noticed Escobar was missing, and gripped his arm. "Where was Escobar when you last saw him?"

The other pointed to a clump of shoulder-high bushes on the seaward side of the road. "Over there."

Victor started toward it, halting in mid-stride. Turning back to the group, he said, "Somebody give me a machete."

Somebody handed him one. He held it hanging down at

72

his side, holding the flashlight in his other hand. He started forward. "Some of you men come with me. The rest of you stay put and don't get lost," he said.

He crossed to the edge of the road, flanked by a couple of big, tough men armed with crowbars, machetes, and long-handled shovels.

The truck beams illuminated everything from the road-way up, but past the shoulder the ground fell away, with plenty of dips and hollows where the light didn't reach. The shadows of Victor and the men accompanying him fell in front of them, blocking the light.

Victor switched on the flashlight, shining the beam in those hard-to-reach places—behind boulders and trees and under clumps of bushes. Sea breezes kept the knee-high weeds in constant rustling motion. The men tramped around noisily, beating the bushes, calling for Escobar and, less frequently, Raul.

Not far from the edge of the road, a couple dozen yards or so, the land fell away, sloping down to the sweeping curve of the shoreline, where surf hissed against the rocks and the sea heaved in constant restless motion.

The rest of the men, the ones who hadn't gone with Victor, crowded at the roadside, watching the searchers poking around in the brush.

Alfonso watched them from the truck. Carlito complained, "I can't see."

He opened the door, swinging his legs so they dangled over the pavement. Alfonso said, "Your uncle told you to stay in the truck."

An outcry sounded from one of the roadside searchers, startling the men. Alfonso stuck his head out the window, craning to see what it was all about, poised to throw the truck into gear and drive away if he had to.

The men outside tightened their grips on their weapons, tense, worried, afraid.

They called to the men searching off-road, "What? What's wrong?"

One said disgustedly, "It's nothing. Ramirez fell into a ditch, that's all."

"Don't tell me it's nothing, I nearly broke my ass!" Ramirez said, cursing.

There were tight smiles and self-conscious foot shufflings from the men on the road as the tension ratcheted down a notch.

Victor said, "Keep your eyes open and watch where you're stepping," and the search resumed.

The truck engine had a heavy idle and its rumbling was especially loud in the cab, tending to drown out other noises. Alfonso felt movement on the seat. He pulled his head back inside through the window, glancing at Carlito . . .

Carlito wasn't there. His seat was empty and the door on his side gaped open.

Alfonso said, "That kid! Can't even stay put like he's told."

Screaming sounded in the brush, a choking cry of fear.

"What's that!—"

"Ramirez again!"

"What's wrong now?"

Victor shone his light on Ramirez, who stood crouching, shouting, "Ahhh! Yaaah!"

He seemed two or three feet shorter than usual for an instant, until Victor realized that the other man was still standing in a ditch. Ramirez was looking down at something, his gaping mouth making a hole that took up the lower half of his face.

He kept bellowing, "Gaaah! Yaahhh!"

Victor crashed through the brush, two or three others close behind, closing on Ramirez. He wanted to grab the man and shake him, but his hands were full with the flashlight and machete.

He said, "Damn you, Ramirez, what now?"

Ramirez stopped shouting, though his mouth still hung wide open. He turned to look at Victor beside him, his neck muscles so taut that his head practically creaked as it swiveled to the side. He jabbed a pointing finger at something that lay in the ditch at his feet.

Victor shone his light down on it. At first, his mind was unable to make sense of what he saw. In the bottom of the ditch lay a crumpled heap of what looked like dried cornhusks wound around a tangle of wire coat hangers. It had been slimed and was wet and glistening and coated with a pale greenish-yellow jelly.

What looked like dried cornhusks was a wrapper of human skin, yellowed and dehydrated, a bag of skin holding what looked like a mess of wire hangers but was really the brittle, pitted remains of a skeleton. The fist-sized lumps of fatty grayish-white material and ribboning seaweed-looking strands were the undigested organic components that had been left behind.

Victor recoiled, dropping the flashlight. That was the signal that sent him and the others, including Ramirez, scrambling out of the brush onto the hard pavement.

Somebody shouted, "Let's get out of here!" but it wasn't necessary, the men were already bolting for the truck.

They grabbed the rails and hauled themselves up, scaling the sides of the vehicle. Some threw their tools into the back, others held on to theirs, while others had first dropped them when they started running. The men who'd been standing on the road mostly hadn't gotten a good look at what was in the ditch, but they hadn't needed to. The reaction of those who had seen it was enough to get a panic stampede going.

Victor was right there in front. He'd probably had the best look at the remains, he and Ramirez, and he was faster getting into action. Not much faster, because Ramirez was right there behind him, along with all the others.

Victor ran around the front of the truck, to the cab's open passenger door. Hooking his hands around the inside of the door frame to pull himself in, he froze.

"Where's Carlito?"

"Isn't he with you?" Alfonso asked.

"No!"

75

"He went out to see what was happening, Victor! He must be with the others!"

"He'd better be!" Victor turned to go, then stuck his head back in the cab. "Stay here and don't start driving until I tell you!"

"But, Victor—"

"Move and I'll kill you, I swear on my mother."

"At least let me turn the truck around—"

"No!" Victor stepped up on the cab's running board, grabbing the flatbed side rails and hauling himself up so he could stick his head over the top and look inside.

"Carlito, Carlito!"

"He's not here, Victor!"

"Did any of you see him? Carlito! *Carlito!*"

Somebody said, "Let's go!"

Victor said, "No! Not without Carlito!"

"He's dead, let's get out of here!"

"Who said that?" Victor craned to see who had spoken, but the voice had come from one of the men in the rear, and he couldn't see who it was or recognize the voice.

"Who said that? Don't want to answer, eh? You dirty coward!" Victor let go of the top rail he'd been hanging on to, dropping to the pavement.

Some men shouted for Alfonso to turn the truck around and drive away. Fists pounded on the cab roof, denting it.

Alfonso squirmed at the wheel, one hand clutching the knobbed stick shift, ready to throw it into gear and be gone. Victor stuck his head back in the cab, pointing at the driver.

"Victor, please—"

"You stay!"

Something brushed against Victor's feet and he jumped back, starting. He did another take when he saw what it was: a human hand, reaching out from under the cab.

A youngster's hand.

"Carlito!"

Dropping to his knees on the pavement, Victor looked under the truck, where a huge glistening mass heaved and struggled.

It wasn't a giant snake or alligator after all. It looked like a monstrous jellyfish as big as a rolled-up mattress, with a human being inside it. That was Carlito, or what was left of him.

It was dark under the truck and Victor couldn't make out what he was seeing too well, plus his mind once again blanked out and refused to believe what it beheld. But he could see Carlito's form hanging suspended inside the jellied mass, kicking and struggling, all except for one arm that hadn't yet been engulfed.

The arm stuck out of the thing's outer membrane, flailing, waving. The hand at the end of it groped for something to hold on to, fingernails raw and bloody from clawing at the pavement in a vain attempt to keep from being pulled under.

Earlier, being run over by the truck hadn't hurt the Drakon, not when it could flatten the parts of its body going under the wheels. Crushing it was like squeezing a handful of putty, the stuff just flowed elsewhere, out of harm's way, being almost infinitely malleable. It had blanketed Raul's body lying on the roadway, humping it off the pavement into the ditch, absorbing it and ejecting the excreta, the parts it couldn't use. When Escobar had gone looking for Raul, it had done the same to him. When more men came, its instincts had pushed it away, avoiding them. It wasn't quite ready to take on that many foes all at once, so it had squirmed through the brush parallel to the road, going to the truck. There was prey there, too, fewer in numbers and easy pickings. It had come up around the back of the truck, where it was darker, squirming under it. While Carlito sat in the cab with the door open, looking the other way, the Drakon had hooked him with a tentacle, stifling his outcries with a flat arrowhead-shaped fluke fastened to his face, and hauled him out of the cab and under the truck. Alfonso hadn't heard anything because of the loud engine noises.

Now Victor, on his knees, grabbed Carlito's hand in both his own and pulled, trying to yank him free. The boy was stuck fast in the thing and wouldn't budge, but Victor wasn't about to give up. Holding tight to the hand, he pulled with everything he had.

There was a sudden release of tension, like an arrow being shot from a bow, and then Victor fell back on the pavement, still clutching the boy's hand, along with the forearm, all the way up to the elbow.

The rest of Carlito was still in the Drakon.

Victor screamed, flinging the hand and arm away. He jumped up just as the creature unfurled another tentacle, whipping it at him. Just as an amoeba can extrude any number of pseudopodia, so could the Drakon.

The tentacle was as thick through as a fire hose, except for the end, which tapered to a curling tip. It knocked Victor's legs out from under him, slamming him to the pavement, stunning him.

The coils wrapped around him, secreting acids that began eating away at his flesh from the outside. The tentacle retracted, pulling him shrieking under the truck.

Carlito was fully absorbed and the Drakon passed the remains out through its membrane, making room for Victor. Its bulk had already increased from the amount of stuff it had absorbed from Carlito.

Each new body that it absorbed added to its strength, speed, and voracity. Also, its metabolic rate was continually heightened with each new ingestion, allowing it to devour and absorb its prey with ever-greater speed.

Victor was dragged on his back under the truck, the sky above being blotted out by the vehicle's undercarriage. The Drakon carpeted him, covering him from head to toe. Adjusting its outer membrane to let him pass through, it took him into the streaming protoplasmic core of itself.

It was like drowning in glue. The stuff was in his eyes, nose, mouth, pores. An arm-thick limb of it forced its way down his throat, pouring into him like liquid cement, thrusting into his innards and expanding, growing.

Then it flooded him inside and out with those incredibly toxic digestive acids.

The men in the back of the truck were screaming and shouting, pounding on the cab and stomping on the flatbed.

"Alfonso, go, GO!"

Alfonso was already in motion, throwing the knobbed shift into gear, lifting his foot off the clutch, and stepping on the gas. Through the driver's seat he could feel the kicking and pounding of Victor's death struggles. Right under him!

The truck lurched forward. It was pointed back the way they had come, toward Claw Cape, but Alfonso wasn't about to try anything fancy like turning around, he just wanted to get away.

Some of the men in the hopper crowded at the back of the truck, looking down off the tailgate as the machine gathered speed to catch a glimpse of the damned thing—and its victims—as they were left behind in the middle of the road.

They saw what looked like a heap of slimed wet refuse, none of them recognizing it for what it was, the last of Carlito. That was all, no Victor or creature.

Alfonso jammed the gears, foot to the floor, but the truck was old and the engine rebuilt and it was a strain for it to pick up enough speed to get out of first and into second gear.

Under the truck, the Drakon clung to the undercarriage, entwining itself among the numerous pipes and knots and coils. It still had Victor, too, slung inside, his body making a hammock-type bulge that hung over the pavement that unrolled beneath it faster and faster as the truck moved out.

This was where the prey was, and it meant to stay with them. Inside it, Victor had stopped struggling and the only movements he made were caused by the jostling of the truck and the shifting liquid flows of protoplasm as the creature kept altering its shape to adjust to the truck's speed and momentum.

The Drakon extended a tentacle out from under the cab and up the side of the driver's-side door. It looked like a fast-motion time-lapse film of a vine climbing a wall.

Victor was done, all nourishment extracted, so the Drakon

passed the refuse through its outer membrane, dropping it on the road. Men on the truck saw it fall and started hollering that the thing was under the truck.

Alfonso manhandled the steering wheel, whipping it left and right to try to shake the thing loose, the ungainly truck fishtailing in response, slaloming down the center of the road.

Some of the men jumped off the moving truck, bailing out before it got up too much speed.

The tip of the Drakon's questing tentacle broadened and flattened, becoming a triangle-shaped fluke as big as a man's hand. It tilted and bobbed, weaving like a serpent's wedge-shaped head as it searched for the vibrations of prey.

It hung outside the cab's open window, level with Alfonso's head. He was looking at the road and didn't see it. But a few men who'd stayed in the back, afraid to jump because the truck was moving too fast, did. They threw themselves over the side, taking their chances.

That was when Alfonso glimpsed something moving in the corner of his eye and glanced out the window, seeing the broad-tipped tentacle right beside him.

His shout was a wordless cry of fear, stifled as the tentacle tip slapped his face with the fluke, attaching itself and covering his eyes, nose, and mouth.

The truck careened, running off the road and crashing engine first into the side of a rocky hill.

The Drakon was unhurt, adjusting its puttylike form to minimize the impact of the crash. Alfonso was not so lucky. His head hit the windshield, starring it, and his chest was crushed against the steering wheel.

Or maybe he was lucky, because the crash had killed him, sparing him the experience of feeling himself being absorbed alive.

The front of the truck was pushed in, the hood accordioned, the radiator cracked and venting hissing steam. Fuel leaked underneath the vehicle, the chemical reek and touch of the spilled gas being inimical to the Drakon.

It flowed out from under the crashed truck, still maintaining its tentacular grip on Alfonso's head. It pulled him headfirst through the open window and outside, flopping to the ground.

Sparks were struck from the truck's electrical system, igniting the pooling gasoline, which burst into flame.

The Drakon liked fire even less than it liked gas. Tucking Alfonso's body inside it, it flowed away from the blaze.

Alfonso was thin and sinewy and not much of a meal, but every bit helped. The Drakon had already absorbed him when the truck's gas tank blew, creating a fireball, smoke, heat, shock waves.

Scattered farther up along the road were the men who'd jumped from the truck before it crashed. Some were injured and couldn't flee, others were shook up but still moving.

The Drakon hastened to them. It got some but not all. A few escaped to tell the tale.

Overhead, high above, a plane flew out of Isla Morgana. On it was the Wolfman, Lawrence Talbot, now having morphed from his murderous lupine form to that of a decent human being cursed with the taint of lycanthropy.

His half-century-old blood feud with the Lord of the Vampires having ended with the staking and physical destruction of Dracula, Talbot now longed only for the peace of death, peace that would come only when he lay in his grave with a silver bullet in his heart, a destiny he now rushed to embrace.

Of course, things would have been quite different had he known of the advent of the Drakon.

But he didn't, and so his fate was sealed.

Know this—when Lawrence Talbot, the Wolfman, was well and truly dead, his soul would slip the devil's grasp and the bells of hell would be silent.

As for the Drakon . . .

FIVE

In an annex to the White Room, in a glass box, stood the New Eve.

"She stands as she has stood there for decades," Countess Marya Zaleska said. "Where is the prince who can awaken this Sleeping Beauty?

"Perhaps you, Dr. Gregor . . . or you, Engineer Mantz."

The three of them stood alone in the chamber, grouped around the feminoid. The hour was late—or early, depending. This West European location was seven hours ahead of Isla Morgana on the clock. Here, it was less than an hour before dawn, while on the island, the night was young.

Not that it mattered much. Daylight had never seen this underground chamber, so Marya need not fear the coming sun's poisonous rays. But underground or not, when the sun rose she must take to her coffin bed, gripped by the catatonic trance that is the sleep of the Undead.

But not yet. There was still some darkness left, giving her time to make plans and issue orders. She and her two companions had just come from the White Room, in the aftermath of the Rite of the Red Orb. Their ceremonial robes had been left behind, but they still wore the clothes they had worn beneath them.

Marya wore a dark suit with a matching jacket and short

skirt, knit blouse, stockings, and hand-tooled Italian leather pumps. Mantz wore a blue engineer's tunic with a mandarin collar and gold piping, khaki pants, and rubber-soled canvas shoes. Dr. Gregor wore a hospital-white suit and white shoes. His glasses were flecked with tiny dry drops of blood, which he had forgotten to clean off.

The room was modest-sized, relatively intimate, with an oval floor, curved walls, and a high arched ceiling that accented the verticality of the woman in the glass box. The white space was lit by softly indirect glowing lights that gave it a hushed, grottolike feeling. Access was provided by a thick bulkhead door, now closed, with a security guard posted outside. It was a restricted area.

Dominating the space was the woman in the glass box. The glass box wasn't really a glass box and its occupant was like no woman born on this earth.

The glass box was a crystal coffin, standing upright on a knee-high pentagonal greenstone pedestal. The coffin's ribs, fittings, and hinges were made of platinum. The coffin itself was over eight feet high.

It had to be, because the women inside it was six and a half feet tall, with a bizarre bouffant beehive hairdo that added another fifteen inches to her height.

She was naked, this New Eve, and undeniably female, if perhaps not certifiably human. A lean, long-limbed Amazon, high-breasted and slim-hipped, hairless below the neck, female in all her parts. Her body showed extensive scarring, particularly at the joints and where the limbs—and neck— joined the trunk. Running down the front of her torso was a massive Y-shaped thoracic scar, recognizable as the kind of incision made during autopsies to open up the chest and body cavities to bare the internal organs.

The breasts and reproductive organs also bore the marks of considerable reconstructive surgery. She was a patchwork creation, with scars scrolling and swirling all over her body in an almost decorative pattern suggesting abstract tattooing.

She was long-faced, with high cheekbones and a long straight finely formed nose. Her features had a kind of

83

strange, unearthly beauty—a Nefertiti for the techno age. Her skin was lunar white with blue tints and highlights. Her eyes were closed.

She and her pedestal-mounted glass coffin stood against the wall opposite the door. Flanking the display were a couple of equipment consoles, automatic monitoring devices that searched ceaselessly and so far in vain for any vital signs. Apart from that, and a few sets of controls for the room's lighting, temperature, and so forth, the annex room was bare.

Marya, Mantz, and Gregor stood facing the feminoid—the female humanoid—each for a moment wrapped in his or her own private thoughts. Finally, Mantz broke the silence.

He began, "Even though Frankenstein's Monster is destroyed—"

"*May* be destroyed," Gregor said quickly. "Frankenstein's creation has amazing vitality and recuperative powers, and I for one am not ready to write him off as finished without making a thorough scientific investigation of the facts."

"Finished or not, the Monster's not going to be of any use to us for a long time, if ever, considering the condition he's in."

"You are wrong, Engineer. The creation is invaluable as a storehouse of biological resources to any researcher, be it animate or not." Gregor frowned, making a fist. "If only I could examine the creature!"

Marya put a hand on his shoulder. Gregor flinched, unable to repress a shudder, though trying hard to repress it. Marya smiled to herself, knowing that her touch often had that effect on the living. That's why she did it.

She said, "You will examine it, Gregor. Our agents will have taken possession of the Monster—what's left of it—within twenty-four hours. Forty-eight hours at the most."

She took her hand off his shoulder, removing with it the leaden sense of dread that had come over him at her touch. He forced a weak smile, but behind the blood-specked glasses, his eyes began to glitter with excitement.

"Why, what's wonderful news, Countess!" he said.

Mantz, thoughtful, said, "I didn't know we had any people on the island."

"We didn't," Marya said. "Over the years we've made many attempts to try to place our people there, but Dracula always found them out and killed them or turned them against us—sometimes both."

"But with Dracula killed, the situation has changed. I've already given orders to take control of Isla Morgana. There are too many things there that the daylight world must never know, for fear that they might betray the existence of those of us in the shadows. Not just the fact of the Monster, but also all the traces of Dracula's long reign on the island.

"Our agents will secure the area and sanitize it. You shall have your monster, Gregor. I promise you that."

Gregor's smile now showed genuine pleasure. "What can I say, Countess? I'm thrilled! After all these years of studying the records and immersing myself in the subject, to finally be able to examine the creation at first hand!"

Mantz said, "You've had the Bride here all this time, and what good has that done? She's still as dead as she ever was."

"Not dead—dormant. A seed of life, waiting to be reborn."

"Bah! Dead, dormant, what's the difference?"

"A very great difference, I assure you."

Marya said, "My own personal experience bears out the truth of Dr. Gregor's words. There's a world of difference between death and mere dormancy."

Her lips quirked in a smile at both men's discomfort with the facts of her condition, something that transcended science and smacked of the Beyond.

Sensing an advantage, Gregor turned to Mantz. He said, "May I remind you, my dear colleague, that my province is surgery and the life sciences. Henry Frankenstein's creation is quite different from the Bride that he made with Dr. Pretorius.

"Septimus Pretorius was a master of the natural sciences, including physics—your specialty, Engineer. Many of his discoveries on the effects of cosmic rays and radiation on living tissue were incorporated in the construction of the Bride. In many ways, she is of a radically different order than her male counterpart, especially in the way she processes the energies of reanimation.

"It is you and your technicians to whom we mere doctors of medicine must look to find the key to reviving the Bride."

Mantz's curt head-bobbing nod acknowledged that swords had been crossed. "I believe that I have discovered that key, Doctor, and it will be my very great pleasure to put that discovery to the test at the earliest possible convenience."

"So you say, so you say."

"I'll do more than that, I'll prove it."

Marya said, "You will have that opportunity, Engineer. The events of this night, the destruction of Dracula and the Monster, have set tremendous forces in motion, both in the occult world and the daylight world to which it is bound. Forces that may work for us or against us.

"To control those forces, to shape events according to our plans, we must have the proper instruments. One such tool is the Bride. Now, with the Monster possibly destroyed—I say *possibly*—it is imperative that the Bride be a fully functioning slave of our will."

She faced Mantz. "How soon can you test your theory?"

"Immediately, Countess."

"So be it. Tonight we will attempt to raise the Bride!"

SIX

On Isla Morgana, the walking dead took their revenge on the living.

Beltran was on horseback, so he was the first to see the stranger come walking out of the early-morning mists that hung over the fields of his *estancia,* his estate in the hills. The sky was light but the sun was not yet up. It was a time of cool blue-gray shadows, blurred at the edges. Dew was on the grass and birds sang in the trees.

Beltran was a power in the hills. He owned a ranch and liked to call himself a rancher, but what he was, was a retired former sergeant in Quantez's police force and a current political gang boss. He and his gunmen terrorized the *campesinos* in this hill district, the families of landless poor who lived and toiled on the big ranches and estates owned by the *padrones,* the wealthy landowners. The workers were slaves in everything but name, and Beltran's job was to make sure that they stayed that way. With violence, brutality, and fear, he and his men did their job well. That's why he was a landowner himself, mounted on the back of a fine horse preparatory to taking an invigorating dawn ride over his domain.

The ranch was in a valley adjacent to the valley where Dracula's plantation lay. A ridge stood between them. Beltran was part of the island's ruling clique and had assurances that he and his property were protected by magical charms and binding spells that kept the zombies and other things of evil safely penned in their master's domain. He was a gang boss, not a sorcerer, and knew or cared nothing about such matters other than that they worked and kept the creatures far away from him. Still, the fields that lay in the shadow of the boundary ridge were kept fallow, both for cultivation and pasturage. Neither beatings nor whippings could persuade the workers to set foot in those areas, and even Beltran's tough gunmen were leery of the border zone. Indeed, he shunned it himself.

Beltran's vest-pocket kingdom consisted of a ranch house, barn, stables, storehouse, a bunkhouse for his men, some sheds and outbuildings, and a cluster of ramshackle, tumbledown huts, little better than lean-tos, that housed the workers and their families. Adjacent to the shacks was a patchwork of tiny vegetable garden plots that the workers were privileged to be allowed to cultivate, as long as half their yield was given to Beltran.

This dawn, the ranch was guarded by a skeleton crew of Beltran's *pistoleros*. Last night, there had been riots in the slums of Magdalena, and most of the gunmen had been sent down to the town to act as a backup for Quantez's forces.

Today, as always, the workers had gotten up in the dark of the night, and had trudged out to the fields and their chores by first light. Entire families labored at their tasks—men, women, and children.

The stable hands saddled up Beltran's favorite horse, a fine chestnut gelding, for the *patrón*'s daily morning ride. Beltran mounted up, heaving himself into the saddle with the help of three or four workers. They were small, slight, and underfed; he was huge and gross. The horse grunted, its back swaying under the rider's weight.

Beltran was habitually armed, never going anywhere without a gun. Today he wore a holstered six-gun sidearm and there was a rifle in the saddle scabbard.

Even before sunrise it was beginning to grow warm, and

when the sun rose up out of the sea, the heat would climb rapidly, burning off the mists and beating down hard on the land. Beltran was equipped with a broad-brimmed straw planter's hat for protection, and even for this short ride his saddlebags were fitted with a canteen of water and some snacks.

The stables and barn both fronted a dirt yard, and that's where Beltran was sitting on his horse, getting ready to ride, when he saw the stranger.

The stranger must have been walking for a long time because he was only a stone's throw away when Beltran and the others emerged from the stable. There were some paling fences and low sheds in the way, blocking the men on foot from seeing the intruder.

Seated on horseback, Beltran saw the newcomer first. Being up high above everybody else was one of the reasons Beltran liked riding. What he didn't like was the stranger. Strangers were trouble.

And there was definitely something wrong with this one. He was tall and thin and half-naked, and he walked in a jerky, shambling manner. Beltran had no one like that working for him at the ranch.

The horse must have sensed his unease, because it snorted, then began pawing its front hooves on the ground.

But why be uneasy? The stranger was obviously unarmed. There was nowhere to hide a gun in the filthy tattered loincloth that was all he wore. He could barely walk. Beltran decided he must be drunk or on drugs or crazy, maybe all three.

No, he didn't belong to the ranch. Beltran's subjects knew better than to stop working and wander crazily in the open.

But they *had* stopped working, the ones who were out in the fields, tending the furrows, some of them so bent and stooped that they could not have stood up straight if they had tried.

Now they stood rooted in place, watching, staring as the stranger came on, closing on the stable and the *patrón* who sat there high-and-mighty on his so-great horse.

By accident or design, a central space was cleared in the

fields, a kind of aisle where no man, woman, or child stood in the way of the walking man.

On he came, long, lank, brownish gray, his movements stiff-legged and spastic. And though Beltran was the kind of man who could find hilarity in a cripple's misfortunes, there was nothing funny about the intruder.

He stepped out from behind the paling fence, where the stable hands could see him. They stopped what they were doing, too.

Beltran was master here. He sat tall in the saddle, stiff-backed, jaw outthrust and chin tilted upward at an impossibly arrogant angle, literally looking down his nose at the invader.

The horse spoiled the intimidating effect, stomping the ground, sidling, shying away. Beltran tugged hard on the reins, cruelly jerking the bit into the horse's mouth so that it neighed with pain.

The stranger entered the yard, coming at Beltran. The stable hands edged away from him and the increasingly agitated horse.

Beltran was becoming increasingly agitated himself, and usually when he got that way he wound up shooting a man. Or worse. He held the reins in one hand and rested the other on his gun butt.

The sun was coming up, its rays gilding a ridgetop in the distance, the ridge that stood between Beltran's land and the valley of the zombies, the direction from which the stranger had come.

And then Beltran *knew*. He should have guessed earlier, but it was a case of things being in context. The gang boss was a murderer and torturer many times over, but he had had the sense to keep away from black magic. He had regular dealings with the zombie masters, he knew such things as zombies existed, he had even glimpsed them once or twice, but he had never seen one in the light of day, up close and getting closer every second.

Worse, he realized that the stranger was in fact no stranger at all. He couldn't remember his name, but he had worked

90

briefly at the ranch six months before. The fellow was a troublemaker, an ingrate who grumbled about slaving night and day for starvation wages. When his grumblings had gotten too loud, Beltran had given him a beating to teach him a lesson, only he had beaten too hard and the man died. The body had been sold to the zombie masters and taken away, and that, as far as Beltran was concerned, was the end of it.

He wasn't supposed to come back. That wasn't the way of things on the island. And yet, he *had* come back. That meant either that he had been sent by a zombie master, or that he had no master and had come to wreak vengeance on those who had made him what he was, one of the walking dead.

And who was a more deserving target of revenge than the one who had killed him?

Beltran reached for his gun as the stranger drew within a few paces of him. He believed in the gun in a way he could never believe in black magic. There must be some kind of trick to this zombie business, some fakery involving drugs and hypnosis. A zombie was a man. Shoot a man and he dies.

But the intruder was dead, Beltran knew he was dead, he had killed him—

"I'll kill you again," he said.

The horse caught the zombie scent. That spooked the animal. Eyes rolling madly, nostrils flaring, it reared up on its hind legs.

Beltran fell backward, out of the saddle, landing on his back on the hard-packed ground. The gun was in his hand when he fell but not after he hit dirt.

He was stunned, the wind knocked out of him. He thrashed around on his back, face purpling, limbs working futilely, an upended turtle.

The zombie darted in, grabbing the horse's loose reins in a white-knuckled fist. White-knuckled because the flesh had rotted away, showing the knucklebones.

At this sudden movement the animal went wild, bucking, rearing, stomping, trampling whatever lay beneath its iron-shod hooves. The zombie made sure that Beltran was beneath them, pulling the reins so the horse remained close to him, trampling.

Beltran broke before the reins did. More blood had been pounded out of him than remained in the pulpy mess strewn in the stable yard. When the reins parted, the horse lowered its head and took off, running across the fields.

By now, the few gunmen who had stayed behind at the ranch while the others had gone into town had heard the commotion and come running, guns in hand.

They pumped lead into the zombie. It turned, as if noticing them for the first time, starting toward them. They kept shooting; like their boss, they believed in firepower.

The zombie grabbed the nearest one and took his gun, breaking the man's fingers in the process. Then he clubbed him to death with it.

The others ran.

Ignoring the workers, oblivious of them, the zombie wheeled around and stalked off, striding jerkily across the fields until it was out of sight.

The *campesinos* watched, awed, until the blurred distant figure blended into the heat waves rising on the horizon.

Then they gathered up their families and ran away, too, but not before looting the ranch house of everything they could carry.

Beltran was not the only one to receive visitors this morning.

At the foot of the valley where Beltran's ranch lay, edging the coast highway, there was a village consisting of a handful of houses and a couple dozen huts and shacks. The inhabitants mostly made their livings from the sea, fishing and smuggling. The richest man in the village was named Cruz. He was a landlubber, a merchant who owned the local *bodega,* a combination grocery store, convenience store, lunch counter, and bait-and-tackle shop.

Cruz was a graybeard, a recent widower who had married a young and pretty wife. Her name was Sarita and she was still in her late teens. Not long ago, she had been a lowly cook's helper in Cruz's kitchen; now she was mistress of the house. Her doting husband would have fired the cook and other servants and replaced them, but Sarita convinced him not to. She liked it better this way, being able constantly to lord it over those who once thought her their inferior.

Cruz spent most of his time in the store, opening it at dawn and closing it after dark. Not too much after dark, though. His house was behind the store, a one-story concrete-and-glass cube.

He was in the store now. Before the marriage, there had been some talk—mostly on Cruz's part—about Sarita helping him out in the store, working side by side with him from morning till night, but she had quickly made him see the error of his ways. Her belief that having a wife who worked was detrimental to his status and prestige was not entirely plausible to him, but her expertise in the bedroom soon had him persuaded.

Now she went into the store only when she wanted something; otherwise she stayed away. She liked to sleep late, lolling around in bed for hours before rising to boss around the servants and spend the rest of the day eating and drinking and watching TV and listening to the radio, sometimes all at the same time.

Today she was annoyed when a shouting clamor in the house woke her up, hours before her usual rising time. The noise stopped almost as soon as it began, but for some reason she couldn't fall back to sleep, and lay there in bed with her eyes open, her heart racing.

Finally she threw back the covers and jumped up, her long glossy black hair fetchingly disarrayed, her slim firm body wrapped in a sheer filmy thigh-high teddy that showed more than it concealed. She stepped into a pair of high-heeled slippers and threw on a robe, stalking out of the bedroom and into the kitchen to give the cook and servants holy hell for waking her up. She relished the prospect of a scene; it almost made up for the discomfort of being rudely awakened.

When she entered the kitchen, the cook and servants were

93

gone. Through the open sliding screen doors they could be seen far off in the distance, running away.

Sarita was not alone. With her was the first Mrs. Cruz, a stocky middle-aged matron with black button eyes. That's how Sarita knew her, because of those distinctive black-button eyes. The rest of her had changed quite a bit.

That was only to be expected, because she had been dead for nine weeks. Sarita had poisoned her, once she had bedded Mr. Cruz and knew she had him hooked. If he suspected that his first wife had been done away with, he made no complaints about it. And Sarita had a friend on the police, so there was no problem from those quarters.

But sometime after interment, some grave robbers must have dug her up and sold her corpse to the zombie masters, who put her to work at the plantation.

And now she was back. Back from the dead, and back in the house. Hands shaped into claws, she came at Sarita.

A cleaver lay on a wooden cutting board near at hand. Sarita grabbed it and swung it at her attacker, chopping some fingers off the zombie's clutching hand and sending them flying.

The fingers were like dried twigs and the stumps were dry, bloodless. The zombie got her other hand around Sarita's throat. She held Sarita against a wall, strangling her.

Sarita tore at the zombie's fingers with both hands but couldn't break their death grip. The zombie held her lifted up off the floor, Sarita's heels drumming the wall.

The drumming stopped as Sarita passed out. Her eyes bulged, her face was purple, and her tongue was sticking out. She went limp, her eyes rolling up in her head so that only the whites showed.

The zombie woman eased her grip. Sarita's back slid along the wall as she slumped to the floor. The zombie grabbed a handful of Sarita's glossy black mane and used it to drag her across the floor to the big butcher-block cutting table.

She hoisted the girl, laying her out faceup on the table. Sarita groaned, choking, rasping, her thick-lashed eyelids fluttering. She came to just in time to see her zombie love rival standing over her with the cleaver in her good hand.

Later, a disbelieving Cruz would return to find a headless, limbless trunk laid out on the table and, on a nearby counter, a serving platter containing Sarita's hands and head, an apple stuffed in her open, screaming mouth.

Worse, he would find the first Mrs. Cruz waiting for him with open arms and a butcher knife in her one good hand . . .

Meanwhile, down by the docks, in the toughest part of the very tough Magdalena waterfront district, there was a dive called the Red Hat Bar. It was a squalid wooden frame building with a flat tilted roof, leaning up against the side of a shuttered, long-abandoned cannery. A couple of warehouses loomed nearby, keeping the Red Hat in almost permanent shadow, no matter what the hour of the day.

There were no signs out front, only a narrow door flanked by a pair of round, portholelike windows that were so dingy and filmed with dirt that they didn't need curtains to keep out what little sunlight filtered down to street level.

Inside was a single square room with a long wooden bar and some stools, and a couple of round tables and chairs. The space had been partitioned with a plywood wall behind the bar. In the rear half of the building, there was a toilet, a storeroom, and a couple of stalls with mattresses on the floor, cribs where whores could take their customers or where addicts could shoot dope.

The Red Hat was a filthy, foul-smelling hole with a vicious clientele that were good for at least a stabbing or two a night. The owners were even more vicious. They had to be, or the customers would have taken the bar away from them and kept it for themselves. That was how the current owners had come into possession of the place, and so far they had held their franchise against all comers.

Early morning was ebb tide for the bar. The previous night's drunks had been thrown out and now the owners and a couple of whores were inside, sleeping it off. The owners were a five-man dockside gang, all related to each other.

Two zombies came in off the street, marching in stiff-legged lockstep after having come down to the docks by a roundabout way winding through alleys and sidestreets.

There was an instant when, with machinelike precision, one zombie hung back a half step, allowing the other to enter the building first, avoiding the low comedy of the two of them trying to go through the doorway at the same time and getting stuck there.

The door was unlocked and so in went the zombies, one after the other. The living who were sleeping with their heads and arms on the tables, and those who were sleeping under the tables, stirred groggily and stared blearily at the newcomers.

A couple of whores who were back in the crib stalls managed to get out the back door, and one of the gang escaped by throwing himself headfirst through a window, crashing in a shower of glass to the cobble-stoned street.

As for the others . . .

It was slaughter. Guns and knives were useless against the vengeful dead. During the melee a fire was started, engulfing the hovel in flames, turning it into an inferno from which none emerged, not even the zombies.

The man who'd escaped through the window recognized the zombies as two brothers, sailors who'd been knifed to death in a bar fight and sold to the body snatchers.

Steve Soto hadn't seen any zombies yet, but he was new to the island. Even so, the malaise was starting to work on him.

He stood on the balcony of his hotel room, taking the air, looking down into the town square. It was empty—of people, traffic, life. The sky was gray, in the shadowland between day and night.

A horse-drawn carriage entered the square. It was an old-fashioned corpse wagon, a hearse, drawn, appropriately enough, by a team of pale horses. The horses had skull faces and red eyes and black plume feathers jutting out of the tops of their head harnesses. They were dead-alive.

Seated on the front of the carriage box was the driver, a

seven-foot giant in a black top hat and black clothes. He drove the hearse to the front of the hotel, pulling up to a stop outside the main entrance. A green-faced monster, he grinned up at Soto.

The hearse had a glass top and sides, letting Soto see inside it. What he saw was a shiny black coffin with oversized gold fittings and handles. Moments later, the coffin lid opened from the inside and the man who was stretched out in its white quilted-satin lining sat up.

He was a creepy-looking guy with inky black hair, white face, and red eyes. He wore a tuxedo and white shirt and a high-collared black cape. His face was hard, heavy-featured, mean. Hard and hateful, with strong white teeth. Fangs.

As Soto watched, he turned into a giant bat, flying out of the back of the hearse and up into the sky. As the bat soared, it grew, its scalloped black wings stretching to the ends of the horizon, covering the sky.

Then it was night and Soto wasn't standing on the hotel balcony anymore, he was in the driver's seat of the corpse wagon. Ahead stretched a razor-edged long white ribbon of road, stretching out to nowhere, bounded on both sides by starless blackness that was neither earth nor sky but pure nothingness, nothing at all.

Now Soto held the reins of the skull-faced pale horses with the black head plumes. His hands were gnarly, chalky gray, with the flesh rotted away to show dingy white bone beneath—the hands of a corpse.

He reached for his gun and held it to his head and pulled the trigger so he could blow his brains out and end it all, anything to get off that road, only the gun clicked empty each time he pulled the trigger.

Then the scene blew up in his face and he awoke.

He dragged himself out of the hotel bed, throwing his feet to the floor and rubbing his face to get some feeling back in it. He felt more tired than he'd been when he'd climbed into bed the night before, after returning from the casino. No wonder he couldn't get any rest, with crazy dreams like that.

Bad dreams can't hurt you, not unless you let them get

97

under your skin and start working on you. Like bad memories.

That's what he told himself.

A shower helped wash away some of the cobwebs from his mind, especially when the hot water ran out after a minute or two and the spray ran cold.

He had a room to himself, while Tony Paul and Dennis shared an adjoining room. Generally, even that would have been too close, but this morning the prospect of seeing his two companions didn't seem too bad.

They were already up and dressed, which was good because he would have been teed off if they were still soundly sleeping while he was wide-awake before the sun had come up.

He pulled on some clothes and got a cigarette going and sat on the edge of the bed in his bare feet, holding his holstered gun in his lap, checking it out.

The holster was neat and self-contained, with a pair of prongs on the inner surface where it could be clipped onto a belt or waistband. He took out the piece, holding it in his palm, loving the feel of it. It was a nice little .38 Special with a snubbed two-inch barrel that made it nicely unobtrusive when covered by a loose-fitting shirt or a jacket. Inside the chambers were six bullets, six tickets to nowhere. Some guys left the chamber under the hammer empty so the gun wouldn't go off if it was accidentally dropped or something, but Soto went for the big six.

He slipped it back in the holster and clipped it onto his hip, covering it with his shirt. It bulged, but what the hell, he'd put on a jacket later when he went out.

He stubbed out his half-smoked cigarette, fired up a fresh one, then unlocked the connecting door.

Tony Paul and Dennis came in. The big man seemed rested and upbeat, but Dennis had a hollow-eyed, hangdog look that made Soto feel better, if only by comparison.

Tony Paul said, "Early rising for you, Steve."

"I hate getting up in the morning. Sometimes I think that's why I got into crime."

"But here you are."

"Yeah. Life sure is funny, huh?"

Dennis stood there, pasty-faced and shaky, massaging the sides of his head with his fingertips. "There's nothing funny about my hangover. Oww!"

Soto snickered. Tony Paul said, "Just because you got comped for free drinks at the casino, kid, don't mean you got to drink the place dry."

Soto went out on the balcony, remembering his dream, trying to shake it off. The sun was up, hidden by some buildings on the opposite side of the square. The light was lemon yellow and there was a haze in the air, not from mist but from smoke. The smoke was coming from farther south along the curve of the harbor, down in the waterfront slum district.

Soto stood at the balcony rail, facing the direction the smoke was coming from. That part of the landscape had a yellow-gray-brown smudge hanging in the air over a couple of crowded acres of tight-packed shanties, barely visible from here. A couple of lines of thin gray-black smoke rose straight up from the locale.

Tony Paul stepped out onto the balcony. He took a couple of deep breaths, slapping his chest. "Ah, fresh air!"

Then he started coughing. "Jeez, it smells like when you roll down the car windows on the Jersey Turnpike."

From behind, Dennis said, "They had some kind of trouble down in the slums last night. I could hear sirens and cars going by all night long."

Tony Paul said, "Riots, looks like."

Soto said, "All the comforts of home."

"Yeah, some tropical paradise," Tony Paul said.

A black police SUV drove by, heading south. Dennis said, "Must be trouble, look at them go!"

Tony Paul said, "That don't mean nothing. These island cops drive like that all the time."

"They look like soldiers, not cops. Some of them carry machine guns, right in the open."

Soto rubbed his chin, thinking. "There's trouble in paradise, no doubt about that. Looks like things started to fall apart right when we got here."

"Maybe it's like this all the time," Dennis suggested.

"Maybe. That's what we're here for, to scope things out up close and personal, get an eyeball on the local situation before the outfit starts moving any money down here."

Tony Paul asked, "This gonna screw up the deal, Steve?"

Soto shrugged. "Too early to tell. Riots don't necessarily mean it's the end of the world. Maybe the locals are just blowing off some steam. That Quantez strikes me as the kind of guy who'll bring things to heel pretty damned quick.

"It could even be a good thing. We can use it as a lever to get better terms on any deal from Sir Hugo and the banking crowd."

Just then a minivan taxi pulled up in front of the hotel. It came in from the north, where the airport was located. A couple of people got out, wearing resort clothes and sunglasses, while the driver opened the rear hatch of the van and started unloading their bags.

"Tourists," Tony Paul said. "They picked a nice time for a vacation."

Soto said, "Let's get some breakfast."

Dennis made a sour face, holding his stomach. "My guts are in such an uproar, I don't think I can hold anything down."

"You can watch us eat."

Tony Paul said, "You know what they say, kid—don't drink the water."

"That's the one thing he hasn't been drinking," Soto said. He stood at the front balcony rail, leaning over it, looking down at the front of the hotel.

Dennis went back into the room. Tony Paul hung back, saying, "What's up, Steve?"

"One of those tourists looked kind of familiar . . ."

But the newcomers had already gone inside, out of sight. Soto shrugged, turning, following Tony Paul into the room. He put on a jacket, closed and locked the connecting door, and the three of them went out of the room, down the stairs to the ground floor.

At the foot of the stairs, a long tiled hallway led to the main entrance, where an arched double doorway fronted the street. To the right was the lobby, stocked with oversized armchairs and a couple of divans. There were lots of tall tropical-looking plants in barrel-sized brown ceramic pots placed around the space to screen out some of the strong hot light that would come shining through the ceiling-high windows when the sun was high.

Also on the right, closer to the main entrance, was the front desk, a long counter of handsome reddish-brown polished wood. The handful of new arrivals who'd gotten out of the minivan taxi stood there, checking in, while a couple of uniformed bellhops stood around, waiting to take their bags to the room once they'd checked in.

On the left side of the hall, a set of glass doors opened onto the dining room. The reddish-brown wood used in the doors was the same as that used on the counter. There were the aromas of food and coffee coming from the dining area, mixed with the smoky smell of burning from outside. Overhead, ceiling fans turned slowly, lazily.

Standing at the front desk, checking in, was a man with a black rooster-tail haircut and oversized dark glasses that looked like a bug's eyes. He wore a cream-colored leisure suit and a brightly colored print shirt, a white vinyl belt, and matching shoes with thick chunky three-inch heels.

Standing beside him was an attractive blond woman, young, crisp, wearing a light-colored safari-type shirt and loose-fitting khaki slacks.

Soto said to his sidemen, "Wait here for a second, I'll be right back."

"Okay," Tony Paul said.

Soto crossed the lobby to the desk, coming alongside the guy with the rooster-tail haircut and the blonde. The man's back was to Soto, but the blonde saw him coming, her expression guardedly neutral. Her face stiffened when Soto took hold of the guy's arm above the elbow and said, "Internal Revenue Service, tax-fraud division. Come with me, Mr. Breen."

101

Breen—that was the guy's name, Jax Breen—stiffened all over, then managed to turn his head enough to see who it was that had put the arm on him.

His oversized bubble sunglasses reminded Soto more than ever of an insect's orbs. Soto could see himself reflected in them, a pair of distorted white ghost faces mirrored in the lenses.

Breen stared at him for a couple of beats before recognizing him. He had a young hairstyle and a wizened young-old face behind the sunglasses.

He said, "Steve Soto!"

Soto let go of the other's arm, but not before he felt the tension going out of it. "Hello, Jax."

"Well, I'll be! I never expected to run into you down here!"

"Like they say, a guy never knows he's in a foreign country until he runs into a guy from the old home turf."

"Damn! You gave me a scare for a second!"

"I'll bet. Just having a little fun, that's all."

"Some fun! You nearly gave me a heart attack, you dirty so-and-so."

Soto flashed a quick, meaningless grin as Jax Breen grabbed his hand in both of his and gave him a big hearty handshake.

Breen's palms were sweaty and his face was pale under its cocoa-butter sunlamp tan, but some of the color was starting to come back into it as the tension creases flattened out.

He said, "What're you doing down here, Steve?"

"Vacationing."

"Don't make me laugh; you never took a vacation in your life."

"What're you doing down here, Jax?"

"Business, what else?"

Soto looked past him at the blonde. The stiffness had gone out of her face, which once again was guardedly neutral. She was in her late twenties, with cornsilk-colored hair in a page-boy style that brushed her wide shoulders. Her lightly tanned face was the color of melba toast. Her dark glasses were down at the middle of the nose and she was looking over the top of them with pale blue eyes. Her outfit was crisp and clean but couldn't hide her strong, well-built physique.

Breen caught the play. "That's Julie Evans, my administrative assistant. Julie, this is an old pal of mine, Steve Soto. We both grew up in the same neighborhood."

She said politely, "How do you do."

She held out her hand and Soto shook it, saying, "Pleased to meet you, Julie." Her palm was cool and firm, the perfunctory squeeze of her grip was strong.

Breen said, "Some joker, huh? Pulling that T-man bit."

"Hysterical," she said.

"Don't let him fool you, Julie. He may look like a hard-ass, but really he's one of the nicest guys who ever stuck a horse's head in somebody's bed."

She had nothing to say to that.

Soto asked, "So what brings you here, Jax?"

"The free enterprise system. Don't laugh. Labor is dirt cheap down here. Manufacturers are always looking for places where they can get work done faster and cheaper, without spending a bundle, not like it is back home, where guys like you have got the unions sewed up to the point where management can't make a profit."

"Stop, you're making me cry."

"All I'm saying is that I know some garment guys that might be interested in setting up a couple of factories down here to make piece goods and whatnot. Why ship the work out to Asia or even Mexico when the islands are right here in our own backyard?

"If everything checks out okay, I figure I'll get some development deals sewed up with the local in-crowd and put together a very attractive package for the investors.

"In fact, if you're interested, I can let you get in on the ground floor with a couple of special sweeteners, on account of you're a friend of mine—"

Soto held up a hand, cutting off the flow of words. "Don't try to scam a scamster, Jax."

"Who's scamming? This is a legitimate business deal."

All the while the two conversed, the desk clerk had been standing there patiently, smiling and nodding, waiting for Breen to stop talking and finish registering.

Julie said, "I'll get us checked in, Jax."

"Thanks, Julie."

She busied herself with the clerk, handling the arrangements and paperwork. Soto said, "If I were you, Jax, I'd take a good hard look around before rushing to sign any contracts."

Behind the dark glasses, Breen's face creased with tension lines, getting that wizened look again.

"Huh? What do you mean, Steve?"

Soto shrugged. "I don't mean anything, I'm just saying look before you leap."

Breen looked around. Julie and the clerk were bent over the counter, shuffling some reservation faxes and other documents. Breen took a few steps away from the counter, stepping into a quiet spot on the sidelines, motioning Soto to him.

Voice low, urgent, worried, Breen said, "Listen, Steve, is this on the level? Do you know something I don't know?"

"I'd like to think so."

"Quit kidding. You know I never joke about business."

"That's not what the tax boys say when they look at your returns."

"Knock it off. I'm serious. You're an inside guy, you know the score. Tell me, is there something about this set-up that's not on the level?"

"I don't know about that, but the word is that they had some riots down in the waterfront districts last night."

"Riots!"

"Sure, didn't you see the smoke? Hell, you can smell it in here."

"We saw it coming in from the airport, but the driver just said it was a fire. He didn't say anything about any riots."

"What's he going to say? He doesn't want to scare you into getting back on the plane and flying out of here. He loses a fare that way."

"Huh!" Breen gnawed on his lower lip. "I don't like that so well. I can get all the riots I want for free back home."

"I don't know how bad it was, I didn't see it. But the cop cars and sirens were going all night long. I don't want to make too much out of it, but I wouldn't say it's nothing, either.

"What I am saying is check it out for yourself before you go making any big commitments."

"I will, I will," Breen said, nodding. "Thanks for the tip, Steve."

Soto shrugged.

Breen tilted his head to one side, vertical creases showing over the bridge of his nose above his glasses. "Tell me, Steve, the riots going to affect your business plans any?"

"We'll see."

"What business is that, anyway?"

"I'm going to organize the workers into a union, set up a little pension fund, stage some job actions for better pay and benefits," Soto said.

"Ha, ha, very funny."

Julie was finishing up at the desk, and Soto noted with interest that the clerk handed her two keys.

"Separate rooms, huh? With a connecting door, I bet," Soto said.

"You've got it all wrong, Steve. Julie's a sweet kid, but our arrangement is strictly business."

"Sure."

"I swear! She's my administrative assistant, and a damned good one, but that's all," Breen said, all aggrieved innocence.

Breen glanced to make sure that Julie was still at the desk. "Confidentially, I think she's frigid," he said behind a hand, his voice lowered.

"She seems a little chilly, at that. Well, maybe the climate will warm her up," Soto said.

A bellhop hefted a pair of suitcases belonging to the newcomers. Julie slung a strap bag over her shoulder and picked up a modest-sized carryall.

Soto and Breen joined her, Breen reaching for the lightest of the bags. He said, "We're going to go up to the rooms and get settled in, and then we've got some business to take care of. Great to run into you, Steve."

"Sure. Nice meeting you, Miss Evans."

She nodded, smiling frostily, then, along with Breen and the bellhop, started toward the stairs. Breen said, "Let's get together later for some drinks, maybe have some dinner, Steve."

"That'd be nice. All three of us."

Julie's thin smile stayed frozen in place as the three walked away. When they reached the stairs, Breen looked back over his shoulder.

He said, "You were just kidding when you made that crack about the unions, weren't you, Steve?"

Soto flipped him a two-finger salute. "Later, Jax."

"Steve? Steve!"

Ignoring him, Soto turned, crossing to the dining-room entrance, where Tony Paul stood waiting. The two of them watched the bellhop, Breen, and Julie climb the winding staircase until they were out of sight.

Tony Paul pursed his lips in a soundless whistle. "Wow, is she built!"

Soto nodded. Tony Paul said, "Who's the guy?"

"Jax Breen; I know him from the old neighborhood."

"And the broad?"

"Julie Evans. She's his administrative assistant."

Tony Paul's eyebrows lifted. "Is that what they're calling them these days?"

"Believe it or not, I think she really is his assistant."

"This guy Breen, what's his angle? Is he connected?"

"He's a crocodile bird."

"A *what*?"

"A crocodile bird. I saw it once on TV, on one of those wildlife shows. They've got these birds, see, that climb right into a crocodile's mouth. The croc sits there with his jaws wide open, and the bird sits in his mouth, pecking out the trapped food particles that're stuck between the croc's teeth," Soto explained.

106

Tony Paul looked like he thought his leg was being pulled. "Bull. You're making this up."

"It's true. It's a good deal for both of them. The croc gets his teeth cleaned, and the bird gets to chow down on the pickings. They've got a good deal going."

Tony Paul was still doubtful. "No kidding?"

"No kidding," Soto said. "That's what Jax is, a crocodile bird. He hangs around the big crocs and makes himself useful and makes a pretty good living out of their leavings. He's into everything and nothing. He's always scamming everybody in these financial con jobs, keeping one step ahead of the law and the investors."

Tony Paul nodded. "I get you. But what happens if the croc's more interested in having a bird dinner than in getting its teeth cleaned?"

"Well, there's always more crocodile birds. Speaking of which, let's go put the bite on some breakfast."

"I sent Dennis in to get us a table," Tony Paul said.

They went through the doors into the dining room, a bright, airy space with a high ceiling. The walls were decorated with shoulder-high patterned tiling. Tables were covered with snowy-white linen cloths and china plates and heavy, gleaming silverware.

There was a nice-sized crowd and most of the tables were full. From the look of things, not only the guests but also some of the businessmen and the bureaucrats from the Ministry on the other side of the square took their breakfasts at the hotel.

Soto didn't have to look too hard for Dennis. He was seated at a table in the corner, near the swinging kitchen doors. That's where Soto would have seated him, too, if he was in charge of the arrangements.

Dennis spotted them and gave them the high sign. Soto ignored him and put a hand on Tony Paul's arm, checking him from moving forward.

The maître d' made a beeline for Soto, recognizing him as a generous dispenser of gratuities from a previous mealtime encounter. Soto and Tony Paul followed him to a nice table beside a window looking out on the square. Soto made sure that he didn't go away empty-handed, discreetly slipping him some paper money.

Someone motioned to him, a few tables away, catching his eye. It was Basil Lodge, seated beside Dorian and two strangers, also *norteamericanos* from the looks of them, a gaunt string-haired middle-aged woman and a pudgy, moon-faced boy-man.

Lodge was well turned out in neat, casual attire, every hair in place, eyes bright, showing no ill effects from his heavy drinking the night before. Dorian was sulky but looked smashing in a pale green sleeveless dress made of some thin, shiny fabric.

Lodge had waved his hand in casual greeting. Soto nodded back. Lodge and company had their food on the table and seemed well occupied with each other, and Soto was interested in breakfast himself, so he decided to wait until later before doing any table hopping.

Dennis got up from his seat by the kitchen, crossing to where Soto and Tony Paul sat. The maître d' moved to intercept him, probably to shoo him away, but Soto indicated that it was okay, and the man went back to his other duties.

Dennis pulled out a chair and sat down. "They had me stuck over in Siberia there!"

Tony Paul said, "Probably afraid you were gonna scare the other guests."

"You saying I don't have class?"

"Kid, some things just don't have to be said."

A waiter bustled up, taking their order and disappearing through the swinging doors into the kitchen.

Soto glanced outside, through the window. Everyday life seemed to be going on pretty much as it had the day before, except for the smoky haze in the sky and the occasional streamers of dark smoke drifting across the skyline.

There was a lot of police-car traffic heading both ways, south to the waterfront district and north to Seaguard Castle, the old Spanish-built fort that was the headquarters of the *policia*.

After a while Dennis started squirming around in his seat, sticking his head forward in the direction of the kitchen, like a man peering for a late bus in the hope that if he looks hard enough, it will come.

Tony Paul rumbled, "Quit rubbernecking, you're making me nervous."

"Where's my food?" Dennis said.

"Sit tight, you'll get it."

"I'm hungry. Anyway, I ordered before you guys, so I should get served first."

Soto said, "If you do, that waiter's tip is going to be looking awfully small."

But Dennis wasn't the only one getting antsy. Patrons at other tables were doing the same thing, staring at the kitchen doors, rolling their eyes, drumming fingertips on tabletops.

"Looks like there's some kind of holdup at that," Tony Paul said.

Soto said, "Yeah, but not the kind of holdup we're used to."

A patron flagged the maître d', probably to complain. They were both looking at the kitchen doors. Nobody had come out of there for a couple of minutes.

The maître d' scurried off to see what was causing the delay. Annoyance and irritation kept edging into his blandly composed features.

He reached the doors, putting a hand on one of them to push it open, when it suddenly slammed into him, swinging outward from the kitchen area.

The maître d' took a heavy hit and was knocked backward, backpedaling a few steps and then sitting down hard on the carpet.

Instant stillness in the dining room, with everybody sitting frozen at their places, silverware held poised in midair.

Dennis guffawed, but nobody even bothered to give him a dirty look, not when they saw what was coming out of the kitchen.

A walking scarecrow of a man, with a skull face, a hole where a nose ought to be, and a death's-head grin.

109

Somebody gasped, *"Zombie!"*

The man stalked into the dining room, oblivious of the maître d', who was crabwalking backward as fast as he could, getting out of its path.

The zombie pointed itself toward Lodge's table and went toward it, hunching along in a weird, ungainly strut, quick-stepping.

Lodge and his table companions stood up. The gaunt-faced woman grabbed the man-boy's arm and started pulling him away, walking backward, neither of them taking their eyes off the zombie.

The table was between Lodge and Dorian and the zombie. Lodge looked grim-faced but game, Dorian was petrified, her face lead gray, with eyes that stared into an abyss but couldn't look away.

Lodge picked up something off the table. Soto couldn't see what it was. He was already moving, out of his chair and charging.

The zombie wanted Lodge, though. Or Dorian, or maybe both. It was hard to tell, since they were standing side by side. The zombie paused, halting, showing uncertainty for the first time since its entrance.

Its head swiveled, fastening hollow eye sockets on the gaunt older woman and the man-boy. She was still dragging him back by the arm, but he was heavy and wasn't cooperating, being rooted in place by fear.

For an instant the zombie seemed to hang fire, unsure whether to go for Dorian and Lodge or the other pair. But the first two were closer, and that decided things.

The zombie's head whipped back around, facing its original targets. Not that Soto believed in zombies. The scarecrow must be some kind of sick lunatic, probably hopped up on drugs. He looked like a crackhead, a crack-cocaine addict. Soto had seen plenty of them and they could do some crazy things when the craving was on them.

Tony Paul and Dennis had jumped up a couple of beats behind him and he heard one of them call his name. *"Steve!"*

Without looking back, he raised an arm in their direction, holding it palm out, shouting, "No guns!"

Tony Paul knew what he was doing, but Soto didn't want Dennis to pull out a rod and start blasting; he'd probably hit everything but the zombie, including Soto.

Not that Soto believed in zombies.

Whatever it was, the scarecrow got tired of the table standing between him and his goal, so he picked it up and tossed it aside.

Plates, food, utensils, tablecloth, and table all went flying.

A dope fiend, sure, that's what he was. That's where that crazy strength came from that allowed him to brush aside a big, heavy table.

Now there was nothing standing between him and Lodge and Dorian.

Soto picked up a chair and slammed it against the back of the scarecrow's head and neck and shoulders. The chair was solid, made of thick heavy wood.

The chair broke. The scarecrow grabbed what was left of it and plucked it out of Soto's hands. Talk about taking candy from a baby—that's how easily he took the chair away from Soto, tossing it aside.

Soto grabbed the scarecrow by the arm, intending to turn him around so he could deliver a vicious karate chop to the neck, but there was one problem: the scarecrow didn't turn, didn't budge. Grabbing his arm was like grabbing a tree branch.

The scarecrow looked like he weighed in at about a hundred and twenty pounds, tops, but Soto couldn't move him. He chopped him on the side of the neck—nothing.

The blow did do one thing, though. It brought him to the scarecrow's attention. The scarecrow turned his head, coming face-to-face with Soto.

Soto felt like he was beholding the literal face of death. The thing seemed to be looking straight at him, but how could that be, when it had no eyes? There were some things glistening in the backs of the socket, moving, but those weren't eyes, they were worms.

111

Soto froze, for an instant as unguarded and vulnerable as he'd been since he first put on long pants. He had no plan, no strategy, no offense or defense.

Tony Paul picked up a knife from a nearby table, came up behind the zombie, and stabbed it in the back.

A puff of dust, like sawdust, blew out where the knife went in. That was all. The knife stuck out between its shoulders like a silver handle on a cooking utensil.

That left Tony Paul flat-footed with astonishment, so that he forgot to duck when the scarecrow backhanded him. The blow sent him sprawling, knocking him half the width of the dining room before he stopped tumbling.

Rapidly revising his no-guns dictum, Soto pulled his piece, stepping between the scarecrow and Dorian, leaving Lodge to take care of himself.

Soto started blasting, emptying the gun into the scarecrow's middle at point-blank range. The zombie jerked with the impact but stayed on its feet. It was lucky that no one was standing behind it because most of the bullets passed through it, drilling it and coming out the other side.

Lodge had something in his hands, whatever it was that he had grabbed off the table before it was overturned. Then Soto realized it was a saltshaker and Lodge had unscrewed the top and was pouring the salt in one hand, where it made a little mound of white grains.

Reaching around Soto and Dorian, Lodge threw the salt in the zombie's face. Most of it fell away, but some of it stayed there, powdering his face like some grotesque white makeup.

Some of the grains had stuck to its death-rictus mouth, its fretted lips and dried-corn teeth.

It smacked its lips a few times, then shuddered from head to toe. It swayed, reeling.

A change came over it, the catatonic rigidity flowing out of its form. Its fixed expression melted, the masklike lines and creases relaxing, easing.

Its fretted lips parted, still powdered with salt, sounds coming from somewhere deep inside it. In a voice that sounded

112

like two pieces of sandpaper rubbing together, it said something, crying out a few words that Soto didn't understand.

Then it collapsed, crashing to the floor. It lay there motionless, a few ribbons of smoke rising from the powder burns where the bullets ripping through it had scorched the edges of the entry wounds.

A tendril of smoke curled from the barrel of Soto's now-empty gun, which he still held clutched in front of him.

There was a pause, which lasted long enough for all the other dining-room patrons to realize the confrontation was all over. The incident had gone down fast, and while it was happening they'd been stuck in place, as if turned to stone by the scarecrow's eyeless Gorgon gaze.

Now—pandemonium. People stampeded, knocking over chairs and each other in their mad rush to reach the exits.

In less than half a minute, the dining room had been emptied out of all but Lodge and Dorian, Soto and his two sidemen, and the scarecrow. Even the maître d' and the waiters had vanished.

So had the gaunt woman and the boy-man.

Soto put his gun away. Nearby, Dennis was giving Tony Paul a hand, helping him up. Bruised and dazed, the big man said, "Wha' hit me?"

"That's a good question," Soto said, putting away his gun. "You okay?"

"Yeah, I think so," Tony Paul said, shaking his head to clear it. "Nothing's broken, anyhow ... Whew! That guy could hit! I fought plenty of guys in the ring, but nobody ever hung one like that on me."

Dorian stood there trembling, staring at nothing, white-faced, teeth chattering.

Soto asked, "You all right?"

She didn't answer, didn't respond. Lodge said, "She's fine."

"Yeah, she looks it," Soto said. "I'd say she's in shock."

"Who wouldn't be?"

"You seem to be doing fine."

Lodge shrugged. Soto took off his jacket, draping it over

113

Dorian's smooth slim shoulders, admiring the fine-grained ivory skin. He said, "Best thing for her is to keep warm."

Tony Paul and Dennis stood over the scarecrow. The silver knife was still sticking out of its back. Scattered below were a couple of exit holes where the bullets had passed through.

Tony Paul shook his head wonderingly. "No blood . . ."

"That was one tough sucker," Dennis said.

Indicating the corpse, Soto asked, "Friend of yours?"

"Hardly."

"Looks like the rest of your breakfast club vamoosed."

Lodge raised an eyebrow, somehow still looking dapper. "Miss Calexa and her son, Alba, you mean."

"If that's what their names are."

"I wouldn't worry about them, they're sure to turn up eventually."

"You're taking this pretty coolly," Soto said, with grudging respect. This Lodge was no softy.

Lodge shrugged. "These things happen."

"Not to me. When a guy gets hit in the head with a chair, stabbed in the back, and shot six times at point-blank range in the guts, he usually goes down."

"You seem to have some expertise yourself in such matters, Steve," Lodge said silkily. "Do you do such things often?"

"I get around," Soto replied, poker-faced.

"I'm sure that you do. You and your friends certainly acquitted yourselves handily."

"Not well enough. We didn't stop him."

"In any case, you have my thanks. And that of my niece as well," Lodge said, putting an arm around Dorian's shoulders. "I'm sure that as soon as she's properly recovered, she'll be only too glad to thank you herself . . . in her own inimitable fashion."

Outside, police sirens sounded, nearing.

Soto said, "That was a pretty neat trick you pulled. How'd you manage to stop him?"

"Quite simple. I applied the infallible antidote to zombiehood. Salt. Simple table salt. When a zombie tastes salt, it breaks the spell of walking death. The zombie realizes he's dead, and promptly dies," Lodge explained.

"There's no such thing as zombies."

"Nooooooo, of course not. Very well. Let us say that this poor deluded creature merely believed he was a zombie, and when he tasted salt, knowing the legend, he convinced himself to die through the process of autosuggestion."

"I'd say the gun and the knife got him, but he was so hopped up on something that there was a delayed reaction before it killed him."

"If you like," Lodge said, being agreeable.

Outside, tires squealed as a couple of police SUVs screeched to a halt in front of the hotel. Doors flung open and men poured out, guns drawn, racing into the building.

Lodge said, "Late again, as usual."

Soto said, "I hope there's not going to be any heat about this."

"Not to worry. Major Quantez is a dear friend of mine, and of course he's thoroughly devoted to Dorian. As are we all." Lodge hugged his niece with the arm that was still wrapped around her shoulders.

"Your buddy said something at the end there, but I didn't quite catch it."

"Do you speak Spanish, Steve?"

"No."

"He did."

"What did he say?"

Lodge readied himself to reply, but Dorian got there first, coming out of her daze long enough to answer the question.

"He said, 'My God, I am dead!'"

PART 2

SEVEN

The earth spun, rolling Western Europe into darkness. The shadow line cut through an area north of the Alps, where Bavaria and Switzerland met in a hazily indefinable borderland, site of the independent mini-state of Visaria. Roughly the size of Rhode Island, Visaria was outwardly similar to such tiny sovereign countries as Liechtenstein, Andorra, Monaco, and Latveria.

The capital and principal city, also named Visaria, sat on the northern shore of Lake Lorelei, where the river Undine took its source, winding northeastward through mountain valleys before eventually joining the Danube.

The city was founded during the Middle Ages, and in the section known as Old Town there still stood a number of buildings that dated back to that time. Much of the city had been bombed out during World War II and rebuilt during the postwar era. For a city whose population had never risen past one hundred thousand, it had an unusually large number of cemeteries and graveyards, many of them quite extensive. The largest were military burial grounds, the region having seen extensive slaughter in both world wars, particularly the first.

The city-state's governmental machinery was located at the lakeside State's Plaza, a broad, open square whose ornate central fountain and rows of surrounding buildings were largely built during the mid-nineteenth century. Fronting the plaza's north side was the Council building, a hulking stone pile complete with working clock tower, where the ruling Board of Electors met.

The plaza's east and west sides were lined with administrative office buildings, done in the same style as the Council site. Facing the south side, however, was a structure radically different in design and type from the Baroque stonework of its neighbors.

This was the Science Palace, a three-story building whose long sides ran parallel to the edge of the plaza. Its stark, simple, clean-lined shape was not exactly rectangular, but trapezoidal, with the outer, shorter sides narrowing slightly inward from base to roofline. Its square-edged central structure rose a story higher than the rest of the building, and was topped by a domed roof tipped by an obelisk spire.

Built in the 1920s, when its Bauhaus-influenced geometrical shape must have been even more startlingly modern, the palace's streamlined style was striking in its use of unornamented steel, stone, and glass.

Now, with the day closing, the building was lit up inside and out, a gleaming white polygon with the lake as a backdrop. The last light was fading from the sky, street lamps were lit, and the corps of office drones who worked in the plaza complex had mostly gone to their homes.

The Science Palace was closed, its doors shut. Inside, a pair of uniformed security guards made their rounds, conducting a final room-by-room inspection to make sure that no unauthorized personnel, no wandering members of the general public, which was admitted during office hours, remained behind.

The guards started on the top floor and worked their way down. They had reached the ground floor and were patrolling the deserted, echoing high-ceilinged corridors and chambers when they were stopped in their tracks by an unexpected sound.

Somewhere in the building, a piano started playing. Its

first few notes were faint, tentative. They might have been mistaken for the sound of crystal chandelier beads rustled by a stray air current. Strings of notes followed as the playing became less hesitant, more sure.

The acoustics in the palace were good, carrying the music throughout the building. The sound came from the rear of the structure, in the Great Hall, a space generally reserved for ceremonial functions and formal receptions.

Opposite the entryway, on the far side of a polished ballroom-sized floor, rose a wall of gridded glass windowpanes, two stories tall. The windows opened on a view of terraced pavilions and landscaped gardens that descended in levels to the lakefront. The sidewalls were hung with murky brown-and-gold portraits in gilded frames, while, just as might be expected, a crystal chandelier hung down from the center of the ceiling.

The chandelier was dark, most of the big room was dim, with the brightest spot being a pale golden glow that emanated from under the tall windows where a standing floor lamp threw a fan of light on a concert-style piano on a raised dais.

Seated at the keyboard was Countess Marya Zaleska, but recently arisen from her coffin bed. Her black hair was tied in a knot at the back of her neck, accenting her fine-boned face and long neck. She looked starved, hollow-eyed and sunken-cheeked, with crimson lips in a paper-white face. She wore a dark long-sleeved knit dress, silk stockings, and high heels.

Seemingly random notes and chords began to coalesce into snatches of melody as she began picking out a tune. It was a folk song, a sweet, simple air, featherlight.

Liquid crystal notes rang out, clear and pure, almost plaintive. Marya's face was a stiff mask of concentration, while her waxy, long-fingered hands were flexible, almost fluid as they moved across the keys.

Outside, all had been calm and still, but now a breeze rose, ruffling the surface of the lake, rippling and distorting the palace's shining reflection.

Inside, scraps and phrases of melody snaked through the halls, swirling along the ceiling, while below, the two guards continued on patrol.

One said, "I know that tune—I used to sing it as a child in school. It's the 'Cradle Song.'"

The other said, "Her playing is not bad."

"Good technique, but a bit cold."

They exchanged glances, not breaking stride as they followed a hallway. Behind them the music unwound, a nursery lullaby.

A pause was held a few beats too long, cueing a new phase of the music—a sinister change. The "Cradle Song"'s main theme was transposed into a minor key, sounding slightly off, mocking.

On the far side of the lake was a line of mountains. Now clouds began to boil off the summits, pouring down their sides and creeping north toward the city.

Marya was more animated now, her face still stiff but her eyes glittering, her body swaying over the keyboard, her hands a white blur of motion.

The lullaby became a funeral dirge with a sly, sardonic undertone.

The first guard shuddered. His partner said, "From cradle to grave." They kept walking, away from the Great Hall, toward the front of the building.

The music continued, a capering waltz through a graveyard. As she played, red dots glowed in Marya's eyes.

Winds gusted, rattling the windows. The sky was overcast, the cloud ceiling low. The few pedestrians out in the plaza clutched their hats to their heads, scurrying bent almost double, hastening to beat the rising storm and the dark.

The two guards reached the end of a corridor, passing through an archway into a rotunda, a wide circular space that soared to the high, domed ceiling. A lofty space that dwarfed human figures. Staircases led to galleries that wound along the shaft's inner walls, projecting at the various floor landings.

Under the dome, the round marble floor was decorated

122

with an intricate mosaic design. At ground level, the designs seemed almost abstract, an inlaid skein of lines, arcs, and swirls. From above, the pattern resolved itself into an image of the zodiac, its rim border marked with the twelve astrological symbols.

The guards detoured into a side room, a security checkpoint. They logged in the time of their completed inspection round, got their hats and coats, armed the alarm system, secured the post, and went out.

They crossed the rotunda to the main entrance, whose oversized front doors were like the gates of some walled city. The doors were already locked. The guards exited via a small door to one side of the massive entryway.

Winds sent loose papers swirling into the air, whipping them across the plaza and out of sight. Lampposts swayed, casting restless nets of light and shadow on the plaza stones.

The rushing wind mixed with the sound of muffled music from inside, whipping it wailing into the heights, sending it spinning off in silvery shivering blasts.

Now off duty, the guards hurried down the palace's broad sweeping flights of shallow stone steps, into the plaza and away.

Low streaming clouds skimmed north across the lake. Rain streaked the Great Hall's windows, a soft percussive accompaniment to Marya's playing.

The music and the storm were in sync. The pianist hammered out great swelling walls of sound, echoing, rolling, more than a little mad.

Clouds opened up, downpouring a hissing torrent. The sky crackled, rumbling. Tiny blue forks of lightning shot out of the bottom of the cloud cover.

Marya's impassioned playing reached a crescendo, her red eyes blazing, her snakelike fingers whipping a pillar of sound out of the guts of the piano.

Over the lake, a sizzling blue-white lightning bolt split the sky, followed by a sullen booming thunderclap.

Marya stopped playing, hands held poised above the keys.

More lightning and thunder followed, not as explosive as

that first bolt, but still vigorous and crackling. There was lots of electricity in the air. The storm had reached critical mass and would continue firing for some time.

Marya smiled, showing fangs. Lightning flashes turned the row of high windows into a glaring white wall, far brighter than anything in the dimly lit hall. Each flash lasted less than a heartbeat, paired with a whip-cracking sky boom.

The keyboard still vibrated. She pulled down the protective cover, closing away the keys, then pushed back the bench and stood, switching off the floor lamp beside the piano. Her eyes glowed in the dark. She went to the window and stood there for a while, watching the storm. The blood-light in her eyes dimmed, fading to almost normalcy.

She stood immobile statue still, while the flickering lightning animated the scene around her, energizing it.

When she had seen enough, she crossed to a sidewall, exiting through a door into a connecting room, a kind of study whose total floorspace was about one-fifth of that of the Great Hall's. There was a desk and chair, with a couple of comfortable armchairs grouped around it. The walls were lined with glass-fronted wooden cabinets and tall bookshelves filled with books.

Except for Marya, the room was empty. No lights, except for the lightning flashes shining through curtained windows and the glow seeping through the bottom of the closed hallway door.

Marya picked her way through the room as easily as if she could see in the dark—which she could. She crossed to an alcove, a recessed niche beside a bookcase. Inset in the wall to one side of the niche was a keypad with a beaded red "on" light.

She pressed a number code into the keypad. The light turned green, triggering a near-simultaneous click from some internal locking mechanism in the wall.

The rear wall of the niche was a sliding panel, which now slid open, revealing an oblong doorway opening onto a landing. She went through the portal. After a pause, the panel automatically slid shut behind her, the locking mechanism resetting with a click.

On the other side of the wall, the keypad's green light switched back to red.

The landing stood in the middle of a stairwell that extended both up and down. It was like a set of fire stairs with restricted access. The landings were lit by electric lights, not overly bright.

The shaft walls were thick, muting the thunder. Marya descended the stairs, following the slanting flights down the well, below the surface of the earth. She *knew* when she was underground, projecting her awareness into the damp earth beyond the stone foundation walls, sensing the worms and beetles and other things burrowing around in the ground.

The stairs went down and down, but that was no problem for Marya, who was tireless. The lower levels were also accessible by elevator, but she shunned all such mechanical contrivances. Science was alien wizardry to her.

When she reached the landing she wanted, she stopped. She had to go through the keypad routine again, only this time it took a different code number to unseal the door.

"So much less satisfactory than a door-guardian imp," she said to herself, stepping through into a short narrow passageway tube, the door auto-sealing behind her.

Still, this world of machine science was ubiquitous, unavoidable. It had to be met on its own terms. Besides, those old imps had their drawbacks as well . . .

By a winding and secret route, she made her way toward the White Room, where the experiment would take place.

In the center of the room stood a crystal egg—the Chrysalis. In it was the Bride.

The egg-shaped object measured eight feet long and was mounted upright in a portable pedestal stand that was braced and secured to remain perfectly stationary.

The egg was man-made, a single giant crystal artificially grown in mineral-bath vats. It had been split in two and the twin halves hollowed out into an oversized human-shaped body cavity. The Bride had been taken from her glass coffin and placed inside the egg, which was then resealed.

The egg was studded from top to bottom with a grid of palm-sized silver disks, arranged in a kind of birdcage pattern. Each disk held a long silver spike that pierced the crystal shell, the points almost but not quite making contact with the embedded Bride. The spikes were conducting rods, designed to carry reanimating energy to key nodes and nexuses of the creature's central nervous system.

Hanging suspended from the ceiling, over the egg, was a vertical column ten feet long and three feet in diameter. It consisted of a stack of quartz cubes separated by black composite disks, all held together in a tubular steel framework. The cubes were eighteen inches on a side, the disks were the size of garbage-can lids. Bundles of spidery metallic rods and wires ran the length of the column, piercing the cubes and disks.

At the tip of the column was a bucket-shaped copper funnel, its wide mouth poised about six feet above the top of the egg.

A complex rigging of metal cables and braces, resembling somewhat the skeletal framework of an unfolded umbrella, held the stacked quartz column suspended from the domed ceiling.

The platform base housing the egg squatted in a snake's nest of power cables and connector and feeder lines. The other ends of the lines were jacked into the sockets of great banks of machinery and stacked equipment consoles that were grouped around the egg.

A dozen or so people clustered around the egg, among them Mantz and Gregor. The rest were half Mantz's technicians and half Gregor's biomedical staff. Techs and biomedics.

They bustled around the egg with the single-minded purposefulness of insect worker drones tending the larva of a future nest queen. They bent to their tasks, machine-tending, inputting data, calibrating, analyzing, adjusting, connecting and decoupling, checking and rechecking.

126

Marya appeared in a secluded spot in the chamber, screened from view by an equipment bank. There was much here that was strange, alien, even hateful to her.

It was an artificial environment, with ventilator ducts supplying canned air and the temperature and humidity auto-maintained at a steady, unvarying rate. Pumps throbbed, air currents swooshed, consoles hummed, and instrument boards emitted a variety of beeps and clicks.

Not that Marya was any paragon of naturalness. But her tomb world of blood, black magic, and Undeath was at opposite poles from the bloodless techno-web of intelligent machines.

At the center of the web lay the attempt to breathe life into a man-made creature, and that was something with which she was indeed familiar: an act of transgression.

"Let us transgress tonight," she said to herself, stepping out from behind the machinery and crossing to where Gregor and Mantz stood under the egg, conferring.

Most of the personnel were too engrossed in their duties to notice her as she glided past. Mantz glimpsed something in the corner of his eye and looked up. He saw someone who wasn't in a lab coat, possibly an unauthorized person, and he started to frown. Then he realized who it was and wiped his face blank.

He said, "Where did she come from? All the entrances are sealed and I didn't see her come in any of them."

"She comes and goes as she pleases," Gregor said, quietly enjoying the other's discomfort.

Marya went to them, gliding surefootedly through the maze of cables and machinery.

Gregor and Mantz greeted her.

"There is the prince who will awaken this sleeping beauty," Mantz said, indicating the suspended column of quartz cubes.

"What is it?" she asked.

"I call it the Lightning Rod. It will pull down the storm and power up the Bride."

Gregor said, "In theory."

127

He and Mantz exchanged glances and curt nods. Mantz said, "The experiment will prove the theory."

Gregor smiled with his lips. Mantz turned away from him, toward Marya. She said, "Electricity has been tried on her many times before, to no avail. Why should it work this time, Engineer?"

"The previous attempts all applied current directly to her. This is the method that has been used to successfully revive Frankenstein's Monster again and again. But the Monster has his own set of ready-made, built-in contact points—his neck-bolt electrodes.

"The Bride has no such electrodes. I am convinced that is why past attempts have failed, because without electrodes her body cannot absorb and hold a charge.

"The biomedical staff has tried to implant electrodes in her and failed. But I'm sure that Gregor could tell you more about that than I could," Mantz said.

"You will recall that I and my staff advised against the implants," Gregor said. "It is so noted in the records, if you would care to refresh your recollection of the facts, my dear Mantz.

"As you know, Countess, I believe that the Bride is of an entirely different order of being than Frankenstein's creation, particularly so in the processing of energy."

Marya peered at the Bride embedded in the crystal egg, her angular form further elongated and distorted by the curvature of the shell. She asked, "How will you deliver the charge?"

Mantz said, "The silver needles piercing the egg like a pincushion are contact points, dozens of them. They will direct the raw force of the current to key nerve-net nodes, simultaneously channeling the energy throughout the body to the central nervous system's ignition points.

"We will literally start her up."

"When?"

"Now. That is, we can commence the process within a very few moments after getting the go-ahead, Countess."

"Then do so."

Mantz motioned his assistant to him, a loose-jointed young man with a straw-colored bowl haircut. They put their heads together for a moment, then the young man went away.

"Hemling says the storm is almost at its height," Mantz said.

"I know," Marya said, smiling. She did, too. The tips of her fangs showed and Mantz looked at every part of her face but them. She was well aware of the unsettling effect the fangs had on those mortals who saw them, even cold, iron-willed logicians like the engineer.

Gregor eyed them intently, almost avidly. But then, biology was his specialty, and fanged immortals were particularly fascinating to him.

Mantz tilted his head back, looking up at his machine. He said, "Frankenstein caught the lightning. So will we. Previous attempts to revive the Bride used artificially generated current. This may well have contributed to their failure.

"We will take our power from the source, from the same place that Henry Frankenstein took his—the storm."

Gregor held up a hand, the index finger pointing ceilingward. "But Henry Frankenstein was not alone in creating the Bride," he said. "He worked jointly with Dr. Pretorius, who had his own theories on stimulating the life force in dead or inanimate tissues.

"Frankenstein's creation was made of pieces of dead bodies, but that is not the case with the Bride. We know that Pretorius said that parts of her were vat-made, grown in a vat—a process similar no doubt to what we call 'cloning.'

"Pretorius also followed different lines of research when it came to engendering the life force in his creations. Frankenstein used the lightning, but Pretorius experimented with something called the Moon-Ray."

Marya, thoughtful, said, "The Moon-Ray . . . Yes. I have heard of this Moon-Ray."

Mantz said, "Indeed you have, Countess. A junior engineer in my department has been conducting a thorough investigation of the subject."

Gregor said slyly, "Over your objections, I believe, Mr. Engineer."

Mantz looked down from the machine, smiling indulgently. He shrugged. "I confess I thought it an unprofitable line of research, with so many other, more immediate tasks clamoring for attention. Yes, Pretorius's notes make mention once or twice of some Moon-Ray apparatus, but that's all we have—notes.

"No schematic drawings, no design specs, no mathematical formulae, not even an adequate explanation of the theory and practice of the Ray. Whatever the apparatus was, if it ever existed at all—"

"It was real," Gregor interrupted. "The notes are quite clear on that. I have studied them myself."

"I'll concede the point," Mantz said. "In any case, it's a lost technology, what I consider an unprofitable avenue of investigation. A majority of the Project Review Board disagreed, and so the project was authorized.

"To date, the project has been unable to produce any controlled phenomena under lab conditions, and so for our purposes, the question of the Moon-Ray is purely academic."

"We'll see, Mantz."

"We will, Doctor."

Nearby, Hemling waved, catching Mantz's eye, signaling that all was ready.

"It's time," Mantz said. "If you will be so good as to accompany me to the control booth, Countess—Doctor."

He and the others went to the control booth, a structure that looked like a milk carton turned on its side, with a long slitted front window that ran for nearly the full length of its upper half. It occupied a raised platform, nestled under the overhanging arch of a rim wall. Bunches of cables radiated out from it to varied machine hookups.

The trio climbed three metal steps to the platform, entering the booth box through a side door. Much of the space was taken up by a multibanked console with chairs that faced the front window. Two of the boards were already occupied by Hemling and another technician.

130

Two more boards were reserved for Mantz and Gregor. Mantz told the technician to yield his place to Marya, but she countermanded the order.

"These colored lights and dials are meaningless to me," she said. "They need tending by one who understands them."

Her hand rested on the technician's shoulder, where she had put it when he had started to automatically rise to make way for her. Her touch kept him from moving, freezing him in place. He could not move. He blinked, his heart hammering.

She lifted her hand and he could move again. She stepped back, standing against the wall, arms folded across her chest.

Gregor and Mantz took their places at the console. Gregor's board was primarily keyed to monitor the Bride's vital signs—if there were any. Now they were flat-lined.

Hemling's board featured a radar screen that imaged the storm, tracking it, its greenish-white sweep hand circling the dial.

The men at the console wore personal communicators, cordless pencil-thin curving headsets with miniaturized components that allowed them to receive and transmit.

Marya was offered one but declined. She didn't want that thing with its tiny insect voice buzzing in her ear.

Outside the booth, the technicians and biomedics were finishing up, going through the checklists for a final time. When they were done, they began filtering out of the room, exiting through bulkhead doors which were placed at opposite ends of the space.

Yellow warning lights flashed. Mantz turned away from the board on his swivel chair, facing Marya.

He coughed nervously before speaking. "I would be remiss in my duties, Countess, if I failed to mention that there is a measure of risk attached to this experiment. In my opinion, the risk is negligible, but since any new venture contains an element of uncertainty, I must call it to your attention. The experiment can be observed safely from outside the chamber."

She said, "I'll take my chances."

The last person to leave the White Room was a technician, who raised a hand in half salute to those in the booth before stepping through the rounded portal, easing the hatch door closed, and dogging it shut.

The wall-mounted emergency light flashers switched from yellow to red.

The four board operators bent to their work, throwing switches, turning dials, inputting coded command sequences. The transceiver headsets kept them in communication with remote units.

Mantz said, "Open the barrier shields."

"Open barrier shields," said Rolf, the technician whom Marya had touched. Through his keyboard he initiated the necessary commands.

Electric motors thrummed as a crack opened in the center of the domed ceiling above the egg. The crack widened, a growing band of blackness bordered by the twin halves of a retractable ceiling hub.

There was a scraping sound as the paired metal plates divided, disappearing into recessed slots. When they were gone, there was a hole in the ceiling, about eight feet in diameter.

The hole was merely the lip of a central shaft which stretched vertically up to the aboveground floors.

In the building's ground-floor rotunda, in the center of the marble floor, at a spot directly under the high arched ceiling, and directly over the underground White Room and its crystal egg, a second set of barrier shields was automatically opened.

This part of the floor was not marble but only marble-faced, with thin stone skin covering fifteen-inch-thick steel floor plates. The shield was in the hub of the zodiac-patterned floor mosaic.

It opened, uncovering the well of the sunken central shaft.

Below, in the White Room, a popping sound accompanied the change in air pressure as the rotunda shield barrier was withdrawn.

Above, a third shield opened, this one set in the center

132

of the building's high domed roof. Directly above that was the roof's obelisk spire, the highest point on the structure.

The tip of the obelisk was a metal-sheathed lightning attractor, with a conducting rod piercing the spire's core.

The shields opened not simultaneously but in sequence, as a safety precaution. It was a mechanical process that could not be hurried, not even by Engineer Mantz.

He used the time to explain the workings of the system.

"First, Countess, the attractor on the roof will draw the lightning. The attractor is also a bolt shaper, using powerful electromagnetic coils to tighten and focus the high-energy bolt along narrow channels.

"The well connecting us with the rotunda is also lined with those powerful coils, directing the bolt to the lightning rod. The rod is actually a filtering device, a buffer that steps down the current to manageable levels."

Marya said, "It is not necessary that I understand the workings of your invention, Engineer, so long as you do."

Rolf's screen showed all green gos for the shield system. He said, "All barrier shields open."

Hemling said, "Barrier shields open, check."

Mantz said, "I check your check."

Gregor said nothing. This part of the process was out of his province.

Hemling's radar screen showed that the storm was holding.

"Now is the time," Mantz said. "Any longer and the storm will have peaked.

"Protective goggles on, all."

The goggles were lightweight plastic visors with greenish-black bubble lenses, held in place by elastic straps at the back of the head. All in the booth put them on, even Marya.

There was something insectlike about the bubble-eyed goggles. With them covering the upper half of her sharp, pointy triangular-shaped face, Marya's head had the look of a praying mantis's.

Mantz said, "Switch on the attractor."

Rolf threw some switches. "Switching on attractor. Attractor on."

Hemling said, "Attractor on, check."

Above, lightning bolts zinged the air around the building. Sections of the town's power grid flickered, then held.

More bolts clawed at the spire. A forked trident speared the spire tip, attaching itself to the metal attractor plates.

Contact! A white-hot jolt of sizzling raw power poured through the plates and into the spire's internal conducting rod, vaporizing both, but not before the bolt shapers had directed it down to the floor well.

The blast funneled through the shaft, into the top of the lightning rod.

White light flooded the underground room, swelling, crackling, dazzling even when seen through the thick-lensed protective goggles.

It was so bright that those in the booth had to turn their heads away. Marya flattened against the wall, instinctively recoiling from the light. It was not sunlight and could not harm her, but its pitiless white-hot incandescence was so much like sunlight in its brightness that she couldn't help but flinch.

It was over in a second, lasting only as long as had the lightning bolt. And the lightning bolt was done, its force spent with a crazy crashing roar of tortured atoms, a deafening crash.

The lightning rod had taken the force of the blast, and the machinery in the room had been hardened against high-voltage electrical discharges, but for an instant the lights dimmed and the machines shuddered.

From the booth, the rod had looked like a stack of ice cubes with hockey-puck dividers between the layers. Now those cubes were all squares of pulsing white light, while snakes of blue electricity coiled up and down the silvery tube framework.

Hemling, awed, said, "It's working! The rod has caught the power of the lightning!"

Mantz said, "Of course it's working! I designed it!"

An electric-blue glow outlined the rod. It was thickest at the bottom, around the copper funnel mouth.

A fan of jagged blue-white energy came spitting out of the funnel. It sputtered, then caught, streaming down, showering the crystal egg with blue-white radiance.

The egg's grid of silver disk-headed contact points glowed, each disk sucking up energy and sending it inward along the silver spike, to the Bride at the heart of the crystal.

The egg's walls seemed to dissolve in the blue-white glow, so that the silver spikes seemed to float in midair. In the center of the energy bath, the Bride was a ghostly phantom outline.

Mantz was exultant. "Look at those readings, Gregor! All that energy flooded into the egg, with none escaping—where does it go?

"Into her, Gregor, into her! The Bride is taking the charge, absorbing it!"

Gregor stared at the board screens. He reached for the goggles to take them off for a better look, but decided against it. The blue-white glare was too bright.

Besides, there were self-adjusting optics in the goggles that allowed for clear viewing of all screen and dial readouts, no matter what the level of light.

He said, "She's taking the charge, no doubt about that!"

"Hah! You see, Gregor, I was right! What are her vital signs?"

"There are none."

"What!"

"Mantz—there are none!"

"Impossible, Doctor. There must be."

"None. They're all flat-lined, not the slightest tick of response."

Mantz looked for himself, saw it was true. He gnawed at dry lips. "Gregor, how can this be?"

"I don't know. She's absorbed enough energy to reanimate ten Brides! With all that power, she should be fully up and running, but there's not a flicker.

"The only thing I can think of—"

"Yes? What is it, Gregor? Speak up, man!"

"She processes energy much differently than her male counterpart, Mantz! Much more differently than even I suspected!"

Meanwhile, the rod's copper funnel had begun to melt under the force of the energy torrent, each molten coppery drop vaporizing as it fell into the blast. As the funnel shrank, the glowing quartz cubes dimmed, fading.

Finally the energy stream sputtered out with the last of the funnel. The cubes glowed with a curious pale ghostly light.

The egg glowed, too, a bubble of blue-white light with the Bride's dark figure at its core.

"Vital signs, Doctor!"

"Nothing, Mantz."

There was a sharp zapping sound, a static-laden electronic *pop*.

Rolf looked up. "What was that?"

Gregor said, "It sounded like the circuitry hawked up a glob of feedback."

Mantz said nastily, "Is that your professional diagnosis, Doctor?"

Before Gregor could reply, Rolf said, "Wait—something's happening . . ."

The blue-white light in the egg dimmed, while the Bride began to glow. She was lit up from within, radiating light from every pore. Her face blurred into shining blue whiteness with midnight-blue blobs denoting her eye sockets, mouth, and sunken cheeks.

Gregor muttered, "This—is not good."

Marya asked, "What is it, Gregor? What is she doing?"

"I do not know, Countess, and that is why it is not good."

Mantz said authoritatively, "It's probably some sort of freakish coronal discharge phenomenon, not surprising with all the energy she sucked up. With that much charge, she *should* be glowing.

"It should play out harmlessly in another minute or so—"

The glow pulsed. Now the silver spikes were glowing, too, their disk-shaped heads studding the egg's outer surface shining blue white. Little blue worms of lightning began to spark and grow, extending from the contact points into the air.

Spidery blue lines of light emerged simultaneously from all the egg grid points. Wispy, rootlike, they unfurled in thickening streamers that grew brighter and bluer with each pulsing beat.

These tentacles of rude, raw force continued to expand and grow. They twitched and swayed, moving to some obscure internal rhythm, weaving a webwork of blue-white energy snakes whose tips quested outward, flicking, darting, probing—

White noise crackled from the console's speaker panels and from the receivers in the board operators' headsets. Gregor tore his off, the others used their mute buttons.

The egg and its wriggling energy streamers resembled some undersea plant, the hydra-headed mass of tentacles gliding and swirling as if disturbed by unseen currents.

The tip of one grazed a wall, brushing a metal plate.

The streamer detonated with the force of a mini-lightning blast, a pyrotechnic explosion that sprayed smoke, dust, and showers of blue sparks. A hole the size of a bowling ball had been punched through the wall at the place where the metal plate had been.

The shock wave rocked the Plexiglas booth window. Wide swatches of red warning lights came alive on the board.

Outside, red emergency lights flashed and alarm klaxons blatted and hooted.

A second streamer touched the top of a bank of machinery. The blast disintegrated a good part of the top, breaking down the array into its separate components and sending them flying across the room.

The pace quickened, with more and more of the energy cords contacting metal objects, grounding, and exploding in potent mini-blasts.

Gregor said, "A mere coronal discharge, eh? I told you, Mantz, I warned you that the Bride was made differently—"

Mantz, suddenly white-faced and haggard, said, "She's rejecting the charge!"

"Yes, you fool, she's rejecting the charge, spitting the full force of the lightning blast back at us!"

The back-blasts were generating pandemonium in the White Room as the Bride spewed blue bolts from each of the egg's surface contact points.

Tentacle tips scored the walls and floor, tearing out great gouges in the surface, blackening and blasting tiles, sending them flying in masses. Metal fused and melted, running like hot wax.

The room lights flickered, swathes of them blacking out. The hooting klaxon alarms were drowned out by the uproar. The room filled with smoke and dust.

In the booth, the power shorted out. The lights went dark and the power went dead.

Mantz shouted over the clamor, "Stay where you are! The auxiliary generator will kick in in a few seconds!"

Nobody was going anywhere, at least not out of the booth, not while the back-blast was still raging outside. The electric lights were out but there was plenty of light to see by, thanks to the auroral display of whiplike blue lightnings flailing the room.

A thump, then a powerful hum vibrated beneath the booth, the sound of the auxiliary generator switching on. Some of the lights blinked back on, but not all, just enough to fill the booth with dirty dishwater-colored light.

Some sections of the console came back on-line, but much of the system had crashed and remained inert despite the frantic efforts of Mantz, Hemling, and Rolf to restore them.

EIGHT

The backlash blacked out most of Visaria. The city stayed dark while the storm moved away, the clouds flickering with a last few sullen blue bolts. The wind picked up, as if to hurry the clouds away.

The black mirror of Lake Lorelei was lit by the white glow of the Science Palace as the lights came back on. The rest of the town stayed dark. On its outskirts, the airport lights blazed on undiminished, being part of a separate grid.

After a moment the lights of a clinic hospital came on. It, too, had its own generators, but they weren't as fast or as good as those of the palace. A few scattered buildings, similarly equipped, showed lights, but the rest of the city stayed dark.

In the White Room, the Bride's charge was spent. The Bride was a dark body in a crystal egg that no longer emitted light. The silver disk heads glowed white-hot for a time, then red-hot, cooling.

The space was filled with dark gray smoke, thick and toxic with the fumes of burned plastic and vaporized metal. Live cables stretched across the floor and hanging down from the ceiling sprayed random bursts of sparks. Some of the banked machine units were still burning.

Smoke rose up through the well, into the rotunda. Doors and windows were opened to let it out.

The underground levels had been cleared of all unprotected personnel. Now, in the halls outside the White Room, an emergency squad assembled, its members clad in antitoxic "spacesuits," helmeted outfits with their own self-contained oxygen supplies.

There was smoke in the halls, and flashing red lights and alarms. The squad members had mini-spotlights mounted on the tops of their helmets, their beams filling the murky corridors with a maze of lances of light.

Somebody found the cutoff switch and turned off the hooting klaxon alarms. With the noise stopped, a person could hear himself think. The red lights kept flashing.

The bulkhead door was unsealed and opened, venting masses of more smoke into the corridors, filling them.

The emergency crew communicated via built-in helmet transceivers. They were equipped with pry bars, fire extinguishers, metal cutters, hydraulic jacks, and other lifesaving equipment.

Smoke poured out the open circular door. The E-crew poured inside, helmet spotlights stabbing through the murk.

The booth was the focus of their concern, but they had to work to get there. A lot of wreckage was in the way. Live wires were handled like venomous snakes, their heads pinned down by insulated poles while they were disconnected and neutralized.

Fire extinguishers sprayed mountains of chemical foam on flaming machine units, fused craters and other hot spots, smothering them. Twisted girders and dangerously dangling beams clanged and crashed as they were cleared and swept aside.

Power from other generators in the complex was directed here, channeled into the massive hidden duct fans that started up with a whine, speeding up into a high-pitched tooth-rattling vibration.

The duct fans were mounted in the ceiling and high walls. Some had been knocked out by the backlash, but most of

140

them were still working. They tore at the smoke clouds, thinning them into a grayish-white veil.

The vanguard of the crew neared the booth. The front and roof were smashed in, splintered. Heaped up against it was the remains of the lightning rod, which had come apart in the crash. The quartz cubes were still hot and the extinguishers buried them in mounds of foam.

Some crew members approached the booth from the side. The support platform was crumpled up around the wrecked structure like a ruffled steel skirt, but one side had been left relatively clear, so the crew approached from that direction.

One of them said, "Nothing could have survived that!"

They went in anyway, clearing away rubble, putting in bracing beams to prop up the structure. Inside, they could see that a couple of the console-board sections, each piano-sized, had been torn loose from the floor and upended against the rear wall, where they had wedged against the curved chamber wall behind it. They formed an inverted V-shape, a protective barrier that had absorbed much of the impact when the rod crashed into the booth.

Under the bracing console sections, there was a space between them and the wall, though both ends were heaped high with loose rubble.

At the near end, where the crew members were working, there was a disturbance at the top of the pile, dislodging pieces and shards that rolled down the sides.

Somebody said, "Something moving in there—"

More of the rubble was cleared away from inside, and a hand emerged, a red hand, slim and tapering, with clawlike fingers. The hand was red with blood.

It pushed its way out into the open, feeling around, fingers creeping like insect legs.

The crew members rushed forward, using three-foot-long spade-bladed entrenching tools to clear away the pile. As they leveled it, they revealed the sheltered space under the wedged machinery.

In the space crouched Marya, she of the red hand. In her

other arm, she held an object cradled to her side, wrapped in rags.

She was in rags herself, her outfit torn and tattered by the blast. She was blood-spattered, drenched in gore. Bursts of red stained her hair, glistened on her face and hands and front.

Still, she looked healthy enough—better than usual, for her. Her eyes glittered and there was good color in her cheeks, under the blood.

There had been no time for escape when the rod came catapulting straight on toward the booth. But her reflexes were super-quick and when the crash tore up the console components, upending them, she had ducked down into the space behind them.

Even so, the impact was stunning and would have been instantly fatal, except that she wasn't alive, she was Undead. It hurt and she didn't like it and after she had gotten her wits back, she was put to great pain and trouble to wrench her twisted limbs out from the wreckage that was pinning them.

Rolf was pulped, Mantz was mangled, they were both dead and torn apart. The scent of all that hot fresh blood in the air was heady, intoxicating. She soaked it in through her pores.

Gregor was trapped in the space with her, alive. His head and shoulders were intact, but from the chest down, he was crushed under one of the components. He was in shock, near death.

She heard the E-crew working toward her, knew that they would reach her in a minute or two. She could have turned herself into mist and floated out, but that took up a lot of energy and she was still stunned. More important, she kept her true nature and her powers a secret from all but a very small circle that included both victims and intimates. Sometimes they were one and the same.

Secrets were power. To reveal her secrets was to yield power. The followers of the cult might suspect what she was, but they kept their speculations to themselves. Besides, not knowing kept them more fearful, which was to be encouraged.

Gregor was dying. A pity and a waste, to lose his keen brain! And Gregor had been right. He had predicted that the experiment would fail in some way. Mantz had had a good brain, too, but he had made a mistake and now that brain was just so much gray jelly smeared across the weight that had flattened his skull.

It was too late for Marya to vampirize Gregor and initiate him into Undeath, thereby sparing that great brain. The process required at least a few hours for the initial bite to infect the victim so that the vampiric trait would take when the rest of the victim's blood was drained.

Marya was not sure she would have vampirized Gregor if she could, since he was an uncongenial type that she would not care to have to look at for the next few centuries.

Besides, there was another way to keep the brain alive.

The crew members neared, closer and closer. Marya crouched over Gregor, who lay on his back, faceup. Pressure from the massive weight crushing his chest and lower body had caused his head and neck to swell and grow purple from hydrostatic pressure. He had lost his glasses and his eyes bulged, unseeing.

She hoped the pressure wouldn't inflict any neuro-damage. She held out a hand, fingers held together, the sharp-pointed nails growing, extending into talons.

With one short, savage slash of her razor-sharp nails, she cut Gregor's throat, splattering herself with hot blood droplets. With the backhand, she slashed again, reversing direction, this time disjointing the neck vertebrae and slicing the spinal cord.

She took hold of his head in both hands, palms pressing his cheeks, and finished the job, tearing his head off his neck. Gore fountained from the neck stump.

She drank. No sense in letting it go to waste. The pounding she had taken had left her weakened and she needed to renew her strength. Gregor's blood was sluggish but thick and rich and she gulped greedily, swilling down a bellyful.

No one would know, not with all the blood that had already been spilled. And if they did know, or guess—what of it?

She held Gregor's head, palming it by the back of his hairless scalp. Something made her murmur, "Yorick . . ."

Gregor's eyes blinked a couple of times but they were distant-focused, unseeing. How long could the brain live without oxygen? Five minutes, then it would start dying, an irreversible process.

Marya opened his mouth and spat in it, a vampire trick. She had survived long and had power and her venomous spittle would give the head a tiny speck of unnatural power that would prepare the way for the coming work.

She turned the head upside down, to keep the blood from running out of the severed neck. She tore off what was left of her jacket and wrapped the head in it.

Then she thrust her hand out of the pile, attracting the "rescuers" to her. They dug away the pile and she wriggled out of the hole, standing up, holding the rag-wrapped bundle against her side.

A couple of E-crew biomedics rushed forward, then checked as she held out a bloody hand, warding them off. They stopped in their tracks.

One managed to speak, voice rasping through his helmet's exo-speaker. "You need help, Countess, you're bleeding—"

"It's not my blood. It's his," she said, unwrapping the head and showing it to them.

The others started. Marya tore into them verbally, eyes blazing through the smoke.

"Don't be fools! The brain in this head is alive and I mean to keep it that way. There's four minutes left before it starts dying, time enough to rush it to surgery and start pumping oxygenated blood to it," she said.

She thrust the bundle into the arms of the nearest medic. "If I lose this head, you'll lose yours. *Move!*"

He didn't waste breath on a reply. He tore open his supply box and turned it upside down, dumping out its contents.

He put the head inside and closed the lid, fumbling the snaps with gloved fingers as he scrambled through the rubble to the exit.

One of his partners was already using his transceiver to radio ahead to surgery to notify them of what was about to be incoming.

Marya slipped past the crew members, sidestepping one who stood by holding a mini-airtank with a nozzle-attached breathing mask, urging it on her. If he'd looked more closely, he would have seen that her chest did not rise and fall from breathing, because she was not breathing.

She was nimble and elusive, moving catlike among the wreckage, making her way to the crystal egg. It had torn loose from its mounting, cradled by a tangled web of twisted metal struts.

It rested on its side, so that the dweller within lay faceup. Marya stood over it, placing her hands on it, peering through the milky crystal at the Bride.

The artificial female seemed unharmed, even untouched by the experience, except for a few scorch marks under some of the contact points.

Marya leaned over the Bride, studying her face from varying angles. Looking straight down at her, her mouth could be seen as a firm straight line, as tightly compressed as a turtle's. But when Marya tilted her head, changing the angle, the Bride's mouth seemed to be turned up in a slight smile at the corners, a smile that was all the more sly and secretive for being so tightly held.

But when Marya shifted the position of her head, changing her angle of vision by a few degrees, the smile was gone, vanished. She peered at the face from different angles and the smile was still gone without a trace, as if it had never been.

Just when she had persuaded herself that it hadn't been there at all, as she was starting to straighten up and turn away from it, she saw the smile again, bold as life.

She thrust her face forward so that it was held a few inches above the egg, staring down at it—

145

No smile.

Perhaps it was an illusion caused by the curvature of the crystal surface. Perhaps her eyes were playing tricks on her.

But she had other senses, not so easily tricked. She sent her bodiless awareness plunging at the other, probing, wary, more penetrating than an X ray.

But the result was the same as always, the same way it had been every time she had searched for some sign of awareness or even life in the inert husk of the Bride.

Nothing.

There was no more sense of personality there than in a turnip. At most, there was a dim flicker of potentiality, of life forces dormant to those without the secret key to free them.

Marya withdrew, dissatisfied. "If I thought there was the ghost of a chance that you really are awake, I'd find a way to find you out, no matter what tortures of hell it took to do it.

"But no. There's nothing there, not a whisper. Soulless clay, without a spark of divine or diabolical fire . . .

"So much the better. When you finally do arise, there must be nothing to oppose my will. You will be my creature, my superhuman slave."

Marya straightened up, taking her weight off her hands where they'd been pressed flat against the crystal surface. One of them had been resting partly on a silver disk head without her knowing it. The disk was still hot, and when she lifted her hands she saw that the edge of the disk had burned into her palm, branding it with a crescent-shaped mark.

She snarled, fangs flashing. The crew had left her to go off on her own after she came up with the head, judging rightly that she could take care of herself. Obedience and submission were cultic virtues—at least, in the lower ranks.

If they had seen her face twist with balked furious power lust, they would have given her an even wider berth.

Marya said, "Wait till you're wearing *my* brand, bitch."

• • •

146

A few hours later, Marya went to surgery to visit the patient. She wore a gray jumper over a black bodysuit and boots. The bodysuit had a turtleneck and long sleeves, covering the wounds she had sustained in the White Room. Long, deep furrowed gashes scored her arms, chest, back, and thighs. They cut deep, but they were bloodless. Under the fabric, her flesh was reknitting itself, the wounds sealing themselves. It was night and she had fed and she was healing quickly.

All but the burn mark on her palm, the crescent-shaped brand. It should have begun to subside, shrinking back into her flesh, but it seemed unchanged. It didn't hurt. Neither did her other wounds. It takes a lot of stimulus to cause a vampire's pain receptors to respond.

Still, the sight of the brand irritated her and she was vexed that it hadn't yet started to fade, while other, more serious injuries were already disappearing.

She caught herself walking with the hand held at her side, palm turned inward, masking the brand.

The surgery was on the same underground level as the White Room, to which it was connected by a corridor. Sealed bulkhead doors at both ends of the passage had protected the surgery from any real damage from the backlash, but the smell of burning permeated it. All levels of the palace, both below- and aboveground, stank of smoke. Exhaust fans labored full blast throughout the complex, but the scorched scent lingered.

Underlying the burned odor were the other, usual smells of the surgery. There were sharp chemical reeks, ammonia, acids, disinfectants. There was the ozone tang of electric motors that powered the pumps, coolers, computers, and instrument banks. The yeasty ferment of nutrient solution and the alien, repellent stink of synthetic blood plasma. Beneath these were the gross and earthly smells of real blood and body parts, an aroma that no amount of chemical scrubbing and deodorizing could do away with.

The site was part lab, part operating room. Now on duty were Dr. Euler Voss and his nurse and lab assistant, Heidi Nyland. Both wore white lab coats over their civilian clothes.

147

Voss was fish-faced, with thinning wiry reddish-gold hair; Nyland had a butter-colored pageboy hairstyle, turquoise-colored eyes in a round pink face, and a round pink body that was chastely covered from the neck down, except for her hands. They were round and pink.

Marya met them in the center of the space, under a drum light which hung from the ceiling. The fixture had a stainless-steel housing and a frosted-glass screen which diffused the light of its array of lamps into a bright, sterile glow.

Marya began, "Congratulations on your promotion, Voss."

"Er—excuse me, Countess?"

"With the, ah, removal of Dr. Gregor, you now head the biomedical department."

Voss flushed, trying not to show his pleasure. "I never wanted to get the job this way!"

"What does it matter, so long as the prize is yours? You're the best qualified for the post. You just get to move up in the hierarchy that much sooner, without having to wait for your predecessor to retire.

"Though I think it's safe to say that Gregor has, in a very real sense, retired."

Nurse Nyland said, "He may be fit for an emeritus role, Countess."

"So I hope. I will see him now."

Voss started forward, saying, "This way, please." He was a half step ahead of Marya and the nurse as they crossed to a partitioned area. They went behind a screen, into an isolated section.

The space was dominated by an oblong pedestal, like two filing cabinets put together. It was a modular life-support system, with the bottom part holding pumps and motors and the top part faced with an instrument panel and filled with monitoring telemetry and control systems.

On the pedestal column's flat top sat what looked like a glass-sided aquarium tank. It held a strange fish indeed: Gregor's head.

A wire-frame harness held the head in an upright position. The head looked small, shrunken. Eyelids were closed taut over bulging orbs. The veins on the sides of the forehead stuck out like pencils.

The head sat in a pan filled with a greenish-yellow nutrient bath. Thin plastic pipes ran into the nostrils, carrying bubbling greenish-yellow fluid. A hooked tube was hung on a corner of the slack, downturned mouth. It operated like a dentist's recirculator, keeping the mouth refreshed and moist with a continual swirling stream of fluid.

At the upper corners on the inside of the tank frame were bulb-shaped metal atomizers with sprinkler faces. Periodically they sprayed the head with a fine yellowish mist, keeping the tissues constantly moist.

"You understand that saving what was left of Gregor was no ordinary procedure, Countess."

"Life is not enough, Voss. What I need is consciousness, the spark of reason. I need Gregor."

"Such matters are beyond my field of expertise, Countess. All I can say is that the monitor readings show the brain is alive and thinking. The brain waves for the higher functions seem relatively unimpaired."

"Though there are some unusual irregularities in the brainwave activity," the nurse said. "Arrhythmic fluctuations, indecipherable peaks and valleys in the scan lines."

Voss nodded. "Not unexpected, considering the massive trauma suffered by the subject. Few men survive their own decapitation! Gregor should be dead."

Marya asked, "But does he know it?"

"There's a question that you can answer better than I or Nurse Nyland. The readings indicate that there's an ongoing awareness in that brain. But how much of Gregor's personality remains, his ego, his unique 'I,' that is a mystery."

"It will be made clear, one way or another. By me."

"As you say, Countess. The brain waves are not those associated with sleep or wakefulness, but with a state somewhere between the two. That reading has held steady since Gregor's—that is, the head's condition was stabilized."

"Have you tried to awaken him yet, Voss?"

149

"No, I thought you would prefer to handle that procedure."

"I do. And I will," Marya said, moving closer to the head in the glass tank. Gregor's flesh had taken on a greenish-yellow tint from saturation in the nutrient fluid.

Voss said, "I can fit him with a speaker earpiece so he can hear you through the tank walls and over the sound of the recirculating fluids. I can even fit him with a subvocal microphone, which will pick up the movements of his tongue and mouth muscles and turn them into words through a mechanical voice box.

"You can talk directly to him, Countess. Carry on a conversation. That is, if there's anything left of Gregor that can hear and talk, or wants to."

"My way is more direct still, Voss."

"And that way is . . . ?"

"Hypnosis."

"Of course," Voss said, neutral-faced and voiced.

"You and Nurse Nyland will remain, to handle any medical needs which may come up."

Voss nodded. "Whenever you're ready to begin."

"Now," Marya said.

Voss nodded again, then turned to the nurse. "Prepare to administer the stimulant, please."

"Yes, Doctor." Nyland went to a tabletop stand holding racked vials of chemicals, serums, and drugs.

Marya said, "Extinguish all unnecessary lights, please. It increases my concentration."

Voss stood at the wall, turning a dial that dimmed the overhead lights. There was a flexi-armature lamp clamped to the edge of the table where the nurse stood, illuminating her and the drug rack. The instrument panels had their own lights, and there were a couple of lab table lamps. They made blobs of light in the mushy dimness.

The tank was lit up from inside by its own interior lights, which took on the color of the nutrient fluids, a kind of undersea yellow green. It gave the shadows a greenish cast.

Marya stood facing the column stand, her head more or

150

less level with the head in the glass box. She was about an arm's length away. She motioned to begin.

Voss said, "The stimulant, Nurse."

"Yes, Doctor."

Nyland injected a few droplets of a clear solution from a syringe into a valve connected to a length of thin plastic piping that fed oxygenated nutrient fluid into Gregor's brain.

Voss said, "The subject is being given a dosage of the drug monocaine, an extract of a rare alkaloid. An extremely dangerous drug in large doses, one that causes paranoia, delusions of grandeur, megalomania, madness, and homicidal behavior.

"It's a poison, like strychnine. But, like strychnine, a minute amount of it can have beneficial effects, stimulating a return of consciousness."

Marya said, "When will it begin working?"

"Almost immediately, since it's being piped directly into the brain."

In no time at all, the head became restless. The swollen veins in its forehead began to expand and contract rhythmically. Muscle tics fired all over its face, mouth twitching, cheeks and forehead spasming, eyelids fluttering.

Marya reached deep into the dark well of her mind, hauling out the special extrasensory awareness that lurked there, the same sense that allowed her to know what transpired outside her coffin while she slept, to summon hordes of bats and rats, to call up the storm.

Voss and Nyland felt that force, shaken by it. It was invisible but as real as gravity and magnetism.

Marya let that awareness float out of her, uncurling like a phantom limb, flowing out to enfold the head. There was already a link between them, thanks to her spitting into its mouth earlier, infecting it with her venom.

That similarity gave her a psychic beachhead, a fulcrum from which to move his mind. The Gregor identity was there, large and strong and crusty, a barnacle-encrusted leviathan wallowing in the depths of unconsciousness.

She called his name: *Gregor . . . Gregor . . .*

Her voice seemed to come from very far away, carrying over vast distances. Voss and Nyland both heard it. But Marya's mouth was closed, she had not spoken aloud.

She communicated not in words but by mind force. The telepathic field she had established with Gregor also included the doctor and nurse.

That gnarled hulk of a mentality continued to evade her. Marya darted some more barbed mind-force harpoons.

Gregor! Gregor!

His disembodied voice faded in, like a distant station on a car radio coming into range: it was hollow, gloomy, rambling.

"... Blazing moonlight ... the roaring red dark, the breakers, the breakers ... chasms of the abyss, a blizzard of stardust—"

"You're drifting, Gregor. Hear me. Hear the voice of your master, who bids you to awaken, rise!"

"I hear."

In the glass box, Gregor's head jerked against the armature, the framework holding it locked in place as it flinched, winced, grimaced.

The eyes snapped open, staring.

Marya leaned forward, quivering with effort. Her eyes reddened, glowed, burned. Shone with bloodlight.

They were reflected as paired sets of red pinpricks imaged in the black pupils of Gregor's eyes. After a pause, the pupils dilated and the irises widened as the eyes came into focus.

Focusing—on her.

"Ah, Gregor," Marya breathed.

His mouth wriggled, lips writhing wormlike. "Countess ..."

"It is not necessary for you to speak, Gregor. Say the thought in your mind, and I will hear it."

"Where's my body, Countess?"

"On the scrap heap."

The head's thoughts blanked out for a time. Then: "What of Mantz?"

"Same place."

"It's too good for him, the fool!"

"What went wrong, Gregor? Why did the experiment fail?"

"Mantz."

"Yes, yes, but why?"

"I told Mantz that she was different. Electricity alone was no good. Her nerves and connective tissues must be overlaid like those of an electric eel, developed to a formidable degree. She absorbed the charge, then shed it."

Marya asked, "How may the Bride be revived?"

"What'll you give me if I tell you?"

"The satisfaction of knowing that you solved the problem that Mantz was unable to solve."

"Then will you pull the plug on me?"

"Why the obsession with dying? A thinker like you lives mostly in his head anyway."

"Will you, Countess?"

"Eventually."

"So."

"You may not believe this, Gregor, but there are ways to make your present condition even more unpleasant."

"I'm sure you could force an answer from me, so I won't put you to the trouble. Besides, I have the feeling—call it a premonition, if you will—that telling you the answer will bring about the result that I desire, namely, my complete and total annihilation."

Marya laughed. "I can assure you, death is no guarantee of that!"

She stopped laughing. "So?"

"Electricity *is* needed to revive the Bride. Mantz got that much right. But it's only part of the process. The current acts as a carrier wave."

"A carrier wave! Are you sure?"

"That's my theory. I must have some expertise on the subject, or why would you consult me?"

"I don't doubt your knowledge."

"Why don't you call up Mantz's shade and see what he has to say?"

"The secret, Gregor! The lightning is the carrier wave."

"Yes."

"Very well. What's a carrier wave?"

"It carries the signal. The lightning is the carrier, useless in itself, but necessary as the means of transmission. It creates a channel by which the active life-force agent is delivered."

"Gregor—*what is that force?*"

"The Moon-Ray."

"Is that possible?"

"For the Bride, yes. The Moon-Ray holds cosmic power. The lightning opens the way for it to work. But the Moon-Ray is the kiss of life to awaken the sleeper.

"Now will you let me die, Countess?"

"Not yet. I still need you, Gregor."

"No surprise there."

"You're a scientist, so surely you can understand that your theories must be put to the test and proved out before any final, irrevocable actions are taken on your behalf."

"You doubt me? No matter. The Bride will live and then I shall die—really, gloriously dead."

"What makes you say that?"

"I—see things."

Marya's fascination grew more intense. "What things? Visions?"

"I thought that would pique your interest, Countess, knowing as I do your obsession with signs, portents and omens.

"Being bodiless, not surprisingly, has made me less time-bound. I float in a limbo lit by visions burning like fires on the edge of a dark gulf. The drugs swirling through my brain must have something to do with that, too.

"These things I see, are they hallucinations? Or shadows of things that are coming to pass?"

"What do you see, Gregor?"

"I see a blood-mad Lord of Bats—a clay man animated by the spirit of destruction—and a Beast of Apocalypse."

154

Marya laughed again, not politely. "You see the past, not the future! It's easy to unravel your riddle."

"Is it?"

"The Bat Lord is Dracula, raging at his own dissolution. The clay man is the Frankenstein Monster, now undone but soon to be raised again by my doing. I am that spirit of destruction that will animate him!"

"So you say, so you say . . . And the Beast?"

"The Beast is Lawrence Talbot, the Wolfman, destined to be tamed by my apocalyptic fury!"

"You are wrong, Countess."

"I—*what!*"

"Talbot is dead. The Wolfman is no more."

She sneered. "He's died before, but the Beast always returns. The Wolfman cannot die."

"He is dead, slain by a silver bullet fired by one who loves him. He connived to bring about his own demise, of course. Now he's slipped the Devil's Brood and found peace, the peace of nonbeing.*

"The peace that I also crave."

"You've found madness, Doctor. Hallucinations, that's all you've seen."

"A bodiless head has oracular powers, Countess. That's why you've kept me alive. And it's true, I have powers of mind that lay dormant before my head was parted from my body.

"No creature as potent as the Wolfman could be neutralized without sending shock waves through the Dark World. Think of me as a sentinel who can see those waves coming in advance of more earthbound creatures."

"You consider *me* earthbound?"

"What is a vampire but a thirsty corpse that refuses to stay dead?"

"Pray that you never find out. Still, there might be something of truth in what you say about the Wolfman being dead."

*See *Return of the Wolfman* (Berkley Boulevard Books).

"You will soon find out for yourself."

Marya brightened. "Better if it is true! Talbot was a weakling, unable to accept the wondrous gift of lycanthropy which the fates had reserved for him. His alter ego, the Wolfman, was a fearsome antagonist, cunning and implacably vengeful.

"That arrogant fool Dracula sealed his own doom when he tried to make the Wolfman his creature. Let them both go down to darkness, and good riddance!"

Gregor's mouth and lips wriggled, squirming, and for an instant Marya had the eerie impression that the head was laughing at her, or at least trying to.

"Nature abhors a vacuum, Countess. So does the Unnatural. Talbot's finish has left a lycanthrope-sized hole in the fabric of the shadowlands. That lack, that gap will not go long unfilled.

"Even now, a new Beast is coming into being, new but from an accursed old line—almost as illustrious as your own distinguished heritage, Countess.

"The coming fiend will be a Beast indeed, sinister, feral, an avatar of depravity and murder."

"If he's that good, he could be of use to me—after being properly brought to heel."

"Muzzle him if you can, but you need him."

"I need no man or beast."

"This one is both, and you need him."

"Why, Gregor?"

"He holds the key to the Moon-Ray."

"Tell me who he is—"

156

NINE

When Marya had learned what she needed to know, she ended the hypno-session. Before breaking the trance, she told the head, "Think about how the riddle of the Bride can best be solved, or your bodiless life span promises to be long and bleak."

"What do you think it is now?" Gregor asked.

Marya reversed the process, withdrawing her field of awareness, the blood-light fading from her eyes. As her glowing eyes dimmed, Gregor's orbs lost their responsiveness and became glassy, the pupils fixed.

Deprived of the vitalizing force of her will, the head went inert, its eyes closing.

Voss and Nyland were still entranced. Marya gave them a posthypnotic command, embedding it in their psyches.

"You will forget all that has passed here now between Gregor and me, until it pleases me to allow you to recall it," she said. That way the memory was not erased but merely submerged, in case she should need to refer to their medical judgments regarding some aspect of the head's words or behavior at a later date.

She clapped her hands once, breaking the spell. The doctor and nurse came back to consciousness with a slight start but with no memory of having been hypnotized. Each was flustered and self-conscious at what they thought was a lapse of daydreaming or inattention in the presence of their demanding and powerful patron, and they sought to disguise it by busying themselves with routine bits of medical business.

Marya said, "That will be all, thank you. I've seen enough.

"I want that brain kept alive and functioning. That's a priority. An attendant must be standing by, monitoring it around the clock, twenty-four hours a day."

She was looking at both Voss and Nyland as she spoke. Voss said, "Yes, Countess," and Nyland nodded. "I'll take the first watch myself," Voss added.

Marya said, "I'm sure I don't have to impress you with the need for discretion."

"All conversations that occur between doctors and, er, patients are secure and inviolable," Voss said.

"I expect no less," Marya said. "No need for you two to interrupt your duties to show me out. I know the way.

"Good night."

She exited, disappearing behind a partition. After she was gone, Voss pinched the bridge of his nose, squeezing his eyes shut.

"Remarkable woman," he murmured.

Nyland massaged her temples with her fingertips. Her head hurt. So did Voss's. They were both saddled with the beginnings of what would soon develop into a pair of throbbing headaches, an aftereffect of the hypno-jag.

As for Gregor, if the head had a headache, it kept it to itself.

Marya stalked through the corridors, restless, intent. The area surrounding the White Room was a scene of purposeful activity as repair and cleanup crews dug in and went to work.

She moved away from the site, heading in the opposite direction. She went through a fire door, out to the landing of a stairwell. Flights of stairs zigzagged down the inner walls of the shaft, around an open central well. It was about a fifty-foot drop to the bottom.

158

The shaft was deserted and Marya was in a hurry. She vaulted the top rail of the landing, plummeting down the central well, stairs zooming up on all sides of her.

She fell feet first, toes pointed, arms held up straight over her head, the jumper billowing up around her shoulders. Somewhere along the way down, she changed.

Her limbs stretched, becoming thinner, more elongated. Wingbones sprouted from her shoulder blades, stretching along the backs of her shoulders and down her arms to her fingertips. Leathery black membranes unfurled, fanning out, stretching along the sides of the body from ankles to wrists.

The face changed, too, becoming longer, more hollow-cheeked, sunken-eyed, inhuman.

The wings spread, swelling like a kite as it catches the wind, or a parachute opening. There was a *thump!* and then a flurry of furious wing fluttering as Marya's descent slowed.

Batwings beat the air as she dropped lightly to the floor at the bottom of the well. She shimmered, shuddering, morphing once again, the transformation process running in reverse.

The bat woman changed back into a woman—into what looked like a woman. The dark jumper was bunched up above her breasts. Marya pulled it down before exiting the well.

At the bottom of the shaft, the light blue-gray painted concrete slab walls gave way to the massive old stones of the original foundation, which were brown, pitted and age-stained, braced with clunky rusting steel plates. There was a musty, damp smell, now laced with the charred smoky scent from the fire.

In one of the shaft walls an archway opened, holding inside it a knobby solid armor-plated door. Rust stained the unpainted metal like a fungus.

Few came to this lowest level, and fewer still used this entrance to access it. It was not electronically secured; the lock was an old-fashioned mechanical job, using tumblers and bolts. The elevator and another set of fire stairs were both easier to use.

Marya owned a key but did not have it with her. She

could have forced the lock, but not without setting off alarms. But what were locked doors to her, who could turn herself to mist?

The technique could be mastered only by the strongest and most skilled of vampires. It was an energy drain, but Marya had already fed this night. She was charged up, with a driving need for action.

She dematerialized, coming apart, visualizing her body as if it were woven of spun sugar and would crumble away to powder at the touch of a thought. Such mental image pictures were helpful in implementing the decorporealizing process.

The forces binding her material form eased, loosening, coming apart in latticed layers. The spaces holding her molecules together widened, letting in the void.

Serpentine vapors swirled around her form as it came apart, disintegrating into a cloud of graveyard dust spinning around its own invisible axis.

Where Marya had stood, there now stood a column of mist, wet, oily, and glistening. It collapsed of its own weight, puddling on the floor at the foot of the door.

It flowed under the door, through the minute crack between the bottom of the door and the frame, pouring into the other side.

The pool of mist now lay inside the door. It rose into a column, hanging in the air in a ghostly blob shaped like a woman. The stones of the wall could be seen through it.

It shimmered, coming together. The ectoplasm knitted and wove, re-forming itself into the shape of a woman.

Marya appeared, wavering, her image moistly glistening. Then the binding forces locked tight and she became solid matter, flesh. Not human flesh, but flesh. The dewiness vanished, replaced by icy crystal perfection.

Communing with the head, changing into a bat hybrid, becoming mist—all these actions had taken a toll on her energy. The ruddiness was gone from her face, which was now taut and white-skinned, drawn tight over the bones of the

160

skull. Her eyes were bruises, her mouth was taut and quivering, the fang tips protruding.

She was famished again, starved. That was why she had used up so much energy in so short a time—to work up an appetite.

Once there had been a castle on this site, and this level had been its dungeon. The castle had long since been razed, but the dungeon remained. Its builders had worked in stone and built the castle to last, and it was easier to use what they had made than to tear it up and replace it.

Many additions and improvements had been made, overlaid on the original stone walls and chambers, but underneath the surface the dungeon was but little changed from its original form and purpose.

A new millennium had arrived, but a dungeon was still a useful thing to have.

Marya was in an out-of-the-way, little-used section, a maze of narrow, stone-walled corridors and passages, dully lit by bare overhead bulbs in overhead lamps with tamper-proof metal grilles.

Marya whisked through the branchings, coming to a more centralized location, a barrel-vaulted main hall. On one of the long sides was a closed elevator door, and there was a fire door in one of the short walls. Marya entered through a doorway in the wall opposite the firewall.

The guard that was posted on duty nearly fell out of his chair when he looked up and saw her coming. As far as he knew, there was no one else but him and the other guards abroad in the halls. The prisoners were all safely locked in their cells.

His initial fearfulness faded as he recognized the Countess. She was known for doing these kinds of things, evading vigilant sentries and slipping through locked and bolted doors with no trace of her passage. She was the only one who could do such things. How she did them was a mystery best left unsolved.

He sprang to attention, assuming a military-style stance,

161

head up, shoulders back, spine stiffened. Marya breezed past him, nodding. She said, "Yes, yes, as you were."

She was a frequent visitor to these precincts and all the night guards knew her. It required a special breed to work on this floor. The guards were all part of a special unit that was separated from the rest of the palace personnel. They had their own private barracks room and mess. They ate and slept together, a kind of isolated elite. They had their own unique uniform, with gray-green jacket and trousers and a round short-brimmed cap.

In the long wall opposite the elevator were two doors made of solid metal, both with eye-level inset viewports, now closed. The guard had been sitting between them.

He hesitated, waiting for instructions. Marya nodded toward the door on the left. The guard hopped to it, going to the door and speaking into a gridded voice panel which was set to one side of it.

After a pause, a buzzer was sounded from inside, electronically unlocking the door. He opened the door, holding it open for Marya, looking like a uniformed doorman at a police-state hotel.

Marya entered, he closed the door behind her, the lock clicking into place. He let out the breath he'd been holding. He was a veteran torturer and death-squad executioner of the Balkan ethnic-cleansing terror campaigns, and he had seen and done things that were unimaginable to sane, civilized human beings.

But the Countess scared him.

She was now in the entryway of the women's detention cell area. To her right was a small side room that served as a guardpost. Ahead stretched a medium-length corridor that was flanked on both sides by closed cell doors, each door fitted with a now-closed viewport.

The guard station was a kind of booth, with a chest-high counter anchoring a wide square window whose clear sliding Plexiglas panels were retracted, opening the space. To one side of it was an open doorway.

Filling the booth was the hulking figure of Gertrude, the

162

turnkey, a former prison matron and onetime nursing-home attendant turned serial patient poisoner. Good times, but working here was the best job she'd ever loved.

She was already off her stool and on her feet, hovering over the wall-mounted rack of cell keys. "Which one, Countess?"

"The big blonde."

"Number Seven. Romy."

Marya held out a hand, palm up. "Just give me the key and I'll do the rest. You stay here and mind your own business."

"Yes, Countess," the matron said, handing over the key.

Marya's fist closed on it and she turned and started down the hall, walking briskly. There was the scent of flesh, quivering life, and hot red blood. It hung over the D cell block like a miasma, making her senses tingle.

Still more delicious were the waves of fear pouring out from behind those cell doors. The prisoners knew who— *what*—was among them, just as chickens know when a fox is loose in the coop.

Their thoughts all but screamed: *Oh no not me please don't let it be me anybody else but me please please—*

At the far end of the corridor, the passage branched off to the left and right, being the short vertical bar at the top of the cell block's T-shaped floor plan. Marya turned left, a few paces taking her to a door at the end of the short passage.

She didn't have to open the viewport and look through it to know what was going on inside the cell. She could sense the nearness of prey, hear the breathless gasps and the pounding heartbeats, taste the fear, and smell the blood.

She unlocked the door slowly and deliberately, rattling the key in the lock and prolonging the suspense to torment the captive's nerves still further. She drew out the opening of the door, too, for the same reason.

She went inside, closing the door behind her, standing with her back to it. The cell was a stark, simple cubicle, lit

163

by a wan overhead lightbulb in a protective metal grille. There was a cot and in one corner a toilet.

Cowering in the opposite corner was Romy. She sat hugging her bent legs, rocking back and forth, hiding her face in her knees. She was hyperventilating, shivering.

No more than twenty, she was a big healthy strapping farm girl with yellow hair, a round face, and a shapely, bigbreasted body. Her coloring and body type were not unlike Nurse Nyland's, though she was only half the other woman's age.

A vital difference: Romy was expendable, Nyland was not. Of course, if it came to that, all members of the cult but Marya were expendable, given a desperate-enough crisis.

Romy was no cultist, of course. She was prey. The D cells were kept filled with a fresh supply of livestock of the human variety, preferably young, healthy, and attractive, whose whereabouts were unknown to their friends and family, if any. There was a D cell block for females and another one for males. Marya needed fresh blood, the rituals demanded sacrificial victims, and the medical departments were always in need of experimental subjects, so there was a pretty rapid turnover rate.

Happily, there was no shortage of fresh flesh, regularly supplied by a thriving subterranean European slave trade. The trade existed on the other continents as well, with the possible exception of Antarctica, but the palace personnel and the cult had found it convenient to work with their own regional suppliers.

Romy was big-boned and Amazonian, almost a head taller than Marya and outweighing her by fifty pounds. At the moment she was paralyzed with fear. She'd been in the cell block long enough to get some faint glimmering of the horrors it held; now it was her turn to experience them firsthand.

Marya leaned over Romy, intent, her profile hawklike. She called the girl's name softly, a teasing whisper.

"Romy . . ."

Romy choked back a sob and kept her head down, not looking up. Marya was eager, impetuous. Her hand shot out, grabbing the girl by the throat and squeezing.

Romy's eyes bulged, her face swelling, purpling. Marya said, purring, "Now that I have your attention, dear . . ."

She eased her grip, just a little.

Romy blurted, "Oh God, please, no . . . *urk!*"

Marya's grip tightened, throttling her prey. "Calling on the opposition? In here that's a capital crime, punishable by death!"

Marya picked Romy up with one hand around her throat, hauling her to her feet. Her free hand took hold of the front of the girl's thin cotton shift and ripped it open, tearing off her bra along with it, exposing her big round breasts and smooth pink flesh and rounded belly.

She threw Romy on her back on the cot and followed her down, stretching out on top of her. Even through her clothes, Marya could feel the girl's body heat, luxuriating in it, like a reptile sunning itself on a hot rock. Ah, these warm-blooded creatures!

Sometimes Marya made an event of the taking, draining the blood from her prey very slowly, drop by bloody drop, feeding on the life all through the long night hours until the final drop was drained and the victim expired with barely enough time for the vampire to climb into her coffin, sated, before the sun came up.

Other times she liked it fast, hot, and dirty. This was such a time. She grabbed a handful of Romy's hair and pulled on it, tilting the girl's head back, exposing her taut neck with the throbbing blood-engorged veins.

She buried her sharp pointed teeth in Romy's flesh, fanging her, fastening her sucking mouth to the girl's pulsing throat.

The vampire's fangs exuded some paralyzing venom that fanned out from the bite, spreading through the veins like ice, a tingling, numbing sensation that froze Romy into an inert lump.

The parasite fed. Greedily.

165

TEN

Wilfred Glendon III was dreaming a dream of blood. Not his first such dream. All his thirty-plus years of life, for as long as he could remember, he'd been haunted by dreams—nightmares—of bloody murder. But this dream was different.

He was flying naked through darkness—flying or falling, he wasn't sure which. So it must be a dream. He plunged through space, a strong, powerfully built adult male in his vigorous prime, helpless to alter or affect his flight one iota.

It was a space without moon or stars. The darkness was not absolute. There was enough of a distinction between black and deeper black to create the impression of great formless masses roiling and heaving.

Perhaps he was not falling after all. Perhaps he was standing still, while the space moved and shifted around him.

He fell out of infinity into the heights of a nightscape. Below were mountains, valleys, a lake, a stark polygonal palace. They rushed up toward him.

His descent slowed as he neared the building's domed roof. He fell through it, and now he realized that he was ghostly, insubstantial. Hands, limbs, and body were transparent, like a double-exposed image.

He slipped downward through the rotunda floor, drifting

underground, layers of floors and chambers rising up around him as he flitted through them.

A stone floor acted as a safety net, slowing him almost to a halt. He was strained through it, popping out of its underside, which was the ceiling of a room below. A small room, a cell.

He floated under the ceiling, bobbing like a captive balloon. He looked down. That's when it became a dream of blood.

Sprawled on a cot was the unlovely corpse of a young nude blond woman, her eyes open and staring. There were two raw puncture marks in her neck, lines of blood running down from them to stain the blanket and mattress. Beneath the blood her skin was dead white, drained. One of her arms hung down over the edge of the cot.

Seated on the floor beside the corpse, sitting cross-legged, was a petite brunette, girl-slim, with an exquisite face and finely molded figure, heartbreakingly lovely.

She held the dead woman's arm to her mouth, kissing the inside of the wrist. At least that's what it looked like she was doing. Her mouth was working and her jaw and neck muscles flexed.

Blood dripped from the corpse's wrist, staining the front of the brunette's dark jumper. Without raising her head, the woman sitting on the floor looked up out of the top of her eyes at the ceiling. Her eyeballs were solid red orbs showing no white. They were hot and glowing and Glendon had the uncomfortable conviction that they were looking straight at him.

She unfastened her sucking mouth from the inside of the wrist and raised her face. Her mouth and chin were bloody, and curved, sharply pointed fang tips protruded from beneath red lips.

The inside of the blonde's wrist had been torn open and punctured when the bloodsucker drank there. It had been drained of all but a trickle.

The she-creature smiled up at him. A tongue came flick-

167

ing out of her mouth, impossibly long and thin and red, split at the end into a pair of forked tails. A serpent's tongue.

She licked her lips and chin, lapping up the blood. Then her tongue slithered back inside her mouth, between fanged teeth and out of sight.

Glendon knew her for what she was.

Vampire.

"And you, Glendon? Do you know what you are?" she asked, her voice sweet, lilting.

"My name is Marya. For you, I am Destiny, and cannot be denied. You are of the Night-Borne and darkness is your heritage. That is why I was able to call up your astral body while you sleep and compel it to come to me. You must join me."

I won't, he thought.

The blood-light faded from her eyes somewhat, and the tension flowed out of her face, making it look younger and almost demure. Except that the points of her fangs showed through her soft smile.

"Tell me the secret of the Moon-Ray, Glendon."

Lost.

"You can find it."

I wouldn't if I could.

"You will."

Never.

Her smile was neither soft nor sweet now. Her voice brittle, she said, "You will show me the way to the Moon-Ray, Glendon.

"But first, I will show you to yourself."

Without warning, she tilted her head back, opening her mouth wide and spewing out a stream of blood. Red black, hot and steaming, it splashed on the floor, pooling.

The pool became a mirror, a red mirror whose surface reflected Glendon hanging suspended above it, under the ceiling.

The crimson image was recognizably his, showing a ruggedly handsome face with a high forehead, sharp cheek-bones, a mouth turned down at the corners, and a hard, flat-eyed hunter's gaze. His expression was shocked, aghast, but the pale eyes were watchful, calculating.

Marya gestured, sweeping a hand above the blood-mirror in a mystic pass. The surface was unruffled, but a change came over the red pool, as though it had been dragged with a net of shadows, blurring the reflection for an instant.

When it cleared, Glendon saw—a hell-beast.

Neither man nor animal, but a satanic creature combining the worst traits of both. Its form was latent with raw energy and destructive power, the urge to kill!

Its hands were claws, gnarled and hairy, distorted. Its hybrid head showed pointed ears, a bristling mane, and slavering fanged mouth. That mouthful of gnashing pointed teeth made Marya's look decorous by comparison.

And yet, there was something of a man in it, a caricature of the human.

Worse, it was he himself—Glendon. Glendon as diabolical man-beast, but still Glendon. Not even the grotesque distortions of that fiendish face could mask its true identity.

Marya, gloating, said, "Lo, behold the Beast! It is you, Glendon!"

His anguished thoughts shrieked, howling, *No, no!*

"The cry of the werewolf! You, Glendon!"

"NO!"

—Glendon was in darkness. Death cell, drained corpse, and blood-drinker—and the image of the werewolf—all were now gone, blotted out by blackness.

Glendon was sitting up, breathing hard, heart pounding as though he'd been running a race.

The darkness was not absolute and he was not alone. Between his breathings he heard a soft gasp coming from somewhere nearby. His hearing was very good, sharp—always had been.

Blurs of light and shadow came into focus, resolving into an orderly pattern of surroundings. Light from a street lamp filtered in through curtained windows on the far side of the room. Closer, behind him and to the side, a line of yellow light shone in under the bottom of a closed door.

169

Nearby, within arm's reach, a throbbing yellow-green disk seemed to hang in midair. It was the face of an electric clock radio. It sat on a night table, its soft glow revealing a heavy-banded metallic wristwatch, a few inches away.

His watch, resting on the night table where he had set it earlier. A homely detail, but real, solid, something his mind could catch hold of and use to reel itself out of nightmare country.

Now he knew where he was: in his own bed. Where better to have a nightmare?

Another gasp sounded, a quick intake of breath quickly stifled, as though the person feared being given away by the breathing.

The gasp was as real as the wristwatch, only it wasn't his. He reached for the night-table lamp and switched it on, flinching from the sudden brightness.

He was sitting up on his side of the bed, back against the headboard, the bedcovers down by his waist. He was not alone.

His bed partner was a young woman in her early twenties, very lovely and very naked. She sat on the other side of the bed, on the edge of the mattress, turning away from him, but looking over her shoulder at him. She clutched a knobbed bedpost, her back to him, her feet on the floor, poised and ready to jump up and run.

Wide green eyes stared at him, partly veiled by the strands of long chestnut-brown hair which had fallen across her face.

Carol. That was her name. He couldn't recall her last name. She had told it to him earlier tonight at the club, where a chance meeting as strangers had resulted in their hitting it off and picking each other up. Her last name had slipped his memory, lost somewhere in the club din and the hazy glow of alcohol and desire. Or had she told it to him at all?

She was a salesclerk at a trendy boutique and a some-time swimsuit-and-lingerie model. He remembered that much, with her lovely face and beautiful body here to remind him.

She had said that she shared a flat with a woman who

would be home tonight, so they had come here, to Glendon's place, a narrow sliver of three-story brownstone in a quiet square in an affluent London residential district.

They were in his bedroom now, on the second floor, fronting the square. The room was handsomely appointed and tastefully furnished, all first-class, but with a certain impersonality that was more like that of a hotel room than a private domicile.

The bed was king size, big enough for two. Or three. Tonight it was just two, with one-half of the combination seeming on the verge of jumping out of bed and fleeing. Tangled sheets and blankets testified to the vigorous workout that had taken place earlier in bed, as did the clothes, his and hers, that were strewn across the floor in a trail from the door to the bed.

Carol was still crouched on the bed's edge, ready to bolt.

"Carol . . . ? What's wrong, darling?"

"You tell me!" She was scared and angry. "Are you high? Are you on drugs?"

"Certainly not!" he said, indignant.

"Or are you a kinkster? Is this your idea of some kind of sick bed game, because if it is, Mr. Glendon, it is *not* a turn-on!"

"I'm quite sure I don't have the slightest idea of what you're talking about, and I suspect you don't either, Carol. Now, why don't you come back to bed and let's settle this in a nice civilized style."

"Civilized? Is that what you call it? You're a fine one to talk about civilized, with all your carryings-on!"

"Now, Carol," he said smoothly, starting to reach for her. She hopped out of bed, totally nude, her fine body stiff with tension.

Through gritted teeth she said, "If you touch me, I'll scream."

He stayed where he was, leaning back into the pillows, hands folded behind his head. "It wasn't so very long ago that you were screaming for more."

"Never mind about that! What about you, with all your howlings and growlings and carryings-on?"

He held out his hands, palms up. "I'm totally bewildered. Won't you please tell me what the problem is?"

Her green eyes narrowed, staring at him. After a pause, she said grudgingly, "You really don't know, do you?"

"Haven't a clue."

"I don't know if that's better or worse. Either way, I don't like it. I'm a normal girl who likes to go out and have a bit of fun with normal people, normal men, Mr. Glendon, normal men!

"I don't like being wakened out of a sound sleep by all your tossing and turning and rolling around. You scared the devil out of me!"

"Sorry," he said. "I must have been having a bad dream."

"Bad dream! Look what you've done to the sheets and pillows, you've torn them all up," she said, pointing.

Glendon now saw what he had previously missed. The sheets and blankets that were tangled around his waist were ripped and shredded, parts of them torn into long strips, as though they'd been clawed. One of the pillows had been ripped open, pillowcase and all, with some of the stuffing showing where it'd been torn out.

Glendon grew thoughtful. Carol saw the change in him and pressed her point home.

"Very nice," she said sarcastically. "Civilized, isn't that what you call it?

"And those noises you made! All that howling and growling, like a wild animal! When I first heard it, I thought there was a dog here in the room, but then I realized it was you!"

She bent over and started picking her clothes up off the floor, not taking her eyes off him. He sat up in bed, idly fingering the shredded sheets.

Carol pulled on her dress, slipping it on over her head, covering up full firm breasts, a high rounded rear, and long legs. Not too much of the legs were covered up, it was a short dress.

Glendon said, "You're not leaving?"

"I'm certainly not staying!" She crossed to a cabinet, on top of which sat her pocketbook. She'd been in too much of a hurry to put on her bra and panties and now she stuffed them inside the pocketbook.

She said, "I'll be having bad dreams myself; you practically scared me out of my skin."

"And such lovely skin it is, too," he said.

She pulled on her shoes.

Glendon tossed back the covers, rolling out of bed so that the bed was between them. He pulled on a pair of pants.

Carol picked up her earrings from the dresser and put them somewhere inside her pocketbook, closed it, and tucked it around her arm, crossing to the door.

She opened the door and went through it, exiting the room. Glendon padded after her, just wearing the pants, barechested and barefoot. He had a hairy chest, hairy back and arms, was hairy all over.

In the hallway there was dark carpeting, wood paneling, and rich melon-colored light. Carol went briskly across the landing and started down the curved staircase, one hand on the railing. Glendon followed.

The house was staffed by three servants, a cook, a cleaning lady, and a manservant, but none of them lived on premises and they all went home at night. Glendon and Carol were alone in the house.

At the foot of the stairs was a hallway stretching to the front door opposite. A black iron chain hung down from the ceiling above the stairwell, supporting a spiky Elizabethan-looking lamp whose amber diamond-pane glass panels shed a golden glow.

The light touched Carol's masses of long brown hair with golden-brown highlights as she crossed under it, her heels tapping on the tan-and-dark-brown checkerboard of the parquet floor.

Glendon stood in the middle of the staircase, hands on the railing as he leaned over it, looking down.

"Carol, where are you going at this time of night?"

"Home, to my nice quiet flat, thank you very much."

She went to the hall closet, barely pausing to grab her coat. Draping it over an arm, she started toward the front door.

Glendon called after her, "I'll get the car and drive you."

"No, thanks."

On either side of the hall, midway to the front of the house, a pair of archways faced each other, opening into side rooms. Carol whisked past them, hurrying to the front entrance.

The door was locked and bolted. Carol started working the locks.

Behind her, Glendon said, "At least let me ring up for a cab."

Carol started. The last she had seen him, he'd been standing on the stairs, and that's where she thought he still was. She hadn't heard him come up behind her.

She said, "Don't go sneaking up on a body like that!"

"Sorry, I wasn't aware that I was sneaking."

"Well, you were!" She finished turning the locks and took hold of the door handle and pulled it, but nothing happened, the door stayed closed. She held it with both hands, tugging, but it wouldn't budge.

She clawed for the locks again, her hands shaking.

"The bolt," Glendon said gently. "You've neglected to throw the bolt."

She threw it, sliding it free, then yanked open the door. Beyond the open doorway lay sidewalk, street lamp, empty square, night. The air was chill, clammy. A light drizzle was falling.

Glendon asked, "What're you going to do, walk?"

"I'll find a taxi."

"At this hour? You're daft!"

"I've sense enough to know when it's time to say good night. Good night, Mr. Glendon—and good-bye!"

She started down the stone front steps.

"Fun while it lasted," Glendon said. She didn't say anything, just stepped down to the sidewalk and started walking away, pulling on her coat.

The house was on a street of restored brownstones, most of which were set well back from the sidewalk. Most of the windows were dark, the houses locked up tight till dawn.

Misty drizzle haloed the street lamp. Surfaces glistened with dampness, stone walls, pavement, railings, bare trees.

Carol reached the end of the street, pausing at the corner to look back over her shoulder at Glendon's house. Light poured out of the open doorway, where his figure stood outlined—watching her?

She shivered, starting across the street, her heels clicking.

Glendon stood framed in the doorway, facing the direction where Carol had gone. He could no longer see her, but he could still hear the tap-tapping of her heels, going away.

Cold moist air swirled around his shoulders and back and chest, raising a shiver. Or was that a shudder?

His eyes stung, tingling and burning. He knuckled them, trying to rub them clear, but this seemed to have the opposite effect, for when he took his hands away, he saw red.

Literally. Red streaks and trails and blurred afterimages danced in front of his eyes. The whole scene—houses, trees, square, night sky—all had a rusty red tint.

A wave of dizziness came over him. He stood swaying, clutching the door frame for support, fingernails clawing the wood.

Red mist filled his head, covering all, smothering down a wave of rising anxiety and dread, suffocating it.

The night air was fresh, intoxicating. He breathed deeply, his senses racing. Something was caught in his teeth, setting them on edge. He hooked a bent finger into his mouth, feeling around, finding the obstruction and fishing it out.

He held it on a wet fingertip, holding it up to the light. It was a tuft of the fabric used for stuffing pillows, identical to that sticking out of the torn pillow on his bed.

He flicked it away, like brushing off a gnat. It sailed over the top rail of the front stoop, dropping from sight. He realized that he was standing at the top of the stoop, in front of his house. He didn't remember stepping out the front door.

The stones were cool, damp and gritty against the soles of his bare feet. He looked down at them, where they stuck out from under the cuffs of his pants. They seemed a long way off, but that might have been because of the red mist swimming before his eyes.

The feet moved, going down the stairs to the sidewalk, then setting off in the direction where Carol had gone. Bemused, Glendon let them have their way, taking him where they would.

Behind him, pouring through the open front door was a fan of yellow light, greasy in the drizzle. The night chill was gone now. He felt hot, overheated, burning up inside the wrapping of his skin. The misty rain felt good on his flesh, wetting down his head and shoulders and bare torso, cooling them off.

He turned his face up to the rain, exulting in the sheer sensuous pleasure of its icy tingle on his steaming flesh.

Carol walked on, about a block ahead, leaving Glendon's square behind. The sidewalk was edged by a line of row houses with brick walls and neat white-painted shutters.

The hour was late, she was alone, her footsteps sounding very loud to her. She turned up the collar of her coat and huddled in its depths, hands jammed in the pockets. Head down, hunched forward, she walked quickly with brisk long-legged strides.

Cars lined the curb, expensive understated machines whose curved polished surfaces were beaded with drops of wetness. Bare trees glistened and the street had a slick, oily sheen.

Carol followed the sidewalk away from the square and toward an area where the blocks were farther apart, the space more open. In the distance, light traffic could be heard, though not yet seen.

Carol came to a cross street, a quiet, deserted side street. Before stepping off the curb, she looked back, prompted by nothing more than instinct.

About halfway down the street behind her, a figure suddenly stepped off the sidewalk, ducking behind a tree.

Carol felt as if her heart had suddenly jumped into her

176

mouth, leaving a cold empty hole where it had been, one that dropped to the pit of her stomach.

She stood staring. She knew someone was hiding behind the tree, but she couldn't see him. It was a fairly narrow trunk and the skulker was doing a good job of hiding behind it.

She said, "Glen . . . ?" Her voice was weak and hesitant, but it sounded overloud to her.

No reply, nothing, and yet she knew someone was hiding behind that tree.

She didn't wait around to see who it was. She turned, hurrying across the street. When she reached the other side, she looked back. The stretch of sidewalk was deserted. There was no telling whether the skulker was still behind the tree or not.

Ahead, at the end of a long street, she could see and hear some traffic moving back and forth across a cross street. She started toward it, walking fast, so fast that it made her legs ache. Her long hair streamed behind her, bouncing along with her strides.

The intersection seemed a long way off. The street was on her left, houses were on her right. She drew abreast of a gap between houses, a dark yard space dotted with bushes.

Something flashed across it, seen out of the corner of her eye, disappearing behind the back of the next house.

The space between Carol's shoulder blades tingled. Hairs stood up on the back of her neck, her scalp crawled, tears started from the corners of her eyes, she couldn't catch her breath.

It was fear.

She ran, houses and yards sliding past her, though her goal seemed no closer. She ran harder and the distance began narrowing, slowly, but narrowing.

Now she neared the corner, where an apartment building sat on a narrow apron of ground, bordered by lines of chest-high shrubbery. Beyond lay the intersecting street, a four-lane avenue that was well traveled, even in the dead of night.

The dark street gave way to the well-lit avenue, where

cars and lorries rushed past. Carol slowed, lungs on fire, staggering.

Behind the screen of shrubs, Glendon crouched, waiting for her, waiting to pounce.

He'd followed her, and when she'd started hurrying away, the chase was on, filling him with a rush of adrenaline-induced excitement that left no time for thought, only action.

He'd darted out from behind the tree, across the sidewalk, and into the shadows on the other side in the blink of an eye. He moved surely and swiftly, the red mist in his head lighting up the scene so that he could see clearly, more clearly than he had ever seen before.

He'd cut across yards, hurdling fences and bushes, moving parallel to her as she raced up the sidewalk. She'd seen him for an instant out of the corner of her eye as he'd pulled ahead, slipping behind the back of a house.

He'd rushed forward, dashing on the balls of his bare feet, flying across the ground. A chest-high wooden plank fence loomed up ahead and he caught hold of the top and hoisted himself over it and down to the other side, moving with lithe acrobatic grace.

It was pure joy to run, leap, and hunt!

He'd known where she was, even without seeing her, just as he'd known when he'd pulled far ahead of her. He'd hopped an eight-foot-high stone wall, dropping down to the damp moist grounds of the apartment building, with its fussy small squares and wedges of bare ground cut by concrete walking paths and bordered by bushes.

Crouching low, his chest parallel to the ground, Glendon had slipped to the edge of the property, crouching down out of sight behind a row of bushes that Carol's present course must surely take her past to get to the avenue.

She thought she'd left him behind, not knowing that he'd pulled ahead of her and now lay waiting. The bushes edged the sidewalk, and when she came alongside of him, all he'd need do is reach out for her and scoop her up off the sidewalk, hauling her through the bushes and into the dark.

It was funny. He wanted to laugh but was afraid it would

come out a growl and besides he didn't want to give himself away. She'd know he was here soon enough when an arm came thrusting out of the bushes to hook her, covering her mouth with his hand to stifle any outcries.

And then, when he had her where he wanted her, terrified and helpless to stop him from doing anything he wanted to do to her, he'd . . .

What would he do? He wasn't sure, but he knew that whatever it was, it was sure to be something nasty.

When he had her, he'd know. His hands would know what to do without being told, his hands and teeth—

Here she was. Her footfalls, her heavy breathing—didn't she know how loud she sounded? Like a brass band. If her senses weren't so fear-numbed, she couldn't help but notice the murder lust that was pouring off him like a stink.

Humans really are the easiest prey, he told himself. He gnashed his teeth, his mouth watering, blood-lust stuffing the inside of his head with red clouds of murder.

All he had to do was grab her—

Someone touched him on the shoulder.

Glendon didn't like that. It was all very well and good for him to be the hunter, but to be surprised himself—unthinkable! His senses were so keen, so alive, even his skin was like a sensory organ, alert to the vibrations of moving things . . .

Who could sneak up on him? Impossible! He must have imagined it. He was sure that he had, for when he looked around to see who had touched him, he was alone.

The unknown disturbed him, and he snarled in defiance.

Carol heard the snarl, coming from the bushes a little more than an arm's length ahead of her. She gasped, jumping to the side, darting sideways between two parked cars into the street, running down the middle of it into the intersection.

Glendon hunkered down, powerful thigh muscles banding as he readied himself to leap and lunge, bringing her down.

A figure appeared beside him, a man. Glendon wheeled

179

on him, thrusting out his hands to grab him—the stranger was gone.

He looked around, head whipping from side to side. The stranger once more stood beside him, but this time on the opposite side of where he had been before.

Glendon gathered himself to strike. The man stood in a patch of light shed by a corner street lamp, revealing his face.

Glendon froze. The man was himself.

Not quite. The man resembled him, they were the same height and build, the same facial features, but there were differences.

It was his grandfather, his namesake, the original Wilfred Glendon. Glendon I.

He'd never met the old gentleman, but he'd pored over enough pictures and photographs of the great man not to be mistaken. He knew that face. Odd to think of him as an "old gentleman," since Glendon I had been less than a decade older than his grandson's present age when he had died.

His grandfather was long-dead, the tragic last victim of the so-called Werewolf of London.

Yet there he stood, less than a few paces away from his grandson. Light shone through him. He was as ghostly and insubstantial as today's Glendon had been during his dream of blood.

The sight so transfixed Glendon that he forgot about Carol, and was only dimly aware of the chaos caused when she dashed out into the avenue, into the midst of night traffic. Horns blared, tires squealed, and then there was the sound of her footfalls safely crossing the roadway to the other side.

More horn honking. An angry driver's voice, shouting something out the window. Then the cars driving away, leaving behind the smell of burned rubber and scorched brake linings.

Glendon was seized with the urge to renew the chase, but his grandfather's ghost was looking straight at him. Glendon I was long-faced, solemn, with sorrowful eyes.

180

The ghost shook his head, as if saying, *No.*

Head hanging, unable to confront the specter's aura of tragic dignity, his grandson gave up the pursuit, slinking away like a whipped dog.

ELEVEN

A spreading shaft of early-morning light tickled Glendon awake. There was nothing to lull him back to sleep, no soft pillows or warm blankets or cushioning mattresses. He was cold, stiff, tired, sore, and disoriented.

He lay sprawled on a floor. He got to his hands and knees, crouching on all fours, head down. He sat back on the floor, trying to rub some feeling into his numbed face, numb where he had been sleeping on it on the floor.

Sleeping? He felt more like he'd been knocked out or had passed out. The inside of his head felt woolly. The inside of his mouth, too.

He rubbed his eyes, trying to focus. He sat in the middle of the entrance hall, on the hard parquet floor. The front door was open about twelve inches, admitting a sliver of daylight which slanted deeper into the hall as the sun rose. The light falling across him had awakened him.

Glendon got his feet under him and stood up, groaning. His feet were sore and tender and were shot through with aches and pains when he put his weight on them. He wore only the pair of pants he had pulled on last night when seeing Carol to the door. His torso was scratched and smeared with patches of dried mud.

He looked at the bottoms of his feet. They were filthy,

absolutely black with dirt. Glendon was an outdoorsman and hiker, and years of trekking on foot in the far places had covered his soles with a layer of thick, tough calluses. But his feet were hurting now.

Muddy footprints trailed from the hallway back to the open door. Glendon went to it, favoring his sore feet, looking as if he was walking on eggs.

The house was still and quiet, deserted except for himself. He recalled that he had given the servants the day off so they could enjoy a long weekend. Also because even though he was the master of the house, he felt uncomfortable having his bedmates parade around in front of the servants.

Not that he had known Carol would be staying the night when he had given the servants the following day off. Before last night, he and Carol had been strangers. But he had known that he was going to go out and look for a woman, and most times when he did so, he was successful in the girl hunt.

He hadn't been so successful with Carol, though. The lovemaking had gone along fine; it was the howling aftermath that had driven her out of the house.

He had some vague, jumbled memories of following her through the streets, running through the night, but those were sheer fantasy, of course. He'd hardly be likely to go running after a woman in the dead of an early spring night clad in nothing more than a pair of pants.

And yet, considering the blackened soles of his feet and his general allover soreness, he could almost believe that it had been real.

He and Carol had had more than a few drinks earlier in the evening, and then a few more when they'd arrived at the house, before going up to the bedroom, but Glendon found it hard to believe that he'd blacked out and fallen into a stuporous sleep on the hallway floor. He hadn't been that drunk!

Still, the evidence suggested otherwise. "I could do with a drink now," he said to himself.

Habitually security-conscious, he was amazed that he

could have been so out of it as to have left the front door open and unlocked. The wind must have blown it almost all the way closed. Good thing, because the bobbies who regularly made their rounds on foot patrol in this well-off respectable neighborhood would surely have come forward to investigate a front door gaping wide open in the middle of the night. A fine thing that would have been, for a police officer to have found Glendon passed out in the front hall of his own house.

No doubt they regularly saw aspects of the private lives of the people they were paid to protect, aspects that were discreditable and worse; their dark sides, so to speak, but Glendon valued his privacy and was sensitive to any black marks against the family name. There had already been too much of that, with that werewolf business and the "Glendon Curse" and all that rot.

Glendon stood at the door, holding it by the handle, looking outside and filling his lungs with deep breaths of cold fresh air. They helped to chase some of the cobwebs away.

He started to close the door, pausing when he noticed some deep scratches and grooves marking the door frame.

"Something's been using this for a scratching post," he said.

He wondered what kind of animal could have done it. They looked something like marks that could have been made by a cat's claws, except for their size. No tabby cat made those deep scoring marks, which stood about four feet up on the frame. A big cat might have made them, a cheetah or jaguar or something like that, but how likely was it for one of them to use the door frame of his London house as a scratching post?

A big dog might have made them, a very big dog, something on the order of a Doberman or rottweiler or Irish wolfhound, but again, the odds said no.

More likely it was the result of someone's clumsiness, accidentally made when packages or bundles were being brought in. As a scientist, researcher, and collector, Glendon was constantly receiving sample specimens, artifacts, and curios from around the world. Most were shipped to his offices at Merrymont College, a part of Oxford University, where he maintained an extensive herbarium greenhouse and lab facilities. But his wide-ranging interests and far-flung correspondences with others in the field assured a steady stream of packages delivered to his house as well.

So it was entirely possible that the door-frame marks had been made by some careless delivery person. Except that his manservant, Jenkins, routinely directed all tradespeople to make their deliveries at the side entrance.

Jenkins was handy, so perhaps he'd be able to repair the damage with some plastic wood filler and fresh paint. More likely, Glendon would have to have the carpenter in.

Not that the expense bothered him. He could afford it, he was quite well-off, thanks to the family fortune. Rich, in fact. Whatever else the Glendon Curse might have done, it certainly hadn't inflicted financial damage.

Looking outside, Glendon saw one of his neighbors across the square exit his house via a front door, dressed for a day's work at the office or bureau or whatever, wearing a light tan topcoat and carrying a briefcase.

Glendon became aware of what a sight he must present if the fellow should happen to glance across the way and see him, Glendon, standing half-dressed and disheveled in the doorway.

The man's focus was on his own routine, however, as he got into his car and started it up. Glendon eased the door closed, locking it.

The muddy smears tracked by his footprints across the hallway floor also irked him. He had only gone out on his front step last night, where could he have picked up so much mud? He made a mental note to clean it up later so the servants wouldn't see it.

Back to the door, facing the stairs, Glendon turned right, going under an archway into a kind of drawing room, where there was a fireplace and comfortable furniture and end tables with lamps and an oversized, intricately patterned Persian rug covering most of the wooden floor.

He passed through the room, carefully detouring around the edges of the carpet to avoid soiling it with his bare, dirty feet. In the rear wall of the room, a doorway opened into a short narrow passage leading to his study.

As he made for it, he glimpsed some kind of movement over to his side and he jumped, gasping. He laughed when he realized that what he had seen was his own reflection in a wall mirror.

He went to it, staring at himself. His hair was unkempt and he needed a shave, his eyes were black-ringed and red-rimmed, and his square-jawed, hard-lined face showed a touch of puffiness and dissipation. He was in good shape, with broad sloping shoulders and a square torso. His chest was thickly covered with curly reddish-brown hair; beneath it, his skin was fair, almost milky white.

He grinned at himself, his reflection showing too many teeth in a mocking grimace. He stopped grinning, turned, and continued on through the doorway into the passage, then into his study.

The study occupied most of the rear of the building's first floor. It was a large, high-ceilinged space, filled with exotic plants, artifacts, and books, books, books. It was a combined workspace, conservatory, and cabinet of curiosities.

There were potted plants, plants in glass tanks and terrariums, and vine-type plants hanging in saucers suspended from the ceiling. A row of man-high bushy green spear-bladed plants in tub-sized planters stood under a tall arched window, their leafy branches exposed to direct sunlight. Other plants were placed in shadowed niches, or bedded under special ultraviolet lamps. Smaller-sized plants filled gaps in bookcase shelves and sat on cabinet tops. There were round spiky star-headed cacti, bunches of green waxy-leafed succulents, and unusually shaped or colored flowering plants.

Dominating the space was a massive antique desk, not much smaller than a compact car. Butted alongside one end, to form an L-shaped branch, was a computer workstation, the stand made of wood shaped and stained to complement the traditional Old World–style craftsmanship of the desk.

The curtains were drawn, the room was filled with gray light, shadows glooming up the corners. Glendon sat down behind his desk, switching on the desktop lamp. It had a long narrow hooded bronze shade and matching gooseneck stand, anchored to the desktop. It cast a fan of yellow light across the dark wood surface, washing it with a golden glow.

On the desktop was a gray metal fireproof box, about the size of a toaster oven. It sat at the head of a green desk blotter, blocking some of the light from the gooseneck lamp behind it.

Items from the box were piled up around the desk. Among them was a rolled parchment scroll; a couple of packets of yellowed, aging letters; some notebooks and brown leather-bound pocket notepads; and a stack of manila folders stuffed with old newspaper and magazine articles.

Glendon sat hunched forward in his chair, staring over the top of the box into space, looking at nothing. After a while he sighed, lowering his gaze. When it fell on the box and its contents, he frowned.

He pushed away from the desk, rising and crossing to a sideboard, where a crystal decanter of fine aged scotch whiskey sat on a silver oval tray, flanked by some tumblers.

Glendon pulled the stopper, splashing a couple of ounces into a tumbler. He carried the drink back to his desk and sat down. He drank the scotch, tossing it back in one gulp.

He shuddered. It burned going down, blossoming into belly-filling heat. He gasped, said, "Hair of the dog . . ."

He turned his attention back to the box and, more importantly, to its contents. Strange, disturbing things.

"Damned things." He set the empty glass down on the desk, squaring his shoulders, resolved to dig into his work. Still, he hesitated.

Reaching a decision at last, he got up, went to the sideboard, picked up the decanter by the neck, and carried it back to the desk. He sat down, pouring another drink but not touching it, setting it to one side of the blotter, where it was out of the way but within ready reach for when it wanted it.

"Which could be anytime soon," he said. Now for the box's contents, the damned things.

"The Ames Testament," he said, half-mocking, half-serious.

The stuff from the box smelled old, musty, particularly the parchment scroll. It had been stored somewhere in the dusty precincts of a forgotten old Thames warehouse, where it had lain neglected for many years—decades—before coming into the possession of the firm of solicitors who handled the Glendon family legal business.

Not long ago, Glendon had dropped by the firm's offices at their request, where he was taken into the inner office of Solicitor Bryce, a dry closet-sized office so airless and heavily paneled in rich aged woods that it reminded Glendon of a humidor.

Bryce was spare and fine-boned, with dry wispy hair, oversized owlish glasses, and sunken cheeks. After the usual opening amenities, he got to the point and explained why he had arranged the appointment.

Bryce said, "It's about this fellow, Ames—Paul Ames."

Glendon had good nerves and strong self-control, so he reacted with little more than a raised eyebrow. "Surely that business has been long-settled? Paul Ames died years ago," he said.

"So he did," Bryce agreed pleasantly.

Glendon pressed. "He died in a madhouse, screaming."

Bryce made an openhanded gesture, indicating that while he didn't necessarily agree with Glendon's characterization of the event, he didn't necessarily disagree, either.

He said, "He was confined to a mental institution for the last years of his life, and did die while in confinement, yes."

"What I said. Paul Ames—there's a name that looms large in the Glendon-family scandals."

"Married into the family, I believe."

"He married my grandmother, Lisa, after my grandfather's death. Very closely after, which prompted no little talk. The way things worked out, I believe he had reason to bitterly recall the truth of the old saying 'Marry in haste, repent at leisure.'

"He spent the rest of a too-long life repenting that he had ever set eyes on Lisa Glendon."

Bryce was solemn-faced, but his thick-lensed glasses magnified his small shrewd eyes into cartoonish distortions.

He said, "Ames certainly suffered an unfortunate string of personal tragedies. The untimely loss of his wife, the shocking violent deaths of their children—all but your father, that is—"

"My father was a Glendon, not an Ames. He was the true son of the first Wilfred Glendon. My grandmother was pregnant with him when she married Ames. Later, they had children of their own—but you know what happened to them."

"Yes. Dreadful business. Brutally murdered, both of them, and within a relatively short time of each other."

"Unsolved killings," Glendon said. "Ames was sure he had solved them, though. He claimed that the murderer was my father."

Bryce tsk-tsked. "His terrible misfortunes unhinged his reason. I fear he was not in his right mind for many, many years."

"He had an obsession about the so-called Glendon Curse. According to him, my father was a worse killer than Jack the Ripper and Sweeney Todd combined. In addition to Eunice and Peter Ames, he was supposed to have killed Ames's aunt, a retired Scotland Yard police inspector, and who knows who else.

"Why, he even said that my father killed his own mother, my grandmother, Lisa Glendon-Ames."

"Monstrous," Bryce said sympathetically, pursing thin dry lips, his glassy orbs wide and swimming. "Well, what can you expect? The man was out of his head, deranged.

"I believe you yourself had an unfortunate run-in with him, Professor Glendon."

"As a matter of fact, I did. It was when I was a schoolboy, about eleven years old. Ames had already been institutionalized a number of times, as well as serving a short prison term for criminal assault against some policemen who attempted to apprehend him for trespassing on the family estates.

"He had only recently been released from a mental hospital, but he was a man on a mission. To put it briefly, one morning he broke into the school building and came into a classroom, trying to kill me. That's what he said he was going to do, anyway. I didn't stick around to find out.

"I climbed out a window and shinnied down to the ground along a drainpipe. I was always good at climbing, you see. When he came out after me, the pipe broke and he fell to the ground, breaking a leg. That's where he was when the police came to take him away. That was the first and last time I've ever laid eyes on Paul Ames.

"While he was chasing me, he said enough for me to get the general idea. Since my parents had perished in a car crash a year earlier, I was the last of the Glendons. By getting rid of me, he'd put an end to the curse.

"So you see, Mr. Bryce, the name of Paul Ames is not one that I can hear without experiencing mixed feelings at best," Glendon said, sitting back in his chair.

Now it was Bryce's turn to lean forward across the desk. "Naturally, Professor, speaking on behalf of the firm, as well as for myself, I deeply regret reminding you of any unpleasant memories, and if there were another way of handling this minor but necessary bit of legal business, it would have so been done, but the fact of the matter is that certain formalities and niceties of the law must be observed, and so here we are.

"In sum, the firm has come into the possession of a piece of personal property belonging to the late Paul Ames. Since you are the closest living relative and only living heir, the property now belongs to you."

Glendon smiled, a slow lazy smile of disbelief. "You're not going to tell me that he's left me some money or something, if only by default. That would be droll!"

"Er, no. At one time Ames had some small ranch holdings in Canada, and some stock in a California aircraft company, but those have all been long since lost.

"I'm afraid he wasn't a very good businessman. He might have expected to come into some money by the marriage to your grandmother, but the Glendon family trust prevented that. The terms of the trust precluded him, or any outsider by marriage, from touching the principal sums on deposit.

"If he'd been in his right mind, he would have seen that this arrangement alone proved that his suspicions about your father were baseless. By the terms of the trust, Wilfred Glendon II was the sole inheritor of the family holdings. By law, the children of Paul and Lisa Ames could not inherit.

"Therefore, your father had no motive for doing away with them, since he would stand to inherit all whether they lived or died. On the contrary, it was Paul Ames and his children who stood to gain if your father had died before producing an heir. If the last of the Glendon line dies out with no successor, then the immediate relatives by marriage would divide the estate.

"Paul Ames was a bankrupt for many years, and died a pauper. In fact, it was the Glendon trust which paid the expenses of his many years of institutionalization. Quite generous, in my opinion."

Glendon said, "A good investment, too, keeping that murderous lunatic in a padded cell where he belonged."

Bryce shrugged, pleasantly blank-faced. Glendon said, "What you're saying is that he left no money."

"Well, yes," the solicitor said.

"What did he leave?"

"A box. A metal box, about the size of a milk crate."

"What's in it, Mr. Bryce?"

"Personal papers, journals, and other small items. Most of it is a hodgepodge, but there are one or two small art objects that are apparently genuine and not without value."

"What kind of art objects?"

"Tibetan. A scroll and a few odds and ends. I'm told that the scroll might be worth something to a museum or private collector specializing in such stuff."

Glendon nodded. "It would be Tibet. Part of Ames's obsession with my grandfather. He did extensive explorations in the Himalayas—made some of his most important finds there.

"Tell me, Bryce, why did it take until now for the box to surface? Why wasn't it with Ames's other few meager belongings when his will was probated at the time of his death?"

"As I understand it, Professor, the box was stored separately, in the attic loft of a Thames warehouse. The building had been condemned for years, but was only recently torn down. It was then that the box came to light. Since our firm handled the legal affairs relating to Ames's continued confinement, the box came into our possession.

"It now leaves our charge, and becomes your legal property." Bryce's eyes narrowed behind the thick lenses, fixing on Glendon.

"Of course, there are papers to be signed first," he said.

"Of course," agreed Glendon.

Bryce's gaze widened and became more diffuse, watery. They stayed that way as he and Glendon made small talk while waiting for Bryce's assistant to enter with the papers. When he did, the forms were signed in triplicate and properly witnessed, signed, notarized, and sealed.

The forms were duly distributed, with a copy for Glendon. The assistant took the other forms away, filed them, and returned a short time later with the box, setting it down on Bryce's desk and exiting.

Bryce and Glendon more or less rose at the same time, signaling by mutual unspoken agreement that the interview was over.

Bryce said, "One more thing, Professor. I feel a word of caution is in order, especially in light of certain sensitive matters regarding Glendon-family history. The late Mr. Ames held some rather peculiar ideas about life and death in general, and the Glendons in particular.

"Keeping that in mind, I must warn you that some of his writings in regard to your father and grandfather contain some material that you may find exceedingly distasteful."

192

"I can stand it," Glendon said. "It's a scientist's duty to look the facts in the face and see the world as it really is, and I suppose that includes Paul Ames's ravings."

Bryce looked doubtful. "Paul Ames was an extremely disturbed individual. This material alone proves that it was necessary to keep him in a place where he could do no harm to others or himself.

"At any rate, it's yours now," Bryce said, sliding the box across his desk to Glendon . . .

Now it sat on Glendon's desk, where it had been sitting for the last ten days, occupying more and more of his time and thoughts. There was no mistaking the extent of Paul Ames's pathological hatred of the last three generations of Glendons, starting from the present Glendon's grandfather.

From the tragic, violent history of the Glendon Curse he had created his own private mythology, a private hell of werewolves and vengeful ghosts and moonflowers that explained the brutal slaying deaths of so many of the family and those associated with them.

And there was a pattern of unsolved murders and grotesque lethal accidents that had afflicted the Glendon circle ever since the first Glendon had somehow crossed paths with the so-called Werewolf of London.

The box contained Paul Ames's record of what he believed was the real and true secret history of the family curse—the revenge of the Werewolf.

The man was mad, no doubt of that. The trouble was that even the bare-bones facts of the family history were disturbing. Even stripped of the mountain of insane speculation which Ames had piled up on it, the underlying framework of the case was truly strange and sinister.

Like the victim of a fixed idea, Paul Ames had seized whatever seemingly relevant material lay at hand, to shore up his makeshift theories. Some of those items now lay on Glendon's desk, where they had been for days, vexing him, haunting him with a problem the ultimate solution of which might well be the worst horror yet.

Glendon picked up the scroll, unrolling it. The parchment

was yellow, wrinkled, oily. The touch of it felt greasy against his fingertips. He was sure that the parchment was made of tanned human skin.

The faded reddish-brown seals stamped on the scroll attested to its diabolical nature. The seals were those of the notorious Red Hat Sect, a long-suppressed society of Tibetan monks whose souls were set on the Left-Hand Path of devil worship. The British had thought that they had wiped out the sect at the turn of the century, during the Stark-Younghusband Expedition. But isolated pockets of the order had survived until the late 1950s, when the Chinese invasion and takeover of Tibet had put the Red Hats at the mercy of an even more ruthless and implacable foe, the political commissars of Chairman Mao.

This scroll was a product of the recent heyday of the society, about a hundred and fifty years ago. A picture was tattooed on it, in red-and-black ink.

It depicted a graveyard scene. In the foreground was a leering man-beast, with pointed ears and sharp teeth and claws. At its pawlike feet were half-eaten human bodies, showing bared rib cages and bones.

Behind and to the side of the man-beast was a mound of skulls.

In the background, a saw-toothed line represented the peaks of a mountain range. Some effort had been made to render the mountains in a detailed and realistic fashion.

Glendon had come to believe that that part of the scroll was a map and that a real location was being depicted, for those who knew how to look.

That's what Ames had thought, too, believing that the graveyard scene showed a real place. He even had a name for it: the Valley of the Moonflower. He wrote about it extensively and obsessively in his journals, covering page after page in a minute, crabbed hand that looked like the tracings of a seismograph needle.

What really had piqued Glendon's interest was the circular border that surrounded the picture, a decorative garland of flowers strung along a chain of human skulls.

The blossoms were clearly shown, curious-shaped bulbs like folded petal hands with flowery liplike petals at the tip.

Glendon readily identified the flowers as the *mariphasa lupina luminosa,* an exotic and ultrarare blossom which, like Paul Ames himself, loomed large in the saga of the Glendon Curse.

Mariphasa was better known as the moonflower. It was believed only to exist in certain mountain valleys in the Himalayas, and even well into the latter half of the twentieth century, most experts in the botanical field were unsure as to whether the plant existed at all, outside the realm of Tibetan folklore.

It was Wilfred Glendon I who had been the first to bring live specimens of the plant back to England, where he had been engaged in a major effort to cultivate and propagate them.

This was an exceedingly difficult task, since according to legend, mariphasa only blooms by moonlight. The plants did not thrive in the English climate, where clouds, fogs, and ambient city lights made a steady supply of moonlight problematical.

To remedy that lack, Glendon had invented an ingenious device, what he called a Moon-Ray Projector, a kind of lamp whose artificial light mimicked the wavelengths and other characteristics of moonlight well enough to nourish and quicken the plants, "tricking" them into blooming.

It was a strange invention. Today's Glendon had investigated the subject as thoroughly as he could, poring over his grandfather's notebooks and correspondence. There was a gap in the section of his private papers relating to the Moon-Ray, and what little Glendon III had managed to learn had been gleaned from passing references to it and marginalia in textbooks and other throwaway writings. The real work, the hard data and blueprints, were long gone.

Today's Glendon had learned that while the idea for the projector was his grandfather's, the device at the heart of it, the actual invention, was based on the work of Janos Rukh, the legendary rogue physicist and discoverer of Radium X.

Rukh and Glendon's grandfather were members of some of the same scientific societies and carried on an extensive exchange of ideas.

Rukh had died under mysterious circumstances, like the Curies a victim of his own radioactive discoveries. His work was decades ahead of its time, with many advanced weapons applications whose secrets had been swallowed up into military intelligence archives.

Which might well explain why all of Glendon I's notes on the Moon-Ray Projector were nowhere to be found.

But the device had existed, and so had the mariphasa, at least according to contemporary newspaper accounts at the time, many of which were stuffed into Paul Ames's dog-eared manila folders. There were photographs of Glendon posing proudly beside the machine and the moonflower plant. Most of the articles took a good-naturedly patronizing tone, along the lines of, "Look what those crazy scientists have come up with now—artificial moonlight!"

As for mariphasa, there was independent confirmation of its existence. Both the British Museum and the Royal Botanical Society had samples of withered stalks and dried leaves of the exotic plant, all that had survived after Glendon's murder. His grandson had seen and investigated those samples, as well as numerous sketches, drawings, and photographs that had been taken of mariphasa.

There was no mistaking its likeness in the places where it was depicted on the Red Hat parchment scroll. Not only in the border, but in the picture itself, which showed a detail of the moon shining down on the plants beside the skull mound, the mariphasas blooming at the end of graceful stalks and bushy fronds.

One of the leather-bound notebooks had yielded an index card which identified the scroll in neat handwriting that was obviously not Ames's: *Tanka prayer scroll from area of Red Hat lamasery near Gotse, ca. 1830–49, depicts "Howling Beast" (Yeti?—ref. unk), with moonflower-and-skull border.*

So much for the scroll. Glendon rolled it up, pushing it away to one side, as he had done so many times before. But he always came back to it, to stare fascinated at it for hours at a time, puzzling over its mysteries.

Now he rubbed his fingertips against his pants, trying to wipe them clean of that greasy feeling. He always did that, too, when he had reached the end of a soul-sinking spell of parchment gazing. That was its purpose, designed by some unknown needle-and-ink Red Hat artist to serve as an incentive for meditation.

Tibetan magic sects of both the Right- and Left-Hand Path, light and dark, all made extensive use of hypnosis and autosuggestion.

Glendon seized on that as a possible explanation of what had come over him lately. The renewed nightmares, more terrible than ever, culminating in last night's bizarre episode and its strange, puzzling aftermath.

Perhaps he had been hypnotizing himself into believing that myth and madness were true, that curses had power even unto the third generation, that werewolves existed—

That he had the taint . . .

The next part of the tale, after Grandfather Glendon had returned from Tibet with his marvelous discovery, to resume his pleasant routine at Glendon Manor, doing his work and raising a family with his beloved younger wife, Lisa, all that and what happened next was contained in another part of the Ames Testament.

It was a true-crime magazine, a sensational tabloid-style document that had been sold over newsstand counters. It was titled, *Special Edition: Secrets of Scotland Yard.* A subtitle added, "Most Baffling and Brutal Cases Now Revealed!"

It had been published more than twenty years before, and the pages were brittle and yellowed. All Glendon had to do was set it on the desktop and flip it open at random, and it would always land at the same place. Constant handlings and obsessive rereadings had done that. Most of this was the work of Ames, but Glendon had pored, wild-eyed and oblivious of time, over the pages on more than a few occasions recently.

The magazine always opened to the big double-page

spread of an article entitled "Was Swami Yogami the Were-wolf of London?" Underneath the title was Ames's scrawled handwriting: *Not the only one.*

Even two decades earlier, the case had qualified as a "True Crime Classic," at least according to the magazine's editors. Absent the exploitation-style tone of hysteria, the facts of the case were related in a straightforward, meat-and-potatoes style and the article was illustrated with file photos that were a generation older than the magazine. A picture of the first Wilfred Glendon stood beside that of his wife, Lisa. There were photos of some of the victims—a hotel chambermaid, a prostitute, and a nude model. The photos of the hooker and the model were a lot bigger than the thumb-sized face shot of the maid. The Scotland Yard inspector who'd been in charge of the case was seen in two photos, and there were some of the Yard detectives who'd done the actual investigative work.

Prominently featured on the "splash" page was a picture of Dr. Yogami, with the caption underneath asking, "Was the smooth swami the mad 'Werewolf' murderer?"

In recent days, and nights, Glendon had stared at that picture until he thought his eyes would burn holes in it. Yogami was a plump moon-faced man, with heavy-lidded eyes and a shiny dark goatee. His origins were indeterminate, and he looked like a Swede masquerading as an Asian. There was something sly and self-contained about him, but was he a killer?

The police said he was. These were the facts of the case:

Shortly after Glendon I had returned home from Tibet, Dr. Yogami also surfaced in London. Whatever his pretensions to occult knowledge, Yogami was a learned and cultured man, who moved in the same scientific and social circles as Glendon.

Around this time, what were known as the Werewolf Moon Murders began. On the night of the first full moon, a bestial killer slew a London streetwalker, inflicting on the victim's body some of the most ghastly mutilations seen since the days of Jack the Ripper. Some equivocal evidence pointed to the possibility of cannibalism, a lead that was firmly suppressed by the Yard throughout the manhunt.

The following night saw another murder, that of a nude model and dancer who was keeping a clandestine rendezvous with one of her many lovers, a married man who worked as a zookeeper. During their liaison, a wolf had been let loose from its cage, escaping. While the keeper pursued it in vain, the killer struck, surprising the girlfriend alone on a park bench.

In this case, the victim's corpse bore even more damning evidence of cannibalism, though the Yard's inspector in charge of the case, Sir Thomas Forsythe (*That ass!* was Ames's notation beside the sleuth's picture), maintained that while the real killer had undoubtedly murdered the woman, her "soft parts" had actually been chewed and mauled by the escaped wolf.

The "canny inspector," as the article labeled him, found his suspicions aroused by Yogami, who presented himself at police headquarters with some absurd theory that the killings were the work of a modern-day werewolf loose in London.

Forsythe was more interested in Yogami himself than in his weird theories. He determined that Yogami actually did, as he claimed, hold the degree of doctor of philosophy, which he had earned at the university of Tokyo, and that he was a devotee of occult studies. He was a member of the Psychical Research Society, the Swami Gurujee movement, the Pan-Gaian Mind Science Lodge, and a host of similar esoteric groups. He was also a serious mountain climber who had been on some Tibetan expeditions and a sometime lecturer and writer.

It was not until Yogami's second visit to the Yard that Inspector Forsythe's suspicions took solid form. Yogami denounced Glendon, naming him as the Werewolf killer. Forsythe had already put Yogami under surveillance, a routine precaution taken after his first walk-in visit.

Now further digging unearthed the interesting fact that Yogami had been in Tibet at the same time as Glendon, and, still more interesting, seemed to have followed him to London. More than coincidental was evidence that other Moon Murders, virtually identical to those terrorizing London, had taken place in other European cities where Yogami had visited.

Unfortunately, the police could not be everywhere at once, and before the sleuth could support his hunch with hard facts, Yogami struck again, sadistically slaughtering the hotel chambermaid who was cleaning his suite. This crime was as foolish and ill conceived as it was horrific, since all the evidence screamed out that Yogami was the killer. Indeed, he made no effort to hide the crime or his authorship of it, more proof of the advanced stage of his homicidal mania.

Yogami then set out to murder Glendon. Surprising the scientist as he worked in his greenhouse lab, Yogami attacked him. A furious struggle ensued, during which Glendon managed to get the upper hand, turning the tables on Yogami and slaying him in self-defense.

One last tragic scene remained to be played out. As the police stormed to the rescue at the manor, not knowing that Yogami was already dead, Glendon was mistaken for the real killer and accidentally shot, felled by police bullets.

"A most tragic error," Forsythe later said regretfully. "Dr. Glendon died a hero, losing his life as he rushed out blindly to make sure of the safety of his beloved wife, Lisa."

As Forsythe later reconstructed the crime, Yogami had somehow conceived an obsessive hatred of Glendon, no doubt fired by jealousy at his rival's superior accomplishments during his Central Asian and Tibetan expeditions. Accusing Glendon of being the Werewolf killer had been a classic, if extreme, example of systemic character assassination, yet it seemed as if Yogami, through the mechanism of projection, actually believed Glendon was the killer.

In the margin beside the inspector's summation, Ames had written, *It wasn't projection when Forsythe came under fang and claw!*

This odd notation, as the present Glendon had learned from his own investigations, referred to the fact that Sir Thomas Forsythe had been murdered long years after he had retired from active duty at the Yard. He'd been fiendishly mangled by a person or persons unknown.

The killing had taken place sometime after the crime magazine had been published.

Too bad, Glendon thought. *It would have made a nice sidebar.*

More and more now, ever since first dipping into the contents of the box, Glendon had been haunted by the terrible suspicion—call it intuition—that the true facts of the case, and the curse, were decidedly different from the version presented in the crime magazine.

Whether valid or invalid, it was this suspicion that had put Glendon on a collision course with the Unknown, a course that was rapidly heading toward its climax.

TWELVE

At midmorning, in a mansion out on Claw Cape, Steve Soto was present at a meeting with Basil Lodge and Dorian. The house sat on top of a low flat rise, overlooking a long sweeping curve of sandy white beach that reached deep into the harbor. It was a low, spacious structure, flat-roofed, with white stucco walls and lots of sliding-glass wall panels opening onto balconies and terraces.

The trio sat outside on a wooden deck-type veranda that was covered by a latticed canopy. The canopy was overgrown with lush tropical vines and creepers whose matted foliage provided shade from the sun.

The sky was hazy, overcast, with a warm moist wind blowing in from offshore. Breakers kept unrolling on the beach with a crashing regularity, each crash succeeded by the sounds of hissing white foam.

Soto, Dorian, and Lodge occupied wicker chairs that were grouped around a glass-topped table. Lodge's chair had a high spreading fan back that made it look like a throne. He wore a blue blazer and khaki pants. Dorian was outfitted in a straight, short, simple white sleeveless dress, a coral necklace, and matching bracelets.

Soto wore the same clothes he had worn earlier, at the zombie breakfast. His gun had since been reloaded.

Lodge's clout with the local law was such that a few words from him to the officer in charge of the police squad that had responded to the emergency at the hotel was enough to square the beef. The lawmen not only gave Lodge and his niece a free pass, they also let Soto and his two sidemen go without asking them so much as a single question, as soon as Lodge made it clear that they were friends of his.

In any case, the police weren't too inclined to ask questions once they saw the dead scarecrow man heaped on the floor like a stack of kindling. They knew about zombies. They wrapped the body in a tablecloth shroud and toted it away.

At that time Lodge had suggested that a further meeting of minds might be to their mutual benefit. Soto had agreed, climbing into the back of Lodge's car when Dorian brought it around to the front of the hotel. Soto had left Tony Paul and Dennis behind. Tony Paul hadn't liked it much— "How'm I gonna bodyguard you if you ain't around?"—but Soto was calling the shots and what he said, went. Besides, there was no need for his stooges to know the terms of any deal that he might cut with Lodge; it was none of their business.

Tony Paul and Dennis had stood on the sidewalk, watching Dorian drive Lodge's snazzy car away, taking Soto with them. Soto hoped they could keep out of trouble for the hour or two that he would be gone.

Dorian drove, and after a minute or two of checking out her performance, Soto had allowed himself to relax, sinking back into plush leather seats. The car had followed the highway south out of town, whipping through masses of hazy blue-gray smoke that hung over the road where it bordered the edges of Shandygaff, the waterfront slum district. The area was cordoned off by heavily armed police squads, who had also set up roadblocks at the entrances to the strife-torn area.

Shandygaff was situated on a sandy flat on the landward side of the highway. The relatively small plot of land was crowded with a jumble of shacks, huts, shanties, and lean-tos, all made from whatever materials could be scrounged for construction: driftwood, empty oil drums, concrete blocks, tin sheets. Hordes of the poor were crowded there, massed together in a perpetually simmering stew of deprivation and violence.

Last night, the boiling pot had overflowed in mass hysteria, panic, and riot. Fires were started, and whole sections of that crowded tinderbox warren had gone up in smoke. Magdalena had a fire brigade, but their services were reserved for those who could pay for them, in the city's built-up section, so the Shandygaff fires had been allowed to burn out of control.

By daylight, most of the fires had burned themselves out, though the charred wreckage still pumped out plenty of smoke, laying a pall on the coastline.

The smoke was left behind when Lodge's car turned off the highway, making a left onto the access road that ran along the cape. It was a private road and its use was restricted to those who lived on the cape and their guests. Police guarded the entrance to the road, screening all comers.

Today their numbers had been doubled because of the social unrest. The guards knew Lodge's car and waved it through without stopping it.

The house was about two-thirds of the way out on the cape, on the harbor side. A gravel driveway ran from the access road to the front gates of a walled estate. The peach-colored walls were eight feet high and topped with rows of iron spikes that jutted outward at a forty-five-degree angle, to discourage wall-climbing intruders.

Automated steel front gates swung inward, opening on a curved white pebble drive that horseshoed in front of the house. Pebbles crunched under the tires as the car rolled to a halt before the front entrance, while electric servo-motors whined as they powered the double-gated doors shut.

The premises were protected by Lodge's own four-man security detail. They were not island police but rather his own entourage of bodyguards.

A central hallway ran from the front entrance to the rear of the house, where sliding-screen doors opened onto the canopy-covered veranda where the trio now sat. Terraced gardens with lush green foliage platformed in broad shallow steps to the beach below.

Now, indicating the seascape, Lodge began, "Marvelous view, eh, Steve?"

"Great. You can sit right here and enjoy a front-row seat as the city burns down."

"Yes, that's definitely an attraction. But it's hardly the city that's going up in flames, Magdalena is not Shandygaff. It's only the shantytown that caught fire. The blaze never reached the edge of the city."

"For how long? Riots and fires both have a tendency to get out of control."

Lodge made a dismissive gesture. "It's nothing, really. It wasn't even a riot, per se. The slum dwellers know enough not to go against Major Quantez."

"Yeah? So what happened last night?" Soto asked.

"The rabble got worked up into a state of hysteria about some monster stalking among them, or some such rot."

"More zombies?"

Lodge smiled thinly. "Not at all. Some nonsense about a sea serpent that came ashore and started preying on Shandygaff, gobbling up the denizens left and right. Apparently the poor fools burned down most of shantytown trying to kill it."

"Maybe they should've thrown salt on its tail."

"Ha, ha. Actually, this could all work out for the best. That waterfront property is potentially too valuable to waste on a mob of penniless squatters. Now that it's been torched, they can go settle somewhere else, while the land is open for development.

"And the fire saves the problem of tearing down their wretched hovels. Just bulldoze the site, and it's ready for development."

Soto said, "I hope you didn't bring me out here to try and rope me into a land deal."

"Hardly," Lodge said. But before he could explain why he had called the meeting, he was interrupted by the arrival of a servant, a compact islander wearing a white coat and carrying a tray of food and drinks, which he set out on the table.

When he had gone, Lodge said, "Try some of this lobster salad, Steve, it's delicious."

Soto waved away the offer. "No thanks, I'll just have a beer." He twisted off the cap, raising the bottle. "Salud."

"Down the hatch," Lodge said, tilting a gin and tonic.

Dorian said nothing. She nodded, smiling meaninglessly, her eyes hidden behind sunglasses, her feelings—if any—hidden behind the mask of her smooth flawless face.

"You must join us, my dear," Lodge said.

She picked up a glass of sparkling water and took a sip, barely wetting her lips.

Soto said, "It's bad luck to toast with water."

"It's too early for anything else," she said.

Soto gulped half the bottle. "It's good. Good and cold."

"Imported," Lodge said.

"Hell, on this island, even a Bud counts as a fancy imported beer," Soto said. He set the bottle down, leaning his forearms on the table.

He said, "So here we are again, sitting by the sea and having a drink. It's all very pleasant, but what's the pitch?"

Lodge laughed. "You come right to the point, I see."

Dorian murmured. "Direct actionist."

"That's right," Soto said. "Time is money. Besides, it looks like things are breaking fast around here."

"Faster than some might suspect," Lodge said. "I liked the way you handled yourself this morning, Steve."

"Thanks, but you're the one who got results with that salt trick."

Lodge leaned over the table. "You strike me as a man of action, Steve. I imagine you're not averse to earning a fair amount of money for a few hours' work, even if there is a certain element of risk involved."

"Depends on the money and the work."

206

Lodge lifted an eyebrow. "And the risk?"

"I'm a gambler. I don't mind taking calculated risks, as long as the odds are right."

He drank more beer and watched Dorian eat. She didn't really eat, she nibbled. Mostly she pushed the food around on her plate with a fork.

He set down an empty bottle. Luckily there were more beers in the ice bucket on the tray which the servant had left at the table. He took one.

"Shaved ice. Nice," he said. He twisted off the bottle cap and drank. "Let's put our cards on the table—even if they are tarot cards.

"Like everybody else, I like to make a few bucks. What the hell, I'm only human. But I have to know what the deal is first."

"Fair enough," Lodge said. "I—we, Dorian and I, that is—we're going on a little jaunt into the hills. I'd feel more comfortable if you'd come along for protection."

"Protection from what? Spooks?"

"I'll take care of the spooks, Steve. No, people. There'll be a few doubtful characters along on the party and I'd feel better knowing there was someone watching my back.

"And my front. And Dorian's."

She said, "You don't have to pay him to watch my front, he's already doing that for free."

"Now, Dorian, you'll embarrass our guest."

"I doubt it."

Soto broke in. "What people? Who do you want protecting from?"

"Major Quantez will be joining us," Lodge said.

"Hmm."

Lodge held up his hands. "The major is a dear, dear friend of my niece and myself. Still, even under the best of circumstances, he's a man who bears watching."

"Under any circumstances," Dorian said.

Soto asked, "Quantez and who else?"

Lodge said, "His men, of course. He never goes anywhere without an entourage of two or three senior officers and a six-man bodyguard."

Soto leaned back in the chair, holding a beer. "That's a lot of men."

Lodge leaned toward him. "Your two associates seem like capable men."

"They can take care of themselves. And they do what they're told."

"With them along, too, the odds might be more reasonable."

Soto was skeptical. "What kind of a party is this, anyway?"

Dorian said, "Treasure hunt."

Lodge glanced at her, but she was looking down at her plate, worrying the food with a fork.

Lodge faced front, shrugging. "No reason why you can't be told, Steve. If we're going to be working together, you'll have to know. If not—but no, I'm sure I can rely on your discretion."

"Don't worry, I never spoil the other guy's grift."

"That's very reassuring."

"As long as it's not costing me money, that is."

Dorian said, "A man with ethics."

"As long as it's not costing me money," Soto repeated. "Look, folks, you want to tell me, tell me. You don't want to tell me, don't tell me. Either way is fine."

Lodge said smoothly, "Actually, Steve, the only reason I was hesitant about telling you is because I was afraid you'd think I was insulting your intelligence."

"I'm thick-skinned. Try me."

"On the face of it, it sounds like one of the oldest swindles in the world. A lost treasure. Why, the islands are full of lost treasures. Every secluded cove in the Caribbean where a pirate ship might have dropped anchor is rumored to have a lost treasure. The only thing there's more of in these parts than lost treasures is people selling lost-treasure maps.

"So you see, it's difficult to talk about treasure without

looking like a rogue or a fool. But this time it happens to be true. There *is* a treasure. And it's not lost, it's found."

"Found?" Soto said.

"Well, it will be, when we get where we're going."

"The treasure's just going to be sitting around waiting there for you to come and pick it up?"

"Believe it or not, Steve—yes."

"Assuming I do believe it, which is a pretty tall order, what's to stop somebody else from scooping it up?

"Like, say, Quantez?"

Lodge sighed, but he was smiling. "That's where the risk comes in."

"Ah."

"Let's just say there are certain reasons, ironclad reasons, why the major and I must go together to claim the treasure."

"Why? More spook talk?"

Lodge nodded. "Something like that. But you have to concede that a man like Quantez—a man who, to put the best face on it, always has an eye out for the main chance—well, he'd hardly bring me along on a plunder hunt without a very good reason.

"Otherwise, he'd just go and grab the gold for himself."

Soto jumped on that. "So it *is* gold?"

"Gold. Jewels. Pearls. Hard currency," Lodge said.

"What, no magic lamp?"

"Let me give you the background. Up until yesterday, the most powerful individual on this island was a man calling himself Baron Latos. He came here many years ago, claiming to be a Hungarian refugee, although a check of the Hungarian peerage lists no such name. He's lived here so long that he must have been a very old man.

"He was certainly a very remarkable one. Apparently he had genuine hypnotic gifts, and he used them to bedazzle the locals. Isla Morgana is a place where the so-called evil eye is still much feared and respected.

"This Latos set himself up as a kind of cult leader, a voodoo man. Technically it wasn't actually voodoo, or *vodou,* as the Haitian variant is called, but rather a syncretic mélange of *vodou,* Santería, *palo mayombe, brujería,* black magic, and devil worship—never mind about the details.

"The point is that Latos was quite convincing at what he did, and he did very well by it. This part of the West Indies is a center of illicit activity, drugs, smuggling, and gunrunning. The big gang leaders and crime lords paid handsomely for the privilege of being blessed by the voodoo man and put under the protection of the infernal powers."

Soto said, "The treasure."

"Ah, yes, the treasure. Baron Latos was, by all accounts, very Old World, old-fashioned, and something of a crank about money. Didn't trust banks—that type. Had a passion for riches that he could see, touch, gloat over. Gold, jewels, pearls, antiquities, if they were valuable enough.

"That's how he liked to be paid. He amassed quite a fortune, and remember, he didn't like banks. He kept his loot in his house in the hills, where he could sit on top of it like a cackling brood hen.

"Until last night. That's when he ceased to exist.

"Now his treasure is there for the taking."

Lodge's eyes gleamed, his face was flushed with pleasure, and he all but rubbed his hands together in greedy glee.

Soto said, "Not to rain on your parade, but what makes you think the treasure hasn't already been took?"

Lodge shook his head. "It's there, Steve."

"His boys would have grabbed it as soon as he kicked. Maybe before."

"They're not the type."

"Ha. Everybody's the type; if they think they can get away with it."

Lodge smiled patronizingly. "You don't understand the cult-follower mentality."

"I understand human nature."

"His followers have been, ah, let us say, *brainwashed* by a master hypnotist. They're oblivious to such things as greed and earthly riches."

"Not like the rest of us, huh?" Soto's narrowed eyes turned up at the corners.

He said, "I'm starting to get it now. Hypnotism—that'd go a long way toward explaining those so-called zombies."

Dorian said, "Don't you wish."

Lodge said, "It's a point of view."

Soto said, "The treasure is guarded by zombies, huh, Basil?"

"Well, yes. But I'll handle them."

"How? I don't know what makes them tick, but if they're anything like that one in the hotel, those babies can take plenty of firepower."

"It's not a question of firepower but of willpower. Zombies are slaves. It's their nature to obey a master. I've knocked around these islands myself for many years, and I've picked up a few tricks from the native *houngans* and *brujos*, the zombie masters.

"Call it the power of suggestion, call it hocus-pocus if you like, but the fact is that it works. You don't have to believe in it. What matters is that they believe in it."

"Could be," Soto said. "But if the zombies are no problem, why don't you just grab all the treasure for yourself?"

Soto answered his own question. "Quantez. That's why."

Lodge nodded, smiling like a teacher pleased by a student's response. "I'd hate to have to put the major's friendship to such a test."

Soto laughed a dirty laugh. "I bet!"

"You sound like you're starting to become a believer, Steve."

"There had to be a reason behind all this mumbo jumbo, and treasure would fit the bill. Gold and jewels I believe in."

He started winding up his own pitch. "Let's get down to the nut cutting. Once you find the gold, what's to stop Quantez from crossing you and taking it all himself?"

"That's where you come in."

"And that's where Quantez goes out, huh?"

Lodge looked faintly scandalized, as if someone had

made an off-color remark, but he was broad-minded enough to let it pass. "That's putting it a little more strongly than I would have, but yes, that's essentially correct."

Dorian's face was raised now, and behind her sunglasses her gaze shifted back and forth between Soto and Lodge.

"That simplifies things," Soto said. "Here's my deal. An even split, fifty-fifty."

Lodge choked on his gin and tonic. He sputtered, face red, eyes tearing. Dorian, blank-faced, rested her fingertips on his forearm.

When he had stopped coughing, he cried, "Steve! *Steve!*"

"Cut the crap," Soto said, cheerfully enough. Cheerful because he was already figuring how he could grab all the treasure.

He said, "You don't want much. You just want Quantez knocked off, which means knocking off all of his boys, too. That's eight, ten kills. That's a lot of guys to whack all at one time, even in a crummy country like this. And they've all got guns, too.

"No, half sounds right. Even then, it's no sure thing, but I'll take a chance."

Lodge used the corner of a linen napkin to blot the tears from his eyes. "I, ah, I daresay that some of Quantez's men will probably drop out along the way, without your having to take a hand in it, if you know what I mean."

"That'll be fine. Anything that cuts them down ups our odds. But it's still half."

"Steve!"

"Half."

Lodge groaned. "You don't have any mercy, there's no pity in you at all."

"Deal with Quantez, see where that gets you."

Lodge purpled, making a disgusted face, snorting. "Pfaw! All right, all right, you know I don't have a choice."

"Deal?"

"Yes!"

"For half."

"Yes, yes." Lodge scowled, drumming his fingertips on the table.

"Okay," Soto said. "Plus some front money."

Lodge yelped. Soto said, "Look, all I have is your say-so that there's a pot of gold at the end of the rainbow. If it turns out to be a chamber pot, I still want to be compensated for my time and effort.

"A little front money. Call it a good-faith gesture."

"And how much would it take to secure your good faith?" Lodge asked, still scowling, one eyebrow arched like a coach whip.

Soto said, "Five big ones."

"This is a stickup. Very well, five hundred dollars."

Soto shook his head. "Uh-uh. Five thousand dollars."

"A bit steep, don't you think?" Lodge's rising voice cracked at the end of the sentence.

"Back home, a guy like me can pull down fifty big ones for a hit. Fifty thousand dollars for one kill," Soto said. Actually, he had never gotten more than half that sum on his biggest jobs, but no one could call him on it if he padded his résumé down here.

"You're not in the States now, Steve."

"Don't I know it! If the treasure's even half what it's cracked up to be, what's five thousand to you?

"Tell you what. When we find the treasure, I'll give the five thousand back to you. That's *my* good-faith gesture."

"I suppose I can't say no."

"You can say it, but it'll be a deal killer."

Lodge did some more groaning before he gave in. "All right, you win."

Dorian said, "A man of ethics."

"Sure. I'm only taking half," Soto said.

Lodge asked, "What about your associates?"

"I'll take care of them out of my end."

"Very generous of you."

"No need to get sarcastic. And no need to discuss our arrangements with them."

"Certainly not. And now that that's settled, we'll have to move quickly."

"It's settled when I get my five thousand, Basil."

Dorian said, "A one-track mind."

"Call it what you like, as long as I get paìd."

Lodge pushed back his chair, rising. "Come with me."

He turned and went inside, Soto following, Dorian lingering a few paces behind. Lodge parked Soto in the drawing room and told him to wait, then went away, into another part of the house.

A couple of minutes later he returned with a packet of fifty-dollar bills, giving it to Soto, who made it disappear.

Lodge said, "I'm surprised you didn't count it, to make sure it's all there."

"I usually do, but this time I thought I'd play it big," Soto said.

"It's done? We have a contract now?" Lodge asked.

"That's right." Softly.

"To business, then." Lodge became brisk, focused. "We'll all be meeting at one o'clock this afternoon at the Ministry, then we'll head out from there.

"It's important that you and your men be there on time so we can get an early start."

"We'll be there. This house in the hills, is it far?"

"No, Steve, it's not far. With any luck, we'll be there and back before nightfall."

Dorian said, "We'd better be."

Soto asked, "What about weapons?"

Lodge said, "Tell me what you need and we'll get them."

"We've got our own pieces, but we could use more firepower. Nothing complicated, handguns and shotguns. We're simple fellows."

"There's no shortage of guns on the island. They'll be ready for you to pick up at the Ministry."

Lodge pretended to look at his watch. "Time you were going. Dorian will give you a lift back to town.

"I'm sure you'll like that."

Soto said, "What's not to like?" He dropped the bundle

214

of bills into an inside jacket pocket, then turned to Dorian. "Lead on."

She shouldered her pocketbook and started out of the room, Soto following. When they had reached the far side of the room, Lodge called his name.

Soto turned, looking back.

"One more thing, Steve. I'd hate for there to be any misunderstanding between friends. If I should fail to return from our road trip for some reason, and be unable to drop a word in the right ears, I'd have to say that your chances of getting off the island alive would be virtually nil. Zero.

"Just a word to the wise guy, hmmm?"

Soto said, "I'd be worried if you didn't have an ace up your sleeve, because that'd mean you're too stupid to live, and I don't figure you for a dumb guy.

"Deal straight with no crosses and we'll be fine."

Lodge nodded. "Take good care of my five thousand dollars."

"What about your niece?"

"She can take care of herself."

Dorian and Soto went through the house, out the front door, and into the drive. The sky was hazy, gray, humid.

She held out the keys. "Don't you want to drive?"

"I don't like to crap around with a stick shift. You drive."

They got in the car and drove out the gates and down the cape road. "Nice breeze," Soto said.

She didn't say anything.

He said, "He really your uncle?"

"He likes me to call him that," she said, after a pause.

She rolled through the checkpoint at the neck of the cape, wheeling north on the coast road. When they were about halfway between the cape and the harbor, she slowed the car, pulling off the road, and following a bumpy dirt path to a secluded bluff overlooking the sea.

She switched off the engine. They sat in silence, eyeing the seascape.

Dorian said, "What'll you take to kill him? Uncle Basil, I mean."

"I'm open to any reasonable offer."

"Me, too," she said.

"I always get paid something in advance," Soto said, reaching for her.

216

216

THIRTEEN

Glendon came to the village of Frankenstein, what was left of it. It was in the lonely country between the desolate south shore of Lake Lorelei in Visaria and the foothills of the northern Alps. The lost village was situated along the winding watercourse of the Frankenthal, in German "the valley of the Franks," named for the pagan Frankish tribes who had made this empty land of rolling hills and river valleys their own during the late days of the Roman Empire.

Now it was an empire of the lost. Sometimes during World War II, the dam that had held the river in check had been blown up, flooding the valley and causing hundreds of lives to be lost. The area had been abandoned and never resettled.

On today's maps, the region was sketchy, vaguely delineated. Glendon had needed to study some pre-WWII maps from the university library archives to get a proper picture of the countryside.

Getting here was not too difficult, at least not in the early stages of the journey. A few hours' train trip through the Chunnel had taken him from England to Paris, where a daily shuttle flight had taken him to the city-state of Visaria. He had been pleasantly surprised at how relatively easy it was to reach the picturesque, Tyrolean-style city on the lake. Apparently little Visaria, with its business-friendly atmosphere, was becoming something of a magnet for Euro-capitalists, businesspeople, and bankers who found the state's laissez-faire, regulation-light climate a good place from which to establish transnational operations.

From Visaria he had taken a hire car to Riegelberg, a modest-sized settlement on the edge of the Frankenthal. He had stayed overnight at the town's only inn, which maintained a few rooms for the use of tourists.

Early this morning, at first light, he had set out for the lost village of Frankenstein, using the only means of transportation available: footpower. Cracked, weed-grown roads and washed-out bridges that had never been repaired denied the area to cars and trucks. An off-road, four-wheel-drive vehicle like a Jeep might have made at least part of the trip, but there was none available for hire.

That presented no real problem for Glendon, who as an explorer and ethno-botanist had journeyed to the far places of the world, hiking through the Andes Mountains, the Amazon jungle, the high plateaus of Central Asia, and many other faraway places.

He was trail-ready, wearing a forager's cap with a short, stiff brim; layers of lightweight, rugged outerwear; and a well-broken-in pair of hiking boots. Slung across his back was a tubular-frame backpack fitted with a complete kit, including a pup tent, bedroll, canteen, food, matches, and other necessities for living off the land. He'd also brought a camera and film and a collecting box for soil and plant samples.

In a waterproof case safely tucked away in an inside jacket pocket he also had his paperwork, his passport and identity documents, his hiking permit, his camping permit, his permit to build a fire on state-owned land, and the like. The smaller the state, the bigger the bureaucracy was a good general rule of thumb, and obtaining state-approved documents could often be a traveler's nightmare, but Glendon had been pleasantly surprised at how easy and hassle-free the experience had been when he went to the Visarian municipal hall. The government clerks had been polite and helpful, extending themselves to cut through the red tape and send him on his way. It had been a pleasant experience.

Soon after he had hit the trail this morning, Glendon had fallen into the steady, easygoing stride of the veteran hiker. The air was brisk and the sunlight thin, but the exercise had soon warmed him up. With its rolling hills, meadows, and valleys, the countryside had reminded him of the terrain along the upper Rhône and Rhine rivers, only somewhat stonier and more alpine.

For much of the way he followed the old highway, an ancient two-lane road whose pavement was so cracked and eroded that it was easier on the feet to walk on the shoulder rather than the road itself.

The highway wound into obscurity, following the path of least resistance through a vista of rolling plains, terraced in gentle rises like the long, swelling billows of a calm day at sea. The pale blue sky was hazed with a layer of thin, high clouds.

This was country where every few hundred yards or so, rose another rounded slope or shallow ridge. Long stretches of it were open, the weedy fields of dry, matted brown grass dusted with a thin powdering of snow. As the morning sun rose, the snow melted into nothingness.

By midday, the parklike meadows had given way to a long, low humped ridge that stretched across the southern horizon. There were many traces of former human habitation, the ruins of abandoned stone farmhouses, and the cratered, bombed-out husks of crossroads settlements that had been destroyed during the war.

The old highway sloped upward along the side of the ridge, leveling out at a gap in the hills, a pass leading into the river valley of the Frankenthal.

The river was still there, winding through the valley floor, sometimes narrow, swift, and deep, other times spreading out in a broad shallow channel, winding through a countryside of brown embankments, fields of golden dead weeds, and dark blue-green thickets and woods.

Glendon paused, admiring the scenery. He checked his

compass and maps, noting his position and verifying that he was on the right track. He didn't use the compass and maps much, didn't need to, even though this was unknown territory to him. He'd always had a good sense of direction and had never really gotten lost in the wilderness.

The old highway now branched off in opposite directions, one following the riverbank upstream, one going downstream. Glendon took the upstream fork, traveling east.

An hour or two of brisk walking brought him to the central valley, where he began to see real evidence of flood damage. Boulders and tall trees and mounds of wreckage littered the sides of the riverbed for a mile, where they had finally been deposited after being carried away by the floodtide when the dam broke.

By early afternoon he reached the village of Frankenstein.

Its remnants stood on a rise above the river, the slopes leading down to a stream bed that was littered with the jumbled ruins of entire city blocks, undermined and overthrown by the flood.

Much of the main body of the village had escaped the waters, though the farms and estates on the once-rich bottomland had been swept away. The ground was marked by lemon-yellow streaks, some of them dozens of yards wide and scores of yards long, residue from the sulfur pits which had been located farther upstream. The stuff had been deposited in the backwash of the flood, tainting and poisoning the farmland. The toxic waste went a long way in explaining why the valley had never been resettled.

The part of the village still standing looked like a relic of wartime. It was mostly the gutted shells of burned-out buildings. Everything was dirty, covered in a layer of fine yellow-brown dirt from the denuded riverbanks and slopes, piled up in little drifts at the corners of upright stone slabs.

Blackbirds roosted in the bare branches of dead trees, the only sign of life in the area beside Glendon himself.

He hiked on, leaving the village behind as he followed the path upstream. His stomach growled with hunger, but he

220

decided to wait until he was farther away from the ruins before eating his lunch. It was a depressing site.

He rounded a bend and came in sight of the wrecked dam. Once it had walled off a rocky gorge, a curving concrete bulwark a hundred feet high that had penned up the river waters, using them to generate power at a hydroelectric plant that was part of the complex.

Now the middle of the high concrete wall was missing, leaving a jagged V-shaped gap that looked as if something had taken a giant bite out of it. Strewn carelessly along the side slopes was rusted metal scaffolding, twisted and torn, the remains of high-tension power-line towers that had been trashed by the flood.

Glendon sat on top of a trailside boulder in the sun, overlooking the gorge, while he ate his lunch. The meal was made up of thin chewy strips of dried high-protein meat and handfuls of trail mix, washed down with sips of water from his canteen. It was standard backpacker's fare, lightweight, energy-plus food concentrate, not tasty but nutritious.

Still, he couldn't help longing for real food, a nice thick juicy steak, served up blood-rare and sizzling with juices. Thinking about it made his mouth water. He could really sink his teeth into some fresh red meat . . .

When he had finished eating, he followed a dirt path down to the river to make the crossing. The massive blocks of rubble from the wrecked dam formed a causeway spanning the river, with the water swirling and chuckling and streaming through the spaces of the stones before re-forming into a solid stream that flowed downstream.

Glendon clambered over the huge blocks, jumping from stone to stone, leaping across the river to the other side.

Flights of stone steps that were once part of the complex zigzagged up the side of the gorge. Glendon climbed them. As he neared the midpoint, he noticed a knob of rock jutting out from the cliffs, about the hundred yards to his right and down. The hillside and riverbank below it were tiger-streaked with giant yellow splashes and stripes.

Projecting from the flattened top of the knob, the base

of a vanished structure stuck out like the stump of a broken tooth.

This had once been the site of the lab of Frankenstein, the charnel workshop where Henry Frankenstein and later his son, Wolf, had conducted their research into the secrets of life and death.

Below, in underground caverns winding deep into the hillside, lay the sulfur pits whose flooding had polluted the river valley. That same dam-busting flood had swept the lab building from its rocky perch, washing it away.

It was a fascinating site and Glendon would have liked to have stopped and explored it, but he passed it by and kept on climbing, driven by some inexplicable force that prodded him on to his goal.

The nature of that compulsion was a mystery to him, and on those few occasions that he had tried to analyze it, it seemed to defy logical understanding.

The impulse had first come to him in the aftermath of the night that Carol had walked out on him. It was something new and disturbing to have one of his female guests quit his bed that way, but that wasn't what bothered him. What had really gotten under his skin was his waking up on the hallway floor with no memory of how he had gotten there, coupled with some extraordinarily vivid fragments of dreams of stalking and blood-lust that he had managed to remember.

He'd had no classes to teach at the university that day, so he had canceled the rest of his appointments and stayed home, closeted in his study with the Ames Testament and piles of other Glendon I material that he had collected to feed his expanding appetite for knowledge about the family history.

Hours had flown by as he'd sat hunched over the desk, poring over the documents, notebooks, and folders full of clippings. He possessed the gift of concentration and had dug deep into the material, until his eyes burned and his head swam.

Somehow he'd fallen into a kind of stupor, looking at the

same sentences for minutes at a time, during which they still failed to make sense to him.

Something from outside caught his attention and broke the spell, causing him to look up. For the first time he noticed how dark it was in the study, beyond the circle of lamplight bathing the desktop. The sun had set and it was dark outside.

Something tapped on the window, a soft, steady tapping. He couldn't see what was causing it, a windblown tree branch, probably. It came again, steady and insistent. The window was on the ground floor, but it was still too high for somebody to stand outside and knock on the glass.

He got up to see what it was, groaning from the stiffness of cramped limbs that had been motionless for too long. He went to the window, starting when he saw something that looked like a broken kite flapping in the air on the other side of the glass. A black kite.

No, not a kite at all, but an animate thing, a blackbird or raven. Raven, from the size of it. It was huge, with a three-foot wingspan.

It wasn't a bird, it was a bat. No mistaking those over-sized pointed "sonar" ears, the ratlike snout and body, those devilish leathery wings.

It was the biggest bat he'd ever seen in the British Isles. It looked like a South American vampire bat. He'd seen bats in the Guyanas that were that big, and in the Amazon jungle, the genuine blood-drinking vampire bat.

But there were no vampire bats in England, not indigenous ones, anyway. And yet, unless his eyes had completely deceived him, or his mind had slipped, that was a vampire bat flapping and hovering right outside his window.

The tips of its pointed wings bumping against the glass panes were what had caused the tapping sound.

Perhaps the creature had escaped from a zoo or private menagerie. He supposed it would be a good idea to call the animal-control people; the bat could be sick or even rabid. And if it was left loose for more than a night or two in the chilly early spring nights, it would probably sicken and die.

It had red eyes, remarkably bright button-sized red eyes. They were glowing. At first he thought it was a trick of the light, a weird effect produced by stray reflections. But the eyes weren't reflecting light, they were producing light, glowing redly.

An eye-catching phenomenon, unique, fascinating. He couldn't look away. The eyes held him, the bat fluttering outside the window, hovering at eye level.

Red eyes blurred, grew, brightening, expanding, filling his field of vision . . .

The next thing he knew, he was waking up at his desk, where he must have been napping with his head pillowed on folded arms. He felt light-headed, airy. Tranquilized, as if the edge of stress had been blunted.

He stretched, yawning then groaning as he tried to work some of the kinks out of his sore, tired muscles. What time was it? A glance at the desk clock showed that it was almost midnight.

That shocked him. He'd been sleeping for hours! He hadn't known how tired he was. The rest had done him good, he felt better. Or at least, different.

Remembering the bat, he wondered if he had dreamed that, too. He must have. There were no vampire bats living in London!

Suddenly he became aware that something on the desktop was out of place. Amid all the controlled chaos of his research materials and the Ames papers, something new had been added, a big scrapbook-sized album whose richly tooled but weathered leather binding indicated that it was at least fifty years old.

He picked up the book, holding it in both hands. He recognized it immediately. It was an album which had belonged to his grandmother, Lisa Glendon-Ames, a kind of combination scrapbook, journal, memory book, and compendium of family photos, letters, and the like. It dated from the period when she had been married to Wilfred Glendon, although the contents had been culled from a variety of sources, many predating the wedding.

Glendon knew the book; he had dipped into it before. There were many interesting bits and references to the family history, more than a few of which he had marked down in the past as subjects for future research.

But he had last looked at it some time ago, long before he had received the Ames papers, and had not looked at it since. Had not needed to, since he deemed it irrelevant to the main line of his current research.

He didn't remember taking it down from the shelf, and yet there it was in front of him, right on his desktop. In fact, it had been opened and partly lying under his arms when he had folded them on the desk and put his head in them, resting it.

Was he suffering from sleepwalking fits? Seemed hard to believe, and yet impossible to ignore in light of the experiences of the previous night and now this.

"I really must be working too hard," he said to himself.

Idle curiosity made him glance at the place to which the album had been opened. An old packet of letters lay there, tucked into the spine of the book. They were lavender-colored and age-dried, like pressed flowers.

He examined the packet. It was one that he knew well and had indeed mentally filed under the "for future investigation" heading. They contained the record of a correspondence with Elizabeth Frankenstein, the wife of Henry Frankenstein. She and the future Lisa Glendon had attended the same school, an exclusive and expensive finishing school for the daughters of the upper crust. They had gone their separate ways upon reaching adulthood but had remained friends.

Strange destiny, that had thrown together as schoolgirls the future wives of Henry Frankenstein, the man who created a monster, and Wilfred Glendon, the savant who was the victim, if only indirectly, of the monstrous Werewolf of London, Dr. Yogami.

That's what Glendon thought then about the Werewolf murders.

He riffled through the letters, the paper on which they

were written brittle as dead leaves, the sheets filled with neat lines of elegant handwriting. They reflected only one-half of the correspondence, namely the letters from Elizabeth to Lisa.

Going through the pages, with whose contents he was already familiar, he came to a well-remembered passage which seemed to be inscribed in letters of fire, so boldly and forthrightly did they stand out from the rest of the text:

> . . . *Henry was very excited today. Apparently he'd been telling that horrible Dr. Pretorius (ugh!) about your Wilfred's ingenious Moon-Ray device, and now they both feel that the invention could help supply the breakthrough they've been seeking in their work. What that work might be is still a mystery to me, since Henry's been so elaborately secretive about it.*
>
> *In all candor, I think I prefer not knowing about it, for I fear that nothing good can come of the too-close, almost unwholesome relationship that has developed between my husband and the "good" Dr. Septimus Pretorius . . .*

There was more, but that was the important part.

The Moon-Ray! The most cryptic of his grandfather's discoveries, as mysterious as the mariphasa plant itself. A machine that made moonlight, for a plant that bloomed only in moonlight!

There was something important here, something vital. As soon as he had read—or rather, reread—the passage, he was struck by a theory, a belief that was so strong that it was almost a conviction, that the secret of the Moon-Ray was the key to solving the mystery of the Glendon Curse and to ending the family history of tragedy.

Odd how that belief had sprung to life full-blown in his mind, establishing itself with rocklike firmness, certainty. Ordinarily his mind didn't work like that. He was a scientist, dedicated to the empirical method as the test of truth. His sudden conversion to belief in the Moon-Ray was more of a leap of faith than the product of careful, rational analysis.

And yet, he did believe it. It was stronger than theory, it was a force. Such unquestioned adherence to an unproven theory gave him a few misgivings, but that queer light-headedness that had come over him since awakening from the dream—if dream it had been—of the vampire bat quickly brushed aside all doubts from his mind.

The logical part of his mind searched for a rational explanation, and found it in the workings of the unconscious mind. For weeks now he had been obsessing about the Ames papers and the family curse, and his subconscious was merely holding up a dark mirror to that mental turmoil. That plus fatigue had caused the nightmares of blood, death, and horror.

That same subconscious had also supplied a solution to the problem. It had created a somnambulistic experience, causing him to sleepwalk to the bookshelves, select the appropriate volume, and leave it on his desk, open to the very page that contained the clue he was seeking. The dreaming submind that never sleeps had solved the problem that eluded the grasp of his waking rationality.

Although he knew the explanation was a little too pat, it fit the facts and he leaped at it. He needed something to explain this sudden impulse, verging on compulsion, to be up and doing, taking bold actions to solve the secret of the Moon-Ray as swiftly and decisively as a general with superior forces takes a city.

All that had followed in the hectic thirty-six-hour period since the great revelation had been geared to that end. He had shunted aside all other obligations, packing his bags and making arrangements to go to Visaria, where the final solution waited.

He didn't know how he knew it, but he knew it.

And so now here he was in the Frankenthal, in the shadow of the Alps, finally within a few miles' walking distance of his goal.

He reached the top of the south side of the gorge. The

land ahead was essentially the same as that on the other side, except that it was emptier and even more lonely. Even the ruins were fewer and more widely spaced.

He trudged on, under a sun that had passed its zenith and had begun its inexorable decline to the west. He went west, following a road that paralleled the course of the river upstream.

The landscape became monotonous, an endless flat plain of bare gray trees, colorless hard-packed dead grass, and reddish-brown earth. It had a worn, weary aspect, like the bottom of a million-years-dry seabed on Mars.

On the flat, upright objects could be seen a long way off. So it was with the tower. It rose in the distance like a truncated road marker or milepost.

It took a lot of hiking before Glendon was any nearer to the landmark. When the sun had been at its height at midday, the temperature had risen to about fifty degrees. When Glendon finally reached the tower, the sun was halfway to the horizon and the temperature had dropped by about ten degrees.

Set back from the south side of the road, about a stone's throw away, was a mound of rubble topped by what looked like a lopsided pyramid.

Glendon went to it, crossing a field of knee-high weeds. The mound was raised about twenty feet above the ground and the pyramidal shape on top of it was another ten feet high.

Glendon said, "The tower!"

He moved closer, walking around the cornerstone-sized paving blocks that littered the weed-grown front field. Nearing the mound, what had looked like a pyramid was revealed to be the base of a square-sided stone tower, the upper half of which had collapsed.

Built sometime in the late Middle Ages, the structure had originally been a watchtower, an observation post for spying out invading armies. More recently, the tower had been an outpost on a different frontier, the far reaches of the life sciences, for it had housed the laboratory of Dr. Pretorius.

It was here that he and Henry Frankenstein had attempted the creation of the New Eve of the coming race of super-humans, with the Moon-Ray acting as midwife to that epoch-making debut.

And it was here that the intended Bride of the Franken-stein Monster had defied the expectations of her creators and the would-be groom by rejecting the Monster as a mate, trig-gering a furious outburst of thwarted mad love that had caused the Monster to throw the switch that overloaded the energy storage tanks, unleashing a cataclysmic explosion that overthrew the tower.

Henry and Elizabeth Frankenstein escaped, but Pretorius, the Bride, and the Monster were all engulfed in the de-struction. Later there were persistent rumors that the Mon-ster had somehow managed to survive, but no such rumors had ever circulated about Pretorius or the Bride.

Could they be buried somewhere under the rubble? Pre-torius would long since have turned to bones, but the Bride was differently made.

Glendon scrambled up the side of the mound to the top. He unshouldered his backpack, setting it down for the first time since taking the trail at dawn. It was like removing lead weights.

He walked around the tower, surveying the situation. On the opposite side, the one facing away from the road, he made a discovery.

A shaft had been sunk in that side of the mound, a tun-nel slanting down into the vaults below the tower. It was similar to a miner's excavation, and had been ably shorn up with braces and crossbeams. Much of the tunnel mouth had collapsed and was buried under stones and dirt, but enough of the digging remained to be clearly seen.

Glendon wanted to investigate further, but this side of the mound was too steep for him to descend, so he walked around to another side of the tower, where the angle was more invit-ing.

As he came around the base of the tower, which until

then had hidden him from the road, just as it hid the road from him, a blur of distant movement caught his eye.

It came from the direction in which he had come, in the middle distance near the edge of a clump of trees. For an instant he glimpsed a clutch of antlike figures moving in the fields.

He blinked, and when he looked again, they were gone. He stood there for a long time, motionless, watching, but whatever he had seen, or thought he had seen, did not return.

Shadows were growing long. Chill winds made the thinning sunlight seem ever more like a transparent yellow wash dimming in the weight of oncoming darkness.

In the east, high in the pale blue sky, was the moon, a wan daylight ghost of itself. Still, the sight of it was somehow thrilling to Glendon, exhilarating.

He retrieved his pack and slung it over a shoulder, then climbed down the easy side slope of the mound.

He circled around to the tunnel mouth. It was old, the few timbers visible being stony with age. The excavation was filled to the brim, choked with dirt and stones. It looked like the diggers had dynamited the tunnel when they were done, sealing it up. The tunnel slanted deep into the core of the mound. Glendon wondered what the diggers had found.

No lone man could clear that tunnel. A work crew could, but would it be worth it to hire some men from Riegelberg to do the work?

The tunnel mouth proved that someone had been here before, a long time ago, someone who knew what to look for. If there was something or someone to be found, the unknown diggers would have found it. No doubt there were many items buried there of genuine scientific interest, but the facts argued that the big prize was gone.

It should have been bitterly disappointing to find that someone had gotten here decades before him, but instead it was oddly comforting. It was confirmation, validation.

His hunch that had bordered on mania had proved right. There was something of value buried under the tower. And what one person could discover, another person could re-discover.

He said, "I was right! I'm on the trail of one of the most important scientific marvels of our time."

He was expert at following trails, picking up the scent and dogging it until he'd brought down the game. Scientifically speaking, that is.

He noticed that his eyes were watery and burning and that his nose itched. Looking around, he saw that he had been unknowingly standing in a patch of gnarly, weedy bushes, which he now immediately recognized.

"Aconite," he said. "Better known as wolfbane."

Odd . . . the wolfbane shouldn't have been in bloom yet, not until much later in the month, if then. These were blooming out of season. An anomaly, really. Perhaps there had been a recent unseasonable warm spell in these parts which had tricked their bioclock, coaxing them to come to fullness at the ragged start of spring, in advance of their rightful time.

The weed had a distinctive musky herbal scent, not easily forgotten once known. The smell seemed to hang around him in a cloud, dusting him with pollen, tickling his nose—he sneezed!

He moved away from it, going around to the front of the mound. It would be getting dark soon and he'd better pitch camp while it was still light.

He picked a site on a walled pavement square not far from the tower. By dusk, his pup tent was set up and a campfire was blazing, with a large stack of kindling standing nearby.

He sat near the fire, using a dead tree branch for a seat, warming himself in the glow, eating a meal from his ration packs and washing it down with swigs of canteen water.

The tower loomed blackly against the colorless sky as the light went out of it. Somehow it reminded him of a lighthouse, marooned on the shoals of time.

He supposed it was risky to light a fire, he being a lone traveler in an unpoliced wilderness, but he was in a devil-may-care mood. He'd had a long hard day's trek and he'd be damned if he'd go without a toasty fire on a cold night like this.

The long hike had tired him out, his eyes especially. They felt weary, irritated. He wondered if he'd experienced a mild allergic reaction to the wolfbane. He could still smell it, or imagined that he could. He could almost see the pollen cloud as a smudged haze floating over the scene, blurring his vision with swathes of swirly red-tinged mist . . .

What he needed was some sleep. The tent was set up but he decided to sleep outside it, under the stars. It wasn't that cold, and besides his sleeping bag was insulated. He set up his bedroll in the lee of a crumbling stone wall, whose surface would act as a reflector, catching the heat from the campfire and pitching it back at him.

He was physically fatigued but mentally excited. He took a couple of long pulls from the flask of whiskey he'd brought with him, its good warm glow easing his nervous tension.

A folded jacket served as his pillow. He climbed into the sleeping bag with his clothes on, except for his hiking boots, which stood nearby.

Wind blew through a nearby thicket of trees, carrying a heady pine scent. The fire popped and crackled, radiating red warmth.

A crescent moon rose over the trees, etched in crystal clarity by the crisp night air. Moonlight bathed him with its sublime soothing rays, soaking into his skin.

He closed his eyes, drifting off . . .

There was a sensation of falling, dizzying, breathless. It woke him up and he sat up in the sleeping bag, his heart pounding.

The moon was much higher in the sky and the fire had burned down low, to a flickering red glow. The paved stones beneath him felt noticeably cooler, even through the heaped fresh-cut pine boughs that served as a mattress.

How long had he slept? Why, he had only closed his eyes for a moment, just to rest them!

232

The firelight was dim, coloring all with a red tint. Despite that, he could see pretty clearly.

Rustling sounds of furtive motion to one side attracted his attention, coming from where he had set down his knapsack. It was being ransacked by what looked to be a pack of little men and women.

Little people, a handful of them, no bigger than fifteen inches tall, male and female. Well formed and well proportioned, nothing dwarfish about them.

They wore garments made from rags, leaves, bits of bone, feathers, and fur. They were armed with foot-long steel slivers that they carried like spears, and swordlike six-inch needles.

They had the knapsack open and they were stealing Glendon's food.

He said, "Hey!"

The minikins vanished, gone to cover.

Glendon was more bemused than anything else. "Little people? This is Visaria, not Ireland. Though they looked like leprechauns.

"No, wait, I've got the answer!

"*Homunculi,* the tiny humanoids grown in the vats by Dr. Pretorius as a prelude to the creation of the Bride!

"Some of them must have survived the fall of the tower and built a colony here. They could be the descendants of the originals, or, given the superhuman qualities of the vatborn, they might even be the originals themselves!"

Glendon crawled out of his sleeping bag to throw more kindling onto the fire, beefing it up. He went to his knapsack and took out a packet of trail mix containing some nuts and dried fruits and laid it out in the open, on the other side of the fire away from him and his gear.

He didn't want them coming too close to him while he slept, not with their sharp-pointed weapons and other impish tricks.

It was an amazing discovery, but he was too tired to grapple with the implications just now. His eyes still burned. That wolfbane was really getting to him. Perhaps his resistance was low because of all the stress he'd recently been under.

The trek had tired him out more than he'd thought. He couldn't keep his eyes open. His limbs felt heavy, leaden. Gravity drew him down, so that he lay on his back in the bedroll.

He fell through the ground, down into the black between the stars.

Images took shape around him. He was dreaming. So he told himself.

Images, faces, scenes, all floating up in the embryonic darkness, pregnant with reason's sleep.

Bats flew, red-eyed. A clay man raged. A she-demon schemed. She had red eyes, too. A wolf howled.

He could see better with his eyes closed. It was like his eyelids were transparent. No, like his whole body was transparent, a ghostly man-shaped bubble floating in red mist.

In that mist, a scene took form:

Strangers came to the fallen tower, a grim-faced black-clad work crew. Their leader was a striking individual, a saturnine silver-haired man with a turnip-shaped head, a V-shaped hairline, pointed eyebrows, and dark mocking eyes in a High Priest's face. A High Priest of Satan.

It was a famous face, one that Glendon immediately recognized. This was Hjalmar Poelzig, Engineer Poelzig, to give him his proper title—or at least one of them.

He had been renowned as one of a handful of world-class engineers in his day, one of the visionary shapers of Europe in that period between the First and Second World Wars. He had built some of the most famous structures of the day, including the showpiece Munich Engel Haus, the Cisalpine Highway Tunnel Number Five, Rotterdam's Cubist Cathedral, and many others.

"The Prague Speer," they had called him. Poelzig's fame as a builder was later eclipsed by his notoriety as a satanic cult leader. Like his detested rival Aleister Crowley, Poelzig regarded himself as the rightful pretender to the Black

Throne. Unlike Crowley, Poelzig was more circumspect about his occult activities.

Yes, Glendon knew who Poelzig was.

And Poelzig knew who Pretorius was. That was evident from the content of the vision, which showed the supreme engineer bossing his crew as they sank a shaft into the side of the mound.

The scene shifted, becoming a montage of images: Poelzig and company digging the tunnel, shoring it up as they went along, burrowing into the core of the mound.

The shaft broke through into the underground vaults. Poelzig led the way, clad in a white hard hat with a built-in miner's lantern, a shoulder-padded black jumpsuit, and a white tool belt. His men were similarly outfitted.

The little people, the *homunculi,* feared Poelzig and went away and hid when he came.

Engineer and acolytes disappeared into the depths, emerging with the body of the Bride. She was wrapped in a canvas sheet, mummylike, making it easier for them to carry her.

She was brought out under the full moon and unwrapped, then placed inside a crystal coffin. A lustful gloating leer transfixed Poelzig's face as he stood over the container, caressingly running his hands over the transparent shell, tracing out the contours of the Amazonian body within. He seemed to thrill to her sunken blue-shadowed eyes and dead blue-white complexion . . .

The tunnel was dynamited shut and the Bride in the clear coffin was hefted on the shoulders of the black-clad claw and taken away, the tomb looters dissolving into red mist along with their treasure . . .

The scene broke up into a blizzard of red motes falling through black space.

A woman stood on one knee beside him, where he lay on his back in the sleeping bag. She was a petite young beauty, with a lovely piquant face. She wore a pearly gray robe with hooded mantle, in a style that took its cue more from Hollywood than from churchly couture.

Her hand was on his shoulder, shaking him.

"Glendon—rise, rise!"

Her lips pulled back as she spoke, revealing fangs, and now he knew her. She was his nightmare vampire queen of blood.

He froze, paralyzed.

"Rise quickly, lest they slay you!"

—She was gone. Everything else seemed unchanged, fire, pavement square, crumbling wall, night.

No. Again the moon was higher and the fire had once again burned down low.

He was seized with a rush of pure terror, a physical thing. It got so intense he thought he couldn't stand it anymore and then a great red fountain opened up somewhere inside his head, spewing a jolt of hot red blood that burst in his brain, a gusher.

Tingling red heat raced through him, eating up the cold chill of fear, burning him up from inside.

It was good. He could breathe again. He exhaled in a long, low throaty murmur that sounded like a growl.

His blood boiled, stewing his brain. Red mist was everywhere, inside and outside his head. The scene was colored by it, even the air. Murky air, thick, swimming, seething.

Like his brain.

He was outside the sleeping bag, standing up. He felt strange, different. The shape of his body, the proportions seemed gnarled, distorted, like an image in a funhouse mirror.

It didn't feel wrong, or bad. Just different. Not bad at all, really.

He looked around. The food he'd left out for the *homunculi* was gone, and so were they. They'd gone to cover, ducking into their hideyholes.

Just as well. They wouldn't make much more than a mouthful each—

What put that thought into his head? Must be feeling bloody-minded tonight.

236

A spotlight was beaming down on him, shining into his face. He cringed, then realized it was the moon.

So bright!

It lit his way as he hopped up and moved away from the campsite. He looked down, surprised to see that he was wearing big furry slippers. Where had they come from?

He was barefoot.

The moonlight was too bright. He shunned it, seeking the shadows. Crouching low, padding soft-footed, he moved stealthily with near-balletic grace that would have amazed him if he had done so while in his right mind.

He jumped up on top of the wall, running along it to the end, then leaping into the air, soaring over some tall bushes to land silently on his feet in a tree-ringed clearing.

He sniffed the air. Somewhere there were enemies in the vicinity, danger. He could smell it. Them.

A rustle of approaching motion caught his attention and he became still more feral, murderous.

Red mists thickened, blanketing him, smothering him, burying him in a haunted fever dream.

When the mists cleared, he found himself lurking in a clump of brush, peering red-eyed at three men standing in a moonlit clearing near the mound.

Two of them were hard-faced, wide-built thugs in their thirties. The third was ten years younger, smooth-faced and wiry.

Not quite strangers. Glendon remembered seeing them before, last night at the inn at Riegelberg. They'd been drinking by themselves at a table and they'd stopped talking when he came in. After a pause, they had started talking again.

Come to think of it, earlier today, when he'd walked through the sleeping village on his way to the foot of the trail, the youth had been loitering around near the inn.

They spoke in low, excited voices, but they might have been shouting, the way Glendon's hypersensitive ears could hear them. They spoke German, a language in which he was fluent. Even without words he would have gotten the gist of what they were about.

The big men were named Fritz and Odo, the youth was Dieter. Odo had a gun. He held it caressingly in his hands, turning it over and over, savoring its potent weight.

Dieter had a stiletto. Fritz had his hands, big gorilla hands. He seemed to think they would be enough.

They wanted to rob and kill Glendon!

He could have screamed with laughter, but that would have ended the game too soon.

They were ready to make their move. All that had restrained them so far was their fear that Glendon had a gun, or that they might spook him into running and possibly escaping in the night.

They reckoned he was asleep now. They planned to split up, trapping Glendon so there was no escape. Odo would go first with the gun, sneaking up behind the campsite and getting the drop on Glendon. Then Fritz and Dieter would move.

That was the plan. Odo went one way, Fritz and Dieter went the other, circling the campsite from both sides in a kind of pincer movement.

Glendon performed a pincer movement of his own, when he slipped unheard behind Odo and got a clawlike hand around his throat—

Fritz and Dieter finally made their way to the site, crouching in the brush just outside the feeble red firelight. The sleeper lay in the sleeping bag, lying on his side, face to the wall, head pillowed on one extended arm stretched out on the stones.

A long wait followed, the scene unchanging except for the firelight, which got dimmer.

The two robbers spoke in whispers.

"Where's Odo? He should have been here by now."

"He should have been here before us, his way was shorter."

More time passed.

"He must have gotten lost, the idiot!"

"Now what do we do?"

"We do it ourselves."

"Maybe we had better wait."

"We can't wait all night. Why chance letting this rich foreigner get away, just because Odo stepped in a rabbit hole?"

"I don't know . . ."

"You're not scared?"

That settled it. The two stepped out of the brush onto the pavement square, Dieter holding his knife out point first, Fritz opening and closing his catcher's-mitt hands.

They closed on the sleeper, who remained motionless. Dieter stood over him, holding the knife at waist height. He kicked the sleeper a couple of times.

"Get up."

No reaction, no response. Dieter said over his shoulder to Fritz, "He's scared stiff!"

"Prick him a few times with that toadsticker of yours."

Dieter crouched over the sleeper, then he slipped on something wet and fell, sitting down hard. The motion jarred the sleeper, causing him to roll over on his back.

A good part of his throat had been clawed away, but except for a few deep-gouged scratches, the face was intact.

Dieter shrieked. *"Odo!"*

His feet churned, slipping in blood. He got them under him and jumped up. "Fritz!"

Fritz was gone, nowhere in sight.

Dieter wheeled around, trying to look everywhere at once. "He was right behind me a second ago—"

Fritz popped up from behind the wall, or at least his head did. A clawed furry hand was holding it.

It threw the head at Dieter, hitting him in the chest. It bounced off and rolled away.

Dieter screamed, turned, and ran. He raced around crazily in the woods until he crashed into a tree and knocked himself down, stunned.

When his head cleared, he sat up to find Glendon grinning down at him. Whatever Dieter saw in the other's face made him scream.

Dieter realized that somewhere along the way he'd lost his knife, not that it would have done him any good.

Glendon didn't need knives, not when the curved sharply

pointed talons sprouting from his fingertips were so razor-sharp. He put them to work digging a hole in Dieter's middle.

That's when Dieter really started screaming.

Glendon awoke, lying curled on the frigid pavement square beside a dead fire. Icy dawnlight hurt his eyes, his head.

He groped around, crawling on the stones, feverish and trembling. He was barefoot, his shirt torn to shreds.

Moving stiffly, wasted, he stumbled across his sleeping bag.

It was occupied by Odo, or what was left of him. Not only had he been clawed and mangled, but some of his soft parts had been eaten, devoured.

Glendon collapsed, flopping to the stones, falling through them into the blackness between the stars—

FOURTEEN

It was midafternoon and raining when the treasure hunters arrived at the plantation. They came in a white SUV, a black SUV, and a rusted orange pickup truck. The white machine held Dorian, Lodge, Soto, Dennis, and Tony Paul. The black machine, a police vehicle, held Major Quantez, his adjutant Lieutenant Luz, grizzled noncom Sergeant Marko, Quantez's driver, and two civilians, Calexa and Alba. The pickup truck held six policemen, two in the cab and four in the back. The back of the truck was an open hopper, so the men in back had nothing but their plastic helmet liners as protection from the rain. Their weapons got wet, too.

"Some party," Soto said. He and his two sidemen sat in the backseat, Lodge had the front passenger side, and Dorian drove.

Dennis asked, "What're you doing here? A woman."

"Because I'm the best driver," Dorian said.

"Sheeeeyit."

Lodge said, "She's driving so you gentlemen will be free to concentrate on the job at hand, namely keeping us alive."

Soto said, "Shut up, Dennis."

"Yeah, shut up," Tony Paul said.

Dennis said, "I was just making conversation."

Soto said, "Make with the silence."

The three-vehicle convoy drove straight across the front grounds toward the mansion. Even when new, the white-columned structure had been an oddity, stunted and dwarfish. Age and neglect had ripened it into a real eyesore.

As it loomed up, Soto whistled. "Tara on a bender!"

Lodge said, "Yes, it was a deliberate attempt by the builder to re-create the plantation-style houses of the Old South in a Caribbean context . . . not entirely successful, I'm afraid."

"We're a long way off from Dixie."

"Indeed."

It was raining steadily, not hard. The clouds were gray brown and oppressive, muting what little color and vitality that still existed in the landscape.

The ground was soft but not too muddy, not yet. The vehicles rolled to a halt in front of the house. Doors opened, bodies piled out, feet squelched against damp earth.

A couple of stick figures were wandering around in the distance, at the edge of the field. One of the policemen in the helmet liner and OD fatigues raised his rifle and popped off a few shots at the wanderers.

If he hit any, they didn't show it. Sergeant Marko stalked over and hit him, knocking him down. He said, "Don't waste ammunition."

"Yes, Sergeant," the man who had been knocked down said mushily, through loose teeth and smashed lips.

When he had picked himself up from the ground, Marko knocked him down again.

"And no shooting until the order is given," the noncom added.

The soldier mumbled something. He was slow to rise until Marko started kicking him to his feet, then he managed to stand up.

Quantez said, to no one in particular, "He's tough but fair."

Nobody disputed the point. Soto and his two men checked their weapons. He stuck a pair of automatic pistols in the top of his pants and stuffed some spare clips into his jacket pocket.

Tony Paul had a sawed-off, double-barreled shotgun, a wicked piece. He filled his jacket pockets with shells. Dennis handled a pair of big-caliber pistols.

Tony Paul said, "Don't hurt yourself with them things, kid."

Lieutenant Luz went to the back of the black SUV, opening the rear door. Out climbed the odd couple from Lodge's hotel breakfast table, Calexa and her son, Alba.

She wore a wide planter's straw hat which was tied under her chin with a pink sash. Alba wore a soft shapeless white fabric hat.

Dennis muttered, "Where do these two weirdos fit into the party?"

"They're witches," Lodge said.

"Yeah, right."

Dorian said, "Uncle Basil should know, he's one himself."

Before Dennis could say anything more, Soto came over to him and said, "I told you to keep your mouth shut."

"Sorry, Steve, I'm a sociable guy—"

"Maybe that Marko character has the right idea."

Quantez went to Calexa and Alba. He said, "Well?"

Calexa turned, facing the house, sniffing the air. She looked at Alba.

"Can it be? Is he really gone?" she asked.

Alba said, "Definitely!"

Quantez said, "Are you sure?"

Alba smirked, not deigning to reply. Calexa did the talking for him.

She said, "Of course he's sure! Alba is one of the world's greatest mediums, a world-class sensitive! If he says it's so, it's so!"

Lieutenant Luz said sourly, "Maybe he can predict what will happen if we can't get these riots under control."

Calexa turned on him. "He's a medium, not a prophet!"

Quantez said, "I will tell you what will happen. We will all have to go to work for a living."

Lodge and Dorian stood nearby, within earshot of the

conversation. Lodge said, "What about you, darling? What do you see?"

Dorian turned her face to the house. A few beats later, her eyes went out of focus. The tight line of her mouth softened, ripe lips parted.

In a soft voice, she said, "He's gone, and yet . . ."

"What?"

"I don't know . . . I get this very strong impression of *doubling*. Like he's gone, and yet's he's here, both at the same time."

Lodge said, "He's left his mark on this place. His brand. That's what you're sensing, not him."

"I don't know." She shook her head, then shuddered. "I don't like to *see* here. It's dangerous. Leaves me open. I know this—others of his kind are here."

"They're nothing without their master," Lodge said. "If that's all we have to worry about, I say let's go in and win."

Dorian smiled warmly at him. "Yes, do."

Lodge tilted his head, looking at her. "I wonder if you'd say the same thing if you were going in there with us."

"Oh, I couldn't. My nerves couldn't take it."

Marko stood nearby with fists on hips, watching as a couple of his men unloaded some boxed crates from the back of the black vehicle. The crates held unlit torches and four-foot-long wooden dowels with sharpened spikes at the tip. And machetes.

In addition to their firearms, some of the police soldiers grabbed stakes and torches. And machetes.

Soto said, "Talk about low-tech hardware."

Lodge, standing beside him, said, "That's two ways to stop zombies. Burn them, or cut them to pieces so they can't keep coming at you. They'll come at you anyway, but it slows them down if you cut off their legs and arms first."

"I'll keep it in mind," Soto said. "What about the short wooden spears?"

"They're no good against zombies, but they're handy against . . . other pests."

All kinds of trash littered the dirt yard, including rusting engine blocks and tin soft-drink signs, a refrigerator door, even an old round four-legged washing machine.

Sergeant Marko spotted an empty fifty-gallon drum lying on its side. Its blackened interior showed it had been used to build fires in. He had some of his men put it back to work, upending it and filling it with kindling. There was plenty of wood around for the taking, all the men had to do was finish tearing it off from where it was dangling from the siding, or break up a few more planks on what was left of the front porch, adding them to the barrel.

When it was full he doused it with gasoline and torched it. It made a *whoomping* sound and was soon burning hot and heavy, too fierce for the rain to make a dent in it, though the wetness made the smoke more black and oily.

A crate of unlit torches was dragged near the barrel fire. Soto said, "That fire's kind of close to the vehicles."

"It's okay. Easier to defend," Lieutenant Luz said, smiling toothily. Soto shrugged.

Lodge and Quantez had their heads together. Lodge said, "I don't like this rain, not so late in the day. It'll bring the dark quicker."

Quantez said, "Then let us not delay now."

"We were supposed to be on the road at one, not two and a half hours later."

"Tell that to the rioters. I could not leave my command until the latest outbreak had been quelled.

"The rabble have been too long without a taste of the whip and spur. They grew bold, the scum. Why, just before I left to join you, I was informed that the rebels had attacked and killed a patrol right under the very walls of Seaguard Castle!

"The situation is at crisis point. I should be with my men in Magdalena, directing the battle against the insurgents."

Lodge said dryly, "I don't know how they can spare you. Perhaps you should leave to join them."

Quantez looked at him blandly. "I'm sure they can get along without me for an hour or two."

Sergeant Marko started forming the men up. Soto stood off to one side with Tony Paul and Dennis.

He said, "Looks like it's time to step up to the plate. Dennis will go in with me. Tony, you stay here."

Tony Paul frowned. "Hey, Steve, you need me. I got your back."

"That's why I want you out here, keeping an eye on the vehicles. I'd hate to have to get out of here in a hurry and find that there's no getaway cars."

"I get you."

"Keep an eye on Calexa and Alba. I don't trust them."

"Those two weirdos? Check."

"Dorian, too."

"Right."

"Those soldier cops look too dumb to come up with any curveballs on their own, but you never know. Watch them."

"You bet, Steve."

"And the zombies, too."

"Yah." Tony Paul put a hand over his eyes, shielding them from the rain, while he looked out across the fields.

"There's a couple more of them than there was a minute ago," he said.

Now there was a handful of jerky stick figures shambling around at the edge of the field.

Sergeant Marko set two of his men and Quantez's driver to stay outside and guard the vehicles and to keep watch for the zombies. And to watch Tony Paul, Dorian, Calexa, and Alba, all of whom were staying behind. Calexa and Alba were Quantez's witches, but they bore watching all the same—all witches do.

A couple of police soldiers lit their torches in the barrel fire and formed up in front of the house's main entrance.

Soto said, "I hope those clowns don't burn the house down. Speaking of clowns—Dennis, you go in ahead of me. I don't want you at my back with a loaded gun."

Lodge had a leather pouch slung over his neck by a strap. He untied the drawstring mouth of the pouch and reached inside, coming out with a handful of rough-grained sea salt

246

with large glittering crystals that he let sift through his fingers back into the pouch.

He said, "Shall we go?"

They went. Waiting for them was the cockeyed mansion, its sides crooked, rooflines sagging, the wings leaning in against the main building. Spread out before it was a yard full of rank growths and scraggly weeds and cactus that was all twisted stems and bladder pods and long thorns.

There were piles of wolf shit and chicken bones and zombie tracks.

In they went, Quantez, Luz, Marko, some soldier cops, Dennis, Soto, and Lodge. The group filed in under the arched double doorway whose doors hung on loose hinges like wings.

Inside, it was dim and musty, with loose floorboards and broken windows. There was dampness and mold, faded peeling wallpaper and cracked plaster, moss, cobwebs, gloom.

The walls and floor were streaked with rank bird and bat droppings. There were rat droppings and piles of wooden shavings on the floor that the rats had clawed for their nests.

Dennis said, low-voiced, "Hey, it's not so bad."

Soto gave him a look. Dennis said, "At least we're out of the rain."

The torches hissed and sputtered, lighting up patches of the ceiling and trimming them with streamers of smoke. The close-packed group started to disperse, widening the gap between individuals, in large part to get some elbow room from the torchbearers.

The straggling file snaked through the rooms, crossing the front hall, going around the grand staircase and into a series of interconnected rooms.

In the rooms were strange things: coffins that were beds, beds that were torture racks, blank discolored rectangles on the walls where mirrors had once hung, withered mummies in chains, a nude limbless carcass hanging upside down on a chain from a rafter beam, a shiny brown coffin whose insides were caked with dried blood.

The last in line of the row of rooms opened into what

had been a drawing room. In the wall opposite the entryway was a massive stone fireplace, with a hearth big enough for a man to walk into without bending his head. It was topped with a marble mantelpiece the size of a park bench, supported by fluted stone half pillars.

The hearth was cold, but it blazed with a sullen molten golden fire that was shot through with yellow, red, and orange gleamings from the torchlight.

On the floor of the walk-in fireplace was a big black chest with wide brass moldings and corner pieces. The lid was thrown open to accommodate the heaped piles of gold and jewels that were overflowing from the chest.

Treasure.

Outside, the rain was picking up, darkening the skies and dampening the barrel fire. Quantez's driver sat behind the wheel of the black machine. The two soldier cops stood under a part of the roofed front porch that was still intact. They were smoking cigarettes, laughing and joking in low liquid voices.

At least they were out of the rain. That was more than could be said of Dorian, who stood by the barrel fire, feeding fresh kindling into it, trying to keep it going. Rain fell on her bare head, wetting her hair down against her scalp. The harder it rained, the thicker was the smoke and the thinner the fire.

Tony Paul stood with his back against a wall of the house, watching Dorian and watching the zombies at the edge of the fields. There were more than a half dozen of them now.

When he turned to look back at the place where he had last seen Calexa and Alba, they were gone. They had pulled a sneak on Tony Paul, irking him.

He looked around. The two guys on the porch were busy horsing around. If they'd noticed the pair's absence, they didn't care. Quantez's driver was staring out into space. Dorian's back was to him as she kept feeding the fire.

Tony Paul slipped away, fading around a corner of the house and away.

Out back there was the graveyard, the chapel, and the old mill. No sign of Calexa and Alba.

Tony Paul shook his head. "The ass end of this dump's no better than the front."

He wondered what was going on inside. Might not be a bad idea to poke around. He walked along the path behind the house, holding the sawed-off shotgun in one hand.

He craned and peered, looking through windows without glass for some traces of the search party. As he drew abreast of the chapel, it caught his attention.

He crossed to the chapel, sticking his head inside to see if Calexa and Alba were there.

"Just the kind of creep joint that'd pull 'em in," he said. But it was empty.

Stepping back out, he heard a soft voice call his name. A woman's voice, sending chills up his spine. But there was nobody around, he was alone.

Then he noticed the below-surface well and the flight of stone stairs leading down to an open doorway in the chapel's stone foundation.

He went down the stairs to the open doorway. Beyond lay a crypt. Enough light filtered in to give an impression of massive rounded stone forms, pillars and archways, tables and boxes.

Dank cool air breathed out from within. He stepped inside. Pools of wetness littered the floor.

Buffered gray light leaked into the chamber, revealing three solid stone tables lined up in a row. On top of each table was a coffin.

The lid of the nearest coffin was open, raised so that it stood upright on its hinges at right angles to the oblong box. It was turned so that it stood between Tony Paul and what lay inside the coffin.

He went around the coffin and looked inside. It held a woman, an old woman, a stringy-haired yellowed corpse with sunken eyes and curved yellow-brown nails. She was dressed in tattered and stained red lace.

Tony Paul's eyes burned, blurring his vision, and when

249

he looked again, he had a very different picture of the thing in the coffin.

She was lovely, with thick wavy hair and a red-lipped mouth and fine-grained glowing velvet skin. At the corners of her mouth were two red stains, streaks that ran down to her chin. Dried strands of the red stuff.

Hard to believe she was dead. Her skin glowed. Lovely stuff! Wonder what it felt like?

He was touching her, running his fingertips over her face. He'd expected warmth but it was cold. He touched her lips.

Something stung the back of his hand as it brushed against her lips. A sharp nip, like a spider bite. That's what he thought it was. It stung!

There was a puncture mark on the back of his hand, already swelling like a little volcano, crowned with a lavalike drop of hot red blood. His.

The skin was broken. It burned, itched. A numbness tingled, a cold burning that spread through him like venom.

He looked down at the lady in the coffin. She was smiling—

No, it wasn't a smile that quirked those red lips up at the corners, it was a pair of long sharp canine upper fangs that did it, presenting the illusion of a smile.

A drop of blood quivered on her lips. His blood.

Her eyes opened.

It hammered him. She was looking up at him. Their gazes met, locked. His eyes grew glassy, muddy; hers brightened, reddening into little fiery balls of blood.

By then, he couldn't look away. He was bending over the coffin, leaning down to kiss her. Her hands came up, reaching for him.

She grabbed him, pulling him down to her so she could sink her fangs into his neck. He kicked while she drank, but she held him so he couldn't get away.

She pulled away first, her mouth clown-painted with smeared fresh blood. She clawed open his jugular, spraying her face with hot sweet geysering blood. She reveled in it, hissing and writhing ecstatically.

Tony Paul shuddered, spasming as his lifeblood vented. His thrashing feet kicked the shotgun he had dropped when he first came under the spell of her hypno eyes.

She hauled him headfirst into the coffin, so that he lay stretched out on top of her. The lid fell shut, closing. It failed to close all the way—his feet hung out over the edge, blocking it.

Not far away, Calexa and Alba had made a discovery of their own, in the graveyard behind the mausoleum.

They found the Frankenstein Monster.

In the house, in the treasure room, as the others pressed forward, Soto hung back. He noticed Lodge was doing the same. Soto kept his back to the wall. With this crowd, that was a good idea anyway, and doubly so now that the gold had been found.

"Right out in the open, in plain sight," Lodge said, speaking out of the side of his mouth so only Soto could hear him. "Convenient, no?"

Soto looked at him, blank-faced. He hooked his thumbs into the top of his belt, keeping his hands near the guns under his jacket.

Quantez and most of the others, including Dennis, were grouped around the golden hearth. Lieutenant Luz stood off to one side, eyeing Lodge and especially Soto.

Quantez started toward the gold, then thought better of it and stopped, backing away a few paces. He gave the order to Marko, who passed it to the underlings.

"Get the gold," Marko said. Two soldier cops moved to obey. One was a torchbearer and looked around for somebody to hand off the torch to. Dennis took it. Behind him, Soto shook his head.

The duo unslung their rifles and set them aside, standing them against a wall. They advanced on the trove of golden fire, bedazzled.

Dennis said, "Watch out for booby traps."

They understood enough English to get the concept. They halted, exchanging glances. Marko gave Dennis a dirty look.

251

He said, "Go on."

The two drifted forward, dragging their feet, unhappy, lagging. Marko stepped toward them, hand unraised.

He said, "Stop hanging back, you dogs!"

They stepped into the fireplace, which was tall enough so they didn't have to duck their heads. Inside the hearth there was room enough for both men to stand at opposite ends of the treasure chest. As they set foot inside it, they looked like they thought the floor was going to drop out from under them.

Nothing happened. Marko guffawed. The two men let out the breath they'd been holding and smiled, looking sheepish. The golden color underlit their faces and eyes, making them glow.

Quantez nodded, grinning, as the two men stooped down, each taking hold of one of the strap-type handles at the short ends of the chest. They pulled, straining forward. The chest was heavy and barely moved. They tugged harder, leaning into it.

The chest began moving. Encouraged, the two men increased their efforts, dragging the chest out of the hearth and onto the main floor.

One of the two was leaning so far forward that his helmet liner fell off his head, landing on the floor. He bent over to pick it up.

By now, the chest was half outside of the hearth. This was the critical point that caused a weighted pressure-pad plate to be released, tripping hidden catches.

There was a dull thud as a locking mechanism came undone, followed by a twanging sound, like a taut steel cable being plucked.

Concealed under the mantelpiece was a double-jointed steel armature, with a powerful coiled spring at the hinge of the two metal arms. One arm was bolted to the underside of the mantel, anchoring it; the other had the ability to move freely.

When the pressure-pad switch tripped the safety catch,

the free arm of the device lashed out, powered by the un-coiling of the jaw spring.

The free-swinging arm of the mantrap was a five-foot-long curved razor-edged scythe. It came flickering out from under the top of the hearth like a switchblade knife.

It missed the man who was bending over to pick up his helmet liner, but got his partner. The blade came whipping in at about the level of the average man's neck height, but the soldier cop was short and the blade took him in mid-head.

It took all of him, helmet liner included, slicing off the top of his head above the ears and sending it flying. It was done as neatly as a butcher's cleaver whacking the tip of a salami.

The body stood upright for a few seconds, weaving, then dropping. The head wound really spewed.

Reaching the end of its swing, the scythe blade hung hor-izontally in front of the mantel, its keen curved edge red and dripping, the steel vibrating.

The soldier who hadn't been tagged dropped belly-down to the floor, crawling away in the opposite direction.

The cycle was not yet done. Behind hollow wall panels could be heard the sound of heavy stone counterweights slid-ing and grinding.

A block of blackness appeared at the base of the hearth's rear wall, growing steadily, rising. The wall really wasn't a wall but a sliding panel, and it was sliding now, climbing upward, pulled into an overhead slot by chains and coun-terweights.

The panel opened on a square of oily blankness, yield-ing a rush of foul air that set the torch flames fluttering.

Quantez yelped, lunging for the treasure chest as if fear-ing it might be snatched away from him. He grabbed a trunk strap and heaved. Marko jumped in beside him, hooking his hands on a corner of the chest and pulling.

Soto almost made his move then, but Luz was watching him, waiting with his hand on top of his gun.

Quantez, Marko, and two of the three soldiers wrestled

253

the trunk into the open. The half-headed corpse got in their way and they kicked it savagely, booting it aside.

The third soldier had unslung his rifle and was now holding it leveled at the hearth, where the sliding panel was now fully open, revealing a square-edged stone tunnel mouth leading back into darkness. The darkness was alive and coiling with a sound of onrushing motion.

The police soldiers hauled the gold clear, leaving a fiery trail of baubles. Dennis danced around them, excitedly waving the torch, getting in the line of fire. Soto would have burned him down without a second thought if it had meant bagging Quantez and company, but Luz was openly watching him, hoping he would try to make the reach.

Soto could wait, as long as Luz didn't make a move.

Something was in the air, and it lay in the black depths of the tunnel, whipping up cold damp invisible currents that stank of rot, pumping them out of the hearth.

Behind them came a sound like a thousand flags fluttering and snapping in the wind.

It was the sound of leathery wings.

Soto glanced at Lodge—he was gone. Not too far from where he'd been standing was a gaping window.

Luz, too, saw that Lodge was gone. He must have thought it was some kind of trick or signal because he reached, clawing at his holstered pistol.

Bats flew out of the tunnel, hundreds of them, pouring out of the hearth in a boiling black cloud.

The soldier who stood in front of the fireplace fired a couple of shots into the mass, the slugs spanging and ricocheting down into the tunnel. He was bowled over by the sheer weight of the horde as they erupted into the room.

Soto ducked, pulling a gun as Luz's shots tore into the wall where he'd been standing.

The bats were vampire bats, the true New World vampires, with furry fist-sized bodies and black leathery wings. They exploded into the space, whirring, whirling, pinwheeling, a bat blizzard.

Men flailed the air with whatever they had, torches, stakes, rifles, machetes, their hands, trying to beat the bats away from their heads.

Luz and Soto were shooting at each other but neither could get a clear shot amid all the chaos.

Quantez ducked behind the chest of gold, using it for cover as he drew his gun and started shooting at Soto. The wheeling bats spoiled his view and he could only throw slugs in Soto's general direction.

Dennis pulled a gun and shot a soldier cop who was standing nearby. The one who had been shooting into the tunnel and who now lay on his back on the floor where he had fallen still held his rifle, and he fired at Dennis. It looked to Soto like he had missed, but Dennis dropped the torch and fell back, out of sight.

A rift opened in the whirling bat horde and Luz took advantage of it, standing in a classic pistol-range marksman's stance with his shooting arm extended, gun pointed at Soto.

Something low, fast, fierce, and red-eyed rushed out of the tunnel, launching itself into the air.

It was a wolf, one of the wolves of Dracula. It had been imprisoned in the underground vaults since the master's passing. It was no longer under the vampire's command, but it was a hungry, angry wolf and not in the best of humors as it came leaping out of the hearth.

It was a magnificent beast, with pointed devil-dog ears and glacial blue eyes and a gray-and-white snout with a fanged red mouth. Thick bands of muscle were bunched at its neck and shoulders as it took its target in midair.

Lieutenant Luz turned his head just in time to see the wolf come lunging at him. The wolf knew about guns and its steel-trap jaws slammed shut on the wrist of Luz's gun hand, taking him down.

Luz lay on the floor, arm extended, reflexively jerking the trigger as he screamed, shooting into the baseboard while wolfish fangs crunched bones and tore tendons and veins and arteries and then the hand didn't work anymore.

Raw flesh and hot sweet blood erupted its ecstatic sensory blast in the wolf's maw, whipping up its kill lust. Better than a bony wrist was a soft pulsing throat and the wolf sank its fangs into Luz's, savaging it.

The soldier who'd fallen down had just managed to rise to his feet in time to get in the way of a second wolf, which came streaking out of the tunnel. He shrieked as the pouncing beast knocked him back down to the floor.

One of the soldier cops still standing fired at the wolves, the other shot at Soto. Quantez and Marko shot at him, too.

It was getting too hot for Soto, who bailed, diving headfirst through an empty window frame, outside.

FIFTEEN

Dorian cringed and started flinching a minute before the shooting rang out inside the house, the shooting and the screams. She stood in the rain with her back to the house, spine straight, arms at her sides, fists clenched. She was pale and tight-lipped with a splitting headache and a hollow stomach and she knew something was going to happen. When it did, she jumped anyway.

The outburst was taking place somewhere in the back of the house, but it still sounded loud. Quantez's driver stuck his head out the window of the black SUV where he sat behind the wheel with the motor running. If it was kept running, there was no fear of dead-starting it and having it come up dead.

He looked back at the house, where the two men who'd been left outside on guard were standing under an overhang, out of the rain.

Inside, the shooting and screaming got more frantic. The two men exchanged glances. One said, "You go in, I'll stay here on guard."

"You go in and I'll stay here," the other said.

They both stayed put, milling around uncertainly, fiddling with their rifles. When a fresh round of shrieking announced the advent of the wolves, the men jumped down from the porch, starting toward the vehicles.

The driver was outside the black SUV, sheltering behind it, pointing a pistol at them. Waving the pistol barrel at the house, he said, "Go back!"

The men halted, indecisive, weighing their chances. Off to the side of them, a few yards away, stood Dorian, her back to the house and her eyes squeezed shut.

The issue was decided when Marko stepped out of the house, standing in front of the entrance, smoking pistol in hand.

"Get in here," he said. The men turned, trotting up to the house, holding their rifles across their chests. Marko stood beside the door, glaring at them as they went inside. He was blood-spattered, but none of it was his blood.

Inside, Quantez and the two soldier cops were pushing the chest across the floor, past the collapsed staircase and down the hall to the door. They'd left behind three of their own, Lieutenant Luz and two more, plus two dead wolves, Dennis's inert body, and a horde of bats. A glittering trail of gold tracked behind the chest, curving around toward the back rooms.

Quantez had stayed behind because there was no way he was going to leave the gold unattended. Now, as the two newcomers joined the group, he was able to yield his place at the chest and step back.

He covered the rear, gun held at his waist, looking around, waiting for something, anything to come bounding out of a dim corner.

He backed up, nearing the open doorway. The others were already through it, hauling the chest outside. Quantez reached down, picking up strands of gold necklaces and jewels and stuffing them into his pockets.

Then he was outside. The rear hatch of the SUV was flung open as the men lugged the chest of gold to it, bowed under the weight. Gold is heavy.

Enough loot had been spilled from the pile to allow the

lid to be closed before the chest was hefted and heaved into the back of the vehicle, sending it settling on its springs.

Dorian put her hands over her ears. Marko shot down the two men who'd been standing guard outside. They wheeled and spun, flopping into puddles in the muddy front yard. Rain slanted down.

One was still alive. Groaning, he raised himself up on his elbows, red leaking from the holes in the middle of him.

"Next time, show some initiative," Marko said, then shot again, finishing him.

Quantez told the remaining two police soldiers to shoot out the pickup truck's tires. They obeyed, blasting. There was a hiss of leaking air as the pickup settled down low in the mud.

The rain had all but extinguished the barrel fire. Marko picked up the gas can which had been used to ignite it. The gallon tin was mostly full. He upended it, splashing gas on the white SUV, soaking it down thoroughly inside and out.

Marko finished reloading his gun and pointed it at the other two low-ranking troops. They looked glum but not particularly surprised. He said, "Throw down your weapons. Just drop them in the mud. Do it!"

They did. Marko used the gun to gesture at the back of the SUV. He said, "Get in."

That surprised them. Quantez said, "You men with guns, gold, and my driver—no, no, that's too much of a temptation. I trust you better now."

The men nodded, bobbing their heads, stammering their loyalty and gratitude.

Quantez beamed, then nodded at Marko. Marko said, "Get in, unless you want to keep your friends on the ground company."

They got in. Quantez opened the passenger-side front door and put a foot in the cab while standing outside. Dorian started toward him, her eyes open now.

He shook his head. "Sorry, this is an official police vehicle. It is against the rules to carry civilian passengers. You'll have to find another ride back into town."

He gazed beyond her, to where Marko was about to put the white SUV to the torch. He nodded. Marko dropped the torch inside the gas-soaked cab.

In a few heartbeats, it developed into a roaring fire. Marko jumped back from it.

Dorian asked, "Why me?"

Quantez said, "Your uncle got away from me. He is free, he and those other two, the witches, free to make mischief. So, I make a little mischief of my own."

He turned, looking at the edge of the field where the zombies had gathered. There were more now, many more, over a dozen.

He said, "Say hello to your friends for me."

The white SUV was burning good and hot now. Marko ran away from it, head down, brushing past Dorian and hopping into the black machine through a side door.

Quantez hopped into the cab, closing the door. He stuck his head out the window, looking back at Dorian and the burning vehicle behind her.

He said, "Keep that pretty head down when the gas tank blows up, unless you want to lose it. Though that might be faster than what the zombies will do to you and the others.

"Too many witches on this island! Time they were all done away with."

The black SUV started forward, pulling away. Dorian called after it, "He's not really my uncle, you know!"

The SUV drove away, giving a wide berth to the zombies. As it passed, they turned their faces to it.

Dorian started walking away from the flaming machine at an angle, her sandaled feet squelching in mud. There was a *crump* as the first blast sounded, the shock wave knocking her down.

The second blast triggered the fireball, a booming thunderclap and a jellied red-yellow-white pillar of fire leaping up from the crumpled wreck, a ruptured metal framework that was a black blot at the heart of the blaze.

A few more shuddering blasts spewed heat and flaming

tendrils of jellied gasoline. They lit up the rainy fading day, making it seem darker still when the sizzling glare died away.

Dorian picked herself out of the mud; her front was coated with the stuff. Her ears rang.

Ignoring the explosion, the zombies still stood facing the direction in which the black SUV had gone, even after it had dropped below a ridge, out of sight.

After a pause, they turned, facing the house, facing Dorian. Another pause, and then they started toward her. It looked like there were a lot more than twelve of them.

They were a long way off, but they were moving.

She turned and went the other way, swinging wide to circle around the house. She knew better than to go inside. Nothing could make her go inside.

She ran behind the back of the house. She knew enough to avoid the chapel and the graveyard, too. She ran off to the side, at a tangent, cutting across a footpath whose broken stones were shiny with wetness.

The old mill loomed up on her left. A ragged figure popped up from behind a waist-high thicket of brush, not far from Dorian. The uncouth figure weaved, shaking its arms over its head.

It called her name, hissing in an urgent stage whisper, *"Dorian!"*

It was gaunt, stringy-haired Calexa, who was motioning to her, indicating for her to come over. Dorian slowed, slipping on wet grass, a wrenching move that tore loose some of her sandal straps so that one sandal was in danger of falling off.

Calexa came out from behind the bushes, taking Dorian by an arm. She said, "Just who I've been looking for! Your uncle was quite worried about you."

"I knew he was alive, I sensed it," Dorian said.

Calexa had her by the arm, steering her toward the mill. Dorian said, "Where are we going?"

"In there. Your uncle and the others are waiting."

"What others?"

"You'll see." Calexa tugged on Dorian's arm, leading her

forward. Dorian tried to tell her about Quantez's leaving them marooned for the zombies, but Calexa was impatient, not really listening.

"I know, I know," Calexa said. "It'll all be taken care of, now hurry along."

They went to a side doorway in the building. The wooden-plank door was intact. Calexa raised a fist to hammer on it, but the door opened from the inside before she could strike it.

Holding the door was one of Lodge's bodyguards from the house on the cape, a muscleman in a black beret, wrap-around sunglasses, a sleeveless body shirt, loose-fitting black pants, and boots. He wore a gun belt with holstered sidearm.

Dorian gasped. "Pierre!"

He nodded, stepping aside and motioning for her to enter. Calexa put a hand on the small of Dorian's back and pushed, shoving her across the threshold, Calexa followed her inside, Pierre closing and barring the door behind them.

Inside, there was light. Firelight—a blaze burned brightly off to one side, out of the rain under a roofed area. The fire was being tended by another of Lodge's bodyguards.

Dorian said, "Reynolds, you, too? What are you and Pierre doing here?"

"That was my idea, darling," Lodge said, his voice coming from deeper into the mill. Dorian looked around, unable to see him at first.

He said, "One of my contingency plans. They followed us here in a Jeep, which is hidden in a gulley below the mill. They were supposed to take care of Mr. Soto and his gangster friends after they had taken care of Quantez and his men.

"I'm afraid our hoodlum associates proved rather more ineffectual than I had feared, however. They're done for and the major has gotten away with the gold."

Lodge stood amid a heap of giant cracked millstones, near the open center space below the hole in the roof, but, like the fire, protected from the rain by the overhang.

Nearby stood a massive wooden pillar, leaning at a tilted

angle. Chained to it in an upright position was the Franken-stein Monster. It sagged against the chains and would have collapsed if they hadn't been holding it up.

It was drained, devitalized, dead, split down the middle and gutted like a butcher-shop carcass hanging on a meat hook.

Lodge moved out from behind the pillar into better view, standing beside the Monster with the rain falling in through the hole in the roof as a backdrop, the slanting downpour turned golden by the firelight.

Lodge looked up at the creature, gazing dreamily at it. He said, "Quantez got the gold but here is the real treasure, the Monster created by Henry Frankenstein. An immortal creature of destruction, a biochemical Holy Grail.

"Unholy Grail, rather."

Calexa said, "And we found it, Alba and I."

"I would have come across it, inevitably—"

"But we found it, Lodge."

"Certainly. But without me, and the timely arrival of my two men Pierre and Reynolds, you and Alba would never have been able to budge it, much less carry it here to the mill and chain it up to a pillar."

"We could have raised it there, by the mausoleum."

"Not even you can draw a magic circle in the rain, Calexa."

"We're not in the rain now. Let's be about the working, Lodge."

Alba floated up from another area of shadows, saying, "Let's."

Dorian said, "The major's left us to the zombies, and they're coming!"

Lodge unruffled, said, "The door is solid and the win-dows have storm shutters. We can hold off the zombies long enough."

"Long enough for what?"

"Long enough to raise the Frankenstein Monster."

Dorian went on, as if she hadn't heard him. "There's still time to get to the Jeep and get away—"

Lodge said, "Get away to where? If Quantez finds out that we're still alive, he'll have us shot. That is, if the rebels don't get us first.

"Even if we were able to win through to the harbor and a boat, we'd be leaving without our hard-won assets. We'd be virtually penniless."

"We'd be alive," Dorian said.

"Why run when we have the most potentially important piece on the chessboard?"

"You don't mean . . . ?"

"Yes, HIM." Lodge reached up to pat the Monster on the wrist, a wrist as thick as a normal man's calf.

"Impossible. You're no scientist."

"I don't intend to use science, Dorian. At least, not as that word is generally understood.

"I'll use the power of black magic. Others have failed because of their inability to master the Monster, but I cannot fail.

"I'll be the first to turn the Frankenstein Monster into a *zombie*."

Calexa croaked, "*We'll* be the first. It'll take all three of us to raise him—you, me, and sonny."

Pierre and Reynolds moved along the row of ground-floor windows near the door, closing and locking the shutters. They were storm shutters, designed to weather a hurricane, but most were old and some were missing. The high square windows had their sills at about shoulder height.

Dorian said, "If Baron Latos couldn't control the Monster, how can you?"

"Baron Latos was old-fashioned, out of date," Lodge said. "I know the rites by which zombies are made. What the Undead has done, a living sorcerer can certainly do.

"Blood must have blood. I will call upon the demons of darkness to grant my plea, to animate this dead thing and make it the blind obedient slave of my will.

"What does the dark demand in return? Sacrifices."

Calexa said, "Blood."

Alba said, "Pain."

264

"Death," Lodge said. "Souls to serve them on the other side."

Alba said, "What sacrifice do they esteem the most? That which is most valued by us."

Dorian kept glancing from face to face, Alba to Lodge to Calexa, then back again.

"What do you mean?" she said.

Alba said, "Can't you guess? You're really not much of a seer at all, just a shallow hysteric with the occasional lucky flashes of insight."

Calexa stood behind Dorian, hands on her shoulders. "You're going to die, dear."

"No!"

Alba added quickly, "Only your body will die, Dorian. Your soul will live on, as a bondmaid to demons." He had a sly look on his face, as though he didn't believe what he was saying and nobody else with any sense would, either.

Lodge sighed. "In any case, what must be done will be done, and quickly."

There was no need for him to signal Pierre and Reynolds, since they had already moved into position, slipping up behind Calexa and Alba. A slight tilt of Lodge's head sent them into action.

Pierre grabbed Calexa from behind, yoking her around the neck with a meaty forearm. Reynolds grabbed Alba, but it was Pierre who had his hands full. Alba froze, Calexa fought and fussed.

Lodge said, "Pacify her, Pierre."

Pierre snapped a sleeper hold on her, cutting off the flow of oxygen to the brain until Calexa had had the fight taken out of her.

Alba's eyes were shiny with tears of rage. "What madness is this? Treachery!"

Lodge said, "No man can serve two masters. The same applies to the Monster. The power is indivisible, unsharable. It can be held by only one—*me.*"

Calexa was trying to say something. Lodge motioned for Pierre to ease up on her a little. He said, "Let her talk.

"Yes, Calexa, you had something to say?"

She rasped, "You can't do it without me, you need my help—"

Lodge motioned for Pierre to tighten up and he did and Calexa was stifled, unable to speak.

Lodge said, "The rarer the sacrifice, the better. Traditionally, the dark gods have most esteemed a virgin sacrifice.

"Without telling any tales out of school, the time has long since past when Dorian could meet that qualification.

"But Alba does meet it. Alba is unique.

"As for you, Calexa, you're long steeped in wickedness and will make a powerful Opener of the Way. The demon lords will welcome you."

She started fussing again, so Pierre reapplied the sleeper hold until she was tamed. He dragged her to a broken section of wooden scaffolding, which stood by itself not far from the pillar where the Monster was secured. A pair of bulky cross braces formed an X-cross. Pierre tied her to it.

Reynolds herded Alba to a tablelike millstone near the Monster. Monster, Calexa, and now Alba were all solidly planted under the roof, out of the rain.

Reynolds stretched Alba on his back on the stone and tore off his clothes, stripping him. His pale, plump, hairless flesh quivered as he was tied spread-eagled across the makeshift altar. He had the composite sex organs of the genuine hermaphrodite.

"The gods will be pleased, this will bring much power," Lodge said, while Pierre and Reynolds looked on encouragingly.

Dorian stumbled toward the door. Lodge called to her, "There are those zombies, dear."

She went to one of the shutterless windows, holding on to the stone sill with both hands as if she were chinning herself. Looked outside.

It was hard to see. It was getting dark.

She said, "They've reached the house . . . they're passing it. Coming this way."

266

Lodge handed Reynolds a pouch. Reynolds went to the window and looked outside. He saw that the coast was clear and unbolted the door and stepped outside.

The pouch was a bag of salt and he reached inside and took out a handful and spread it outside the door, in front of the threshold.

"Don't use too much outside, the rain will just wash it away," Lodge said.

Reynolds stepped back inside, bolting the door. He spread handfuls of salt on the floor beyond the door. He scattered more of the stuff on the insides of the windowsills.

Pierre was busy gagging Calexa, wrapping strips of cloth tightly around her mouth.

"Gag her tightly," Lodge said. "We don't want her working it loose and calling down some foul witch's curse on us."

When Pierre was done, he began piling scrap wood around Calexa's feet, dumping in big double armfuls of kindling.

"That's good enough," Lodge said. "Now stay back, all of you. You'll be safe enough outside the circle—you're not doing the magic.

"Move back—further back; Pierre, go over where Reynolds and Dorian are. None of you may come near the circle for fear of breaking it."

Calexa returned to consciousness, in a fine fury. She writhed vainly against her bonds, eyes rolling, jaws working against the gag in her mouth.

She froze when she saw Lodge approaching her, knife in hand. At the sidelines, Dorian stepped forward, saying, "No, don't!"

Reynolds held her back, restraining her. Lodge said, "Don't worry, Calexa, I'm not going to kill you, not yet. I just need some of your blood to draw the circle."

He held a saucer-shaped object in one hand. "I'm afraid we don't have a proper ceremonial bowl, but this old hubcap will serve the purpose quite well. Ritual observance is all very well and good, but out in the field, one must improvise.

"Besides, it's the intent that's of prime import in these matters. But I'm not telling you anything you don't know, Calexa.

"Still, I'm sure you never expected to find yourself on the other side of the altar—a most unique perspective.

"One that I must confess I don't envy you."

Pressing the knife-blade tip to her neck, he made a small but deep incision in a vein, drawing blood. Blood spurted from the hole in her neck, jetting in sync with her pounding heartbeats. Lodge held the hubcap so it caught the blood, which pooled thick and purple red. The wound was serious but not mortal, at least not immediately.

He tapped her for about a half-pint of blood. She grayed, eyes rolling, fainting.

Lightning flashed and crackled, thunder boomed. Winds rose and the rain fell harder.

Lodge stood by the fire, heating the tip of the knife white-hot, then dipping it in the bowl of blood. There was a hissing sound and the blood bubbled.

Lodge began walking in a counterclockwise circle, dipping the fingertips of his left hand into the hubcap saucer of blood and flicking the red stuff on the floor as he walked.

He said, "I draw the magic circle."

His circuit took him around Calexa, Alba, and the Monster. As he sprinkled the blood, he stayed inside the growing circle, careful not to break it. He muttered invocations and Names of Power, calling on the guardians of borders to witness his deed.

Finally he returned to the point where he had started, having enclosed himself with the other principals in a magic circle of blood. The circle would protect the operator, the magician, from the dark forces he was about to conjure up.

Since neither Dorian, Pierre, nor Reynolds would be calling up the darkness, they would be more or less safe outside the circle. Still, it was best to stay a safe distance away from the site of the working, for fear of malign influences coiling around the protective barrier.

The fire, too, was inside the circle. Lodge plucked a firebrand from it, holding it out in front of him like a wand.

He said, "There's only one sure way to kill a witch, the age-old remedy—burning."

Set on top of a waist-high fragment of broken millstone were three glass jars with oily rags sticking out of the tops. The jars were filled with oily, yellow-tinted fluid, thick and viscous.

Lodge picked one up, holding it away from him. "These homemade firebombs were intended for use against zombies, but they're just as useful against witches."

He used the torch to set fire to the oily rag stuffed into the top of the glass jar. The rag ignited quickly, creamy yellow flames curling up from it.

Lodge threw the jar at Calexa's feet, where it burst, freeing a hot scorching bushel basket of jellied flames that spilled onto the kindling and the victim.

Fire leaped up, with a puff of white smoke, the flames leaping up higher and higher, entwining Calexa with fiery vines and tendrils, engulfing her in an inferno.

She writhed, burning at the stake, the smoke of her burning pouring up thickly through the hole in the roof, into the clouds.

The storm broke. Sheets of falling rain slanted sideways. Palm trees flailed, branches breaking off.

Dorian was screaming for it to stop while Reynolds held her back. Not that there was anything she could have done. It was too late for the victim.

Calexa's hair vanished in a puffball of flame, leaving her bare scalp stubbled and scorched. Fire burned away her gag, leaving her mouth free.

In a rush, she shrieked, "I curse you—*aiiiieeeeeee!*"

She burned, screaming, accompanied by a frenzy of thunder and lightning.

Outside, prowling around the mill, Steve Soto heard those screams. Earlier, while hiding out in the graveyard, he'd seen the fleeing Dorian intercepted by Calexa and directed inside the mill. He'd worked his way toward the site, zigzagging across the broken ground, using all available cover as he closed on the hulking ruin. When he'd seen the zombies coming, making for the part of the building holding the side door through which Calexa and Dorian had disappeared, Soto slipped around the corner to the building's short side.

The zombies hadn't seen him, or if they had they were ignoring him. Why not? He didn't have any beef with the zombies. They were still arriving at the building, straggling along a long, loose, disconnected line from the house to the mill.

The sky had darkened, the thundering, flashing clouds thickening, descending, more oppressive, like a lid that was being lowered on the scene. The darkness was thick and the lightning was glaring, and between the two it was difficult to see much of anything.

The storm had really blown in out of nowhere, but Soto supposed that that was the nature of these tropical storms.

Screaming started inside the building. It sounded like Dorian. He didn't go crashing in to rescue the damsel. Steve Soto had stayed alive for a long time by looking before leaping.

A couple of old wooden crates littered the yard where he was standing. He piled them up against the side of the wall, under a shuttered window. The shutters were closed but a lot of the slats were missing, and by standing on the stacked crates he should be able to see inside the mill.

He mounted on top of the crates, balancing carefully. They were rickety and he didn't feel entirely comfortable trusting his weight to them. The gusty winds and sheets of rain didn't make it any easier. Some of those sizzling lightning bolts and thunderclaps sounded like they were coming damned close.

He stood on top of the crates, holding on to the trim outlining the window, face pressed to a place against the shutters where the slats were missing.

He looked inside, where all hell was breaking loose. It

270

was so crazy that it took his brain a minute just to process what it was exactly that his eyes were seeing.

It was Dorian who was screaming, but she was okay, or at least in no immediate danger. She was being held in place over to one side of the structure, against the wall. Soto recognized the man who was holding her as one of Lodge's bodyguards from the house, as was the man who stood nearby.

Deeper in the mill, toward the center of the mill but not under the hole in the roof, was one of the damnedest things Soto had ever seen, and he'd seen some doozies, especially since coming to the island.

Lodge was playing black magician, burning a woman alive at the stake. Alba was stretched naked across a stone, trussed up like some sacrificial offering. Nearby, chained standing to a pillar, was a grotesque caricature of a human being. At first, Soto thought it was some kind of lifelike native idol or statue. It couldn't be real.

But Calexa was really burning to death. It was rough stuff, hard even for a tough hood like Soto to stomach. The thing in the flames was all blackened and shriveling in the roaring blaze, but it still kept moving and screaming.

The screaming especially chilled his blood. There was a raw honking quality to it that rasped his nerves. He found himself saying under his breath: "Come on, damn you, die, damn you, why don't you just shut up and die?"

But she wouldn't. He didn't want to pin a sucker tag on himself, but he had to do something, if only to silence the human torch. He pulled his gun, intending to plant a couple of slugs in Calexa to end the agony, then put the blast on Lodge, too.

He raised his gun toward the gap in the shutters, angling for a clear shot, finger tightening on the trigger—

Shots rang out, a whole string of them. Soto's first thought was that he was sure he hadn't pulled the trigger, then he was jerking under the impact of slugs that ripped through him, sieving him and spinning him.

He lost his balance and fell, the crates toppling. He hit

271

the ground hard but barely felt it because he was already so torn up that there wasn't all that much of him to feel.

He lay sprawled, limbs outflung in different directions, lying on his back with the rain pouring in his face. With great difficulty, he raised his head, tilting his neck so he could look at his torso.

A handful of holes were punched through his chest and belly. Exit wounds, bullet exit wounds. He'd been shot in the back. Shot? Hell, ventilated!

His killer emerged from behind the screen of bushes edging the clearing, the place where he'd been hiding when he'd ambushed Soto, gunning him down.

He crossed the open space, smoking pistol in hand, to stand looming over Soto, looking down at him.

It was Dennis.

He said, "You don't look so tough now."

"You, Dennis . . . ?"

"That's right, Steve. When the shooting started back in the house, I hit the floor and played dead until all those idiots cleared out of there. I went to duck out a back window and that's when I saw you, sneaking out of the graveyard.

"I followed you and caught you when you weren't looking. You should've been looking. You taught me that, Steve. Guess I learned my lessons pretty good—better than you."

Soto asked the big question: "Why?"

"How do you get to be the new top gun? You take down the old top gun. That's you, Steve, and now you're history.

"I haven't seen Tony Paul around and I've got a feeling he's history, too. But if he's not, I'll just do him the way I did you. He's even stupider, so it should be easy.

"With the two of you gone, I'll be the top shooter in the outfit back home. Let's face it, Steve, the fact that I was able to catch you napping shows you're overdue for retirement.

"Too bad about that treasure getting away, but that Quantez is a slippery dude, slipperier than you. Still, you could get rich off of his leavings."

Dennis reached into a jacket pocket, pulling out a fistful

of jeweled gold chains. "Check it out. I picked it up off the floor, when it fell out of the chest. Must be worth about five grand, easy.

"There's more lying back in the house. Think I'll just go back there and scoop it up. It'll be a bonus, like getting paid for hitting you.

"Not that I needed to get paid for this, Steve. I'd have done it for free. All that errand boy crap you were always handing me got really old."

Soto took a breath, hearing his lungs bubble and wheeze from a chest wound. He wanted enough breath to get his exit line in.

He said, "You'll always be an errand boy, Dennis . . . a punk—"

He was still holding his gun and he meant to whip it up and put the blast on Dennis, but his body wouldn't respond and he barely had the strength to lift the gun off the ground, and while he was struggling with it, Dennis shot him again.

Soto fell back, exiting. Motionless, but exiting . . .

Dennis stood holding the gun, idly watching smoke curl from the barrel. His other hand made a fist that playfully swiped the air.

"Son of a bitch! I did it!"

Lightning, crashing thunder. During the brief pauses in the din he could hear more crazy noises coming from inside the mill. Lurid colored lights shone through the gaps in the shutters.

Dennis said, "Wonder what's going on in there? Never mind. That's how Steve got his, by getting snoopy and forgetting to watch his back. I won't make that mistake!"

He crossed the clearing back to the bushes, parting them and slipping to the other side to retrace his footsteps to the house.

In the mill, the sounds of the shooting had been drowned out by the storm and the screaming. Calexa was dead now,

273

consumed, a human ash pile collapsing in a heap amid the kindling, sending showers of embers skyward.

Lodge readied himself for the final stroke. He stood over Alba's flabby quivering form, holding the knife high. He drove it down into Alba's chest and started cutting. It took a fair amount of strength to cut through the breastbone and muscle and connective tissue, but Lodge was inspired and the knife was sharp and the gods were thirsty, just as they had been in the days of the ancient Aztec empire when High Priests with obsidian knives had first performed the ceremony.

Lodge tore open a hole in the chest cavity and reached in with his bare hand and drew the still-pumping heart from the breast of its still-living victim.

It was beating still as he carried it in both hands as an offering, bringing it to the Frankenstein Monster. It was throbbing and slippery, as if trying to escape from his grip.

The Monster's head drooped on the end of its neck, chin resting on his chest, jack-o'-lantern mouth hanging slackly open and gaping.

Lodge stuffed the heart into the Monster's mouth, cramming it in between its jaws. The heart's blood, the most potent magical agent in the spell, squirted down the Monster's throat. Some spilled on his chin.

Lodge stepped back, his hands dripping blood, raising those hands above his head. Usually unflappable, he was shrieking now, caught up in the Dionysian ecstasy of the *sparagmos,* the rending of the sacrificial victim.

He called on the dark powers to accept his offering of two satanic souls to eternally serve in hell, to accept his offering and find it good and heed his prayer—

A lightning bolt came blasting through the hole in the roof, striking the Monster.

The blast filled the cavernous mill with white sun-heart glare. The shock wave knocked Lodge off his feet, sending him flying backward, tumbling head over heels.

For an instant the white glare acted as a kind of X ray,

revealing the Monster's oversized skeleton in black silhouette.

The flash faded, and the Monster's fleshy form was once more visible. Its neck bolts hissed and sputtered, glowing white-hot. As the glare from the blast faded, the neck bolts continued to blaze brightly.

The concussion from the bolt had extinguished the fire, snuffing it. It was dark in the mill, except for a bright greenish-yellow glow centered in the Monster's neck electrodes, but which had suffused the rest of its form with a glimmering foxfire shine.

Lodge picked himself up, feeling gingerly for broken bones, finding none. He'd been thrown through the air by the blast, and he ached all over.

Over to the side, Dorian and the two bodyguards huddled together, crouched against the wall, slowly rising to their feet, stunned.

Outside, even the zombies seemed to have been taken aback by the blast, and clustered around in front of the mill, walking in circles and bumping into each other and bouncing off.

Steve Soto was conscious. He didn't know how or why, but there he was. He lay sprawled on his back, his eyes open, the rain washing over him.

The storm was breaking, the wind and rain lessening. Soto felt strange. He could feel the rain hitting him, and the wetness of the puddle in which he lay, and the soft yielding earth beneath his bullet-riddled body. But his senses were afflicted with a kind of numbness. He couldn't tell if the rain was cold or warm. He could feel his body, the weight and shape of it, but little else. His torso felt all solid inside, like a potato, his limbs seemed to have been formed from clay, with as little feeling.

He'd taken a lot of slugs. He should have been dead. His luck hadn't run out yet. Or maybe it had. The lack of feeling in his body, the numbness in his extremities, could all be the result of a bullet severing his spinal cord and wiping out all feeling.

That'd be worse than being dead, to wind up as a paralyzed vegetable. It should have scared him, but it didn't. His emotions were all played out, as if they were used up and he didn't have anything left. Somewhere in a corner of his mind was a little seething nugget of dread, but it was smothered by the all-pervasive blankness.

He tried to sit up. His limbs worked, responding. They were clumsy, though, as though they'd gone to sleep. He sat up with his back to the wall.

Even in the rainy dimness he could see the raw holes in his chest and belly. By all rights, he should have been dead. Hard to believe that all those shots had drilled him without piercing a vital organ!

That was Dennis for you. He couldn't even manage to pull off a kill properly. Too bad for him.

Boy, was he going to get a big surprise!

Soto felt around his shattered chest, sticky with blood. He'd been shot right through the lung, and he wasn't even wheezing, even though he was a prime candidate for a sucking chest wound.

No wonder he couldn't feel anything! He'd probably gone into shock from trauma and loss of blood. He might not have more than a few minutes, a few seconds left.

He stood leaning against the wall, rain falling around him. He was aware of a lack of something, something missing that bothered him, and he couldn't put a finger on what it was, but it was something important, vital. What?

He came in for a pretty big surprise himself when he realized what it was.

He wasn't breathing.

In the mill, the Monster's greenish-yellow skin glowed, phosphorescent. The glow in its neck bolts dimmed and faded, but its flesh continued to shine.

The Monster shuddered, racked with muscular spasms

from the smoking top of its scorched squared-off head to the tips of its gunboat-sized shoes.

His neck-bolt electrodes shone silvery bright, scoured free of all encrusted rust and corrosion.

His veins swelled, expanding and contracting. Various body parts heaved and slid. The stomach cavity was stuffed with masses of viscera that Lodge had shoved back in there earlier, when he and the others had first found the Monster. Chains had been wrapped around its middle, holding its guts in place.

When the lightning had struck, the chains had acted as high-grade conductors of electricity, carrying the charge through to the Monster's innards.

Now, in the stomach cavity, the viscera began to stir, making quivering peristaltic motions, like fat sluggish eels writhing en masse.

They slid among each other, swelling, shining with secretions, reknitting themselves, repackaging the coiled intestines in the places where they should go.

Gnawed places that had been chewed by the maddened, bloodthirsty wolves now began self-sealing, tooth punctures closing, flesh growing to bridge the gaps.

Lodge stared, marveling. "The lightning has restarted its metabolism! It's remaking itself, healing!"

The jolt of power seemed to have jump-started the Monster's life processes. It was the amazing hybrid vigor of the creature, thanks to its cosmic-ray-charged body chemistry, the cells mutating into hyperlife, remaking the reanimated transhumanoid.

There was a humming sound, as of a hive of furious insects buzzing away—the sound of months, if not years, of the body's healing processes being compressed into a matter of minutes.

The coiling viscera could now be seen only dimly, through a tough gray-white-green membrane that had grown to cover them. The membrane began building up its flesh, layer by laminated layer, quick-growing thick slabs of muscle interwoven with cartilaginous connective tissue, honeycombed by squirming wormlike nerve bundles.

Was it the product of satanic sorcery or Frankensteinian super-science? Whatever the reason, the miraculous transformation continued. Awed, filled with dread, Dorian and the bodyguards pressed closer, advancing one tentative step at a time.

When they were still a good distance away, Lodge called for them to stop. "Don't come any closer to the magic circle, the spell hasn't exhausted its power yet."

They hung back. The Monster's body rebuilt itself layer by layer, from the inside out, the outer membrane toughening and coarsening to a gritty epidermis that was wide-pored and shot through with shiny flecks, as if micalike mineral particles were embedded in its skin.

The Monster choked, a ragged death-rattle cry in reverse, coughing out the dead air trapped in its bellowslike lungs. Its chest heaved, swelling, taking a great gasping breath which seemed to Dorian to have sucked all the air out of the space.

Lodge, wonderingly, said, "Breathing! That's strange— zombies don't breathe!"

Dorian said, "This thing is as far beyond a zombie as a zombie is beyond an ordinary hypnotic subject. With its origins combining science and black magic, there's no telling what it is that you've brought back into the world."

Irritated, Lodge motioned to her for silence, not taking his eyes off the Monster. "Be quiet, dear, or I'll sew your lips shut with rawhide thongs."

The sound of his voice must have jarred something in the Monster's awareness, for it opened its eyes. Deep in the pits of its black-olive pupils were jewellike points of gleaming emerald light, a reflection of the tremendous inner energy powering the creature.

After a pause, its eyes came into focus. It tilted its head down and looked around, taking in its surroundings and the people that inhabited them.

Looking down at itself, it saw and recognized its new wholeness. It grinned—not a pleasant sight.

Lodge frowned. "Grinning? That won't do!"

Dorian said, "Zombies don't have feelings, emotions. That's something else that you've called up."

The Monster turned its head at the sound of her voice, looking straight at her. It leered, smacking lipless mouth edges that were stained red from the heart it had sometime since gobbled down.

That glaring leer made Dorian's blood run cold, choking off her words. Beside her, Pierre and Reynolds stirred uneasily, shuffling around on their feet.

Lodge put on a bold front, swaggering up to the Monster and glaring up at him.

He said, "Look at me, you hideous gargoyle! Behold the face of your master, who brought you back from night's black shore to walk the earth as my slave!"

The Monster looked at him, a change coming over its face. Its expression of cruel amusement and mocking mirth at its resurrection was replaced by an iron devil mask.

Beneath the ledgelike brow the eyes were blazing emeralds. Its lipless fish mouth curled over yellow-brown horse teeth in a withering sneer, arrogant, hateful, triumphant.

It stepped away from the pillar, snapping the chains that bound it, breaking the pillar in two so it fell crashing behind him. It stood free, massive feet anchoring it to the floor, keeping it upright though it swayed and reeled with the first stumbling steps. It flapped its big arms around for balance.

Lodge said, "Zombie or devil, you're bound by the laws of black magic! I brought you back, you must obey me!

"That is the Law!"

The Monster raised an arm from its side, indicating something on the ground behind Lodge. Lodge turned to see what it was.

It was a broad wide swath of dirt, that was all, an imprint in the dust made by a body that had slid along the floor. In fact, it had been made by Lodge, marking his passage when he'd been sent flying by the lightning blast that reanimated the Monster.

At first Lodge was puzzled, not quite making the connection. Then his gaze widened to include a broader angle of his surroundings and he realized that the marks went directly across the line of sprinkled blood marking the limits of the magic circle, wiping out part of it, opening a gap in the ring.

Lodge turned ashen. He felt suddenly old and frail, weak, as if his skin was a drumhead stretched across his bones. Every heartbeat seemed to age him another ten years.

"The magic circle—it's broken," he said. "Must have been broken when I was thrown across it by the blast . . ."

White flecks of spittle clung to his liver-colored lips. He said, "B-but that means that the protective barrier was broken during the rite—the circle that keeps the demons outside, keeping them from destroying any mortal who dares to call them up to do his bidding . . ."

He got the picture in the last second before the Monster started moving, coming at him. The Monster picked him up like a twig and turned him upside down, effortlessly holding him aloft.

Taking hold of Lodge's ankles, one in each hand, the Monster tore him apart down the middle, ripping him in two like a wishbone.

With a casual toss, the creature threw the wreckage away, sending the body halves flying across the mill.

Dorian screamed. The Monster turned, starting toward her. She whirled, running for the door. Pierre and Reynolds were already there, tearing away the bolt, throwing open the door.

A crowd of zombies stood just outside the door, waiting to get in. They rushed through the open doorway, arms extended, clawlike hands reaching and tearing for human flesh.

Pierre and Reynolds were pushed backward, shoved deeper into the mill by the zombies thronging inside. From behind them came the Monster's big-footed juggernaut tread, closing on the living humans.

Dorian dodged to the side. Reynolds had been the first out the door and the zombies got a good hold on him, sinking their clutching hands and teeth into his flesh, taking him down to the ground.

As they did so, the Monster came crashing down toward

Dorian, reaching for her with shovel-sized hands. Shrieking, she ducked, evading his grasp. The creature was carried by its own momentum into the press of zombies pouring through the open doorway.

A zombie grabbed for her, tearing long scratches on her arm as she pulled loose from it.

In the back of the zombie ranks there was a stir, a disturbance. A figure had come in from outside, plowing into them, shoving them aside as it bulled its way into the mill.

It was Steve Soto. He fought his way to Dorian, knocking the zombies aside, scattering them left and right. For some reason, they offered him no resistance. It was as if they didn't see him, didn't know he was there.

Dorian reached out to him, her arm straining at the shoulder joints. He pushed aside the last zombie or two in his way and grabbed her wrist, closing his hand around it in a death grip.

He pulled, yanking her to him with such force that her feet left the floor. Something brushed the back of her head and she turned around to see that it was the Monster's fingertips, hanging a hairsbreadth away from her.

Soto yanked again, swinging her past the Monster, just beyond its reach. The creature didn't like being thwarted and its face reflected a mad green-eyed fury.

At that moment Pierre, wrestling around with two or three zombies that were trying to drag him down, backed into the Monster, bumping into it.

Snarling, the Monster grabbed him around the neck with one hand, squeezing. Pierre purpled, his face swelling until it seemed about to explode.

The Monster tore Pierre's head off his neck, wrenching out the spinal column with it, pulling it clear through the top of his shoulders.

Taking hold of the other end of the spine, the Monster began flailing around with it, swinging it over his head, using the knobbed skull at the end of the column to knock aside the zombies standing between it and the door.

But by now Soto had already dragged Dorian through the

door, outside, into the wet misty murk of near dusk. Still clutching her wrist, Soto hauled her around the corner of the building and into the clearing where he'd been shot by Dennis.

They kept going, running behind the back of the mill. In front, the Monster crashed through the doorway, not bothering to duck, taking out a good part of the door frame as it lumbered into the open.

It staggered around, swaying, clumping this way and that, hooded eyes green-glaring, seeking the woman and the man who had dared to take her from him.

Dorian heard the brute crashing and bellowing as she and Soto dodged around the end of a line of trees, putting a screen of thick heavy brush between them and the Monster.

After a while they heard it moving away, across the front fields and the distant road that lay at their far edge.

Dorian swayed. Soto's hand was on her arm, half holding her upright, steering her. His hand was as cold and stiff as an iron claw.

The rain had all but stopped, but dripping trees sprinkled them with moisture. Dorian said, "Thanks."

"It's nothing. Consider it payment for services rendered," he said, his voice flat, emotionless, a rasping monotone.

"Well, thanks anyway."

"You've got to get out of here, Dorian."

"Pierre and Reynolds came here by Jeep. It's hidden down in the gulley on this side of the mill."

"Can you find it?"

"Yes, I think so."

"Good. Take it and go. Go now."

He wasn't holding her arm anymore, but the place where he'd been gripping it was sore and numb. She rubbed it, squeezing some feeling into it.

He said, "Get going, there isn't much time."

"What about you? Aren't you going?"

"No."

"You must!"

"I've got business to take care of here."

"You can't stay here, Soto. Worse things than monsters and zombies walk here after dark."

"They can't hurt me."

"You've been lucky enough to stay alive so far, but don't press your luck. You're a gambler, you're supposed to know when to cash in your chips and go home."

He chuckled, a hollow sound like wood rasping on wood.

"I already cashed in my chips, Dorian."

"What? What do you mean?"

"I'm dead," he said.

"Are you mad!"

There was still enough light to see by, so he pulled open his jacket, exposing his torso and chest. In case she didn't get the message, he took her hand and placed it against him, so she could feel the blood and the bullet holes.

She gasped, recoiling. He let her go.

He said, "I got shot while Lodge was casting the spell. Killed. I was dead. I am dead. That zombie-making spell of his worked better than he thought, because it turned me into one.

"You see, I'm a zombie, too."

She reeled, staggering. He reached for her arm, to steady her, but she flinched, backing away.

He said, "I guess you believe it now."

After that, there was nothing else but for him to escort her to the head of the gulley, on the floor of which a Jeep was parked, hidden behind a screen of brush.

Soto said, "Lodge is dead, so whatever hold he had on you is finished. You're free—so go."

She asked, "What about you? What will you do now?"

"Looks like I'm in it for the duration.

"There's nothing more to say and I don't feel like saying it, Dorian. So go.

"Just get out and go."

Baffled but understanding what she had to do, she stumbled down the side of the hill, into the brush. There were no keys in the ignition, but she had a key to the Jeep on her key ring. She fitted it into the lock and started the engine, its noise sounding loud down amid the dripping greenery.

Soto stood at the top of the hill, watching her start the Jeep and drive away. She switched on the parking lights only, driving through the gulley without headlights, the vehicle lurching and bumping, crushing through the brush, heading away from the plantation.

With a little luck and smarts, she just might get away.

Soto turned, heading back to the house.

Inside he could see a single point of light shining on the ground floor, visible through the windows as it moved from room to room. It was shed by the torch Dennis held in his hand, one that he had found lying on the floor and managed to relight with his cigarette lighter.

He walked crouched low, bent almost double, following a crabbed course from the front of the house to the rear. Every now and then torchlight would pick out an answering gleam in the dimness, a golden glimmer of some loot that had fallen from the chest.

He worked his way through the row of rooms, nearing the drawing room where the treasure had been found. He had his gun in hand. He wasn't thrilled at going back into the room, but that was where the greatest amount of gold had been spilled.

Most of the bats were gone, flown out the windows into the dusk, but there were still plenty hanging from the ceiling beams and dark corners, fluttering and scratching at the woodwork with their talons.

The drawing room was the same. Dead men, dead wolves, too many bats hanging from the ceiling, the tunnel mouth gaping at the back of the hearth.

Dennis stood under the arched entryway, thrusting the torch into the room before him, sweeping it slowly from side to side while holding it at chest height, trying to pick out those fugitive golden gleams.

No real gleams seemed to meet him. Disappointing, but the baubles would be harder to find in here, what with all the blood and bodies to block the view.

He went deeper into the room, walking softly. Golden glints glimmered at the foot of the hearth. In his zeal to get to them, he tripped over a corpse and almost fell. That sobered him, tempering greed with caution.

Nearing the hearth, he bent over to pick up a ruby in a golden setting, a teardrop of fire. He had to pocket his gun to free a hand to pick up the treasure. A few paces away was another golden gleam.

Something else gleamed back behind the hearth, in the black tunnel mouth. Three sets of red eyes, the eyes of the wives of Dracula's Undead harem.

They came floating and fluttering out of the hearth. One was dressed in white, one in red, and one in black. The one in red had yellow hair and looked rounder and better-fed than her two sunken-cheeked sisters.

They fanned out, swaying, posturing, thirsty mocking corpses.

Dennis had his gun out. "That's close enough, girls."

Teeheeing, they advanced, carefully placing one foot in front of the other, gliding in a kind of stately slow motion.

"I ain't playing, you wacko broads."

Still they came. Dennis shot the blonde in the chest. She staggered with the impact, but that was all. She looked up coyly out of the tops of her red eyes, smiling, showing her fangs.

She lifted the hem of her moldy red lace gown to her waist, exposing herself, but it was only a distraction. The white-clad she-vampire came in from the side, lunging.

Dennis gave her a faceful of torch, setting her white bridal veil on fire. It spread quickly, shooting across her dress, crackling up, enshrouding her with flames, turning her into a two-legged funeral pyre.

Shrieking, she turned and ran back into the tunnel, a fiery comet trail streaming after her. She fell off a landing, dropping from sight.

The black-clad vampire clawed at the torch, trying to knock it from Dennis's hand. He waved it in front of him, warding off the two vampires, backing away.

They didn't seem inclined to follow him too far from the hearth. That might have been because it was barely sundown and they didn't want to risk exposing themselves to any stray light beams remaining in the sky.

Backing away to the far end of the room, Dennis turned, ready to thrust himself through the doorway and out the nearest window to make his escape.

Only the doorway was blocked.

By Soto.

Dennis's scream was cut off as Soto's hand shot out, grabbing him by the throat. His free hand plucked the torch away from Dennis.

Dennis pulled his gun and stuck the muzzle against Soto's belly above the belt buckle and pulled the trigger, blasting.

Soto's body jerked with the impact, the muzzle flares scorching his shirt and making it catch fire.

But Soto's grip on his murderer did not slacken. That's when Dennis really started screaming.

"It can't be! It can't be! You're dead, Soto! I killed you, you're dead!"

"Yeah, there's a lot of that going around lately," Soto said.

He threw Dennis deep into the room, so that he fell crashing near the hearth.

The vampire in red and the one in black wafted out of the tunnel, bending, reaching. Fangs gleamed in the torchlight as they closed on Dennis.

He said, "Stay away, you bitches!"

The two halted, as if frozen in place, then parted, each stepping to the side, opening up a center space.

It was filled by the vampire in white, who emerged from the tunnel. She stank of burning. Half her hair had been burned off and there was massive fresh scarring on her face and chest. Her bridal white was soot-grayed where it was not actually black and scorched.

She bent over Dennis, her fanged mouth open and gaping, her hands shaped into wicked claws.

She said, "Bitches, eh?"

Night fell.

SIXTEEN

It was dusk when the black SUV rolled out of the valley to the place where the road intersected the coast highway. They were in sight of the shoreline. The storm had broken and thinning clouds let some fading colorless light into the sky, though the vehicle had its headlights on.

The junction to the plantation road had been restricted by a police roadblock. The police were gone, but the roadblock remained, a pair of wooden sawhorses angled across the two-lane road, blocking it.

Marko turned to the two men in back. "Go move those blockades."

They got out of the SUV and walked around to the front of it, standing in the glare of the headlights as they moved aside the barricades, opening the way.

They finished and were walking back to the SUV when Marko stuck his gun out the window and shot them down. Fire speared from the muzzle of his gun, streaking lines into the victims, who fell sprawling.

Quantez said, "We will travel faster now that our burden is lighter."

The driver turned left, heading north along the coast highway toward Magdalena. Beyond the city lay their destination, Seaguard Castle.

The castle was a slab-sided old Spanish fort, a couple of hundred years old, built in the days of treasure galleons and buccaneers. These days it served as headquarters and home base for the police.

Now, at dusk, the fort was in a ferment. Night was coming. Last night had been bad, with Shandygaff residents rioting over those crazy "sea serpent" stories. Major Quantez had been unavailable and out of communication all day, leaving a leadership vacuum at the top of the chain of command.

Worse, it seemed as though the fortress itself had been infiltrated. The force was on full alert. Corner guard towers shone spotlights down into the courtyard, flooding it with light. Well-armed squads stood posted at strategic locations, ready to move into action when the signal was given.

Not long before, in late afternoon, a routine patrol making the rounds circling the outside of the castle had made an alarming discovery. They found a wrapper of skin filled with crumbling bones that had once been a man.

It was the guard dogs that had found it. They'd gone wild long before they came near to it. Because of the previous night's riots, the castle dogs had been pressed into crowd-control duty against the shantytown dwellers. Consequently, no canine patrols had made the circuit of the castle for a good part of the night and all of the day.

This was the first such patrol, and before it had completed even one circuit, the dogs found the corpse. It was under the castle's west wall, its most inaccessible area. Masses of brush hemmed in the narrow clear strip between woods and castle wall.

The dogs found the corpses stuffed under some bushes. But that paled in comparison with what was found nearby.

It was a well sunk in the ground, a secret entrance to the castle. It was covered by a broad flat stone that was hidden under dirt and weeds. It had never been spotted before, its existence undreamed of, and it would have remained a secret still if it hadn't shown signs of recent use.

The lid had not been properly replaced but had been left

ajar, revealing a two-inch gap between stone and ground. Bushes and weeds were crushed around it, and there were curious wide serpentine grooves marked in the earth.

When the lid was pried up by a squad that came to investigate, they discovered a vertical shaft, ten feet deep, lined with rough-hewn stones that showed signs of great age. Iron staples protruded from the walls, serving as handholds.

At the bottom of the shaft was a five-foot-tall square-sided tunnel, leading to the vaults below the castle.

The side of the shaft and the floor of the tunnel were smeared with a dried sticky substance, like the trail of slime left by a snail. Only this snail would have to have been as big as an anaconda to leave so wide a trail.

The police officials paid little attention to this fact. They feared rebels, not monsters. Subversives with a suitcase full of plastic explosives could undermine the castle's ancient foundations, bringing the towering structure crashing down.

The commander left in charge of the fort in Quantez's absence wasted no time in organizing to counter the threat. He formed up two heavily armed terror squads, sending them below on a search-and-destroy mission.

One team descended the conventional way, through the dungeons of the central keep and into the cellars. The other entered through the newly discovered secret passageway.

Both teams converged on the vaults from different directions. The men wore hard hats with miner's lights. They were armed with assault rifles, handguns, and grenades. The leaders of the two squads communicated with each other and the commander by hand-talkers.

The vaults were an eerie underground world. There was about ten feet of clearance between the bottom of the foundation overhead, and the ground dirt below. The space was honeycombed with a forest of thick stone supporting piers arranged in vaulted arches.

It was dry and musty, peopled with rats and lizards, armadillos and bats, centipedes, scorpions, and spiders.

No rebels were to be found, as the armed squad members fanned out, infiltrating the space, clearing each vaulted area before securing the next.

The dirt floor was free of any footprints but those of the action teams. There was one set of tracks, though, those grooved serpentine marks winding through the dust.

The trail began where the secret tunnel gave onto the dirt floor. The hunter squads followed, trailing it deep into the winding recesses of the vaults.

The tracks led to the foot of a vaulted bay filled with a mound of skulls—then ended.

The vaults had once been used for burial grounds and the bay was heaped high with a mound of skulls, higher than a tall man's head.

Somebody noticed that the slime trail angled up the side of the vault wall, across the arched roof, and down the back wall, disappearing behind the mound.

It was also seen that the mound was not exactly flush with the back wall, but stood apart from it, so that there was a space between the two.

An energetic volunteer with a strong stomach tried scaling the mound to see what was on the other side. About twenty well-armed members from both teams were grouped around the front of the bay, wondering what to do next.

Skulls dribbled down the mound, rolling across the dirt floor as the volunteer heaved and flopped his way to the shaky top of the mound.

A squad leader called to him, "What's back there?"

"A c-coffin," was the tentative reply.

"What else would you expect to find down here?"

"It's m-moving."

"What!"

"It's shaking! Maybe there's a bomb inside!" The climber flung himself backward, sliding down the mound to the dirt floor.

The others scattered, taking cover. Nothing happened.

After a while somebody asked the volunteer, "Are you sure you're not seeing things?"

"I'm sure! And you will be, too, when that thing goes off!"

Outside, aboveground, the last rays of daylight were fading, sliding out of the darkening sky.

The coffin vibrated, rattling against skulls and stones.

The skull mound began to quake, jellylike. The floor quivered. The walls hummed, shaking loose bits of mortar and mold.

Red light flashed, triggering a blast that scattered the skull mound, scattering them like the filament of a windblown puffball.

It was a cannonade of skulls, skulls catapulting through the vaults, shattering on stone, rolling across the floor.

The blast had been an eerie silent explosion, shivering the scene with powerful psychic pressure waves as well as physical phenomena.

The squad members picked themselves up from the dirt, shaken, dazed.

Now that the bay had been pretty well cleared of skulls, what had been hidden behind them was revealed.

A handsome, heavy black coffin, standing upright, wedged in a corner.

It shuddered. The lid was not fully secured and banged against the edges, making a stuttering hammering din. Smoky pearl-gray mist curled out from the gap, shot through with ruby-red rays of light.

Some idiot opened fire on the coffin, stitching holes in the lid, venting more pearl-gray smoke and blood-light beams.

Suddenly the lid burst from its hinges, sailing away like a magic carpet despite its weight.

The edges of the coffin were fringed with pearly-gray tendrils that curled and waved. Inside was a pillar of darkness in the shape of a man, red-eyed and white-fanged.

He sprang out of the upright coffin, dynamic, trailing clouds and coils of infernal energy.

"Behold the triumph of Dracula! Back from the dead, and stronger!"

Throughout his unnatural life, Dracula had prolonged his existence by leaving little to chance. When the sun rises, he must sleep in his coffin on a bed of his native soil. That was why, no matter where he made his stronghold, he always had a number of extra coffins cached nearby. If, as had happened, his enemies should discover his lair and destroy his coffin, he always had others to fall back on.

So he had done on the island, salting coffins away in various hiding places in the hills and on the coast. He had dwelt here for decades and had many coffins secreted. One was planted below Seaguard Castle, in the vaults.

The Vampire Lord's stunning return to the world of the living had been accomplished in the following way: Last night the Drakon had raged in Shandygaff, feeding voraciously, gobbling dozens of men, women, and children to use their raw materials to build a new body. When dawn neared, it had been too far away from the plantation to reach it in time, but some shadowy survival instinct homed in on the nearest coffin. The Drakon had crawled outside the castle, prying up the secret hatchway, diving down the hatch, squirming through the tunnel, and slithering through the dust to the bay where the coffin lay hidden behind the skull mound. Defying gravity, it climbed the stone walls and ceiling, pouring itself into the coffin.

While it slept, the transformative processes continued, so that when the sun finally sank, Dracula was once more resurrected.

And hungry.

A soldier opened fire, spraying the vampire with autofire. The bullets passed through Dracula, smearing against the stone wall behind him.

Dracula grabbed the shooter, burying his fangs in his neck, holding him off the ground as he took a good long pull of the hot red fluid.

Others shot at him, filling the space with gun smoke, bullets, and noise. The slugs ventilated their comrade, again passing harmlessly through Dracula.

He tossed the drained body aside, red streaming down

the sides of his mouth. "You mortal clods lack the wit to appreciate my magnificence, but that doesn't make your blood any less tasty.

"How thoughtful of you to present yourselves to me for the slaughter!"

Dracula came at them, grabbing the nearest, twisting his head back, exposing a taut pulsing neck, fanging it in a spray of blood.

The racket of shooting faded, petering out as the team members ran for their lives. Weapons were useless against Dracula and many of the fugitives threw theirs away so they could run faster.

Dracula moved among them in the vaults, stalking and slaying.

Meanwhile, the black SUV of Major Quantez rolled up to the castle's main gate as the panic inside was reaching its height. Men fled out from under the archway, running for their lives. Shots sounded from inside the courtyard, but nobody was shooting at the men who ran and they weren't shooting back at any attackers.

Marko would have shot them, for cowardice and desertion, but Quantez stopped him.

"Put away your gun. It is too late for that now. All it will do is call attention to us," Quantez said.

Without being told, the driver turned the SUV around and drove away from the castle, back to town.

Like Dracula, Major Quantez had a few contingency plans. He had the driver go to the waterfront, to a private pier where a fast boat waited.

At Quantez's order, the SUV smashed through a wooden rail barricade at the foot of the pier, driving out to the end of the pier. Moored to the slip was a cabin cruiser with fast lines and powerful twin motors. In accordance with Quantez's standing instructions, the boat was fully fueled and ready to cast off.

The hardest part was getting the chest of gold out of the back of the SUV and into the boat. Heaving and straining, carrying it for short distances, setting it down, and picking it up again, the three men finally managed to haul the chest to the boat.

Quantez climbed into the boat, standing at the side on the afterdeck while the driver and Marko hefted the treasure chest off the planks, across the gunwale, and into the boat.

They had no sooner done so than Quantez shot them. Marko was also planning a double cross and was holding his gun down at his side when Quantez's slug caught him. The driver clawed at his chest where he'd been tagged, side-stepping off the floating dock into the water.

Quantez would have liked to stow the chest out of sight belowdecks, but it was too heavy for him to manage that now, given the hurry he was in.

The engines started right up, kicking over easily, throbbing with a steady hum of power.

Quantez hopped out onto the floating dock to free the mooring lines, then jumped back in the boat. Standing at the wheel, he worked the throttles, easing the boat away from the dock and out into the harbor.

He pointed the boat toward the channel between the seaward tip of Claw Cape and the buoy lights marking the tiny offshore cay. The passage was navigable, if one was careful and clever and knew these waters, and was no superstitious fool to be put off with old wives' tales about ghost pirates and cities in the sea. The passage's unsavory reputation was a selling point, as far as he was concerned. It was the quickest, quietest route off the island.

Salt sea breezes ruffled his hair. He felt his anxieties calming as he pulled away from the harbor. He glanced back at Magdalena, a crescent of colored lights piled jewel-like on a dark curving shore edged with a scallop of foaming surf.

At sea, the clouds were breaking up, causing moonbeams to slant down through the rifts. Scraps and streamers of clouds whipped across the night sky.

That's what Quantez thought the flying triangle was, an unusually sharp-edged cloud scrap that was managing to hold its shape as it blew out to sea.

But it was more regular than that, more solid. It kept its

shape, a flying black triangle with two neat red running lights at its nose.

It soared above the boat, a couple of hundred feet aloft, keeping pace with it. More clouds parted and now he could see the thing better.

It looked like a giant black beach umbrella which had been sent soaring up into the heights. No, a bird, a big black bird. Damned big. Judging by its wingspan, it was the size of an eagle, a condor.

It dropped, pulling out of the swooping dive when it was less than a hundred feet above the boat.

The damned thing was so close Quantez could hear its wings flap. They were fully extended, holding that triangular framework to soar on the winds, requiring only an occasional flap and flutter of wings to keep it on course.

It kept pace effortlessly with the boat. It unnerved Quantez. It could only be a bird of ill omen, of evil.

He opened up the throttles, but the flier kept pace. Its nose down-tilted, diving, swooping straight down at him. Even when he told himself that it couldn't be happening, that giant night birds didn't dive-bomb boaters, the black delta shape was coming in low, swooping down on him in a tight flat curve.

It came right at him, gliding over the water. It was huge. What he'd thought were twin red running lights were eyes, shining orbs of blood-fire. It had a spade-shaped head and pointy dagger-blade ears sticking out of the top of its skull.

It was no bird, it was a bat, a bat as big as a condor, a thing that couldn't be! But it was. There was no mistaking those black leather scalloped batwings.

Hanging down from its underside were two prehensile furry limbs ending in taloned claws that were widespread and reaching.

Quantez threw himself to the deck and the giant bat flashed over him, its claws slicing the air above his head.

It overflew the boat, gliding low over the water ahead of it, abruptly pulling up and climbing, pancaking upward and around.

It came in for another try. Quantez steered the wheel with one hand, gun in the other, shooting at the bat as it came swooping toward him.

The bat pulled up short, spreading its wings suddenly in a kind of braking maneuver that set it hovering above the boat. Its talons caught hold of the top of a wooden deck rail, holding on tight.

Quantez pumped slugs into it, shooting it in the body and wings. The bullets streaked through it and kept on going, lances of fire spearing into darkness.

Soon the gun was empty. And so Quantez threw it at the bat. That was all it was good for. Not even that, because it hit the hideous creature and bounced off.

Quantez backed away, hitting the backs of his legs against the treasure chest and toppling backward. He fell sprawling on his behind on the deck, his flailing hands, scrabbling for a handhold, contacting the shaft of a gaffing pole.

The gaffer was an eight-foot-long spear with a barbed and hooked pointed tip for hauling big fish into the boat. It made a good weapon.

The bat morphed, becoming a bubbling black inkiness that shifted into a man-form, a devil man, a human devil with red eyes, white fangs, and clutching clawlike hands, wrapped in a swirling black batwinged cape.

Dracula.

He started toward Quantez, who held the pole like a spear, aimed at Dracula's breast.

The vampire said, "You stole my treasure, but I could sense where it was, guiding me to you.

"He who dares plunder Dracula, dies!"

He lunged. Quantez thrust with the pole, trying to spear him. Dracula sidestepped, grabbing the pole in both hands, tearing it free from the other's grip. The vampire snapped it in half, scaling both pieces out over the water.

He closed on Quantez, grabbing him by the throat—

There was a brutal grinding, a blow and a shock, as the pilotless boat ran aground on some half-submerged reefs, tearing its bottom out on the razor-sharp coral.

Dracula and Quantez were tossed about, breaking Dracula's grip. The boat uptilted, seesawing on the rocks, its bow lifting up into the air. A horrible mechanical racketing sounded as the twin-engine screws beat themselves into scrap metal on the rocks.

Seawater rushed in from all directions, sending the deck awash, weighing down the boat so it sank back into water, sliding stern first into the sea.

Dracula howled. "My gold!" He hauled the chest out of the water, holding it under one arm, water swirling around his legs.

He said, "Curse you, the chest is too heavy for me to fly away with. Now it will be looted by the sea god's minions!"

He grabbed Quantez by the neck, shaking him. The major thrashed, kicking a length of anchor chain, rattling it.

Dracula seized the chain, tearing it loose from its fastenings. He tied one end of it to an iron ring that was bolted to the side of the chest. Then he fashioned a loop around the other end, throwing it over Quantez's head and wrapping a few turns of it around his neck.

Dracula said, "Your soul belongs to me, slave! Guard my treasure well until I return for it!"

Water, black but topped with coffee-colored creamy foam, closed in around the boat as it slid stern first off the rocks, plunging into the channel.

Nimble Dracula hopped to the upper deck, standing balanced on a rail as the stern of the boat submerged.

Quantez struggled, his head still above water, but the chain holding him tethered to the heavy box.

The boat sank, waters closing in over his head.

Dracula stepped off the top rail, launching himself into space like a man doing a swan dive. He changed in midair, morphing into a giant bat, wings bursting out from his shoulder blades and opening to their full length.

The bat flapped low and fast over the wave tops, skimming then, then nosing up, soaring into the starry heights.

Below, a bubbling white outward-expanding circle marked

297

where the boat had gone down. Shark fins sliced the water, arrowing in toward it.

The bat flew back to shore.

Nothing like a taste of sea air to stir up an unhealthy appetite. When Dracula returned to Magdalena, he went on a wild tear, turning the night into a roaring, rollicking blood-orgy.

Who was safe from a creature who could turn himself into a bloodthirsty bat, swooping down from the sky to take a victim on the wing?

The vampire indulged his whims and appetites, going where the hunt took him. He would terrorize the poor for a time, slaughtering and blood-drinking, wiping out whole families. Then when the sport began to pall, he preyed on the rich in their well-guarded homes and yachts.

Magdalena society high and low was astir like an overturned anthill by the time the night began to ebb, and the darkness before dawn was at hand.

The giant bat flapped toward Seaguard Castle, now standing empty and abandoned by all but the dead. There were many dead, sprawled where Dracula had left them, littering the courtyard, ramparts, and watchtowers.

The terror he had spread this night had been something of an object lesson. The mortals would never again dare to invade the vaults during the daylight hours, while he took his rest.

In the nights to come, he would consolidate his hold on the island, burying his crimes along with those who knew too much about the Undead plague blighting the island.

Within a few days, the human cattle would have convinced themselves that the evidence of their senses was a lie, and that the macabre murder carnival had been carried out by police and rebel death squads blood-feasting each other and the usual luckless innocent civilians caught in the cross fire.

The first gray streaks of light in the east sent a warning shiver along the bat's back. It flew in low toward the square-sided central keep, swooping through a great arched entrance into the building, gliding swiftly into a long high-walled central hall.

A number of bodies were strewn about the halls and staircases. Most of them had not had their blood drained by Dracula to slake his great thirst, they had just been slain for the sport of it.

Through open windows that faced east he glimpsed flashes of the lightening sky as he flew through the keep. The sun would soon be up, but he was inside, shielded from its poison rays.

At the end of the hallway a curving staircase led down and down. The bat dove headfirst into the stairwell, folding its wings back against its streamlined bulletlike body as it plunged down several floors to the bottom of the shaft.

Then the bat morphed back into Dracula's human form. Long cape streaming behind him, he went through a doorway, following zigzagging flights of stone stairs into the depths of the vaults.

Soon he was in the lowest levels, threading a labyrinth of high-walled narrow stone corridors. He needed no torches or lights, since he could see in the dark.

He came to an open trapdoor in the floor, whose stone staircase accessed the vaults, the standard route to the underground level in the keep.

Dracula went below, where corpses were scattered around the dirt floor, contorted in the postures of violent, unnatural death. The site reeked of pain, fear, and death, black emanations that suffused it with satanic power. It was heady, intoxicating, going to his head like a remembrance of thick, rich Tokay wine, back in the lost age when he had drunk not blood but wine.

To the Undead, blood truly was the wine of life.

Dracula stalked through the vaults, cape swirling. As he neared the place where his coffin lay, he had to step over more bodies.

Humans. Cattle, bred to slake primal appetites of their vampiric superiors. And of all vampires, who was more superior than Dracula, Lord of the Undead!

"Not Lord of the Undead. Overlord! Dracula, Overlord of the Undead! Who can dare to defy *me*?"

Dracula swept around the corner of a massive upright stone pier, noticing that it was shot through with four- and five-foot-long spiderweb cracks. They looked fresh. Probably the pillar had sustained the damage from the shock wave unleashed by his final metamorphosis from the Drakon, when the skull mound had been blasted aside and he had burst from his coffin.

That could be a problem, because the pillar was central to the whole system of vaulted and arched underground piers and bays which supported the castle. If it collapsed, it could bring the weight of the entire structure crashing down on this lowest region.

Such an eventuality might require him to return to his coffin cache at the plantation. He'd been away from it for too long. He wondered what his harem of wives had been up to in his absence. He anticipated the looks on their faces when they realized that their absolute lord and vampiric master wasn't destroyed after all.

Yellow-brown skulls were scattered about the dirt floor, a sign that he was nearing the bay with his coffin. Ready for a long satisfying stretch of coffin slumber, he hurried up to the entryway—

And stopped dead in his tracks. Or undead.

One thing stood between him and his coffin:

The Frankenstein Monster.

The last time Dracula had seen the Monster, it had been lying dead and gutted. Now it was back to its full prime, bigger than life.

Yes, he'd been away from the plantation too long.

It was almost funny. Dracula could have laughed, except that he wasn't the type who enjoyed a joke at his own expense.

How had the Monster found him? Instinct. It *knew*. There was a bond between them, an unearthly link. Occult ties, and now ties of blood, blood which had passed between them.

300

Of course, the Monster would have to find him just before sunrise, leaving Dracula with no way out except one.

Habit.

Conditioning, force of habit. For decades the Monster had been Dracula's slave, a weak-brained subject of his will.

What had gone before could be again. Dracula focused his will, his concentration slightly off due to the omnipresent knowledge of the coming dawn, something he felt in his skin, in his cells.

His eyes glimmered with blood-light. He began, "You have done well to come to your master, my faithful slave. I am your master. Surrender to the joy of submission to your superior, your—"

The Monster came to him, or at least at him, charging.

Dracula was not one to be manhandled, least of all by a lumbering oaf, a lump of living clay that he thought of as his mindless creature, when he thought of it at all.

Quick as thought, Dracula was around the Monster and behind it, jumping up onto its back. The vampire clawed at the Monster's eyes and throat, and tore at the back of its neck with his fangs.

It was like a mountain lion fighting a grizzly bear. An eyeful of Dracula's claws left the Monster momentarily blinded. The Monster reached behind him, trying to grab Dracula's biting head and crush it.

The Monster staggered but couldn't shake Dracula off its back. It slammed into a pillar, trying to crush him against it. That seemed to work, so the Monster did it again, really throwing itself against the stones, mashing the vampire against them.

Cracks splintered the vault archway, jarring loose stone blocks which began thudding down around the combatants.

Dracula's grip was easing with each bone-crushing smash against the stones. The Monster lowered its head, charging straight at the pillar, battering Dracula and itself full tilt against the pillar.

The pillar broke in two along the cracks that were already there. The Monster and Dracula were tossed onto a heap of massive blocks as the bottom half of the pillar came undone, fragmenting.

The Monster had Dracula on his back in the rubble, hands on his neck, trying to tear his head off. Unlike humans, Dracula was made of stronger stuff, and resisted.

But then, looking up, Dracula saw doom unfolding, doom for him and the Monster.

The bottom half of the pillar was gone, a mass of loose blocks on which the Monster had Dracula pinned down.

Without the bottom half of the pillar, the upper half could not stand. It slammed down like a piledriver on the Monster and Dracula, pressing them together under a couple of tons of stone.

With one pillar down, the overhead arch lost its form, coming undone. Stones showered, beams fell, mountains of dirt poured and roared as the castle started collapsing on its foundations.

Burying Dracula and the Monster under a mountain of man-made rubble.

SEVENTEEN

Séance and shadows. The shadows came first for Glendon. They were everywhere, ringing him all about, pressing against the cone of light that shone down on him from overhead where he sat restrained to a chair in an otherwise darkened room.

He'd been cleaned up and given fresh clothes; he could see that much just from looking down. He wore a pair of what looked like surgical scrubs, a loose-fitting gray-green top, and pants. His feet were bare.

He sat in a chair that suggested a cross between a dentist's chair and an electric chair. It was square-shaped, solidly built, with a high straight back and solid armrests. Canvas restraint straps, the kind used by hospitals to secure violent or psychotic patients, held his wrists bound to the armrests. A similar restraining harness crisscrossed his chest, binding him to the chair, and his ankles were strapped to the chair legs.

A ceiling spotlight threw a cone of yellow light down on him and the chair. The rest of the space was dark and he couldn't see much outside of the circle of light, but he could see that he was seated facing one end of what looked like a long conference-type table.

Farther down the table, he thought he could make out a

double row of motionless shrouded shapes, lining opposite sides of the table. But the room was so dark that he could distinguish little else about them.

Somewhere nearby a door opened, letting more light into the room. It came from behind him, to the left. He turned his head, trying to see, but the restraints did not allow him enough movement to discern what was happening.

Or who was entering. He was aware of movement, fresh shadows thrown by a figure standing in a doorway, then stepping across the threshold, closing the door after entering and banishing the light from outside that had been shining through the open doorway.

There was motion nearby, the rustle of garments, a soft tapping as of heels moving across the floor to him.

A woman stood beside him. She was of medium height, slim but shapely, clad in a long-sleeved, charcoal-gray knit dress whose hem reached down to her slender ankles. The dress was split up the sides, showing her stockinged calves and neat black pumps with three-inch heels.

A long-fingered white hand moved into his field of vision, holding a plastic bottle of clear fluid with a plastic straw-type extension. She fitted the tip between his dry cracked lips and squirted some warm, thin fluid into his mouth.

He hadn't realized how parched he was and sucked it down. At first, it hurt to swallow, but after the first sluggish trickles had crawled down his dry throat, it was soothing and refreshing. He sucked more, gulping greedily, and was sorry when the flow halted and the bottle was taken away.

The fluid left a faint, not unpleasant chemical aftertaste.

It hurt to speak, but Glendon forced out the words.

"Where—where am I?"

She said, "In a room at the Science Palace in Visaria." Her English was clearly enunciated, flawless and unaccented, but with a precision that somehow suggested it was not her native tongue.

Glendon asked, "How did I get here?"

"You were found in the Frankenthal and brought here."

304

"What's here? A madhouse?"

"It only seems that way," she said, sounding faintly amused. She moved around in front of him, resting a hip on the edge of the table, leaning forward into the light so he could see her face.

It was the face of the she-devil in his dream of blood.

One of his dreams of blood, he silently amended. He could recall another, more recent and vivid, a nightmare of murder, mutilation, and cannibalism that had taken place at the old ruined watchtower. That was the last thing he remembered before coming to in this place, in a confused, half-aware montage of blurred faces and controlling hands, long corridors and elaborate labs and operating tables.

He actually had thought that he was in a madhouse, until he saw the face of the woman seated across from him. Knowing her for the haunter of his dreams, he sensed that he was in a place that would make a madhouse seem tame.

"I know you," he said. "The demoness."

"My name is Marya, Glendon. Marya Zaleska. *Countess* Marya Zaleska, to add my rightful title. But you and I need not stand on formality.

"Here we can relax and be ourselves. Our true selves. And after all, you are a kind of royalty yourself, in a manner of speaking."

"What do you mean?"

"You are the grandson of the famed scientist Wilfred Glendon, the discoverer of the Tibetan mariphasa and the inventor of the Moon-Ray.

"A distinguished lineage, made even more so by your being a third-generation lycanthrope."

Glendon started involuntarily, checked by the restraint straps which he had momentarily forgotten.

"Apparently you're the one who's mad, Countess."

"You might have been able to convince yourself of that before, Glendon, but not after the incident at the watchtower. You've been blooded now, not once, but three times.

"Once for each of your slaughtered victims."

"I didn't kill anybody. I couldn't!"

She raised a hand, holding it palm out. "Spare me your absurd denials, Glendon. I know who you are and what you are.

"And so do you—now that you've killed.

"Don't deny it. Revel in it. The swine you killed were three common cutthroats—scum. They would have killed you cheerfully and laughed about it later at the beer garden, over drinks paid for by money they would have lifted from your corpse.

"Little did they know that while they thought they were stalking a lone, defenseless traveler, they were really on the trail of a werewolf."

He began, "It's insanity, such things can't be—"

"You cannot deny your heritage of blood and death. It's your destiny. No one can escape the consequence of such a birthright. Who knows that better than I?

"You suffer from the hereditary taint of lycanthropy, Glendon. It has been passed down in the genes by the males in your line, ever since your grandfather begot a son on his wife, Lisa, after he'd been bitten.

"What else is the Glendon Curse if not werewolfism? It destroyed your grandfather and his wife, your father and mother, and many other victims caught up in the curse.

"Your grandfather and father died because they lived a lie. They tried to deny the great dark gift they had been granted, the power of the Beast in a world that respects only fear and brute force.

"They were ashamed, as if the lives they took to survive had any meaning or value compared to the greatness, the exaltation, of hosting a demon inside one's skin!"

Glendon said, "I daresay you would know more about that than I."

"Yes, I know. I, Countess Marya Zaleska—*Dracula's daughter.*

"And I am a friend, Glendon, the only one who remains to you, now that you have experienced the great awakening into the knowledge of what you truly are."

"And what's that?"

306

"The Beast, Glendon. You have become the Beast."

"Conceding for the sake of argument that there's some grain of truth buried under this occult nightmare, there are ways to fight it."

Marya quirked a smile, showing pointed fang tips.

"The mariphasa? You will find that specimens of the plant are even harder to come by in today's world than they were in your grandfather's time.

"And even if you had it, how could you propagate the plant and make it blossom, without a Moon-Ray projector?"

When he did not speak, she continued. "You are silent. You do not know. That is why you came to Visaria, to the Frankenthal, to search for traces of the secret that Pretorius might have had."

Glendon frowned, thoughtful. "I wonder how much of my sudden, irresistible compulsion to come here to seek the Moon-Ray was of my own making, and how much of it was your doing . . ."

"I? I am but a mere female, Glendon, the weaker sex. How could I make you do anything?"

Her laughter mocked. He said, "There are ways, Countess—drugs, hypnosis, brainwashing. The more I think about it, the more likely it seems to me that this whole mad business of werewolves and murder is nothing more than some kind of hypnotic suggestion that's being worked on me.

"I killed no one, but somehow you've managed to hypnotize me to believe that I'm guilty of the most fiendish murders!"

She eased her hip off the edge of the table, standing up. "You think you're fighting me, but you're not, Glendon. You're fighting yourself."

She leaned down and kissed him on the mouth, a soft, light kiss that took him by surprise, her lips brushing his.

"I told you once that I'd show you to yourself, Glendon. And so I shall."

His lips tingled where she had kissed him. There was a numbness there, like a shot of novocaine, blossoming outward from his mouth, fanning across his entire face. When

307

it reached his eyes, they blurred, going out of focus, dimming . . .

Blackness, grayness, then sight returned and with it, awareness. Glendon had lost track of time and couldn't tell if his blackout had lasted seconds, minutes, or hours.

He was still in the chair, still strapped down to it and seated facing one end of the table. The spotlight overhead had been dimmed, so that he no longer sat isolated in its glowing cone.

At the opposite end of the table, a pair of red eyes hung in the darkness, shining.

The Countess did something with her hands, making mystic passes in the air. In the center of the table, a red glimmer appeared, flickering into being, slowly and steadily brightening.

It was a crystal ball, the size of a medicine ball, inset in a hollow base in the tabletop. Instead of being clear, transparent, the glass was red.

The globe shed a smoky crimson light that slowly picked out the surroundings.

Marya sat at the far end of the table, facing him, her hands resting on the tabletop. On the ring finger of her right hand was a blood-ruby that seemed a miniature duplicate of the crimson globe in the center of the table.

She and Glendon were not alone, and yet, they were. Twelve were seated at the table, Glendon and Marya at the ends, and ten corpses that were lined up five to a side.

Ten corpses, males and females, young and old. A third of them were withered mummy types, petrified into grotesque misshapen forms. A few of the others were quite fresh and even comely, in a store-mannequin kind of way. But there could be no mistake that they were not sleeping, but dead.

They were all holding hands. Hands or skeletal claws that lay flat on the table, each hand tied by golden cords to that of its neighbor.

Glendon's neighbor on his left was a middle-aged woman, blowsy-looking, plump, recently dead, clad only in a garment that was a cross between a hospital gown and a shroud.

Her hand stretched across the table, reaching to the armrest of his chair, where it had been tied to his hand. Her flesh was cold and clammy.

On his right was a monk-hooded, wizened cadaver, old and dry, empty-eyed, noseless, with a fretted fanged monkey mouth. His hands were claws and one of them was tied to Glendon's right hand.

The fluid he'd been given to drink earlier must have been drugged, for the squirming worm of horror at the core of his awareness was smothered under blankets of lazy uncaring, a pleasant sensation of bodily lassitude and lightheadedness.

Marya leaned forward across the table, her eyes blood-orbs, her fangs bared, an impossibly long forked tongue flickering snakelike across her lips.

Somehow, Glendon found his voice. "So you're not human after all."

"Neither are you.

"Listen to me, Glendon. Within you lies the key to the secret of the Moon-Ray. But you can not find it without my help. That is why I called you to me, drawing you to me with astral cords, binding your will.

"Let me tell you what will happen, Glendon. My voice will take you away—is taking you away now. You will sleep. While you sleep, your untenanted seat of reason will hold another—a guest.

"That is the purpose of this séance."

She joined hands with the two cadavers seated in high-backed chairs on her left and right. She clasped their dead hands, squeezing them.

She said, "Now we are all together and the circle is joined, though not complete. Twelve are present, you, me, and the dead.

"Soon another will join us and we shall be thirteen, completing the magic number.

"Rest, Glendon. Sleep. Let go and surrender to quietude, the peace that is beyond the tomb but not beyond understanding."

The crimson globe pulsed, washing the scene in blood-light. Glendon's thoughts became slow, heavy. His eyes closed, the red light shining through the lids.

The blood-light was slow, thick, sludgelike, suffocating. It was swallowing him up and taking him away. His consciousness ebbed . . .

He was under, disconnected, disembodied. He was a pole of power, she was another, and the linked corpses were the force multipliers in the circuit, amplifying the occult energies.

This was necromancy, trafficking with dead souls. And other comings and goings.

Marya's voice filled the space, echoing down the slow pulsing crimson tides of blood-light.

She said, "Invisible bonds link the dead to their living descendants. Like calls to like, blood to blood, spirit to spirit. And never more than in the case of a curse, which forces the innocent to carry on the deadly hates of their forebears.

"By those ties, and by my will, I call on you, Wildred Glendon, the first Glendon, finder of mariphasa, inventor of the Moon-Ray, and the original founding lycanthrope of your bloodline.

"By those ties I call you, by my will I call you. Ghost or spirit that you are, you are bound to earth by the existence of your flesh-and-blood descendant, your grandson.

"His body will host your essence, so spirit, appear! Heed the call, return to this vale, and make yourself manifest in the living, breathing shell of your blood-kin!"

Glendon, entranced, unconsciously strained against his bonds, writhing in the chair.

A crack opened up in the world, letting in a wind from Beyond, an icy force. Red-black shadows boiled and bubbled in the air above Glendon's head.

From out of the chaotic cloud dropped a white jellied blur, a ghostly human outline, floating through Glendon's skin and sinking inside him.

A stream of images, faces, scenes assaulted him, swamping his clouded awareness.

310

They were the memories of the first Glendon, Glendon I, now relived at a blinding pace by the stunned, flickering consciousness of Glendon III, dispossessed of his rightful place in his own body and mind:

... In Tibet, in the Valley of the Moonflower, Glendon was bitten by a werewolf who was Dr. Yogami. But it was not Yogami but Glendon who was the real Werewolf of London. Yogami had killed the hotel chambermaid, but the Glendon werewolf had killed the streetwalker and the nude dancer. Killed Yogami, too, when he caught him stealing one of the precious mariphasa blossoms Glendon used to check the onslaught of his own lycanthropic compulsion.

The Glendon werewolf would have killed that fatuous ass, Paul Ames, if police bullets hadn't slain him before he could rip the throat out of his lovely, faithless Lisa.

What he could not accomplish in life, his curse achieved after death. His son, Glendon II, begotten on Lisa after his father had been infected with lycanthropy, inherited the werewolf gene and became the instrument of Glendon I's beyond-the-grave vengeance.

Glendon II became a werewolf, killing his mother and step-siblings, Inspector Sir Thomas Forsythe, Aunt Nettie, and others who had been involved in the travails of the original Werewolf of London.

That auto wreck that had killed both of Glendon III's parents was no accident, no fluke. His mother and father had been driving on a night when the full moon came out. His lycanthropized father had attacked his mother, losing control of the car and causing it to crash and burn, destroying the evidence of what had really happened.

All this today's Glendon learned in a single blinding flash of insight as his body was possessed by his grandfather's ghost, for in that mystical bonding, they instantly shared memories.

But Glendon I was strong and cold, while his grandson was drugged and weak-willed from Marya's mystifications.

In the chair, Glendon's body was surrounded by a nim-

311

bus, a ghostly white blurred outline that was superimposed over, and in, his own flesh.

His face was blurred and shining, the contours seeming to change, altering to the more high-domed, gaunt-faced visage of his grandfather.

Marya said, "Wilfred Glendon!"

"Who calls?"

"Glendon III, your grandson and heir!"

"He is my host, but it was you who summoned me, Marya Zaleska."

Her blood-eyes narrowed slightly. "So. You know who I am."

"There are few secrets hidden from those of us on the Other Side, Countess, especially those pertaining to your kind."

"What kind is that?"

"The Undead. What business have you and I to do together?"

"We are alike, lycanthrope. We both have a demon in our view."

"Indeed. But I did not ask for mine. It was forced on me. I was a scientist who sought only knowledge and to benefit mankind."

"The more fool, you!"

"Even that accursed Yogami, with his occult pretensions, tried to fight the curse."

Marya laughed, sneering, showing her fangs. "Don't play the martyr with me, Beast! As you said, there are few secrets on the other side. I know that it was you, your malign influence reaching out from beyond the grave, that activated and powered the Glendon Curse.

"You used your werewolf son to destroy those who had offended you!"

"Who had better reason? Yes, I sparked the taint in my young son, contriving events so that he would slay his own mother, my wife, beautiful, treacherous Lisa.

"Paul Ames was to die, too. He escaped the claws of the

312

werewolf, but knew that his darlings and friends were murdered by his stepson and could never prove it.

"He died in a madhouse, screaming and sobbing his sick soul out.

"But the rest was none of my doing. The satanic energies I had unleashed were not so easily bound.

"As for my grandson, it is my wish—and my prayer—that somehow he may escape his destiny, if he can."

Marya said, "Death does not necessarily bring wisdom. Foolish ghost! Man, vampire, or shadow, who can escape destiny?"

"Remember that and be guided."

"Since you know so much of earthly doings, you know what I want."

"Yes, the secret of the Moon-Ray."

"Give it to me!"

"A poor bargain. What do you offer in return, Countess?"

"With the Moon-Ray, your grandson may cultivate the flowers of the mariphasa, and escape the curse with which your blood afflicted him."

Glendon's laughter was hollow, as if echoing in a well. "Now who lies? I know you, Countess. You will never let him go when you can have a Beast to serve you."

"What of it?" she asked, shrugging. "Would you condemn him to suffering your fate, to seek the ghastly deaths of those he loves?

"In my service he shall be spared that, at least."

"Who will spare the world from the horrors that result when you use the Moon-Ray on the Bride of Frankenstein, to spawn a new slave super-race to dominate and terrorize the living?"

"You were a scientist. You know it's only a matter of time before the secret is rediscovered anyway. Give it to me, and at least you buy some small measure of peace for your grandson."

"A Faustian bargain, eh? Very well."

"You will do it?" She was all tense eagerness.

"I will do it for him, in the hope that it will help to ease the long hard way before him.

"But beware, Countess. Do not call me up again. Even vampires are not immune to ghostly vengeance."

"You dare threaten me!"

Glendon's body suddenly pulsed, flaring up in a crackling energy aura. The aura was the color of the Moon-Ray.

Like electricity, the charge jumped from Glendon through the corpses' hands that he held, and from them to the next corpses in line whose hands were clasped, and so on down the line, moving in a circle around the right and left sides of the table.

The two-pronged charge ripped through the corpse circuit, zapping Marya.

She bucked from the force of the current, sitting upright, rigid, straining. She would have let go of the dead men's hands if she could, breaking the circuit, but she was paralyzed, unable to do so.

Glendon's eyes were balls of moon-fire.

Now, from all the séance members grouped around the table, lines of force leaped, arrowing toward the crimson crystal globe. When they met at the center, the globe melted.

It liquified, puddling into a shiny molten mass that spread outward across the tabletop, in sizzling moon-fire rivulets that crossed and branched, met and merged, wove and interwove until they had formed a mazelike pattern.

The molten crystal seethed and bubbled, eating into the surface of the table.

The corpses rocked, swaying with the current, giving the illusion that they were convulsed with mirth, shaking in their seats.

Smoke, white and toxic, rose hissing and curling from where the molten crystal pattern was branding itself into the tabletop.

The smoke vanished as the last of the molten crystal was consumed, inert.

A last blast remained, as the strands and streamers of

314

moon-fire energy were withdrawn, reeled back across the table and into the corpses.

The moon-fire charge reversed its path on the corpse circuit. The two bodies flanking Marya imploded, collapsing, shriveling, deflating into dust.

The same thing happened to the next two corpses in line, and then to the next pair, and so on along the circuit path until the last of the corpses had fallen into dust.

The power flowed into Glendon's body. The ghost of the original Glendon used the surge of force to free him from his earthly host, rocketing him out of the material world.

A ghost shape flitted out of Glendon, almost too quick for the human eye to see, flashing out of sight and away.

Marya screamed.

Glendon III, today's Glendon, once more occupied his rightful place in his own body. He was weak, dazed, but Marya's shriek roused him from his stupor.

She sat with her head down, forehead resting on the table, her hands clenched into fists on both sides of her head.

Between her and Glendon, the other chairs at the table were heaped high with mounds of graveyard dirt and fragments of dry bones.

Tendrils of smoke wafted from the design branded on the tabletop, an intricate, mandalalike pattern of interlinked boxes, circles, semicircles, triangles, interlinked by various wavy lines.

Marya raised her head off the table, looking up, the bloodlight in her eyes dimmed to a pair of sparkling red points.

Glendon spoke, his voice steady, even.

"Too bad, Countess. You've failed."

She smiled, exulting, triumphant, flashing a red-lipped mouthful of dazzling white fangs.

"No, Glendon, I've succeeded!"

She leaped to her feet, overturning her chair behind her. She thrust out an arm, pointing down at the pattern branded into the tabletop by searing moon-fire.

"See that, Glendon! Do you know what it is?

"It's a schematic drawing, a diagram of the main operative circuit of the Moon-Ray, the key to building the projector!

"With it, and the race of super-slaves I can spawn from the newly reanimated Bride, the worlds of living and the dead will bow down before me, going under my heels.

"Tomorrow is mine, Glendon! None can escape destiny, and it is my destiny to rule supreme.

"Tomorrow belongs to the dark!"